ACCLAIM FOR

"Love lost, love regained, forgiveness, regrets, second chances…these are all themes in *Win, Love, or Draw*, a solid debut novel from Texas native Crystal Barnes. Throw in a few villains, heroes, and even a feisty gun-totin' female, and you've got the perfect setup for a heart-pounding adventure balanced with beautifully timed moments of comedic relief. This delightful historical offers readers an exciting read and more than enough romantic tension to keep 'em hangin' on for the ride. Highly recommended!"
—JANICE THOMPSON, AUTHOR OF *MISMATCHED IN TEXAS*

"Crystal Barnes's first novel, *Win, Love, or Draw*, takes the reader on an exciting journey to Cater Springs, Texas, circa 1877. This book has everything you could ask for: a pretty, strong leading woman; a handsome, gun-toting man; and take-your-breath-away shootouts! The book is also a beautiful love story with a common thread of forgiveness running through the pages. Barnes shares my love for the great state of Texas, and it comes through in her writing. I'm proud to recommend this debut novel by author and friend Crystal Barnes."
—ANNETTE O'HARE, AUTHOR OF *NORTHERN LIGHT*

"'Let's Make a Deal' is a diverting story by newcomer Crystal Barnes that conjures a headstrong young woman of the Old West. She agrees to an arranged marriage but stands her ground when it comes to consummating the union—until she actually falls in love."
—*PUBLISHER'S WEEKLY*, FOR "LET'S MAKE A DEAL" FROM *A KISS IS STILL A KISS: A SHORT STORY COLLECTION*

ALSO BY CRYSTAL L BARNES

MARRIAGE & MAYHEM SERIES

Win, Love, or Draw

OTHER WORKS

"Let's Make A Deal" from
A Kiss is Still a Kiss: A Short Story Collection

"Husband Hunting" from
Out of the Storm: A Short Story Collection

Marriage & Mayhem
Book 1

Win, Love, or Draw

~~~

Crystal L Barnes

© 2015 by Crystal L Barnes

Printed in the United States of America

All rights reserved. No part of this publication may be reproduced, stored in a retrieval system, or transmitted in any form or by any means—for example, electronic, photocopy, recording—without the prior written permission of the publisher. The only exception is brief quotations in printed reviews.

This is a work of fiction. Names, characters, incidents, and dialogues are products of the author's imagination and are not to be construed as real. Any resemblance to actual events or persons, living or dead, is entirely coincidental.

All Scripture quotations are taken from the King James Version of the Bible.

Cover design by Crystal L Barnes

To God be the glory.

Without Him, I wouldn't be on this wonderful journey of writing. He has placed in my life so many amazing people who helped make this story possible. Each one is special to me, and thank you doesn't begin to touch my gratitude.

A special thank-you goes to my "Sam."
Whether you intended to or not,
God has used you to teach me so many things,
for which I'm eternally grateful.

God be praised.

[Charity/Love] beareth all things, believeth all things, hopeth all things, endureth all things. Charity never faileth.

—I Corinthians 13:7–8a

1

Tuesday, November 13, 1877
Cater Springs, Texas

Catherine McGarrett jolted to a halt on the bustling boardwalk outside Koch's Mercantile. Tighter than a cinch strap, her focus fastened on an unexpected form farther up the dirt street. It couldn't be... Her heart stopped, then slammed with renewed vigor against her rib cage. A chill skidded down her spine that had little to do with the crisp November breeze and everything to do with the apparition riding through the middle of town.

"Ouch! Mama, you're hurtin' me."

"Huh?" Catherine dragged her gaze from the busy road filled with wagons and cowboys to the five-year-old who picked at her grip. "Oh, I'm sorry."

She loosened her hold on his arm, all the while striving to keep sight of the fetching rider with the black duster and tan horse. The brisk wind whipped a strand of her blond hair across her cheek, but she paid it little heed as she followed the pair's progress. Her wayward husband invaded her dreams often enough. What were the chances her mind would play tricks on her in the daylight?

"Benin, I know this might sound silly, but do you see a dark-haired man with a black Stetson riding toward the livery?"

"You mean that fella on the buckskin there?" Her son pointed at the figment of her imagination. "Yes'm, I see 'im."

"You do? Well. Good." Catherine released her son, lest he feel her sudden shaking. "I'm glad to know I'm not imagining things. Let's put our purchases in the wagon, shall we?"

Benin's gaze bore into her while they rounded to the back of their buckboard.

Loud yapping broke the hum of ordered activity. A mangy mutt dashed across the street in pursuit of a striped cat, racing straight toward the cowboy. Harnessed horses reared. Wagon drivers shouted their displeasure and fought to keep their rigs from spilling into the street. The sandy buckskin veered around the chaos with ease. Well trained.

Her mouth went dry.

Were any of the general's men in town? A quick scan of the various establishments and sidewalks yielded nothing, but then again, she only knew one of their faces. No, they preferred to terrorize her from the shadows. Wait. What was she thinking? The general and his cohorts wouldn't know what Sam looked like; they'd never met him. Besides, that might not even be him. A breath she hadn't realized she'd been holding seeped from her lungs.

Benin handed her his small parcel. "Mama, do you know that man?"

Her pulse skittered even as her eyes welcomed another peek at the broad-shouldered, narrow-hipped rider. "Let's just say, if I don't, he looks much like someone I do." Too much.

"Who?" Benin's dark head swung back toward her.

How she'd ended up with a son who looked so little like her, she'd never know. If it weren't for his coffee-colored eyes, no one would think them related. Would Sam notice? She rubbed at the headache forming between her brows.

"Questions, questions. You're full of questions today. Stop dallying. We've got work waiting at home." Catherine hurried Benin ahead of her onto the wagon bench and took the reins in her gloved hands.

"Have I met 'im?"

She sighed and rested the reins on her knees. Benin had inherited one other trait from her. Persistence. "You recall the man we pray for every evening?"

"Is that him?" The boy whipped around in his seat, then reached for the reins. "Come on. Let's go see if it is."

She tugged the reins away, making the horses shift. "No."

"Why not? Don't ya wanna see 'im?"

Part of her shouted *yes* while the rest of her trembled with uncertainty. Turning the horses toward the south and home, she steeled herself against her conflicting desires. "It's not important whether I want to see him. Lord knows I do, but he has to want to see me. If that's really him—and I'm not saying it is—he knows where to find us when he's ready to talk."

Still, she couldn't resist one last glance inside the livery when they passed.

A glimpse of steel-gray eyes stole her breath away.

"Samuel McGarrett. As I live and breathe, is that really you?"

Sam chuckled and led his buckskin, Sandy, farther into the shadowed livery. The scents and shuffles filling the interior welcomed him as much as the grin on his friend's face. "Yeah, Matthews, it's me." He shook the tall rancher's hand. He'd always appreciated a man he could look in the eye. Not many crossed his path.

"Well, if that don't beat all. I haven't seen you in a coon's age. Hey, Schreiner, come on over here and meet a friend of mine who's finally found his way home." Joe Matthews shifted his focus back to Sam. "It's been—what? Three, four years?"

"Five." Actually, five years, seven months, and four days, but who was counting?

Matthews let out a low whistle. "That long, huh?"

Sam nodded toward the burly man with the leather apron. "What happened to Grayson?"

"Oh, he kicked the bucket shortly after you left. Schreiner here bought the place from his widow. Schreiner, meet my old school chum Samuel McGarrett. Sam, this is our town blacksmith, wheelwright, livery owner, and best horseshoe thrower around, Hans Schreiner."

"Howdy." Grinning, Sam shook the beefy hand Schreiner

extended. "Remind me to test that last claim some time."

"Ja, sounds good."

"So, how long you here for? You passing through or sticking around a bit?"

"That all depends. Is she..." Sam rubbed his hand over his mouth.

"Still around?" Matthews nodded.

Schreiner's brown eyes widened. "You that McGarrett? The sheriff's son?"

Sam heaved a sigh. "Guilty."

The slight frown that marred the big man's face wasn't much of a surprise. Everyone in a small town knew everyone's business...even when they'd been away for years. Sam shifted in his boots and stole a glance at the passersby outside. "Where's she, uh, living now?"

"Same ole place on the south side, next to her sister's." Joe smirked. "I'm sure you know the place."

Like the back of his hand. "Yeah, just a bit."

Joe accepted the reins Schreiner passed him, slipped the man some money with a nod, and faced Sam. "If you're planning on sticking around and need some extra work, look me up. I've got some green horses that could use a bit of that magic touch of yours. In fact, if she won't let you on the property, come by the ranch. I'm sure Ma would love to see you, and you can meet my wife."

"Joe, the bachelor, got married?" Sam blinked. "When did that happen?"

"In May. It was her pa's dying wish." The grin that covered Matthews's face marked a truly happily married man.

"Must've been your wish too." Sam hadn't sported that look in a long time, but he still remembered how it felt. Would he ever tout it again?

Joe chuckled. "If I'd've known then what I know now, I wouldn't've bucked at the idea near as much." Joe snapped his fingers. "Hey, I've got an idea. You got business in town, or can you ride with me a ways?"

Some of his business could wait, and the other part lay outside of town. "I'll follow you to the cutoff." Sam swung into the saddle with a creak of leather and tipped his hat to Schreiner. "Nice to meet you."

The blacksmith bobbed his head and picked up his tongs.

Sam trailed Matthews from the livery. Once they cleared town, he moved alongside his friend. "What's this idea?"

"I was thinking on sending Ma over and inviting—" Joe leaned forward in the saddle. "Is that her?"

"Who?" Sam's focus whipped straight ahead, and he inadvertently pulled on the reins.

A wagon, slanting to the side, filled the middle of the road. Beside it stood a honey-haired, Stetson-wearing woman with hands planted on her slender hips. A beauty even from a distance.

Memories darted across his mind faster than speeding bullets. A joyous picnic. A white gown. A passionate kiss. Horseback races. Quiet meals. Loud arguments. Angry frowns. And finally, a parting wave.

Sam gulped and nudged his horse into a canter behind Matthews. Ready or not, he was fixing to face the one woman who could make him tremble in his boots, the one woman he hadn't laid eyes on in almost six years.

God, if ever I needed You, it's now.

<hr>

"Why did this have to happen now? I knew I should've waited until next week to come to town for supplies." Catherine set her fists on her hips and kicked a clod of dirt rather than the separated wagon wheel she longed to vent her frustrations on. No sense in making a bad situation worse.

"Mama, someone's comin'."

Her hands dropped from her hips. "What?"

Benin pointed back up the road.

A familiar paint cantered toward her with a rancher on board. Joe Matthews. Well, good. At least she wouldn't have to figure out how to fix this on her own.

A second horse, a buckskin, came alongside the first, a broad-shouldered man in a black duster on board, riding tall in the saddle.

Her pulse quickened. "Breathe, Catherine, just breathe. That might not even be him." But even as she tried to convince herself otherwise, she had no doubt who rode the second horse. Only one man ever sat a saddle like that. What should she do? Call out a greeting? Pretend she didn't recognize him? Grab her son and run for the hills? That last one held merit. Then the general couldn't hurt them. Her boots, however, had other ideas. They wouldn't budge.

Dead. They were all dead because she couldn't find it in her traitorous heart to run.

"Howdy, Mrs. Cathy, Ben. Looks like y'all have fallen into some trouble."

Catherine nodded, yet her focus remained fixed on the dark-haired wrangler with the haunting gray eyes who pulled to a stop a few feet in front of her.

"Cat."

Her breath caught. Words took wing. She hadn't heard anyone call her that in years. Nearly six, to be exact. No one had ever called her that but...

"Sam."

"You look good."

Her heart soared. Catching it along with a flyaway strand of hair, she shoved them both into place and strode for the rear of the wagon. Maybe she could run. Just a bit. "You too."

Fisting her navy skirt, she climbed into the back of the leaning buckboard, well knowing she wouldn't find anything to fix the wheel, but if she continued to stand and stare at Sam, she was liable to make a complete and utter fool of herself. Not that he hadn't done a good job of that all on his own, but she'd strived hard not to prove people correct about the notion. She had brains. She wouldn't have the successful horse ranch she had today if she didn't.

Hooves clomped closer while Catherine dug between the supplies. From the corner of her eye, she caught the sandy color of the buckskin.

"Want some help?"

She'd wanted help from him for years, and she hadn't gotten it. Why start—

Catherine straightened. If she refused him now, would he leave again? Without talking to her, without an explanation for his actions, without a chance to change things from the way they were to the way they ought to be?

She swallowed her foul-tasting pride. "You don't happen to have something to fix that wheel in those saddlebags of yours, do you?"

"Well, with some rope and a long pole, we could limp the wagon back to the livery. I've got the rope." Sam glanced at Joe. "We might have to get creative with the pole or borrow one?"

"I'll go back to town. Schreiner should have one. I'll take the broken wheel with me and let him know we're fixing to bring him some work. Benin, you want to give me a hand, pal?"

Catherine's gaze flew to Joe. Had he lost his mind? Leave her alone with Sam? Her heart beat erratically. "I—"

"Can I, Mama, *please*?"

Sam's gray eyes widened and sought hers, then flicked to the boy.

Uh-oh. Whatever was fixing to come out of Sam's mouth, she doubted her son needed to hear it. Not yet anyways. "Sure, Benin, you can go. Just don't be any trouble for Brother Matthews."

"Yes'm." Benin flashed a toothy grin, helped Joe with pieces of the broken wheel, and took his place on the rump of the pinto, behind the rancher. "Thanks, Mama. We'll be back in a jiffy."

Joe Matthews tipped his hat her direction and turned his gelding toward town. Soon tufts of dirt kicked up behind them.

"Mama? He's your son? How do you have a son? How old is he? Where did he come from?"

The buckskin shook her head, clearly picking up on her rider's anxiety.

She knew the feeling. Catherine stared into wide stormy eyes for the span of a heartbeat, then bent, grabbed a couple bags of coffee, and started unloading the wagon. "He's five."

"Five? Five! He isn't...I mean you weren't...why didn't you... I think I'm going to be sick."

2

Sam straightened at Cat's approach, his head pounding from the bombardment of questions and self-recriminations swirling within. "Is he really mine?"

She halted midstride. Fire snapped in her dark eyes.

He gulped. Wrong question.

"If he's not yours, then whose do you think he is?" She threw up her arms and stalked toward the wagon. "I can't believe you, standing there, asking me that question. We lived as husband and wife more than a year. You ought to know me better than that. Of all the unmitigated gall." She whirled to face him and jabbed her thumb toward her chest. "What do you think I am—some hussy?"

"Whoa, whoa. I'm not accusing you of anything. All I want to know is if he's my son. I have a right to know that, don't you think?"

"I have a right to know a lot of things, but you don't see me demanding answers."

Sam flinched. That was some jab of the spur. He let the comment slide though. She might be hankering for a fight, but that was the last thing he wanted. All he wanted was the truth, a straight answer to a straight question. "You could've told me I had a kid sooner."

"How could I? You haven't been here. You've been gallivanting across the countryside like some...like some... Oh, I don't know. Like some antelope. I wasn't even sure you were still alive."

"So he's not mine?"

"Of course he's yours. Didn't you even look at him? All I can see is your face every time I do." Her shoulders drooped, and she turned away with a shake of her head. A few steps and she climbed in the back of the wagon.

A son.

He tipped his head back and forced air into his lungs.

He'd left his wife pregnant and alone, all because—

Cat was right. He was a heel of the worse sort. *God, I'm sorry. I had no idea. But You did...* Sam swiped a hand across his face. *Why did I run from You for so long?*

He had to make this right, but how? Where were all the words he'd planned and practiced on the way back to Cater Springs? Working his hands along the brim of his black hat, he approached the buckboard, halting when a weighty sack of feed landed by his feet with a thud. Was she trying to hit him? It would serve him right.

"Cat, I-I'm sorry. If I'd've known—"

"Don't."

"What?"

"Don't say that you would've stayed for our son but not for me." She twisted and seized another bag, but not before he glimpsed tears glistening in her brown eyes.

The ache in his heart spread until his whole body hurt. Sam caught the next sack of oats and dropped it on top of the previous. When she reached for another, he grabbed her wrist. The jolt of touching her rocked him clear to his toes.

Cat focused on his hand and then his face. Questions, hurt, anger, sorrow, and so many other emotions floated in her watery gaze.

Everything within him longed to pull her closer, to wrap his arms around her the way he used to and let the world fade away, but too much stood between them now. Too many years.

He released her.

"You're right, Cat. I...I never should've left. I should've returned right after that cattle drive, but I didn't. I'm sorry. I wish I could go back and change things, but I can't. Will you...can you forgive me?"

A sigh seeped out of her. "I already did."

Her three simple words knocked the air from his chest harder than any punch he'd ever taken—and he'd received his fair share—but this couldn't be that easy. "You did?"

"Yes, but if you think that means I trust you, you're dead wrong."

Fair enough.

She turned and picked up another sack.

He promptly took it and set it with the others. Confusion tugged his brows together. Didn't forgiveness and trust go hand in hand? Maybe not. He could forgive a dog for biting him, but that didn't mean he'd trust him enough to get close again. Sam stood before his wife, but the mileage between them just stretched before his eyes. "What more can I say?"

Cat hoisted more feed. "You know what I want to know, Sam."

Surprisingly, he did. She wanted to know why he hadn't come back sooner. Clearly, Pa had kept his word and the knowledge of Sam's work to himself. He fiddled with a splinter on the wagon's side. "I was...helping people."

"People? And that was more important than helping your *wife*? What people?"

He couldn't tell her he'd been helping Pa when he'd first left. He couldn't tell her about the others he'd helped either. Knowing more would only endanger her. "I wish I could tell you."

"Why can't you?"

"I just...can't."

The next bag landed inches from his toes. With the anger in her eyes, he had to admire the woman's self-control.

"Can't or won't?" Cat shook her head and reached for a flour sack. "Forget it. I don't have to know. I've gone without knowing so long, why should it matter now?" She chucked the bag over the side to land with a thud and a puff of white.

Guilt washed over him, but not enough to untie his lips. Instead, he grabbed a barrel and started helping her unload the supplies so they could move the wagon once Joe and Benin returned. Wait. Benin?

Sam stopped and looked at his wife. "You named him after my grandfather?"

"Yes." Cat grunted with the toss of another sack. "Benin James McGarrett."

Make that her father and his grandfather. A smile tugged at his lips until a new question surfaced that didn't make him want to smile in the least. "Does he know who I am?"

Swiping a sleeve across her brow, she paused and returned his perusal. "We have prayed together for your soul and safe return ever since he was born. I told him earlier the man I saw riding through town looked like you, but I wasn't sure. He's a smart kid, so yes, he probably has a slight inkling you're his father, since a complete stranger called me by a nickname and I didn't correct him."

Sam slid out the last barrel. "So what are you going to tell him when he gets back?"

"I..." She sank onto the end of the wagon. "I don't know." She peered at him when he sat beside her. "Part of that depends on you."

"How so?" He clenched his hands together to keep from touching her. Uncertainty darkened her gaze and made him want to shield her and vanquish her every fear. Fear that had taken up residence because of him. Yep, he was a wretch of the worst sort.

Cat stood and walked a few paces away. "As much as I want you to be a part of our lives..." She faced him, a determined glint in her eyes. "I'm not going to let you come in and upend his world and leave again. I refuse to let that happen."

She wanted him to be a part of their lives? That was a good sign, right?

"Who said I was leaving?" The only reason he'd ever leave again was if... Oh, but he'd made sure that could never happen.

"Look, I want to trust you—heaven knows I do—but you don't know what the last—" Cat pivoted. Hugging her waist, she drew a shuddering breath and gazed heavenward.

What had he done? Where was the beautiful, once-understanding wife he'd left? Had he ruined everything? Would she shut him out, not even give him a chance to redeem himself? He stood and walked toward her. Tentatively, he cupped her arms. She stiffened for a moment but didn't move away. Maybe there was still hope.

"Cat, please, let me make this right. Give me a chance." He breathed in her lemony scent, which might be why he took total leave of his senses and pressed a kiss to her shoulder.

She stiffened and jerked away. "Don't. There...there'll not be any of that."

"But—"

"If you're going to stay, it's going to be on my terms. I'm not going to be left in the same state if one day you decide to just up and leave again."

"I told you. I'm not leaving." How could he make her understand? He stepped forward.

Cat countered with a back step. "I mean it, Samuel."

Sam raised his hands and retreated. "All right. I got it. No kissing."

"And you sleep in the barn."

"What?"

She folded her arms across her chest.

"All right. All right, I'll sleep in the barn." A haymow would be better than what he'd put up with over the years, but he had looked forward to at least a soft mattress and a warm building. He'd hoped for an even softer woman beside him, but some things took time. Elijah Stone had warned him the road to restoration wouldn't be easy. Clearly, he'd been right. Hopefully, he hadn't been right about the other aspects of the past six years. Aspects better left behind.

※

Catherine prayed for the trembling to stop while she stared up the dirt road. It had been ages since another's touch had affected her so. She wanted nothing more than to turn and throw her arms around Sam's neck like she used to, but what if she did and he left again? She doubted her heart could sustain another shattering disappointment.

Finally, a rider appeared at the top of the hill coming from town. Not much longer and she wouldn't have to be alone with Sam. *God, I thought I was ready for this, but now I'm not so sure.*

"Here they come. What're you going to tell Benin?"

She still searched for those words. "I'm going to say we're taking the wagon back to town and you're staying here with our supplies."

"No, I should be the one to drive that wagon. I don't need y'all getting hurt if something doesn't hold."

Catherine bit her tongue and swallowed the rebuttal that begged to spring forth. "Fine. You take it to town with Joe. Benin and I will stay with the supplies."

"I can't leave you out here by yourselves."

Her tongue had to be bleeding. "What do you suggest then?"

He frowned and flicked his attention to the wagon and back. "You got a gun with you?"

The man wanted to put a weapon in her hands. Wow, he must've lost some scruples. "No, I don't." And even if she did, experience had taught her carrying a rifle didn't always make a difference. Bad things still happened.

Sam mumbled something and shoved his duster aside. Bone-handled six-shooters hung from a notched belt strapped to his waist and thighs.

Oh, God, help me. What on earth had her husband become in his absence?

"Here. If I'm going to leave my wife and son sitting on the side of the road, they're going to have something to protect themselves with."

"What exactly do you expect to happen?"

Sam scanned the surrounding hills as if searching for something...or someone. "You never know."

Unfortunately, she did. And that same knowledge reflected in her husband's gray gaze.

He clasped her hand and set the cool metal in her palm. "Remember what I taught you?"

"Of course." How could she forget when she'd replayed those moments target practicing together too many times to count? Only later had she realized he'd been preparing her for his absence, preparing her to take care of herself because he wouldn't be around to do it. She jerked from his grasp. Gun in hand. The desire to point the end at Sam flicked through her mind, lingering a bit longer than it should have.

Something must've registered in her gaze, because her husband took a step back, his brows drawn.

Joe and Benin pulled to a stop beside them, thankfully disrupting the moment.

"Mama, we got your stick." Benin slid from the saddle with Joe's help and stared up at Sam when he took the wooden pole from the boy with a nod. "Hey, that's a dandy gun. Did I miss you shootin' a rattler 'r somethin'? Can I shoot it?"

Catherine flicked her gaze to Sam, then back to her eager five-year-old. "No, you can't. We're just borrowing it while the men take the wagon back to town, so if we do see a rattler or something, we'll be able to protect ourselves."

"Aww, why can't I shoot it? It's not too big like our rifle."

"Benin, I said no."

He hung his head. "Yes, ma'am."

Sam tousled her son's—correction, *their* son's—hair as he left his horse's side carrying a rope. "Maybe we can get in some practice shooting together later."

"Really? Can I, Mama?"

"We'll discuss it." She directed her comment more at Sam than the boy. Learning to shoot a rifle to kill a deer or a hog was one thing, but pistols, like the one in her hand, were too often used to kill creatures of the two-legged variety. She'd be hogtied and dragged by a stampede of horses before she'd let a son of hers start down that path.

"Okay. I'm gonna go help the men."

After stuffing the Colt in her apron pocket, Catherine folded her arms and watched the three work. Make that, two of them work while one watched up close. With Joe's help, Sam ran the thick pole under the end of the back axle until the wagon ran horizontal again. One end of the pole extended forward above the front wheel, and the other dragged the ground past the rear of the wagon. They lashed it firmly into place before Sam climbed onto the driver's bench and tested its hold by turning the buckboard to face town.

"That ought to do it." He tied the reins around the brake handle and jumped down. "Thanks for your help, Matthews."

"No problem. Y'all need help with anything else, or you through with me?"

"I think we can manage from here."

"Are you sure he shouldn't accompany you back to town?"

Sam's eyes narrowed at her. "I'll be fine. I've done this before."

Maybe so, but he'd also left before and not come back. She'd feel much better sitting on the roadside with no more transportation than her own two legs if someone else accompanied him and made sure he returned.

Joe Matthews hesitated in mounting his horse. "Are you sure? I don't mind."

Sam grabbed the buckskin's reins and moved toward her. "There's no need. I'm sure you're anxious to get home to your wife."

Catherine scrutinized her husband. Was there an underlying meaning behind that statement?

Joe smiled. "Speaking of my wife…she'd probably hogtie me for sure if I didn't wrangle out a promise from the two of you to come to dinner soon."

Not a bad idea. "How about tonight?"

All eyes shifted to Catherine. She shrugged. It beat spending the evening arguing with Sam, and it would assure he'd stick around for at least a few more hours. Well, possibly.

"Really, Mama? Ya mean it? Hey, Brother Matthews, ya think your wife could gimme a lesson with her knife? I wanna be able to throw it like y'all so's I can take down Sam Bass if'n he comes back this way." Benin pretended to flick a knife through the air.

Sam's brows shot up. "Knife throwing? What kind of woman did you marry, Matthews?"

Joe grinned. "The best." He tipped his Stetson at Catherine. "I'll be expecting you folks around dinnertime."

Sam dusted his hands together. "How about tomorrow instead of tonight? Give the ladies a bit more time to prepare?"

Catherine studied her husband. He knew as well as she did that Joe's mother always cooked more than plenty for each meal and could make a pot of vittles multiply in size in a matter of minutes. Was he really just being considerate, or was he up to something?

Joe gathered his reins in one hand. "Tomorrow's fine."

"Should I bring anything?"

Joe paused his horse beside her. "Seeing as how I invited y'all, I'm going to say no. If I don't miss my guess, I reckon you'll have enough occupying you until then."

Catherine glanced at the matched pair standing near her. "Thank you, Joe."

"My pleasure, ma'am. See y'all tomorrow." The pinto carried his rider up the next hill and disappeared.

Catherine drew a deep breath but hesitated in turning to face her son and husband. How would Benin react when she told him with all certainty that Sam was his father? How did she even start the conversation? How—

"Mama, is what you su'pected earlier 'bout this here fella true? Is he my pa?"

Hanging her head, she rotated and stared at the dark-eyed boy who'd stolen her heart from the first moment she'd learned of his presence. She slid her hand onto his cheek and fiddled with the too-long hair hanging behind his ear.

"Yes, baby. He's Samuel Houston McGarrett, your father." Catherine didn't dare look at her husband. She'd hoped to have this conversation when he took the wagon to town, but perhaps this was better.

Her son's lips pressed together before he faced the man he mirrored in so many ways. "You really my pa?"

Sam knelt in front of Benin. "It would seem so."

"We've prayed for you."

"That's what your ma said."

"Why'd ya take so long to come home? Did ya get lost?"

Catherine's heart caught. How many times had she asked God that question? She'd had no idea her son longed for the same understanding. She slid her hand onto Benin's chest and held his back against her.

Sam's gaze roamed her face, then fell to their son. "In a way. Mainly, I was just stupid."

Tears rushed to the surface. When he said nothing more, a surge of anger followed. That was all the explanation they got from him! She could've told him that much. Leaving anyone when you promised them you'd come back, when you promised to love and cherish them until death did them part, was indeed stupid.

Catherine grabbed Benin's hand. "Come on, son. Let's find some wood to make a fire to keep us warm while your pa takes the wagon to get fixed."

"We're not goin' with 'im?"

"Someone has to stay with the supplies."

"Ya want I should take Pa's horse 'n' ride home 'n' have Mr. Mo bring us the other wagon?"

Catherine paused. Would that be better than waiting around on Sam, or should she give him a chance to prove he wasn't planning on leaving?

She brushed a strand of hair from her face. "That's a smart idea, Benin…"

An indiscernible expression hovering somewhere near hurt and uncertainty clouded Sam's gaze.

Catherine swallowed a sigh. "But I think it's best if we wait. It shouldn't take too long, should it?"

If she wasn't mistaken, Sam stood a little straighter. "Shouldn't take long at all." He strode around his horse and reached into his saddlebags. "Here's some matches for that fire." Sam handed the small tin to Benin and passed the buckskin's reins to her. "I'll be back quick as a whistle."

"You'd better."

3

The traces jingled in rhythm with the horses' plodding steps. Part of Sam waited to hear the whiz of a bullet from his Colt fly past his ear. Cat looked none too happy about him driving off with her wagon, but all things considered, he didn't blame her. He wouldn't trust him either. It was a miracle she hadn't shot him on sight or sent him packing, and to find out she'd actually prayed for him all this time was nearly incomprehensible. When the Word said God's ways and thoughts were higher than his own, it surely wasn't yanking his lasso.

A cool breeze rushed around him, urging him to turn up his coat collar. Texas weather had more ups and downs than the hills surrounding him—much like his lovely wife's moods. How did the woman go from spitting mad to utterly calm in such a short time? He'd never been able to understand her, and it seemed time hadn't done him any favors. Her anger made sense. Her acceptance didn't. How could Cat not hate him for what he'd done to her?

And his son! He couldn't believe she hadn't filled his mind with accusations and bitterness toward him. If the child hated him, he surely wouldn't be so thrilled about target practice. Unless he planned to do his mother's bidding and use him for the target? Sam shook his head. With Cat's reaction to keeping the pistol in general and the look she'd seared him with when the boy had jumped on the idea, he didn't see them going off with guns anytime soon.

He'd missed so much of his boy's life. How did he make up for missing five years? Was it too late to catch up? Could they still form a bond? Maybe if Cat would let him, but there was no guaranteeing she would. She could change her mind about allowing him to stay at any moment. The way her fists had balled at her side hadn't boded well. Could she have truly forgiven him? And if she had, could he ever forgive himself?

Sam hung his head. How on earth were they going to fix their marriage with a child looking on? Those questions in her coffee-colored eyes might spring from her lips at any time. He wasn't planning to fight with Cat, but not answering her questions or not answering them the way she wanted would surely set her off. That wasn't the kind of impression he wanted to leave on his son. If only he could get her alone for a while.

A flash of movement caught his eye. Sam studied the top of the nearest hill to his right. A chill climbed his spine. His fingers itched to grab his gun, but he waited.

Nothing moved.

"It was probably just a deer or a rabbit, right fellas?"

The knot in his gut argued otherwise. Sam slid the gun from its holster and urged the team to pull a little faster. If trouble had indeed managed to follow him home, there was no sense in keeping himself a sitting duck longer than necessary. His mind flicked to his wife and son sitting on the roadside, and he wished the horses would sprout wings.

"Father God, I sure hope I'm wrong, but if I'm not, please keep them safe."

⁂

Catherine sat in the dried grasses and stripped a twig. Benin poked at the fire with a long stick from a nearby mesquite tree. The long, dried seedpods crackled and shriveled to a crisp, the dire consequence of getting too close to the flames. Why did she feel like those seedpods, like she was inching toward a fire and certain doom? She'd hoped and prayed for Sam's return, but what consequences would follow?

Surely the general wouldn't like this.

The only question was—how would he demonstrate his displeasure? Would there be more threats? Something more severe?

Her heart clenched. Maybe it wasn't safe letting Sam back into their lives.

The twig snapped between her fingers, and she hurled it into the flames. She was so sick and tired of being afraid. Maybe she should use Sam's return for their good, their freedom. Then again, telling him everything might not be worth the risk. Sam was practically a stranger now. She only knew what he used to be. It stood to reason he'd changed over the years.

After all, she was no longer the naïve teenager who'd tumbled headlong into marriage. She'd believed herself in love, and truly she had been. In fact, the attraction remained, but love was more than attraction. More than a feeling. It was a choice. A choice he'd neglected for years. A choice she'd have to continue to make daily. Why did that seem easier when she wasn't staring at the embodiment of betrayal?

Catherine rubbed her fingers against her forehead, then propped her chin in one hand and rested her elbow on her knee. What she wouldn't give for her Bible right now. First Corinthians 13 beckoned. She'd memorized the thirteen verses over the past five years, but she longed to read them again, especially some of the middle verses. The whole chapter described charity, or love, but those middle ones were her favorite. "Love 'beareth all things, believeth all things, hopeth all things, endureth all things. Love never faileth.'"

"You say somethin', Mama?"

"Just thinking out loud, honey."

Benin nodded and returned to poking, like she talked to herself all the time, which wasn't too far from the truth. Paul said in Ephesians to "speak to yourselves in psalms and hymns and spiritual songs," and she made a regular habit of it.

Did Sam still love her? Was that why he'd returned, or was it for some other selfish reason or sense of duty? Duty. Ha! Sam wouldn't know duty if it bit him on the backside. Duty would've kept him home or at the least in touch with her. No word for nearly six years. Six! What had he done during that time? How had he spent his days? Did her friend Roxie's words from last year hold any truth?

"Mama, can we target practice while we wait?"

"No." Sam's pistol weighted down her skirts, but she wasn't about to waste any bullets.

"Why not? He said I could."

"He said you *might*. Later. And I said we'd discuss it. If you ask me again, I won't let you do it at all, understand?"

"Yes, ma'am."

Was that what having a husband home would do, make her son rebellious? Benin rarely argued when she put her foot down like she had earlier.

"Mama?"

"Yes?"

"Why do ya think Papa wears two guns?"

"I don't know, honey." But she'd sure like to.

"You think he's a gunslinger, or maybe a bounty hunter, or a Texas Ranger, or maybe a US Marshal?"

"Where on earth did you come up with a list like that? Who's filled your head with such ideas? Should I keep your grandpa from coming out so often?"

"Aw, Mama, it's not all Gramps's fault. Mr. Mo 'n' Roscoe, they tell me stories too, 'n' my friends at church, 'n'—"

"I get the picture." Catherine reached over and tugged him down beside her. "Look, I know you're curious about your father. I've got questions for him too, but don't be upset if he doesn't tell you his whole life story all at once."

Her heart smote her. Hadn't she been expecting such a miracle? She sighed.

"Does that mean I'm not s'posed to ask 'im any questions?"

"No, no, it doesn't mean that. I'm just warning you that there are some things your pa might not want to talk about. Some things we'll have to wait for him to tell us in his own time."

How could she preach to her son and herself at the same time? *Okay, God, I get it.*

"All right. Mama?"

"Yes?"

"He's not gonna leave again, is he?"

Catherine brushed the lad's dark hair off his forehead and pulled him close. "I hope not, Benin. I really hope not."

Because if he did, she might be liable to track him down and shoot him herself.

※

Sam paused his pacing in the livery doorway when a silver-haired man pulled a palomino to a stop outside the office next door. After the fellow swung down, Sam cupped his hands, brought them to his lips, and blew out the hollow dove call his father had taught him as a child.

The palomino looked over and shifted to face him, nearly throwing the old man off balance.

"Pecos, I ain't got time for this. Behave yourself."

Sam swallowed a laugh and sounded the call again. The gelding trotted his direction, his reins slipping from the sheriff's unsuspecting hand.

"Why you dumb—" The old-timer stopped midstride and rubbed his eyes. "Samuel, that you, son?"

Sam patted Pecos's neck and smiled. "Hi, Pa."

"Well, ain't you a sight for sore eyes? Bring me back my horse, and come give me a proper greetin', boy."

Sam closed the gap between them and accepted his father's bear hug. It'd been too long. A large nose snuffled his shoulder and broke them apart.

Pa chuckled and grabbed the reins trailing the ground. "This horse always did cotton to you better'n me."

"He must like you some if he's put up with you this long."

"I doubt he will, now that you're back." After securing the horse, Pa rubbed a hand over his gray whiskers. "You seen Catherine?"

"I've got her wagon being fixed in the livery there."

"Oh." Pa ducked his head and strode through the door of the sheriff's office.

Sam stayed on his heels. "*Oh* is right."

"Shut the door before you let me have it with both barrels, will ya?"

He did so while his pa circled the scarred desk filling up one side of the room. Sam folded his arms and leaned against the door. "Why didn't you tell me I had a son?"

Pa sank into his creaky chair and tossed his gray Stetson onto the hat stand in the corner. "She made me promise not to."

"Why in the world did you agree to such a fool-hardy notion? I deserved to know."

"And ya do."

"Yeah, now. You made me miss out on five years of my boy's life."

"Don't go layin' blame at the wrong door, son. You're the one who up and decided to leave in the first place. I offered to do it myself."

"Yes, but too many people knew you're a lawman. You needed anonymity. I just wish I'd have known what it'd cost me." Sam sank into the ladder-back chair across from the desk. "Now, I'm wondering if it's too late."

"'Cause of Catherine?"

"No, although I don't know how long I can take sleeping in the barn."

"She's already relegated you there, huh?" A deep chuckle rumbled from Pa before he sobered. "If it ain't Catherine, then what is it?"

For a moment, Sam let his mind wander back to a time he'd rather forget. "Let's just say, I'm not sure the past will let me."

Pa sat forward. "I thought you settled everything. Did you bring trouble to my town?"

"I did my best to see that I didn't, but I got the sneaking suspicion someone was eyeballing me from the bushes on my way into town with Cat's wagon." Sam shook his head and stood, donning his hat. "I've probably been looking over my shoulder too long. Anyway, I need to go check on that wheel. Why don't you come out to the place tomorrow? Make sure she hasn't shot me."

"I've got a standin' invitation for dinner every Friday. I'll see y'all then. You can survive a few days without me. Good to have ya back."

Sam nodded and, after a parting hug, strode for the door. He paused with his hand on the latch, reached inside his jacket pocket, and withdrew a brass star. "I almost forgot. I don't need this anymore. It didn't do me much good outside your county anyway."

"I'm sure it helped, but if you don't need it anymore, then why you still wearin' that?" Pa nodded toward Sam's gun belt. "Keep it. Besides, there's one last thing I'd like you to try your hand at."

"No, Pa, I'm done. I—"

"Sam Bass was spotted in the area."

Hadn't Benin mentioned that name earlier? He'd chalked it up to a boy's active imagination. Was he wrong? Sam's hand slid from the door latch. "The Sam Bass who was part of the gang that robbed the train in—what? Nebraska?"

"One and the same."

"They're saying that's the biggest heist ever. Sixty thousand dollars' worth of newly minted gold coins."

Pa nodded. "I lost his trail up near the old Ackerman place a few days ago. If someone with better eyes were to say…"

"No, Pa. Not this time. If I left now, Cat would string me up the nearest tree. Not—"

"Take her with you."

"*What*? Have you lost—Pa, it's November. I'm not taking her out in the cold after some wanted thieves."

"I'm not askin' you to catch the men. Just find their trail again for me. Tell me which way they're headed. Besides, it ain't been that cold, and cold has a way of tuggin' two people together, if ya catch my drift."

Sam knew exactly what he meant, and the idea held merit. Plus, it would give him some time alone to convince Cat he'd changed, maybe even convince her to let him move into the house. The more he was around her, the more they could talk. Pa said it'd been a few days since he'd lost the trail. That'd surely put enough distance between her and any real danger. "What about Benin? I can't take his ma off after only meeting him hours ago."

"He don't call me Gramps for nothin'."

"You'd keep him?"

"I raised you, didn't I?"

"Well...yeah." Sam removed his hat and worked his hands along the brim. "You really think she'd agree to it?"

"So what if she doesn't. Make her go. She could use a few days free of that ranch. She works too hard as it is. Between me, the boy, and the hands, I think we can manage."

"Wait. What? What ranch? What hands?"

"Ain't you seen the ole place?"

"No. Now what's this about a ranch? Hasn't she been living off the money I've sent?"

"She ain't touched it. Anytime I tried to give her some, she refused, so I quit tryin'. It's just been earnin' interest in the bank."

"So what has she been living on all this time?"

"Horseflesh. She just got contracts to supply horses to the United States Army and the Wells Fargo stage lines this comin' year. Believe it or not, but your woman has some of the best-trained horseflesh around. She must've learned a thing or two from you before ya left."

"Or from her father."

"Her father?"

"Yeah, he worked with horses before he died during the Indian raids. He's the one who gave her that paint."

Pa blinked. "I didn't know that."

Sam nodded. "Honestly, I'd be more surprised if you did. She doesn't talk about it."

The older man scratched his chin in his all-familiar manner. "Sam, t—"

A knock jarred the door seconds before the burly blacksmith's head appeared. "Your wagon is ready, McGarrett. Guten Tag, Sheriff."

"Howdy, Hans."

"Thanks, Schreiner. Add that to my wife's bill and have the total ready for me. I'll be right over."

Schreiner's eyes widened. "Ja, will do. Sheriff, I also have nameplate carved and ready to hang. It reads 'G. W. McGarrett, Sheriff,' just like one the boys shot down."

Sam returned his attention to his pa. "Shot down?"

"Just some boys with more time than good sense. They finish payin' for it, Schreiner?"

"Ja, they have mucked stalls all week."

Pa's grin parted his whiskers. "All right, let them hang it when they get done today. I'll come out and do a little remindin' when they do. We shouldn't have any trouble from them now. Well, at least not for a while anyways."

"Ja, sounds good." The blacksmith slipped out the door.

Sam readjusted his hat and returned to their conversation from before. "You said it's been about three days since you lost Bass's trail?"

Pa folded his arms and leaned back. "Yeah, and there hasn't been a drop of rain. You shouldn't have any trouble findin' it. It starts at the cavern on the Matthews' land and heads northeast toward the Ackerman place."

Sam rubbed his hand across his chin. He could find the trail. Of that he had no doubt. But what about Cat? He couldn't leave her again so soon. She'd never let him come back.

"Pa, as much as I'd like to help, I can't say yes without talking to Cat. I'll try to talk her into it though. Maybe the Lord'll be on our side and she'll actually come willingly. He surely knows I'm already in hot enough water with her as it is." Sam grabbed the door handle. "We were invited to supper at the Matthews' tomorrow. Why don't you drop by before then, and I'll give you my answer? Maybe you can stay with Benin if I can convince Cat to go."

"Fair enough. Hey, why don't I plan to take Benin campin' or huntin' regardless? Give y'all a day or two to talk without little ears around?"

That was a mighty tempting offer. "What about Bass and his gang?"

Pa shrugged. "I've done what I can. The rest is up to you and the good Lord."

"Sounds like a plan." With a deep breath, Sam opened the door. "Guess I'd better go see which way the wind's blowing."

4

"If you think for one minute I plan to go along with your harebrained scheme, you've cracked your crock." Catherine peeked over her shoulder into the back of the wagon to make sure Benin was indeed asleep. "I told you I'm not going to let you come in here and turn his world upside down, and me leaving would do exactly that."

"How could spending time with his grandpa upend his world? He sees the man all the time."

"But he's never spent the night away from me."

Sam's gaze narrowed. "You sure this isn't more about you than him? It's a good thing I came back when I did. You're turning him into a mama's boy."

Catherine stiffened. "How would you know the first thing about what he's turning into? You don't even know him. Besides, what's wrong with him taking after me? It's sure better than taking after a man who ups and leaves his family."

A muscle twitched in Sam's jaw. "I told you I'd be back."

"Yes, I remember, but you neglected to mention it'd be some six years later."

Sam studied her, his blue-gray eyes reminding her of a gathering storm. "Do you even want me here? You say you've forgiven me for leaving, but you keep throwing it back in my face."

His comment stung and held a ring of truth, but she brushed it off. "Do *you* want to be here? You've not been back twenty-four hours, and you're already talking about leaving again—to hunt outlaws, no less. Is that what you've been doing all this time?"

"I'm not discussing what I've been doing. The past is just that. The past. I'm talking about tomorrow and the next couple of days."

"Days! How long are you expecting it to take to track down these heathens? And why does it have to be you? Why can't your father do his job and go after them himself?"

"I told you. He lost the trail. He's just wanting me to see if I can find it again."

"He taught you how to track. What more are you going to find that he can't?"

"His eyesight's not as good as it used to be. Come on, Cat. Come with me. It'll only be for a little while." His hand slid around hers, kicking her pulse into a full-fledged gallop and reminding her of every reason why she should tell him *no* and why she'd always told him *yes*. The man could charm a dog out of his last bone.

"I...I'll consider it." If she got far enough away from him to form a coherent thought.

The corner of his mouth edged up. "That's better than a no."

"But it's not a yes, understand?"

"Yes, ma'am."

Catherine expected him to return both hands to the reins, but he held on. Amazing how different holding his hand was compared to holding Benin's. Even through his gloves she felt his strength. With everything in her, she wanted to cling to him and never let go, but the last time she'd held on so tightly, he'd run for the hills. Literally. Would she ever be able to be that close to him again? Trust him so implicitly? Depend on him?

She glanced over and found those amazing gray eyes studying her. GW said his father had had eyes like that. Eyes that seemed to look straight through a person. Eyes that were unforgettable. Eyes that invaded dreams and stole precious sleep.

Catherine blinked and looked away, reclaiming her hand.

She needed to maintain her distance to handle this situation properly. One wrong move and the general would make her life a living nightmare. She'd always dreamt of Sam's return, of how she'd throw her arms around him, kiss him, and everything would go back to the way it was. Better even.

But that wasn't the way things were.

Any moment she'd wake up and find herself still dreaming. How could she know he'd truly come to stay? If she said no to his crazy hunting expedition, would he still leave without her? Might that be a test of his loyalty? Perhaps she should refuse, see if he'd put her first, stay with her.

Catherine studied Sam from the corner of her eye. Did she dare? She sat a little straighter. Yes, she did. "I'm not going."

"Pardon?"

"I'm not going to go off traipsing after some wanted ruffians."

"Why not?"

"I just told you. It's not safe." Plus, the general wouldn't like her traipsing off either.

"They're probably miles away by now."

"You don't know that, and if that's true, then why still go after them?"

"Ugh, are we really doing this again? Cat, I've told you why. My pa asked me to, and I want you to come with me."

Catherine crossed her arms and dared him to make a move without her. "If you go, you go without me."

Sam's jaw tightened, and his mouth firmed into a hard line. Seconds ticked by, then his face transformed and his eyes softened. "Will you at least go to the Matthews' alone with me tomorrow night? I'd hate to see my pa come out for nothing. He'd at least get to spend some time with Benin. And we could have some time to talk?"

"I, um… Sure. I guess that would be all right." She studied him. That was way too easy. Or was she being too hard on him? A sigh drifted from her. "I suppose GW could take Benin camping too. He'd enjoy that. But I am *not* going traipsing after any thieves, understood?" She had enough trouble in her own backyard.

"Understood." Sam flicked the reins, encouraging the team up the last hill. He tossed her a smile. "Now tell me, what's this I hear about you turning our place into a horse ranch?"

Catherine leaned back in the seat and tried to ignore the way his smile tugged at her insides. And failed. Miserably. She'd hoped that one day he'd be proud of what she'd accomplished. She'd worked hard to build something they could share in, something they could one day hand down to their son. "I had to occupy myself somehow while you were away."

"Clearly, your pa rubbed off on you more than I thought."

"To be fair, I remembered some things you taught me too."

"Yeah?"

She nodded, then exhaled and studied her dusty boots. "I remember a lot of things."

The plodding of the horses and creak of the wagon filled the heavy silence.

Sam rubbed a hand on his thigh and readjusted his grip on the reins. "I, uh, thought my memory was pretty good, but it didn't do you justice."

"How so?"

"You're even prettier than I remember."

Catherine's heart skipped a beat as pleasure warmed her cheeks and tied her tongue in knots.

"*Ehemm*...there's the ranch. Anything I need to know before we pull up in front of the house? Like maybe, are you still living in the house I built?"

With a hard swallow, she forced aside her feelings. There was business to attend to. "Yes, same house. I only added the additional corrals and the bunkhouse. Oh, I guess I'll have to introduce you to my foreman and the hands."

"You mean *our*, right? And please tell me you aren't the only woman out here with all these men."

"What exactly are you implying? I am a married woman, and everyone around here knows that."

"It's just not right. One woman amid a bunch of men."

Catherine frowned. "Maybe you should've thought of that before you left."

"Look, I sent you plenty of money. You didn't have to start raising horses and hiring strangers."

"What are you talking about? I haven't seen a dime from you."

"Are you loco? Pa told me himself he tried to give it to you."

Her stomach dropped to her toes. "That was from you? I thought he was just..." She leaned her face into her hands. This day was becoming too much. All those years scrimping and saving had been for naught? Sam had tried to provide for her? He hadn't left her to starve? But then...

She straightened. "Why didn't you send the money directly to me? Why go through your father?"

"I—" Sam broke off and looked toward the grounds of the Bar M Ranch. "I had to."

They were back to *that* again. No explanations. Catherine forced her fingers to not curl into fists, but it took some effort. Time. She took a deep breath. In time, he'd give her the answers she sought.

If she didn't strangle him first.

5

Sam stopped the wagon at the hitching post in front of the house. Memories tugged at him of all the times Cat had emerged from the simple cabin with a kiss and a hug after a long day in the saddle. Those moments together were often more refreshing than a tall drink of water on a sweltering day. His gaze strayed to his wife. Did she remember those times too?

Cat moved to disembark.

"Wait. I'll help if you'll give me just a second."

"Oh, um, sure."

Sam hopped down. He'd always thought Cat enjoyed him helping her. Had she simply forgotten, or did she really not want to be near him?

The front door swung open while he rounded the wagon. A black woman of generous proportions stepped onto the porch, a spoon in her hands. Sam's gaze darted to his wife. Why hadn't she admitted there was another woman on the property? Why let him assume the worst? She could've told him the truth and avoided a whole argument. Had she not changed at all in his absence?

"Miz Cathy, well, glory be. We wuz beginnin' to wonder 'bout you." The large woman's ebony eyes strayed to Sam, and she crossed her arms. "You have trouble on the way?"

Sam had no doubt the spoon in the woman's hand had been used for far more than stirring in her days. The uncanny need to hide, or at least hide his knuckles, washed over him. Shaking off the sensation, he helped Cat down.

"We're fine, Ida. Just had some problems with a wheel." Cat

stepped away the instant he released her, which stung just a mite. Did she have to treat him like he had the plague? How was he going to win these people's respect if he didn't have hers?

"Would you ring for the others to join us?"

"Sho' thang, Miz Cathy. Am I gonna be addin' another place to the table?"

"Yes. Not tomorrow night though. Joe Matthews invited us to share supper with his family, and the sheriff will be coming out to spend time with Ben."

"Yes'm." Ida clanged her spoon around the inside of the triangle hanging from the porch post. "Hope these men don't think they's gettin' suppa' this early."

Two wranglers, with chaps flapping, rounded the barn. A third, with skin that matched Ida's, emerged from the shadowed interior of the whitewashed building. They veered toward the rear of the cabin until Ida shouted and turned them toward the small front porch.

At a tap on his shoulder, Sam rotated to find Benin kneeling on the feedbags piled against the wagon sides and reaching toward him. Sleep weighted the young boy's eyelids and flushed his cheeks. With a slight hesitation, Sam pulled his son from the perch. The lad's arms encircled his neck, but instead of insisting to be put down, he laid his head on Sam's shoulder.

Sam's brows climbed toward his hairline, and his gaze strayed to his wife. A faint smile touched her lips before she turned away. Ida eyed him suspiciously before silencing her spoon.

Standing there, holding Benin, Sam soaked in his son's acceptance. A wave of love so profound, and deeper than he could've imagined, washed over him. Did every father feel this way? How could his wife, *his* father, not have told him about Benin? He'd missed so much of his boy's life. Sam gave himself a mental shake. That was over now. He'd see that Benin was taken care of. He'd teach him what every little boy, what every man, needed to know, starting with how to know God. From there, he'd teach him to ride and train horses, track animals, catch fish, survive in the woods... The list was endless.

Sam hoisted the child a little higher, settling him more comfortably in his arms. A stair-stacked group gathered opposite his wife, eyeing him and talking in hushed tones.

"Everyone." All attention shifted to Cat. "I've got some good news to share with you. As you all know, I've been praying for my husband's safe return for quite some time. Today God has answered my prayers. This is my husband, Sam McGarrett."

Eyes widened and a few mouths gaped, but what caught his attention most was his wife's choice of words. She considered his return good news? She didn't act like it.

"Sam, this is Larry."

The tallest of the three men gave a nod of his dishwater-blond head, his mouth a firm line.

"Curly."

A brown-haired young man with close-cropped curls straightened and nodded.

"And Moses, who generally prefers to go by Mo."

The dark-skinned fellow stepped forward, hand outstretched. "I's always knew you'd be a-comin' back. Unlike some people." Mo looked askance at Larry. "Welcome home, sir."

Sam shook the man's hand, surprised the others didn't make the gesture too. "Thanks."

"Mo is also my foreman and Ida's husband. I think you've figured out who she is. They live in the cabin on the other side of the kitchen."

"Pleased to meet y'all." Sam swallowed the shock that his wife had a former slave as a foreman and that these wranglers actually consented to work under such a man. A rarity indeed. Personally, he didn't care what color a man's skin was as long as he stayed on the right side of the law and did his work without shirking, but not everyone shared his opinions.

"Where's Roscoe?"

At Cat's question, Benin's head popped up. Clearly, the tyke hadn't gone back to sleep.

"He finished his chores, so's I let him exercise one of the hosses 'fore supper. He should be back in a gallopin' fury nows that that supper bell's done ringed." Mo grinned at his wife, then looked at

Sam. "Roscoe's our boy. He's nine."

"He's my friend."

Sam peered at the lad in his arms. "I'm mighty glad to hear that."

"Men, y'alls can go on back 'n' finish up with them hosses. I'll help the ladies unload their foodstuffs, then bring y'all the feed."

Larry and Curly nodded at Mo and started for the barn with nary a word.

"They're not much for talking, are they?"

"Naw, they talks plenty once they gets to know ya, Boss. Yous wants I should unsaddle your hoss?"

Boss? Did the man switch loyalties so quickly, or was he simply that welcoming? Sam peeked at Cat. He couldn't tell if she was bothered by the title or not. "Call me Sam, and thanks for the offer, but I'll take care of Sandy here in a minute. She can be a bit temperamental with strangers the first time."

Mo nodded and moved toward the wagon. "If'n y'all'll excuse me…"

"Thank you, Mo."

"Sho' thang, Miz Cathy. Ida, honey, you wanna ride with me 'round to the kitchen?"

"I ain't forgot how to walk." Ida turned and strode back into the house. Soon a door smacked shut on the other side of the shotgun cabin. Mo chuckled and drove the wagon around the house.

Sam looked to Cat for explanation. "Ride to the kitchen? I thought I built it in the house?"

"We built a separate kitchen with a dining area a couple years ago when the house nearly caught on fire. It sits about halfway between this cabin and Ida's."

"Makes sense."

"Can I go help Mrs. Ida?"

Cat smiled up at Benin. "No, but you can help Mr. Mo."

Benin squirmed to get down and hurried to round the house as soon as his feet hit the dirt. He paused at the corner and peered back at his ma. "Can I have a lemon candy?"

"If you're good and eat all your supper, I'll let you have two."

"Yippee!" Benin took off again.

"Pa got him stuck on lemon drop candy too, huh? You still partial to peppermint?"

Cat peeked up at him. "Sometimes." She stepped inside the house.

Sam moved to follow until a snort from behind stopped him. "Don't act so jealous, Sandy. I'll be back."

But first he was going to take advantage of a few minutes alone with his wife. Her choice of words continued to surprise him.

Catherine's steps faltered. Why did every word her husband said have to remind her of the past? *I'll be back.* Couldn't he have found a different way to state that? Was he trying to make her remember? She picked at a fingernail while he shut the door against the cool November winds. When it latched, she rotated and stared up at him. "Why did you say that?"

Sam's brows rose, then he shook his head with a small smile. "Believe it or not, I was just fixing to ask you the same thing."

"Me? About what?"

"I was wondering if you truly meant it when you said it was good news that I'd returned."

She stopped her fidgeting and moved to straighten an already straightened living room. "Of course it is."

"You make me wonder. I didn't even get to kiss you hello, and we've already argued more than once. Just makes a fella wonder if he's truly welcome."

Catherine paused with her hands on the back of her rocker and looked over her shoulder at her husband, who stood unmoved by the front door. She returned her focus to the doily on the chair, plucking at it with her fingers.

"I'm sorry, Sam. I don't mean to be difficult. I'm…I'm just…"

His approaching steps filled the small room, and then his warm hand settled on hers. He stood so close his breath stirred the hairs that had escaped her bun. "You just what?"

She just wanted to turn and throw her arms around his neck, just wanted to forget the last six years ever happened, just wanted to start all over, but she couldn't because... Catherine drew a shaky breath and forced herself to speak the truth.

"I'm scared." Tears pricked her eyes.

"Of me?"

She nodded, paused, and then shook her head, unable to speak lest she lose the close rein on her emotions.

"So which is it?"

Catherine's shoulders lifted in a shrug. How did she tell him all the things she felt when she couldn't even explain them to herself?

His hands moved to cup her arms. "Darlin', I can't fix it if you don't tell me what's wrong."

Darlin'? A sniffle escaped along with a solitary tear. She swiped it away, but not before Sam saw it. He turned her, and his finger slid under her chin. She refused to look at him, to give him the chance to see all the things she couldn't say.

"Cat, if you don't look at me, I'm going to kiss you."

Her eyelids flew up.

His stormy blue eyes searched her face, and a hint of a smile teased his mouth. "Is that what you're afraid of? Kissing me? I'm sure you'll remember how if you want to give it a try."

Her traitorous gaze slid to his lips, and whether he believed it or not, there was nothing wrong with her memory. Kissing him was like sweet nectar to a hummingbird, a drenching shower on a parched land, a warm fire on a freezing night...and a noose around a thief's neck. Even apart from the general's ultimatum, letting Sam close was like signing her death warrant, because if she did and he left again, she'd surely die from the heartache. It was only by the grace of God she'd managed thus far, and part of her said He'd carry her through it once more, but another part feared to ever tread those painful waters again.

She took a step back, out of his reach and out of kissing distance.

"I see." His eyes clouded. "Some other time then." He rotated, his gaze falling on something besides her, allowing a full breath to finally fill her lungs. "I like the room. You've changed it up some. Do you use the loft for Benin liked we'd, um, planned?"

More reminders of the past. They'd spent so many hours planning their cabin, their family, and their life together on this property. She'd never been happier than the day he'd carried her over the threshold. Too bad those plans hadn't come to fruition...and remembering them only hurt. "Yes. If you'll excuse me, I should go help Ida."

"Sure. Is there something I can help with?"

The sadness in his eyes pricked her conscience. If they were ever to find that happiness again, she'd have to put forth some effort. No matter how much she wanted to escape the memories and pain. "You still have a thing for horses?"

A corner of his mouth tugged up. "What do you think?"

"Well, there's a horse in the corral, if you'd check on him..."

"What's he look like?"

"Trust me—you'll know him when you see him. I rescued him from an overbearing brute a couple months back."

"Rescued?"

Catherine shoved her hands in her apron pockets. "I've only done it a couple of times, and he looked like he needed help."

"I'll go take a look."

Satisfied Sam's upset had subsided somewhat, Catherine nodded and slipped out the back door. She leaned against the wood and urged her heart to resume a normal pace. *Oh, God, You've got to help me. I have no idea what I'm doing anymore.* She wanted answers, but after the way Sam had slammed the door on her inquiry earlier, she was afraid to ask.

Sam stared at the closed door for a heartbeat. Replaying their conversation, he moseyed out the front door, grabbed Sandy's reins, and strolled toward the barn, scanning the homestead his wife had transformed into a prosperous horse ranch. A bunkhouse, three corrals, a chicken coop, woodshed, kitchen, smokehouse, springhouse, foreman's house, and a barn. How could a woman who'd accomplished so much be scared? Did her fear only apply to him, or perhaps more accurately *them*, or was she scared of something else altogether?

He caught a glimpse of the curly-headed ranch hand circling a palomino in the farthest corral. The taller blond man—Larry, wasn't it?—saddled a big bay gelding outside the fence. Could it be she feared someone on or off the ranch? Had she been threatened? His wife didn't frighten easily, or at least she hadn't years ago, except maybe when it came to heights. Was her skittishness his fault, or was there something else afoot here?

Shaking his head, he continued toward the barn. Being out on the trail so long had him looking for trouble where there wasn't any. Cat just needed time to trust him again, and he'd prove that she could. Somehow.

6

Catherine hammered a nail into a loose rail of the corral fence, then swiped a sleeve across her forehead, knocking her hat back a fraction. Only in Texas could someone break a sweat in the month of November.

"Why didn't you tell me that needed doing?"

She straightened at Sam's approach. "I know how to use a hammer." She scooted down to the next loose board and reached in the bucket at her feet for another one of the nails Benin and Roscoe had straightened for her to reuse.

Sam's hand settled around hers when she held the tip against the slat. "Let me help."

Relishing his touch more than was wise, she took a deep breath and passed over the hammer. The nail disappeared into the wood in two taps. The last one had taken her about five. "I thought you were going to check on Thunder?"

Another nail sank into the slat. "Thunder?"

"The horse I rescued."

"That's his name? Well, I reckon it just about fits him again. He's a beauty. Nice lines. I take it the man who owned him before liked wearing Spanish spurs before he all but ran him into the ground?"

Catherine nodded and passed him another nail when he pointed to the bucket. "I don't know why everyone thinks a stallion has to be controlled with such brutality. If you can't handle a high-spirited horse, don't buy a stallion. Get a gelding."

"You don't have to tell me. I saw his scars. Looks like some of them were deep."

"Deep?" Sam's horse trotted over, and Catherine rubbed her nose. "How close were you able to get to him?"

"I patted him. Why?"

She wagged her head. "I should've known. You're the first man he's let get close enough to do that. Normally, I'm the only one that can tend to him."

"I can understand that. I'd much prefer the nursing of a pretty little lady than a hairy old man myself."

Catherine licked her lips and searched for another slat that needed fixing, but she couldn't squelch the pleasure of his words.

"Say, you didn't sell that man another horse, did you?"

The pleasure vanished. "Yes, Sam, I'm a complete and total idiot. Of course I didn't sell him another horse. He was getting onto the stage and was fixing to shoot Thunder."

The hammer dropped to the ground. "You approached a man with a drawn gun. Are you insane?"

"You'd rather I'd let him shoot the poor thing?"

"That's not what I meant, and you know it. What if he'd turned his gun on you?"

"I never said I approached him alone, Sam. Gracious, you act like I have no brain in my head whatsoever."

"I…well…why didn't you say so?"

"How could I? You were too busy jumping down my throat."

Sam rubbed his chin. "I…I'm sorry. You're right."

Catherine gaped at her husband. He'd never apologized so quickly in all his born days.

"Who went with you?"

"Your father."

"Oh." Sam cleared his throat. "Cat, I—"

"Mama." Benin hurried between them.

She would've scolded him for interrupting, but his timing was a relief. Sam threw her completely off balance. She didn't know what to expect from him anymore. "What is it, baby?"

"Curly asked me to come get ya. Thunder's stall's all clean, 'n' he needs your help puttin' him up."

"Tell him I'll be right there."

"Yes'm."

Catherine sidestepped Sam, then paused. "If you really want to help, there's a few more loose boards on this side and a couple on that side there I wanted to get to before supper."

"Yes, ma'am."

She started after Benin.

"Cat?"

She turned.

"Will you take a walk with me after supper?"

"I...I don't know. That broken wheel put me behind on what I needed to get done today."

"A short one?"

Catherine tugged on her gloves. "Will you answer my questions?"

"Depends on what they are."

Why couldn't he just give her one straight answer? Why did he feel the need to keep things from her? Why not be completely honest? *Remember, Catherine, time. He needs time.* Rather than say something she'd regret, she pivoted on her heel and strode into the barn.

Sam hammered one more nail into place and shook the fence to test the hold. When would he ever learn how to talk to his wife? He wanted to be honest with her, but it seemed anytime he did, she got mad at him. Why couldn't she accept there were some things she was better off not knowing, was safer not knowing?

The supper bell chimed, setting his mouth to watering. He hadn't had a home-cooked meal since he'd left Elijah Stone's place. Cat could turn quite a deft hand at a skillet. Hopefully, Ida was just as skilled.

Sam gathered up the hammer and nails and set the items on a shelf in the empty barn. Well, empty except for the line of filled stalls on each side. These people sure knew how to respond to a dinner call. The food must not be too bad. Sam strode down the center aisle. Long, inquisitive faces peered out at him, and he rubbed a few. Cat had quite a growing stock, and if he didn't miss his guess, some, if not all, of the mares would foal come spring. She'd done rather well without him. He didn't know whether to be upset or proud. Did she need him at all?

The barn door closed with a creak. He'd have to oil those hinges. His steps slowed as he neared the kitchen. He owned every inch of this property, but his reception thus far made him feel more like an intruder. He'd had to convince the men earlier to let him help unload the feed. How long would it take for things to change? Not for the first time, he wished he'd never left. Taking a steadying breath, Sam forged inside.

Silence fell on the room. Everyone was already seated except for him and the cook.

"Howdy. Smells mighty good in here." He shed his coat, hanging it on the last empty wall peg. A faint *ting* drew his attention downward. The brass deputy star glared at him. He snatched it up and shoved it in his pants pocket, hopefully before Cat noticed. Next time he'd insist Pa take the badge back. If she saw it, she'd only ask questions he couldn't answer, which would only upset her.

Benin slithered off the bench beside the foreman's son and rushed toward him. "Mama saved you a seat, Pa."

"She did?" Sam's gaze searched for hers but met the top of her bent head. Had she seen the star, or had her head been down the whole time?

"Yeah, right at the head of the table."

"Oh, really?" A corner of his mouth tugged upward. Sam ambled toward his assigned spot at the far end of the table near hers.

"Wait, Pa. Miss Ida don't let nobody sit at her table with dirty fingers."

As if to reinforce Benin's statement, Ida folded her arms, the ever-present wooden spoon dangling from her hand.

Sam tossed her a smile meant to charm and ruffled his son's hair. "Thanks for the head's-up, partner. I like to keep the cook happy."

Benin beamed at the attention, then showed Sam to the washbasin before escorting him back to the table. Cat tried to be inconspicuous, but he caught her staring. Hope stirred anew in his chest. If his son could accept him, maybe his wife could too. She had, after all, saved him a seat at the head of the table. That had to mean something.

His fingers couldn't resist touching her shoulder before he took his chair. "Thank you."

A slight nod was all he got. Sam swallowed a sigh. *Lord, help me. How do I break down these walls of hers?*

"Do I get to bless the food this time, Mama?"

"Sure, Benin."

Heads bowed around the table, except for Larry's. What was with that man? He seemed to have a Texas-sized chip on his shoulder. A lot of men weren't talkers, but it was the *way* Larry didn't talk that set Sam on edge. Why had Cat hired the man?

Catherine barely registered Benin's young voice, Sam's presence all too keen beside her. How many times had she wished to see him in that seat? How did she keep him there? How did she keep from being short with him? It seemed she was constantly on the defense.

"Oh, 'n' thank You, God, for helpin' Pa find his way home. In Jesus's name. Amen."

"Amen." Sam squeezed his son's shoulder, a faint shimmer in his eyes. He then cleared his throat and accepted the bowl of stew she passed him.

Catherine continued ladling stew for the others while Ida divvied up the cornbread. How did Benin make welcoming his father home seem so easy? To be fair, to him it probably was. His heart didn't bear the scars hers boasted, and it was her job to see that things stayed that way.

She served up the last bowl and set it before her. Carrots and taters played hide-'n'-seek in the dark, savory broth, but the tempting smells were lost on her. How did she protect Benin this time? He needed his father. One look in his shoe-button eyes testified to that. But his father was the one man who could hurt him most. If anyone could bear witness to that, she could. Sam probably didn't even realize the power he held. She rubbed at the tension building in her temples.

"Are you okay?" Sam's face appeared inches from her own.

Sincerity and worry radiated from him.

When was the last time someone had looked at her like that? A question sprang to her lips, but she held it in. Now wasn't the time or the place.

"I'll be fine." She hoped.

"You never answered my question earlier."

"Question? What question?" Catherine peeked at the table full of people, eating and conversing, paying them no heed.

"About that walk."

"Y'all are goin' on a walk. Can I come too?" Benin peered hopefully between her and his father.

So much for no one paying attention. Now everyone stared their direction. They knew Sam wanted time alone with her. Larry's eyes narrowed. She gulped. *Oh, God, what do I do? I want time with Sam, but Larry will squeal on me in a heartbeat. Sam might not be the law, but as my husband, the general will probably see him as just as much of a threat, if not more.*

Sam ruffled Benin's hair. "I think it's best if it's just me and your ma this time, partner, but how about I come and tuck you in before then?"

"Really? Will you tell me a story?"

"You bet your sweet Sunday I will."

Benin grinned liked Sam had given him a whole bag of lemon drops. How would she ever compete with Sam? Wait. What was she thinking? Their son's affections weren't something to compete for. Benin needed them both. He deserved to have his father's attention for a change.

"Cat?"

"What? Oh. If I can finish my chores before it's too late, maybe we can take one after Benin is in bed."

Now Sam looked like the one with the bag of lemon drops. Mercy, but she'd always loved his smile. Her heart fluttered in her chest. A walk alone with Sam in the moonlight. If only she could make that happen. But with Larry watching on, that could never be.

Sam jolted awake when sharp points jabbed him in the backside. He scrambled from the hay. Another prod to his posterior sent him sprawling from the stall. "Ow!"

What was going on? What was attacking him? Reaching for his gun, he hurried to his stocking feet.

An hourglass-shaped shadow separated from the darkness. "I said, 'get!'"

"Cat?" Sam dodged another strike and put away his revolver. "What's wrong?"

The pitchfork nearly connected with his stomach.

He stumbled backward toward the door. "Cat, talk to me. What's the matter?"

"You good-for-nothing. You ain't hurting my family." She added an emphasizing thrust.

Arms raised, he backed out into the moonlight. "I'm not out to hurt you. I'm not out to hurt anyone. Please put down the pitchfork, and we'll talk about whatever it is that's bothering you."

Silver light touched Cat's face and glowed against the pale fabric of her nightgown.

Nightgown? He inspected her face again as he took another evading step. Why, she was asleep! She didn't even know what she was saying. Did that mean she meant every word?

A sharp stab hit his gut and nearly dropped him to his knees.

Yep, she meant them all right. But was she dreaming of him or someone else? With her next lunge, he dodged and knocked the weapon from her grip.

A fist swung toward his face.

Boy, the woman was quick on her feet. He caught the next punch with his palm and wrapped her into a confining hug. "Cat, stop. It's me, Sam. I'm not going to hurt you."

She mumbled something incoherent and leaned against his chest, the fight seeming to drain from her. When a whimper seeped through her lips, he loosened his hold and scooped her into his arms. She curled into him, tucking her head under his chin. He didn't know whether to be relieved or concerned.

More mindless murmuring followed.

What was going through her head? Stepping over the pitchfork, he started toward the house. He'd witnessed her sleepwalking a few times in their married life, but never had she acted so violently toward him. Washed dishes, cleaned house, watered the horses, but never had she turned a pitchfork in his direction. He shifted his grip and opened the cabin door. Careful not to make undue noise and wake Benin, he carried Cat to her bedroom and settled her on the mattress.

With a sigh, she rolled away from him and hugged a pillow to her chest.

His pillow.

A deep ache pulsed through him. How long had she slept that way? Ever since he'd left? He rubbed a hand through his hair and scanned what he could see of the room in the shadowed darkness. Their room. Memories bombarded him. Why hadn't he realized how much he'd been risking when he'd left that day years ago? Moonlight glinted off the honey waves of his wife's hair. Would she ever welcome him in here again? That episode in the barn made him wonder. She might think she'd forgiven him, but he'd felt the force of her anger.

Sam shuffled toward the door and gave a final peek over his shoulder before exiting the room. *God, You're gonna have to help me win her back because I'm in way over my head here.*

∽⚜∽

Water dripped into Sam's face, jolting him out of a Cat-filled dream. "Aww, Sandy, really?" He swiped what probably wasn't *just* water from his cheek and forehead and climbed from the hay for the second time in one night. "How did you get out of your stall? Can't a man get some shut-eye around here?" He grabbed the mare's halter and led her to her stall.

The back door of the barn creaked open.

Sam's hand flew to his gun. Was Cat coming after him again? "Who's there?"

"It's Larry." A horse, breathing heavily, trailed the wrangler inside. The gray light of predawn accompanied them both and hid the man's face.

When a lantern flared to life in Larry's hand, Sam squinted. "You always ride before daybreak?"

"Not always." Larry hung the lantern on a hook and went about his business unsaddling the bay horse.

Couldn't the man string more than two words together? Sam's unease with the wrangler returned to settle on his shoulders like a wet blanket. "How long have you worked here?"

"Three years."

"What'd you do before?"

"This 'n' that." Larry put the saddle in the tack room and returned with a brush. "How long you been carryin' that star?"

Sam tried not to stiffen. "That's my business, and you'd be wise to keep it to yourself."

Larry's hand stilled. "Or what?"

Was the man looking for a fight? "Or you might be finding yourself a new job."

A smug grin settled on the wrangler's mouth as he resumed his brushing. "Your wife might have something to say about that."

What was that supposed to mean? Was the man more to Cat than a worker? Sam's gut tightened. "Watch how you speak about *my* wife, or you'll be off *my* property before breakfast."

Larry led his horse to an empty stall. "Whatever you say, *Boss*."

Sam's fingers curled into a ball, itching to knock the smirk off the wrangler's face.

A creak behind him announced another's arrival.

"Mornin', Mista Sam. Larry. Y'all beat me to the milkin'?" Mo snatched a pail off a hook by the front door.

Larry frowned. "That's a woman's job."

"Not today. It be yours." Mo extended the bucket. "I gotta split some wood for my Ida, 'n' Mista Sam probably plannin' on gettin' that walk in 'fore breakfast since theys was too busy to enjoy it last night. Ain't nuthin' like sharin' a sunrise with yo' gal."

"Thank you, Mo. That's a mighty good plan." Sam had a question or two he wanted to put to his wife. He left the two to their chores and stalked toward his house. The door opened as he grabbed the handle.

"Oh!" Cat put a palm to her chest. "Sam, you scared me."

No recognition of last night lit her eyes. Figured. Just like the other times. Well, last night could wait. He wanted to talk about this morning and the past three years.

"Walk with me." Sam snatched her hand and tugged her outside before she could argue otherwise.

"What's the matter? Will you slow down?"

A short distance from the creek, he strode around a pecan tree and stopped.

Cat plowed into him, then staggered backward. "What is going on? Why did you drag me out here?"

He flung his arm toward the east, where a hint of pink touched the top of the hills. "To watch the sunrise together." His fists settled on his waist. "Care to explain to me what's going on with you and Larry?"

"Me and Larry?"

"Yes. You. Larry. Why does he think you'd defend him if I wanted to fire him?"

Cat blanched. "Y-you fired him?"

"I came close, and I will if I don't start getting some answers. What's going on?"

She turned, hugging herself as she'd done on the roadside the day before.

Sam grabbed her shoulders, ready to make her face him, but stopped when he found her shaking. Another scenario, not at all to his liking, flittered into his mind. The sleepwalking episode didn't help his imagination. "Cat? Darlin', did he do something to you? Did he…"

She shook her head, and the air rushed from his lungs.

He rotated her and tipped her chin. "But you're scared of him, aren't you?"

Her lack of an answer was answer enough.

"He'll be gone before breakfast."

Cat snagged his forearm. "No, you can't. Y-you'll just make it worse."

"Make what worse?"

Her lips pressed together.

"Mama?" Benin stood on the back porch dressed in his nightshirt. Cat moved to head that way.

"No, I'll take care of him, and you stay away from Larry until we can talk more about this, understand?"

If he didn't miss his guess, a small measure of relief filled her brown eyes. She nodded.

Sam brushed a lock of golden hair from her forehead and tucked it behind her ear. With a hand on each shoulder, he turned her toward the east. "Enjoy your sunrise. We'll talk more later."

He'd guarantee it. He gave her a small squeeze, then strode toward his son. Something was going on around here, and someway, somehow, he would get his wife away from prying eyes and convince her to talk.

Catherine gripped the roots of her hair and fought down a scream. This couldn't be happening. How could her control over the situation be unraveling so quickly? She'd done everything the general ever asked of her—given him food, money, her silence—but less than twenty-four hours with Sam threatened to undo it all. Her gaze lifted to the vast beauty painted across the horizon. *Oh, God, what do I do? Please help me.*

Her husband had always been a great judge of character. She should've known he'd see right through Larry. What on earth was she going to tell Sam? He would ask again. No doubt about that. He wanted answers from her. She wanted answers from him. They were at a standoff, and she couldn't say a word without endangering everything she held dear.

The day had just started, but she got the sinking feeling it was going to get a lot worse before it was over.

7

Sam paused outside the kitchen door about an hour or so before suppertime and debated whether to knock or simply enter. He owned the place, but he didn't want to get off on the wrong foot with these people. Especially the cook. He wasn't overly fond of questioning every bite that made it to his lips, and the woman already seemed set against him, if those frowns meant anything.

Before he could decide, the door swung open, and a little body charged into his legs.

"Whoa, slow down there, partner." He lifted Benin into his arms. "Where you going in such an all-fired hurry?"

"Mama said Gramps was comin' today, but Miss Ida won't tell me why."

Sam chuckled and started to close the door, but on second thought went inside the warm kitchen. "Actually, I was just coming to explain that to you."

"You were?"

Sam smiled at Ida and sank onto a nearby stool, settling Benin in his lap. "I was. I thought Mrs. Ida would like to know too."

"I knows how to mind my own bizness." Ida scowled, but she stayed busy near his end of the table and didn't shoo him outside with her spoon.

"Why is Gramps comin' today? It's not Friday, is it?"

"No, it's Wednesday. Gramps is coming to see *you*. Actually, he asked me if he could spend a few days with you. Would you like that?"

"Oh, boy, a few days? Would he take me campin' or huntin'?"

"Camping might've been mentioned." Sam tried to keep his face

57

emotionless but failed upon his son's excited squeal. "With Thanksgiving coming up, you might be able to talk him into some turkey hunting too. I bet Mrs. Ida here makes some good turkey and dressing."

"Do you, Miss Ida? I forgot."

The woman actually smiled at the boy, her white teeth gleaming against her dark skin. So she wasn't made of stone.

"I ain't sho', Benin. It's been an awful long while since I cooked me a turkey. I mighta forgot too."

"Is it different from cookin' a chicken? 'Cause you make the best chicken around."

"Not much different. The onliest difference is it's bigger than our roosters."

"Oh, wow! A big chicken. You thinks Gramps would let me shoot it, Pa?"

Sam's grin grew as his chest warmed. He'd never tire of hearing that name fall from his boy's lips. "I don't know, but when I was your age, he taught me how to call a turkey."

"Call him what?"

Ida chuckled, and Sam swallowed a laugh of his own.

"We'd call the turkey closer so he'd be easier to shoot."

"Oh." The creases lining Benin's forehead cleared for a moment but returned with fervor. "Will you be comin' too, Pa?"

The opportunity he'd been waiting for. "Not this time. You see, while you spend time with Gramps, I'm going to spend time with Mama. I might even take her hunting."

"Girls don't hunt."

"I'll have you know your mama's gone hunting with me before."

"No foolin'?"

"Honest Injun. She shot the deer's antlers clean off."

"Why'd she shoot his antlers? That's not how you kill 'em, is it?"

"No, that's not how you kill them. She, um, missed." Sam grinned, remembering how she'd accidentally missed on purpose.

"She needs practice."

"Yes, she does, but I'm not sure if that's what we'll do yet. I'm going to talk to her after supper tonight at the Matthews'." And somehow convince her to open those tight lips of her.

"I forgot 'bout that. Do I have to go? Can I stay here with Gramps 'n' start learnin' turkey calls 'stead of goin' to supper?"

"I think Brother Matthews'll understand. He likes hunting too."

"Good." Benin's mouth pressed into a line exactly like Cat's did when she was deep in thought. Another question was coming. "Will ya take me on a huntin' trip next 'n' teach me how to shoot your gun?"

"I intend to teach you all about hunting, and I'm sure we'll make lots of trips together now that I'm home."

"Oh, boy. Did ya hear that, Miss Ida?"

"I did, 'n' I think I heard your grandpa ride up. Run 'long now 'n' go see."

"Yes'm." Benin slid from Sam's lap and scrambled for the door. He stopped before opening it, hurried back, and threw his small arms around Sam. "I'm glad you're back."

His heart swelled, and he winked at the lad. "Me too."

Benin grinned, then raced outside.

Sam stood to follow but paused when Ida cleared her throat. "Yes?"

"Mista McGarrett, I's don't know what you're up to, but you better not hurt Miz Cathy. She's a strong woman, but she ain't made of no steel."

"I'll remember that, Mrs. Ida, and please call me Sam." He donned his hat, tipped it in her general direction, and left.

Time to get his wife to himself.

─── ⚜ ───

Catherine spotted the scrap of paper on the table with her name on it the moment she stepped from the bedroom. Sweat broke out on her forehead. That wasn't Sam's handwriting, which only meant one thing...

The general.

Oh, God, please... Her hand shook as she lifted the note.

Deep voices and clomping steps carried through the closed front door. She quickly stuffed the missive in her skirt pocket and reached for her cream-colored Stetson hanging beside the door. Her bonnet kept her ears warmer but blocked her peripheral vision. She'd learned her lesson about that the hard way, and now she despised riding and not being able to see around her. She'd have to make do with cold ears. Maybe she'd have time to knit herself a scarf this winter, with Sam back.

Taking a deep breath to steady the bees swarming in her stomach, Catherine headed outside.

Benin hurried her direction. "Mama, guess what?"

She crouched to his level. "What?"

"Gramps is gonna teach me how to call a turkey."

"Really? I didn't know you could do that."

"I can't, but Gramps can. He taught Pa, 'n' now he's gonna teach me."

"Well, it sounds like you're going to have a good time."

Benin's head bobbed with enthusiasm.

Catherine smiled and stood to face GW. "I told Benin that if he was good, he could have two lemon drops. No more. Also, I don't care if you are camping—please don't let him stay up too far past his bedtime, and please don't go too far from the house."

"Yes, Mama." GW grinned and wrapped her in a hug.

She lowered her voice. "I don't know whether to choke you or kiss you for helping Sam arrange this."

GW winked. "I prefer the kiss."

Catherine swallowed a laugh and pecked him on the cheek. She pointed her finger at the silver-haired man and then her son. "You two behave."

"I'll behave just like me."

"George Washington McGarrett, do I need to change my mind about letting my son go with you?"

The sheriff chuckled. "No, ma'am. Y'all have a good time. Benin'll be just fine."

"Benin's not the one I'm worried about."

"Cat, would you quit your clucking and mount up? I'd like to eat sometime tonight, if you don't mind."

"I am not clucking." Catherine frowned at her husband, who stood between their horses, and moved toward the chestnut gelding waiting patiently beside Sam's buckskin. She checked the saddle's cinch, but before her foot touched the stirrup, Sam tossed her into the saddle.

"Yes. You are."

Catherine gathered the reins in one hand when her horse stepped back. She shook a finger at Sam. "You better mind your manners, mister, or I'm staying here."

"Didn't your mama ever teach you it's not nice to point?"

"Ugh. Why I—"

Sam smacked the rear of her horse, and Buster took off down the road.

She barely managed to keep her seat as Sam shouted their good-byes behind her. He charged up beside her while she hauled back on the reins.

"Are you out of your mind?"

With a laugh, he galloped by.

Her horse, not to be outdone, struggled against the reins and started after them. Catherine pressed her lips together and gave Buster his head. Without prompting, the animal stretched into a full, smooth gallop, and soon they gained ground on the buckskin and her heavier rider.

The blowing wind filled Catherine's ears and chilled her cheeks as the thrill of a racing steed filled her. She never tired of this. The pounding hooves. The powerful muscles. The utter freedom. Nothing compared to it.

Buster galloped alongside Sandy. Sam's eyes widened, and his chin dropped.

With a laugh, Catherine charged past. She wasn't sure how many minutes they raced along, up one hill and down the next, before Sam shouted at her to slow down, but it wasn't long enough. She'd forgotten how wonderful it was to let go and toss care to the wind.

"Woman, are you trying to run that horse to death? Pull up."

Catherine did and patted Buster's sweaty neck while Sam came alongside. She gave him a triumphant grin.

Sam snorted and shook his head. "You can still ride like the wind."

"And you're still slower than molasses."

He threw back his head and gave a rich, deep belly laugh that had her joining in. My, how she'd missed this, the companionship of a man. Well, not any man. She'd missed Sam. She hadn't realized how much until that moment. He could bring her out of her shell better than anyone, even her sister. He could make her laugh, make her cry...make her feel. Maybe that's why her emotions felt like they'd run the same gamut the horses had. Up, down, up, down.

"What's got you so quiet over there?" Sam thumbed his hat back.

"Uh, oh, nothing."

"I'm not so sure. One minute you're laughing, and the next you're clammed up. You know, it's okay to talk to me."

"It's nothing. Really. I've just..." She shrugged. "...missed this."

"You want to know a secret?"

"Hmm?"

"So have I." The corner of his mouth turned up. "You're the only girl I never minded losing to."

"That's because I'm the first you didn't have to let win."

"Maybe." His smile grew. He nodded toward her stirrup. "I was wondering what you had to do to get ready to go riding. Now I know. When'd you start wearing those under your dresses?"

Catherine tugged her skirts back over her jeans. "You aren't supposed to say anything."

"You'd rather I let you ride into the Matthews' yard like that?"

She frowned but let the matter go. She would rather not have everyone know she had breeches under her skirts. Most men frowned upon it. It seemed to only stir Sam's curiosity, which wasn't necessarily a good thing.

They climbed the next hill and ambled down the same in silence. Silence between them seemed to have happened a lot since their sunrise discussion. She dreaded when he'd broach the topic again.

Sam cleared his throat. "There's your sister's cutoff up ahead. Did you, uh, want to drop by?"

"I'd rather not be late for supper. All those nieces and nephews of mine won't make a quick stop possible. Maybe we can bring Benin and come visit them soon."

"How many does Constance have now?"

"Five and a half. Two boys, three girls, and another one on the way."

"Mercy. How many is she planning on having?"

Catherine frowned. "There's nothing wrong with a big family."

"Never said there was, darlin'. In fact, I'm pretty sure Benin would love some siblings to play with."

Ignoring his jab, she focused on the road ahead of them. They were almost to the LW Ranch. If she wasn't mistaken—and given her total lack of direction, that was entirely possible—the Matthews' place should be at the bottom of the next hill.

She propped her hands on the saddle horn, deciding to give Sam a bit of the hard time he'd been giving her. "So, what do you think Sister Hatch fixed for dinner?"

"Sister Hatch? Did Joe get a new cook?"

"Not really. No. Sister Hatch is Warren Hatch's wife, Joe's mother."

"You mean that ole hermit who used to cook for Mr. Asher married Joe's ma? When did that happen?"

"Brother Hatch is not an old hermit. He's a sweet man, but yes, he did marry Joe's mother. They got married earlier this year."

"Well, this is a day full of surprises."

"Oh, I'm sure you'll be even more surprised when you find out who Joe's wife is."

"You say that like I've met her before."

"You have."

"Who is she?"

"I'll let Joe do the honors."

Sam sat back in the saddle and stared at her. "You just have to keep doing that, don't you?"

Catherine grinned unrepentantly and led the way down the hill into the Matthews' yard.

Sam followed Cat, wanting nothing more than to charge forward, swipe her from her saddle, and kiss her until she told him everything. What had he been thinking telling Cat he'd abide by her rules? He was daft to agree to such nonsense. He had every right to kiss her, and if she continued teasing him and smiling at him, why, he'd be tortured simply being near her.

He slowed his horse as they cantered into the yard, and he studied his honey-haired wife. That was it. That was why she'd demanded his distance. Retribution. No doubt he deserved every ounce of her bad humor, and he'd figured he couldn't just sweep back home and into her good graces. But did she have to make it so hard?

Stopping at the hitching rail, Sam dismounted and circled to help her down. He might as well face it—any hard time she gave him, he'd well and truly earned. Right now, he simply had to pick himself up by his bootstraps and remember the prize ahead of him. Her heart. A high prize indeed.

With a sigh, he focused once again on behaving himself and released his wife the moment her boot tips hit the well-packed dirt. He'd behave himself if it killed him, and with as sweet as his wife looked, it just might.

The front door of the large log house swung open, revealing a short, graying woman. "Well, slap me silly. Joe told me, but I just couldn't believe it. Samuel McGarrett, you better get your mangy hide on over here and give me a hug."

Leaving his wife to finish tying her horse, Sam hurried up the front steps of the wraparound porch. He swept the older woman, who'd always smelled of something delicious, into his arms and lifted her off the ground.

"Ooo. Boy, put me down. I wanted a greeting, not a heart attack."

Sam laughed and set Mrs. Isabel Matthews Hatch on her feet.

"What's going on out here?" A raven-haired woman stepped through the screen door, wiping her hands on a checkered apron.

"Howdy do, Miss Asher. It's good to see you again. How's your family doing?"

"Actually—"

"Actually, her name's Matthews now, and to answer your question, I'm just fine." Joe appeared behind the petite woman and settled his hands on her shoulders. She peered up at Joe with an adoring smile so reminiscent of the looks Cat once gave him, Sam found himself glancing over his shoulder to find his wife.

She stood near the porch post, her arms folded across her chest, her head cocked to the side. "I told you you'd be surprised."

"No fooling." He snagged her wrist and tugged her over. Pleasantly surprised when she came willingly, he placed his hand on her waist and held her close. She stiffened almost imperceptibly and tilted a questioning gaze to his.

"It's good to see you two together again. You always did make a handsome couple."

"Thank you, Mrs. Hatch." Sam winked at Cat and was rewarded with a slight blush. My, oh my, but he was the most blessed man to ever walk the earth.

"What's with the formality? I'm Aunt Isabel to you, just like always."

"Yes, ma'am." Forcing himself to stop staring at his lovely wife, Sam settled his attention and his free arm along the older woman's shoulders. "You know I always thought I'd be calling you Ma instead of Aunt."

"Me marry GW? Boy, you do go on." She patted his stomach. "But speakin' of callin', I better call the fellas before the vittles get cold. Y'all go on inside and find you a place at the table. We're havin' your favorite, pot roast with potatoes and carrots, cornbread, and fresh-churned butter."

"You always did know how to make a man's mouth water." Not quite ready to let go of his wife now that she'd let him this close, Sam kept his arm around Cat and followed Joe and Sarah Matthews inside. Hopefully, Cat would be this amenable after supper when he brought up what she'd avoided all day.

Catherine squirmed in her chair. The words in the general's note made her itch to leave, but if she did, she'd have to explain, and that would only make matters worse. *God, please show me a way out of this.*

"Joe, my pa tells me you had a run-in with that robber Sam Bass. I hear there's quite a bounty on his head. Why'd you let him get away?"

Catherine's head came up. She studied her husband as he buttered a slice of cornbread. Hadn't he let that situation go? Why bring it up again? She had enough trouble coming from the general. She didn't need more from Sam.

Joe put his knife aside. "It's not that simple."

Sam broke the cornbread in half and dipped it in his gravy. "What happened?"

Her focus on her husband, Catherine mashed her potato. He seemed curious but not overly so, and the happenings were new. Everyone in town still discussed it. In fact, she hadn't heard the whole story herself. She only knew it involved Joe and a cavern on the Matthews' ranch.

Joe forked a bite of roast. "I'd been tracking a cat who'd become partial to my beef, when I stumbled upon Bass with two other men. I knew something wasn't right, so I hid in a cavern. Unfortunately, they decided to camp in the cavern too, and I was stuck hiding in a crouched position for more hours than I wanted. When they fell asleep, I snuck out to go fetch the sheriff."

"So did you help Pa track the Sam Bass Gang when they left the cavern?"

"No, he insisted I come home and keep watch over my family. I heard the sheriff lost the trail near the old Ackerman place. It's too bad."

"Yeah, a real shame." Sam scratched his chin and glanced Catherine's way.

With a duck of her head, she avoided his gaze. Catching that gang might be a good cause, but protecting her son ranked higher on her list by leaps and bounds.

Sister Hatch pushed away from the table and stood. "Well, I think we've had enough of this rehashin'. Who's ready for some custard pie?"

Hearty agreements went up, and a short while later Catherine set her coffee next to her empty pie plate. She sank back in her seat with a sigh. "Sister Hatch, I don't know anyone who makes a better custard pie than you do. I'm so full I don't know how I'm going to climb on my horse."

"You're always welcome to stay the night. We have plenty of room, don't we, Sarah?"

"I—yes, we do." Sarah Matthews frowned slightly at her mother-in-law. Joe looked ready to choke on his last bite of pie. Not the expressions of those eager to share their home with interlopers. Besides, what newlyweds did? She sure hadn't.

Catherine forced herself not to look at Sam as the memories washed over her. "Thank you all the same, but I need to get back home. I've got a bi—busy day tomorrow."

That was close. Hopefully, Sam hadn't caught her near-slip of the tongue. How ever was she going to meet the general's demands without Sam knowing?

"Well, that's too bad." Sister Hatch stood and started gathering the empty plates. "Joe, why don't you help Sam saddle their horses?"

"Sure thing, Ma."

"Warren, honey, will you take the rest of that tea out to the springhouse and bring me in some more water? I don't think we've got enough in the reservoir to do all the dishes."

"Sure, sweet pea." Warren Hatch stood and moved toward the door with a slight limp.

The men trickled out of the house, the husbands to their assigned duties and the hands to their evening chores.

Catherine pushed from her seat before her nerves got the best of her. "Is there anything I can do to help?"

"No, no, you're a guest. Why don't you and Sarah take your coffee to the living room? I've got things under control here."

Sarah set down her napkin and stood. "Are you sure, Isabel?"

"I'm sure. Now off with you."

The black-haired woman smiled at Catherine. "We'd better do what she says."

"I think you're right." Catherine grabbed her cup and followed Sarah into the next room. "When are you due?"

Sarah paused midstep. "You noticed? I didn't think I was showing that much."

"You're not. I've just been in your condition before, and Isabel loves to put people to work, unless it's for a good reason..." Catherine let the sentence dangle and sank onto the couch opposite the crackling fireplace.

Sarah settled into a rocker beside the couch. "Guess it's not that hard to figure out when you put it that way." Her hand went to her slightly rounded middle. "I bet you're glad to have your husband home. I'm already dreading the thought of next year's cattle drive. I won't be able to go, what with the baby and all. How did you stand Sam being away so long?"

"A lot of prayer." Speaking of her husband, Catherine stood and moseyed to the window. What was taking them so long to saddle two horses?

"Cathy, is something wrong? You seem a bit on edge this evening. Is it Sam?"

"Huh? Oh. My mind's just all over the place lately. I'm sorry."

"That's all right. It'd say it's completely understandable in your situation."

She had no idea.

"I'd probably have fallen to pieces long before now."

"The day's not over yet."

Sarah laughed at Catherine's quip.

Only she wasn't joking. Not completely. The note in her pocket threatened to undo her well-kept composure, which apparently wasn't so well kept if Sarah had noticed her unease. Had Sam? A hand touched her elbow, jerking her head around.

"Cathy, I...I know I haven't been married long, but if you need someone to talk to..."

"Don't worry. I'll be fine." Lord willing. "I would appreciate your prayers though."

"Of course." Sarah sent her a reassuring smile before nodding at the window. "There's our men now. Y'all have a safe ride home. Feel free to visit anytime."

With a word of thanks, Catherine stepped outside and swung onto her horse. Paper crinkled in her pocket, nearly causing her to knee her mount from underneath her. *God, You've got to get me through this night.* She wanted to tell Sam more than anything, but three years of silence wasn't broken easily.

Especially not when her life wasn't the only one at stake.

8

The shadows grew longer and merged together as the sun lost its glory. Days were much shorter in November. They'd be making most of this ride in the dark. At least the near-full moon should provide enough light. Swaying with the rhythm of the saddle, Sam peeked at the first twinkling stars, then at his wife riding beside him. Over halfway home and the leather of his saddle made more noise than she did. He slipped a knee around the saddle horn, feigning a comfortable pose in hopes of relaxing her. "Ready to tell me about it?"

No response. Not even a glance his way.

"Cat?"

With a start, she gave a shake of her head, and her horse mimicked the motion. So, he wasn't the only one picking up the tension rippling off her in waves.

"Cat, did I do something wrong, or is your silence linked to what you wouldn't talk to me about this morning?"

More silence. A headshake wasn't even offered.

After about the tenth try of engaging Cat in conversation, Sam finally gave up. The woman's lips were clamped tighter than a penny-pincher's fist. When they arrived home, she tossed him her reins and disappeared inside before his foot slipped from the leather stirrup. He stared at the closed door he'd made and hung with his own two hands. The door that now separated him from his wife.

"God, something's wrong here. Please help me get her to talk to me. Show me what to do." With a sigh, Sam took the horses to the barn and went about settling them in for the night.

About an hour later, while lying in the hay waiting for sleep to claim him, a thumping noise caught his attention. With sock-muffled steps, Sam made his way to the barn door and peeked out.

Cat's silvery silhouette rounded the porch post.

Clearly, he wasn't the only one having trouble sleeping, but where was she headed at this hour?

She veered his direction.

His brows rose. Had she had a change of heart and wanted to talk to him, or was she coming for the pitchfork again? That was a thought. Could she be sleep walking again? Not ready to take any chances, Sam moved the pitchfork well out of reach and went for his boots.

The barn door creaked open as he stomped his heel into the boot and stood. He waited for the scratch of a match, but it never came. Then again, a good amount of moonlight did stream through the door.

"Buster?"

A whicker responded to Cat's call.

Why did she want her horse? "Cat, something wrong? Why are you up?"

"I'm leaving."

He nearly tripped over his boots. "What? Why?"

She trailed to the tack room, emerging moments later with the saddle and bridle he'd put away only hours ago.

"Cat, what's the matter? Talk to me."

"We can't talk here."

"O...kay. Where can we go to talk?" Maybe she'd reconsider his former offer, and he could still help his pa. "Want to go to the Anderson cabin? We can be there in a few hours."

"Fine."

His brows shot up at her easy acceptance. "I'll get my horse."

"Make it quick. Time isn't on our side."

That was an odd comment, but rather than question and risk her changing her mind, he hurried to saddle his mount. He considered waking one of the men and letting them know what was going on, but Mrs. Ida knew a bit of his plans, at least the part about getting his wife to himself and a possible hunting trip. That would have to do. Hopefully, with their absence and that of their horses, the woman could put two and two together and figure out they might not be back for a while. He swung onto the horse as Cat cantered out of the barn. She surely wasn't wasting a moment.

Silver moonlight and abundant shadows showered their path as they left the barnyard.

Swallowing a smile, Sam moved alongside Buster and veered him toward the northeast. His wife still had no sense of direction. They'd gone about a quarter of the distance to the cabin, when Cat started to wilt in the saddle. For half a heartbeat, he considered turning them around, but just as sure as he did, she'd refuse to talk to him come morning. He pulled them up near a stack of boulders.

"Cat, why don't you ride with me for a while?"

A few incoherent mumbles parted her lips.

He'd take that as agreement. Sliding his arms around his wife, he lifted her smaller frame and settled her in his lap. The wind whipped around them, and Sam adjusted the reins to tuck his jacket more firmly around Cat. Tonight was shaping into a cool one. After tugging his hat lower, he turned up his collar and got them underway.

If he remembered correctly, and he most always did, the Ackerman place ran along the northeastern border of Matthews' land. From what his father had mentioned, he suspected the trio of outlaws had moved northward. Maybe toward the Dallas area.

Come morning, he'd start on finding their trail and on worming answers from Cat as well. Wonder what'd changed her mind. Studying her shadowed profile in the moonlight, Sam's lips curved upward. At least she'd let him ride along. Why had she wanted to leave? She'd seemed so adamant about not coming with him before. What had changed? Was it because Benin was safe with Pa? Perhaps she'd tell him in the morning. He doubted they'd be doing any talking that night, but he could handle this kind of silence, with her curled into his warmth. Much better than her chilly silence earlier.

Stifling a yawn, Sam steered his horse around a cactus patch and other scrub brush and angled up another hill. These next few days would be a challenge, but he'd counted on that the whole way home. Cat was a challenge, always had been and probably always would be.

He was determined this time to figure out how to meet that challenge, or die trying.

Uncertain how long they'd ridden, Sam sagged with relief when he spotted a small cabin that looked more like a dilapidated lean-to through the abundant shadows. Old man Anderson hadn't been the best of carpenters, but it was a shelter with a fireplace. Hopefully, without a bird nest built in the chimney.

Sam slid from the saddle with Cat in his arms and walked on tired legs toward the off-kilter door hanging from old leather hinges. He booted open the wood and watched a shower of dirt descend before stepping inside.

Total darkness greeted him.

Uncertain where to put Cat or even where to step next, he shuffled to his right and tugged with his fingertips at the scrap of fabric covering the solitary window. A loud rip filled the silence before gray moonbeams shafted into the tiny dwelling and landed on a sagging rope bed shoved against the opposite wall.

Sam took one step and pressed a boot against the ropes. The wood frame creaked, but the supports held. Tentatively, he lowered Cat and emptied his arms. With a weary sigh, he strode back out the door. His buckskin, Sandy, stood where he'd left her, head hung low. Cat's chestnut mimicked the stance.

"It's been a long night, huh, girl?" He unfastened the cinch and removed the saddle from his horse. After placing it inside the door, he tied the mare to a low branch on a nearby oak and repeated the motions for Cat's gelding. Rolling his neck to relieve the tension, he ambled back inside. The moon had nearly run its gamut across the starlit sky. He wouldn't get much rest, but he had to have at least a few hours before he had to face whatever Cat revealed in the morning. He had a feeling whatever she had to say would be a whopper of a tale.

⊱━━━⊰

Catherine blinked against the daylight streaming through the window. When had she moved her bed to face the east? It normally faced the south, didn't it? What happened to her blue curtains? She repositioned to get a better look, and her head pounded like it would burst.

A loud snore rattled the cool room and jolted her upright.

Gripping her forehead, she searched for the source. Sam lay near a small crackling fireplace, his head propped on his saddle. Wasn't he supposed to be sleeping in the barn?

"Sam."

The man bolted to his feet, his gun freeing its holster with a quiet swoosh.

Her brows shot upward. Who woke up like that? "Sam."

The gleaming barrel swung toward her.

Catherine gripped the bed frame.

With a blink, Sam stuffed the pistol away. "Sorry. What is it?"

"I, um…" Her heart and head beat out an unsteady rhythm. Maybe now wasn't the best time to ask him why he was in her house. Wait. Was this even her house? She blinked, then rubbed a hand over her eyes, but the scene before her stayed the same. Where was she, and why did she feel like she'd been rode hard and put up wet? "I wanted to know where we are."

Her husband swiped a hand through his dark locks before glancing around the small space. "The Anderson cabin."

"What?" She shot to her feet. "I told you I wouldn't come here."

A frown turned down his lips. "That's not what you said last night."

"Last night? I never said a word to you after we left the Matthews'."

"Yes, you did. You said we couldn't talk at the house. I suggested here, and you agreed."

"I did not. I would've remembered that. I wouldn't do that. Not now. Not when—" She bit down on her tongue.

"'Not when' what?"

"Nothing. I'm not saying another word until you tell me what you were thinking, bringing me out here against my wishes."

Sam's jaw worked from side to side. "You really don't remember a thing." He shook his head. "I should've known you were sleepwalking." Mumbling under his breath, he grabbed a stick and prodded the coals, sending sparks shooting up the chimney.

"Sleepwalking? I haven't done that in…" Her blood chilled. "W-what did I say?"

"Nothing much. Just that we couldn't talk at the house, and you agreed to come here."

Her secrets were still safe. Relief bulked her knees. Thankfully, she was still positioned in front of the bed and wilted onto the frame. She stared at her husband's broad shoulders as another unsettling question came to mind. "Did we, uh…we didn't…"

Inquisitive, yet inscrutable, eyes rested on her for the span of several heartbeats until she fought the urge to squirm.

"No." With a toss of the stick in the growing flames, he spun on his booted heel and strode from the small room.

Now that was the man she'd married. He always walked away before they finished a conversation. The sagging door creaked on a stiff breeze. Who would let a cabin get in such disrepair? Where had he said they were at? The Anderson cabin?

Her gaze shot to the window. No. Oh, no. He'd brought her out here to track that dumb outlaw. *Oh, God, please say it's not so.*

Catherine yanked the paper from her pocket. *Sunset.* Less than twelve hours. She pushed her way outside. "Where's my horse?"

Sam shifted to face her from his place beside his buckskin. "What?"

"Where's my horse?" Without waiting for him, she circled his mount. Buster nickered a greeting. She scanned the area around them. "Where's my saddle?"

"You walked right by it on your way out the door. Where do you think you're going?"

"Go get it. Never mind. I'll do it." Ignoring her thumping skull, she strode into the house, hoisted the saddle and blanket into her arms, and returned to her horse. She slapped on the leather as quickly as possible, then reached for the reins.

Sam jerked them out of reach. "You didn't answer me. Where do you think you're going?"

"Give me the reins. I've got to get home."

"Cat, the boy will be fine. Pa's watching over him. Don't worry."

"It's not just Benin." She gripped the sides of her aching head. "Oh, what have you done? I have to get back."

"You're not making sense. What more do you have to worry about besides Benin? Does this have something to do with Larry? What are you not telling me?"

"The ranch! Oh, forget it." She rotated on her heel and marched away.

"If you're headed home, you're going the wrong way."

Blast her sorry sense of direction. "Then which way is it?"

"You start talking, and maybe I'll tell you. Now, what's going on, Cat?"

"I've *got* to get home."

"And I've got to help my pa."

Desperate and heartsick tears pressed in behind her eyes. "It always comes down to this, doesn't it?"

"Comes down to what?"

"You're always more concerned about helping someone else than you are about the needs of your own family."

"Needs? What needs? And I *am* concerned about my family. What do you think I'm doing here?"

"Oh, right. If it's helping your father, you're ripping and raring to go."

"Sure, I try to help my pa, but look around, Cat. He's not the one I wanted out here with me." He released the reins and grasped her shoulders. "I wanted *you*. I did this for *you*."

"So dragging me out here against my will was for my own good? Oh, I can't wait to hear this explanation. How is that?"

"It wasn't against your will. Weren't you listening to me in there?" A deep-throated growl parted his lips, and he dipped his head. After a moment, his hands dropped from her shoulders, and he straightened with an unexpected calm in his gray gaze. "We needed time alone, Cat. Benin doesn't need to watch us ironing out our problems."

Her arms uncrossed. "I...I hadn't considered that." She released a heavy sigh, grabbed her reins, and moved from his grasp. "You make plenty of sense, Sam, but there are plenty of things you don't know, and one of those is I have to get back to the ranch. Today. Now mount up and show me the way home, or I'm giving Buster his head and letting him pick his way back."

"Why're you in such an all-fired hurry to get back? Why today? And why couldn't you have told me this the other day when I *asked* you to come with me?"

"I'll start answering your whys when you start answering mine. Now come on." She mounted and stared down at him. "Unless you're ready to talk, that is."

Sam frowned but moved to his mare's side. "Have it your way. Give me ten minutes to scout the area, so I can at least tell Pa I looked around."

She *did* need a moment in the necessary, and some water would be nice. "Fine."

"Glad you approve." Sam reached into his saddlebag and withdrew a navy bandana with the corners knotted together. "Here. Have some breakfast."

He tossed the parcel to her, then moved off to the side of the house, if one could call the dilapidated shack a house. How could he have brought her to this hovel? Catherine untied the knots and extracted a piece of jerky. The dried meat hovered near her lips while her mind strayed to the ranch. What was she going to do if she didn't get back in time?

Sam had a good notion to veer to the left and keep them going in circles, but the near panic in Cat's eyes when she'd spoken earlier kept his horse on the straight and narrow for home. What had her so worried that she wouldn't talk to him? Had Larry threatened her? Or did this have more to do with their troubled marriage? The memory of the odd sensation of being watched while he drove the wagon to town the other day came flooding back.

No, there was more to this than their marital problems. Something wasn't right.

His gaze flittered back to Cat, who hadn't spoken a word since he'd mounted up and turned them southward.

He had to convince her to talk. Sam waited for the path between the scrub brush to widen and fell back beside her. "How are you doing?"

Her gaze stayed glued to the trail. "I'm fine."

How did he begin? He drew a deep, steadying breath and plunged in with both feet. "If I give you a couple answers, will you fill me in on what's going on?"

She looked at him, really looked at him, her dark-brown eyes searching to the very depths of his soul. "You really mean it?"

He dipped his head.

With lips pressed together, Cat looked forward once more. "All right."

Sam lifted his hat and brushed a sleeve across his suddenly sweaty brow. "What do you want to know first?"

"Why didn't you come back after wrangling horses for that cattle drive?"

"I had unfinished business I had to see to and...I was tired of all the fighting."

"Fighting? What fighting? Sure, we had discussions, but I wouldn't call them fights."

He snorted. "Loud discussions."

The clippity-clop of the horses' hooves and the familiar creak of leather filled the silence that settled between them. Sam waited, sure more questions would come.

Cat tucked a stray hair behind her ear. "I'm sorry I drove you away."

"What?" He inadvertently pulled the reins. Sandy stopped and shook her head. He did the same, then nudged the mare forward. "What gave you that idea? I never said it was all your fault. Last I checked, it takes two. Once I cooled off, I realized that. I should've talked to you more instead of getting upset."

"And walking off."

"Cat, I'm not like you. I can't let things go at the drop of a hat. I have to have time. Time to think, to pray, to…be alone." Sam steeled himself against her reaction. Surely she wouldn't like hearing he had to be away from her.

"That's why you always did that? To think and pray? Not just to get away from me?"

He blinked. "Yes. Didn't you know?"

"I had no idea."

Sam nudged his horse closer and reached for her hand. "As much as I've always enjoyed being near you, darlin', it is possible to have too much of a good thing." He offered her a smile, praying she'd understand.

She studied their interwoven fingers before turning her gaze on him. "Why didn't you tell me?"

"I thought you knew."

Cat shook her head.

"Well, you do now." He stroked his thumb across her knuckles, relishing the feel of her smaller hand in his. "Does this warrant an answer to my question now?"

She pressed her lips together in her familiar fashion and withdrew her hand.

He missed it immediately. "Cat?"

"You're not going to like it."

Sam stiffened. "Tell me anyway."

9

Catherine shifted in the saddle, trying to find the words to tell Sam the situation she'd stumbled into during his absence. The fact that he'd dragged her out to the middle of nowhere didn't boost her confidence in him in the least, but he *had* answered her question and explained his reasoning. Feeling like she stood on the edge of a crumbling abyss, she forced herself to respond with the truth. "I have someone I have to meet by sunset today."

"Today? What for?"

"To protect us."

"Protect? From what?"

"From the general."

"The general? Cat, will you please stop talking in riddles and tell me what's going on?"

"From the beginning?"

"That'd be nice."

She rubbed the sweat from her palms. Was it really worth the risk telling Sam? It wasn't so much her life that concerned her. It was Benin. What would happen to him if she went against the general's orders and shared the unspoken with Sam? Her rebellion would affect them all.

Catherine forced her grip to loosen on the reins. Sam deserved to know, and telling him would take some of the burden off her shoulders.

Perhaps he could even help.

Her gaze slid the length of him, from his thick-muscled arms to his broad shoulders to his narrow waist, until it rested on the bone-handled six-shooters nestled in the holsters strapped there. He was the first man who truly looked able.

"How well can you use those things?"

"What things?"

"Your pistols."

"I thought you didn't like them?"

"Just answer the question."

Sam eyed her strangely. "Suffice it to say, they've done me well."

Cat pressed her lips together. Hopefully, that meant he was slicker than a greased pig and faster than lightning. All their lives might depend on it.

She drew a deep breath. "A couple years after you left, I was riding fence during the spring and checking on the horses."

"When did you build a fence?"

"Earlier that year. My nephews helped me do it. Now please let me tell this without interrupting, or I might not be able to get it out."

Sam nodded, so she continued.

"I thought I heard a horse in distress, one of my mares that might be foaling early, so I hurried to investigate." Her heart started to pound, and her blood ran cold as the sights and sounds from that day resurfaced.

Catherine tightened her hold around her sleeping two-year-old and urged Buster into a fast walk toward the horrendous cries piercing the warm spring air. She did *not* need this. If Nan foaled too early, it was very possible she'd lose both the mare and the colt, and she needed every last ounce of horseflesh she owned to make it through the year. Nan was one of her best broodmares, her only broodmare, and Catherine had high hopes the Lord would bless her with twins this year.

The cries stopped, and deep voices carried to her, followed by grunts and groans. She pulled up short behind a twisted oak when she spotted a group of men hovering around a prostrate form. A lean, dark-haired man with a black slouch hat nodded to a portly, graying fellow.

Seconds later, a gunshot rent the air.

Catherine muffled a scream while her horse backstepped. Benin awoke with a cry.

"Who's there?"

Cradling Benin to her, she wheeled her mount in the opposite direction.

"Stop, or I'll shoot." An ominous click emphasized the man's words.

The boy on her lap and the dead man on the ground insisted she pull back on the reins.

Footsteps crunched closer. "Well, well, well, what do we have here?"

Benin buried his face in her shirt and clung to her. His cries turned into whimpers. Anger, pure and hot, shot through her. These men had no right to scare her son, let alone take another's life. Her right hand slid toward her saddlebag.

"Madam, before you attempt something foolish, might I remind you that more than a half-dozen guns are already cocked and pointed your direction." The man's voice rang smooth, polished, more like what she'd expect from a banker than a ruffian.

Catherine stilled and waited, wishing one of them would step into her line of vision.

"What we gonna do with her?"

"Now, I believe, gentlemen, that is entirely up to her. You see, madam, you've put me in quite the predicament. No one was supposed to witness that scene a moment ago." Boot steps thudded closer. "It might benefit you to know that he chose his fate. You see, he decided to turn on me even though he knew the consequences. Such a very bad decision. He left me no other choice. What is a man if he does not keep his word? And mark my words, madam, should you decide to repeat what you've seen here today, you shall meet with the same fate as this unfortunate fellow. You wouldn't want your child to grow up without a mother, would you?"

Catherine rubbed Benin's back while her heart threatened to beat out of her chest. She shook her head.

"Wise choice." The stench of burning tobacco wafted her direction. "Now tell me, what's your name?"

Catherine pressed her lips together until something cold and hard touched her lower back. Sweat dripped down her temple.

"The general asked you a question." Another, more gravelly, voice.

"Catherine." Peering down, she caught a glimpse of a man's dust-covered boots. If only he'd come a little closer, she'd have more to tell the sheriff.

"Catherine what?"

A sharp click resounded behind her.

"McGarrett." She bit out the word.

"As you can see, Mrs. McGarrett, my men know I have very little patience. When I ask a question, I expect an answer, and when I tell them to do something, I expect them to act. Now here's how this is going to transpire. One of my men will accompany you back to your home, and if you even *think* of running to the law, he has my permission to shoot you. Now, where do you call home?"

Catherine gritted her teeth. These men were not going to take over her life or her ranch.

Benin whimpered in her lap and drew her gaze to his dark head.

She slowly released a sigh. "The Bar M."

"Aw, a fine piece of real estate."

Catherine stiffened. How did the man know about her ranch? Why did they call him General? Were they some kind of rogue soldiers who couldn't accept the war ended over a decade ago?

"Now I know where I've heard your name before. You're the McGarrett woman who couldn't keep her man at home, aren't you? Well, we can't leave a poor, defenseless woman to struggle all on her own, now can we, boys?"

Deep, throaty chuckles filled the air behind her, sending an eerie chill down her spine. Why, oh why, had she opted to check the fence today instead of tomorrow?

"Here's what we'll do. My lieutenant here—you can call him…Larry—will accompany you back to the grounds of the Bar M and become your new ranch hand. He will report to me if you so much as sneeze in the direction of the law."

Shuffling, then a mixture of hushed baritones interrupted the general.

"I see. That does present a problem." The band's leader cleared his throat. "Mrs. McGarrett, my men just reminded me that your father-in-law is the county sheriff."

Catherine swallowed the smirk that tugged at her lips.

"You will not speak a word to him of today, and whenever he visits you, must make sure that Larry is privy to your conversation, or he has my permission to shoot you both. Do I make myself clear?"

"Abundantly."

"Good."

Catherine rubbed a hand against her leg and peeked at Sam. "After that, Larry followed me home and never left. He watches my every move like a hawk."

Sam remained stoic, a tick in his jaw the only hint he'd heard her. That and the white-knuckled grip he used on the saddle horn. Remembering his words from earlier, she let the silence continue, giving him time to think. She needed his help. Sam might not care enough to help just because of her, but perhaps he would for their son's sake and that of Sam's father. Either way, at least her child had another parent to take care of him now. If—heaven forbid—something happened to her, at least Benin would be taken care of.

Catherine straightened in her saddle, her fingers fisting the reins. However it turned out, she refused to have this hanging over her head any longer.

The general wanted to see her.

The general would get his wish.

"You're not going."

Catherine's gaze swung up. "What did you say?"

"I said you aren't going. This so-called general wants to meet with you 'cause I'm back, right?"

"I think so."

"Then I won't come back. You'll ride onto the ranch alone."

Her heart and hopes plummeted to her toes. If it weren't for her boots, they'd have hit the dirt and been trampled by the horses. "I'll still have to meet him whether you come back or not. I doubt he'll send a message saying he's changed his mind."

"No. 'Cause I'm going to find him and do my level best not to shoot his mangy hide before I throw him in jail."

"I...you...y-you've lost your mind."

"And you've lost yours if you think I'm letting any wife of mine go traipsing into an outlaw's camp."

Her heart rose to beat irregularly in her chest. Maybe he did still care after all. "How can you possibly find him before this evening? You don't even know what he looks like. What about all his other men? You'd be one against who knows how many."

"Two against who knows how many. I'll try and get Pa to go along. As long as it doesn't rain, I should have easy enough tracks to follow."

"How do you figure that?"

"Larry got a message to you yesterday before we left, right?"

Catherine nodded. "I peeked at it before we ate supper."

"Then there should be fresh tracks to follow all the way back to their hideout. When you get to the house, all you have to do is get Pa a message to meet me."

"Where?"

Sam scratched his chin. "Which direction does Larry normally ride off?"

"South. Sometimes west. Why?"

"I've got to have someplace to start. Does he always ride that big bay gelding?"

"Mostly. Yes. Sam, are you really considering doing this?"

"Of course. Why wouldn't I?"

Tears sprung to her eyes without warning, and a sob caught in her throat. After so many years of waiting and praying, was this really happening? Were her prayers finally being answered? A glimpse of freedom sparkled in the distance, the relief overwhelmingly unbelievable.

"Darlin', are you fixing to cry?" Sam's hand slid around hers, pulling a tear to the surface. "Hey, it's going to be all right."

The sob escaped. Her vision blurred.

Her horse shuffled to a stop, then strong arms lifted her from her saddle and over onto Sam's lap. She covered her face with her hands while relief poured from her eyes. She couldn't believe she was falling apart like this in front of him, but she was powerless to stop it. For years, she'd longed to share the horrors of that day with someone. She'd longed for this to end. For the freedom to let her son roam their land without fear. For the ability to walk one step without looking over her shoulder.

"Shh, now, don't cry. We'll make it through this." Sam cradled her to his chest, and his horse started walking.

As the tears started to dwindle, she listened to the steady thump of his heart and allowed her mind to wander. How long had it been since someone held her like Sam did now? Were there other woman he'd held like this in his absence? Other women who'd known him as well as she, better even? Her heart constricted.

Leaning away, she peered into his gray eyes. "Is it true?"

"Is what true?"

"Roxie sent me a letter from Crystal Falls. Said she saw you"—Catherine gulped—"with another woman."

Sam stiffened, and guilt marched into his gaze.

Her heart cracked. She cinched a wall around it before it shattered into a million pieces. "Let me down please."

"Darlin'—"

"I want on my own horse." Tears pressed in, but she refused to give them free rein.

"It's not what you—"

"Please. Stop."

Sandy clomped to a standstill, and Catherine slid to the ground. Grabbing her reins, she swung on board Buster.

"Cat—"

"Take me home, Sam."

After a moment of strained silence, Sam dipped his head and nudged Sandy forward. Catherine fell in line, wishing she didn't have to watch his broad back the whole way home. How could he betray her in such a way? Leaving her was one thing, but breaking their vows... How could she ever forgive him for that?

―⁂―

Sam longed to break the heavy silence further chilling the cool air, but he'd seen Cat's face. She was determined to believe the worst. Anything he said right now would go clear through that pretty little head of hers. It didn't matter that he'd only done what was necessary to complete his assigned task. It didn't matter that he'd never let things stray further than a chaste kiss. It didn't matter that he already felt like a heel for his actions. His gander was cooked.

The road home multiplied in length.

Not only the road home but the road to her heart.

Sam skirted around a spindly oak and chanced a glance back at his wife. As much as she tried to hide it, he saw the pain written across her face. He hated that he'd hurt her again. Why had he ever justified his actions as being right? The end clearly didn't justify the means. Somehow, he had to convince Cat to talk to him. No, to listen to him.

Evidently, protecting her with silence wasn't doing their relationship any good. He'd have to tell her the whole story. She'd kept the happenings with the general quiet for so long. Perhaps he could trust her with his past too.

Maybe then she would talk to him again.

10

Catherine readjusted her position in the saddle and glanced at the sun, which sat well past its zenith. "How much farther?"

"We should be coming across your sister's old house soon. I figured we'd stop there and water the horses and figure out the rest of our plan from there."

"Plan? What makes you think I still want your help?" Her heart smote her. Bitterness wasn't the answer, but the hurt that raged in her demanded release. *God, I need Your help.*

"Cat, you might not love me or believe me anymore, but I'm still your husband. I'm still going to help you."

Love him? Love a man who broke his vows? Who left her alone for almost six years so he could do whatever his little heart pleased?

Love beareth all things...endureth all things.

God, I'm sick of enduring. I'm sick of being hurt. I'm sick of always having to be the one to put up with whatever happens to me with a good attitude.

Love covers a multitude of sins.

Catherine swallowed a groan. *God, I know You want me to love and forgive him, but I...I can't...at least not on my own. You're going to have to do it through me. Show me how to do this.* She drew a deep breath. *Help me to love him the way You do, even when I don't feel like it. Because right now I surely don't.*

A small cabin made of part river rock and part timbers came into view at the bottom of the next hill. Her sister's old place still stood in good repair. She'd always loved this location, but Constance and her family had quickly outgrown it. Rather than add to it, they'd built a new place on a different portion of their property, near a stream.

Sam pulled to a stop at the small barn, which sat a stone's throw from the house. "We'll let the horses cool down a minute. Then I'll draw them some water."

Catherine nodded and slid from the saddle, grateful to give her body a break. She was used to long hours in a saddle, but today's ride proved more than taxing. After a pat to Buster's neck, she led both horses into the small corral. Sam wandered in the direction of the well.

Welcoming the distance from him, Catherine moseyed to the far side of the corral and folded her arms across the top rung of the fence. A couple of rungs were missing, but she didn't have the energy to care. She looked forward to home, but even that place held troubles. What she wouldn't give to be able to take her horse and disappear. "God, I'm so tired. I just don't want to deal with any of this anymore."

However, to give up and leave would be letting the devil win. The general wouldn't let her get farther than Cater Springs anyway, and then there was Sam... A sob caught in her throat, and she pressed her fingers against her mouth to keep it in. She'd thought he was past hurting her. How wrong she'd been. Tears blurred her vision for the second time that day. *Why, God? Why did he have to do it? Why did it all have to happen this way? What are You trying to teach me?*

Catherine laid her forehead on her arms and fought for control of her unraveling emotions. A hand touched her shoulder. She jolted upright and stumbled out of Sam's reach.

"Darlin', it's not what you think."

"How do you know what I think?" She drew a breath meant to steady, but her lip trembled. "How could you?"

"It was necessary to get the job done." Sam sighed. "Or at least I thought so at the time." His troubled eyes pleaded with her. "I promise you I only kissed one of them once. That's it."

"One of them?" The restraints holding her crumbling heart together strained to the breaking point. "You mean there were more?" Shaking her head, she rotated on her heel, but he caught her arm.

"Honest, Cat, nothing happened. They meant nothing. They were just a means to an end. I don't know what your friend told you, but she got it all wrong."

"Apparently not. You just admitted you...you *kissed*...another woman."

Sam tugged her closer. "I'm sorry. Can't you see that?"

"Looks can be deceiving."

"So can feelings." He captured her face between his hands, lowering his mouth toward hers. Before she could respond, he stopped. A war raged in his eyes. "I promised you no kissing. You might not believe it, but I'm still a man of my word."

His hands fell away, and he strode toward the watering buckets outside the fence.

Catherine stared after him, oddly bereft at the lack of his touch. Shaking her head, she sank against a corral post. She must be going daft. The man just admitted he'd kissed another woman.

But he kept his word not to kiss her.

He admitted he'd courted other women while married to her.

But he'd also apologized.

He admitted they'd been a means to an end.

But he hadn't said what end.

Catherine rubbed her hands across her face and resisted the urge to kick something or, rather, someone. Ugh, why did everything with him have to be so confounded confusing! Where did that leave them? Did she ask for the rest of the story? Did she listen to God and forgive him? What did she do? Her knuckles turned white as she gripped the fence. Her little boy would never understand why she'd pray for years for his father to come back and then kick him out the next day. With a sigh, she looked heavenward. *God, as much as it hurts, I want to do the right thing here. Please help me.*

When in doubt, wait it out. Catherine hadn't heard her mother's old adage in years. Why did it come to her now? Her gaze roamed heavenward. Was that what God wanted her to do? Wait?

Maybe it *was* best to put off any hasty decisions. She certainly wasn't thinking clearly. Perhaps she should wait until after the mess with the general was cleaned up before deciding how to clean up the mess that was her marriage. Yes, maybe that was best.

Catherine pushed away from the fence and walked to a refilled bucket located outside the corral. She quenched her thirst, dropped the dipper back in the bucket, and finally returned Sam's scrutiny. "So what's your plan?"

"What? I-I mean..." He shook his head as if to clear it.

"Look, I want to make sure Benin is safe. When this mess with the general is no longer hanging over our heads, then we'll talk. Fair?"

His brows jumped. "Fair enough."

"So?"

Sam removed his hat and ran his hand along the brim. "Well, I have to get word to my pa to meet me on the south end of the ranch."

"I can do that. Where do you want me to tell him to meet you?"

"Maybe it'd be better if we met on this side and circled around together so no one gets suspicious."

"Okay, so where?"

"Is that split oak—you know, the one that the lightning struck—is that still standing?"

Catherine nodded.

"Have him meet me there."

"What if something happens, and he can't meet you? How will I let you know?"

Sam settled the Stetson back in place and rubbed his chin. "Forget the tree. We don't really have time for me to wait anyway. Tell him I'll leave subtle marks on the trail. He can meet me at the hideout if he can get away."

He moved toward his horse.

"Wait."

He turned.

"What if something goes wrong?"

"What could go wrong?"

"I don't know. I just have this sinking feeling in my stomach. Are you sure I shouldn't just go like the general said?"

"You're not going, understood? Let me handle this." Sam motioned toward her horse. "Time's a-wasting."

Catherine studied his self-assured stance and his confidence while he swung into the saddle. "You've done this before, haven't you?"

The leather ceased its creaking. Sam peered at her, then tugged on his gloves. "Something similar, yes."

Catherine swallowed back her trepidation and her questions and walked toward her horse. She paused with her hand on the saddle. "Sam, I don't think this is going to work."

"And why not?"

"Larry will still expect me to leave with him this evening to go meet the general. If he senses something is up, he'll put the other outlaws on the alert and make things ten times harder."

"I hadn't considered that." Sam rested his hands on the pommel for an instant, then grabbed the reins and backed his horse away from the corral. "Have Pa truss him up before he comes out to help me."

Catherine pressed her lips together, nodded, and mounted. "How much farther do we ride together?"

"We split company here. Take that path to the main road leading back to town, and go to the house. You can do that on your own, can't you?"

She bobbed her head.

"Good. I'll see you tonight or at the latest, tomorrow."

Sam walked Sandy next to Catherine and extended his hand. She hesitated a moment before she slid hers inside his.

He squeezed it gently. "When we get through this, I'll tell you anything you want to know."

"Anything?"

"Anything."

"All right."

His fingers slipped from her hand and lifted to her cheek. "Be careful, Cat." His thumb brushed across her lips. "I love you."

He kneed his horse and galloped out of the yard.

Catherine trembled from the bombardment of emotions coursing through her while Sam progressed up the hill to the south. She'd waited years to hear those words fall from his lips again. Why did he have to say them now? Why, when she second-guessed everything he said? Why, when she might never see him alive again?

She shook her head and urged her horse down the path. This was all a big mistake. She should've never said anything. She should've never agreed to this. This was her fight, her battle, and here she was riding home while the man she'd spent years praying for went off to face possible death. How could she have let this happen? If he died, it would be all her fault. Not that the rat didn't possibly deserve it, but she didn't want the fault on her conscience.

Catherine tapped her horse into a trot. She'd better hurry and let GW know what was transpiring. If he couldn't get away, then Ida could watch Benin, and somehow she'd help finish what should've ended many months ago.

Sam slowed Sandy to a walk and picked his way down the rocky hillside. He must be a dunce for leaving Cat with those words, but he might not get a chance to say them again. He should've said them long before now, but how on earth was he to know she had some crazed friend in Crystal Falls who'd spotted him and sent her a letter?

It was just his luck that Cat would find out. Why couldn't someone have tattled when he'd been shot and laid up for months? No, Cat's friend had to air his indiscretions instead of his accomplishments or injuries. How would he convince Cat he'd changed now? He'd hoped she'd never know the depths to which he'd stooped to get a job done. Stone was right. He should've let all the skeletons out of his closet the moment he'd gotten Cat alone. There he went letting his foolish pride trip him up again.

Sam paused at the crest of the next hill. A hint of white broke through the trees in the distance. That would be the barn. Odd color, white, for a barn. He'd have painted it red. Yet another difference between him and his honey-haired wife. The gulf between them seemed to be getting wider and wider. The exact opposite of what he'd come here to do. Why did things sound so good in his head, but when they came out, she took them all wrong? Would they ever be able to communicate without someone yelling or getting hurt? Sure, he'd only been home a short while, but how long would it take for things to change for the better instead of the worse?

With a sigh, Sam kneed his horse and started circling to the west side of the ranch. Maybe once he showed her how much he still cared by bringing these outlaws to justice, she'd believe him when he said he wanted to make things right.

If he didn't get killed first.

11

"Miz Cathy, Miz Cathy!"

Catherine yanked Buster to a stop beside the sheriff's palomino and vaulted to the ground. She'd never seen her cook so frantic. "Ida, what's wrong?"

"Benin. The sheriff. Oh, Lord, 'ave mercy." Ida stopped waving her dishcloth and gulped air like a drowning man.

That's when Catherine saw the cloth wasn't just red.

It was saturated.

With blood.

Her heart plummeted. They were too late.

She gripped Ida's shoulders. "Where are they? What's happened?"

A harsh moan emanated from inside her cabin, followed by a loud thud.

Releasing the older woman, Catherine raced inside. "Benin!"

She halted on the threshold.

GW lay sprawled in the opening to her bedroom. Blood seeped through bandages tied across his right shoulder. She hurried to his side. His left eye was swollen shut and tinged with blue. Who had done this?

"GW." She patted his cheek. "Oh, dear God, please help us."

Ida knelt across from her.

Catherine gripped her arm. "Where's Benin?"

"I dunno, Miz Cathy. The sheriff took 'im huntin' this mornin'. He wundered in like this jus' a short while ago, bleedin' an' nearly unconscious."

"Was he shot?"

"No, them's stab wounds, ma'am."

Catherine cupped her hand to her mouth and breathed a prayer. "Get Mo and Curly. Have them put him back in my bed." She hurried to her feet and headed toward the door.

"Where's you goin', Miz Cathy?"

"To get my boy." Catherine yanked the rifle from above the doorframe and went in search of her bullets.

"The men're mountin' up, gettin' ready to do that theyselves."

Catherine jerked the box off the highest shelf by the door and started filling her gun with ammunition. "Stop them. Don't let them leave this yard without me. They don't know what they're getting into, but I do."

"Ya do?"

Catherine nodded and stuffed the box into her pocket. "Get them. Please." She leaned the rifle against the wall and knelt beside GW when Ida scurried out the door. "GW, come on. Wake up for me. Tell me what they said."

His eyelid fluttered, then he blinked out his right eye. "C-Catherine, that you?"

"It's me."

He lifted his head, but she put a hand to his good shoulder.

"Don't. I think you've lost too much blood. I'll get the men to help you get in bed."

GW wagged his head. "No, got...to...help Ben." He struggled to sit up. He wouldn't be stopped, so she steadied him until he leaned against the doorframe.

"Tell me what happened. Sam and I will take care of it."

The older man licked his lips and stared at her. "I'm sorry, Catherine. He took him."

"Larry?"

"H-how'd you know?"

"It's a long story. I'll fill you in on it later. Just tell me what he said."

"He said your life for the boy's. He said..." Air hissed through his teeth, and he cupped his side. "He said to meet him at Gable's Gorge.

Alone." GW caught her arm when she moved to rise. "But you can't. That's a death trap."

"I have to. He's my son." Catherine pried loose his grip. "Don't worry. I'll tell Sam first."

He nodded and squeezed her hand. "I'm sorry, pumpkin."

"It'll be okay, Pa."

A grin touched his cracked lips. "You ain't never called me that before."

She smiled and pecked him on the cheek. "I'll be back."

After grabbing her rifle, she strode toward the door.

"Catherine."

"Yeah?"

"Save me a piece of the feller who did this to me."

"I'll do my best." Catherine paused on the porch when Mo and Curly hastened onto it. "Get him in bed, then come back out here."

The two nodded and disappeared inside.

Catherine patted Buster on the neck as she moved past him toward the horses the men had ready and waiting. "Sorry, boy, you're staying here this time. I've put you through enough today." She rubbed the nose of the next chestnut gelding with the four white socks. "Rusty, you might not like me so much once this day's over."

Stepping over, she slid the rifle into the scabbard on his saddle.

"Miz Cathy, you want I should take care of Buster for you?" Ida's son peeked at her between the two horses, the fear and worry evident in his scrunched brows.

"Would you do that for me, pal? I'd really appreciate it."

Roscoe slipped Buster's lead into his hand. "You will bring'um back, won't ya?"

Catherine paused, turned, and leaned down in front of the nine-year-old. "Do you remember how we prayed for Benin's pa to come home?"

He nodded.

"We had to trust God and believe that one day He would bring good into our lives and bring him safely back? Well, this is just like that. We've got to trust God to take care of Ben." Her voice wavered.

She sucked in a breath and settled her hand on the lad's shoulder. "You stay here and do me a favor. Pray. Trust God. He can do what we can't and help us do what we never thought possible."

The lines smoothed a bit on Roscoe's brow. "I'll be prayin' till I see y'all ridin' in."

"That's a good boy. Thank you."

When the lad and horse moved off, she caught Ida staring at her.

"I'll be doin' the same, Miz Cathy. Don't you worry none. God ain't failed us yet."

Catherine swiped at a rogue tear. "Thanks, Ida."

The men tromped back onto the porch.

"That shoulda's painin' him somethin' awful, Ida. Ya might wanna check on him."

"I's prayin', Miz Cathy." Ida brushed past Curly and disappeared into the cabin.

"Where's your husband, Mrs. McGarrett? Isn't he going to help?"

"He's out finding the outlaw camp."

"Outlaws?" Curly's brows rose, and he glanced at Mo.

"Look, I know y'all have a bunch of questions I don't have time for. I have to catch up to Sam, warn him, and still get to Gable's Gorge by sunset." Catherine climbed onto her fresh mount. "I know you both want to help, but I can't risk them seeing other people and shooting my son." She backed Rusty away from the hitching post. "If we're not back by morning, y'all have my permission to start gathering the townsmen and neighbors."

"Be careful, Miz Cathy."

Catherine touched a finger to her Stetson and left at a gallop. She'd head for the lightning oak and pray she could find the subtle signs Sam had left for his father...and that she didn't get lost along the way.

Sam nicked the base of another live oak with his knife and kept walking, leading his horse by the reins. He hadn't found Larry's trail, but he continued to press toward the southwest, all the while replaying his conversations with Cat in his head. Her willingness to talk once this was over gave him hope they might still have a future together. He only knew he didn't want to spend another year without her by his side. One moment in her presence hardened that resolve.

Stepping along the rocks, he worked his way down the hill and through the trees. Occasionally, he stopped and clustered a few stones together as another marker. He sure hoped Pa caught up to him before he found the camp. Making half a dozen men surrender would be a whole lot easier with another gun along.

Part of Sam wished Cat had come along too, in spite of her anger and irritation with him. He could spend all day watching her and not tire of it. She had a subtle grace mixed with confidence he respected. There wasn't another woman like her on the face of the earth. During the last day and a half around her, he'd felt more alive than he had in years. Somehow she had that effect on him…and he loved it.

Sam skirted around another particularly large boulder and skidded to a halt. Blood pooled on one rock and splattered others. Deep ruts scarred the ground here and there. Caution guided his Colt into his hand. Had an animal died here? If so, where was the carcass?

That's when he saw it. A bloody handprint smeared across the farthest boulder.

Sam scanned the area. Nothing moved, not even his horse.

This was no two animals butting heads. This was a life-or-death standoff.

But who'd lost?

He stepped over to the handprint boulder and searched behind it and into the trees. A small blood trail led to a set of hoofprints near a mesquite. They headed northward.

Back toward the Bar M.

Not good.

Sam searched the ground, hunting for more signs. Another set of tracks led toward the southwest. These sank deeper into the dirt, which meant a larger horse than the first. Maybe a big bay? He ran a hand across his face, closed his eyes, and tried to picture the man Cat had introduced as Larry. He'd been on the tall side. Maybe six feet or right near there. Dishwater-blond hair. Sturdy build. Larry would probably have a boot print about the size of Sam's. Maybe a tad smaller.

Sam studied the dirt closer and finally found the man's tracks. Yep, Larry had most likely done this, but who had he fought? One of the hands? Someone else? Whoever he was, he was long gone and in a very bad way.

Another set of footprints caught his eye.

Little ones.

A chill washed over him.

God, please tell me I'm wrong.

"Rusty, I think we've taken a wrong turn." Catherine slid from the saddle and turned in a wide circle. Every mesquite tree, live oak, and cactus patch looked the same. She'd found the lightning tree, but clearly her sense of direction had twisted from there. The sun continued to sink, and the closer it got to the horizon, the more her angst increased. She had to find Sam and get to that gorge.

Benin's life depended on it.

"Oh, God, please let me find him in time." Catherine tugged Rusty over to a boulder and climbed to a higher viewpoint. The chill November wind seeped through her coat. Rubbing her hands together, she searched again for one of Sam's distinguishing marks.

Nothing presented itself.

"Do you think we should go down the hill or toward the sun?" She stepped into the saddle. "Maybe if we head toward the sun, I'll warm up a little. I do think it's getting colder out here."

Rusty walked forward at her nudging.

After a moment of clomping, she tugged him to a stop. "What is that?"

She turned him toward the top of the hill. It wasn't much. Just a small bit of order. Three stones stacked on top of each other. Catherine dismounted and nearly shouted for joy when she spotted a partial boot print near the grouping of rocks. "Thank You, Jesus."

Sam had clearly been changing his markings. Why hadn't he told her he planned to do that? She released a breath of frustration and studied the landscape. Either she was getting better at tracking or Sam was getting sloppy. She could actually tell which way he went. Hope resurfaced, causing a grin to split her face. Maybe she could find Sam in time so she wouldn't have to face the general and his men alone. Perhaps there remained a chance she'd survive this ordeal after all.

Scattered stones and occasional hoofprints led her downward, weaving by the occasional marked tree. When she rounded a boulder and came across a bloody mess, she gasped.

"Dear Lord, have mercy." What had happened here? A smeared handprint marred one of the farthest boulders. Had harm befallen Sam? "Oh, God, please say it's not so."

Catherine picked her way that direction, fearing she'd find a slain body on the opposite side. Only more trees and rocks met her view. No Sam. The air seeped from her, and she sagged against a boulder.

"Maybe he's not dead. Maybe he's still alive. But which way did he go?" She pushed off the rock and moved to the left, searching the trampled ground for the tracks she'd followed before. When she finally found them, she set off at a brisk pace.

No one in her family would die because of her tonight.

12

"Here he is, General. Just like you wanted." Larry shoved Benin toward a lean man with a dark, short-brimmed hat.

Sam clenched his fist and forced himself to remain hidden in the live oak's upper branches. Backlit by the lowering sun, the leader's features remained indistinguishable. The general snapped at a portly fellow and pointed to the boy. Porky jumped to his feet and hurried Benin toward a small fire.

Larry picked at his teeth with a toothpick. "How long you gonna give her to show?"

"Are you certain she received my message?"

"If the old coot didn't bleed to death before he reached the ranch house."

In a blink, the general leveled a derringer at the end of Larry's nose. "My orders were to not kill him. Are you telling me you disobeyed a direct command, Soldier?"

The toothpick fell from Larry's mouth as he hurriedly shook his blond head. "N-no, General, I wouldn't think of doing that. I...I just roughed him up a bit. You knew the sheriff wouldn't make it easy to take the boy."

The sheriff? All that blood had been from his father? Sam gripped the branch to keep from tumbling off his perch. *Oh, God, please...*

"That's better." As quick as the small pistol appeared, it disappeared up the general's sleeve. "Now tell me what you told him."

Sam scooted a bit further out, grateful Texas live oaks weren't deciduous trees and he had leaves to hide his eavesdropping.

"I said that she'd have to exchange her life for the boy's and that she'd have to come alone to Gable's Gorge."

"Very well." The general scratched a match with his thumbnail and lit a cigar. After a few puffs, he dropped the match at Larry's feet. "Take Bone and go keep watch for her at the opening."

"Yes, sir."

"And, Lieutenant..."

"Yes, sir?"

"Should she not show up this evening, I expect one of you to stay awake and keep a lookout."

"Yes, sir." Larry strode away, tapped a short, brown-haired man on the shoulder, and pointed back in the direction he'd come. The two talked for a brief moment, then moved toward their horses.

Sam hoped he'd tied Sandy far enough out of the way she wouldn't be discovered and give him away. The general wandered closer to the campfire and took a seat. Benin sat, leaning against a felled log, his little arms wrapped around his legs and his face buried in his knees. Sam's heart broke, and his anger surged. He had to get his boy out of there. After nightfall he'd slide down and sneak Benin out, but how would he warn Cat not to try something foolish in the meantime?

"Well, well, well, what do we have here?"

An ominous click drew Sam's attention downward.

The open end of a rifle barrel greeted him.

Uh-oh. Change of plans.

Catherine slowed her mount at the sight of a buckskin farther ahead. Was that Sandy? She swung down and lowered her voice. "Sam? Sam, are you here?"

The horse lifted her head and looked Catherine's direction.

Yeah, that was Sandy all right, but where was Sam? Why didn't he answer her? "Sam."

She stopped Rusty beside Sandy and tied him nearby. "I'll let you two keep each other company. You wouldn't want to tell me where your rider went, now would you, girl?"

Sandy resumed munching on the knee-high grasses.

"That's what I thought."

Catherine searched for boot prints but stopped when she saw the ground dropped away a few feet ahead. Crouching, she inched forward until she peered over the edge. To the left, she saw a large oak tree, and farther in the distance, the tumbled mass of a rockslide that turned the ravine into a makeshift canyon. To the right, two men sat with rifles across their laps where the walls of the ravine grew closer together at a bend. With a gasp, Catherine scurried from the edge.

She'd found Gable's Gorge.

Catching her lip between her teeth, she sank onto her heels. Where had Sam disappeared? He had to be here somewhere. Had he snuck in? Been captured? Was he somewhere on the rim? Catherine scanned the rocks, trees, and grasses. No one. Maybe he'd followed to the hideout on foot. Was the hideout in the gorge or somewhere nearby? After scooting farther away from the sentries, she peeked over the edge.

Smoke swirled up from the far side of the large oak, whose branches touched the top of the rim.

"Gotcha." Catherine quickly and quietly worked that direction. When the tree lay in reach, she went to her belly and scooted to the drop-off. Moving a branch aside, she squinted against the setting sun to see the group gathered around a small campfire. The branch slid from her shock-slackened grip and slapped her in the face.

"Mmm." She grabbed her nose. When the pain ebbed, she peeked again. Her eyes weren't deceiving her. Both her son *and* her husband were trussed up in the middle of camp like two Christmas turkeys.

Catherine laid her forehead on her arm. What now? "God, You've got to help me. Don't let them die. Show me what to do."

She'd counted on Sam's help to get them all out of this alive. Now it might very well come down to her life for their boy's, but what would they do with Sam if she made the exchange? Would they kill them both? What would happen to her son if they did let him go? And there was no guarantee they would. Would they recapture Ben since he knew their faces? Would they kill him too? Her heart seized. She couldn't allow that to happen.

Lifting her head, she studied the situation again. Four men. Two sentries. One general. *God, what way do I go?*

Her gaze rose to the orange-and-crimson hues painted across the clouds. How much more time did she have before they acted? Were they expecting her to abide by the former note to arrive before sunset, or did Larry's new demands reign supreme? The sun was setting, and her family remained alive. Perhaps she still had options.

Could she possibly sneak into camp after dark and free Ben and Sam? With the tree, she could get past the guards with no problem. The lingering question—could she climb a tree in the dark without breaking her neck? After falling from the barn loft as a child, she'd never been too fond of heights. It'd been years since she'd fought her way up one of those trunks, and this time she'd be working backward, from the top down. For anybody else she wouldn't dream of doing this, but for her son…

Catherine pressed her lips together and tried to figure out a path down. Most of the limbs within her reach started out quite slender before thickening to a width she'd deem worthy of holding her weight. One sat a bit lower that would do, but she'd have to dangle over the edge to get to it. A shiver raced along her spine, and it had nothing to do with the cold air. Sam might call her Cat, but she doubted even a feline could descend that tree without making a sound, and waking a bunch of outlaws who wanted her dead wasn't the plan she had in mind.

She'd have to find another way.

※

Sam strained at the ties that bound his hands behind his back while scanning the outlaw camp. Porky, who the men surprisingly called Ham, added wood to the fire. The general leaned against the ravine wall, working quietly on his cigar. Three others hid behind hands of five-card stud, probably waiting their turn at sentry duty.

Or for Cat to show.

Sam bit back a groan. How could he have been so foolish as to let himself get caught? He released a sigh. He knew why. His gaze strayed to the dark-haired boy sitting silently beside him, dried tear tracks on his dusty face. "It's going to be okay, partner."

Benin's brown eyes, so like his mother's, turned his direction. Sam hated the fear and uncertainty there.

"Are they gonna hurt Mama?"

Sam blinked. That was not the question he'd expected to be on his five-year-old's mind. "They'll have to go through me first."

"But you're tied up."

Nothing like stating the obvious. "I know, Benin. I'm working on that." Sam examined the men. No one seemed to be watching them, but that could change in an instant. "Look, son, I have a knife hidden in the heel of my boot. If I shift my legs toward you, you reckon you could get it out for me?"

"Hey, you two, quit your jawin', or do I need to gag you?" Ham stood from his seat by the fire.

Benin leaned into Sam, his little body quivering. Sam bit the inside of his cheek to keep from spouting off and making his captors angrier.

The general waved off the portly man and moved to stand before them. "So, you are finally in a talkative mood? Good. Now maybe you'll answer my questions." He flicked ashes from his cigar onto Sam's leg. "What did your wife tell you?"

Sam blew off the cinders. "Tell me about what? In case your man didn't mention it, I haven't been around a whole lot for talking of late."

"He told me you two didn't come home last night."

"Well, if you hadn't seen your woman in years, wouldn't you want to get her alone?"

The general smirked, the scar on his cheek whitening with the motion. "That may well be true, but you still haven't answered my question."

"Question? What question?"

The gun appeared in a snap. "I do not like games, Mr. McGarrett." The general shifted the barrel toward Benin. "Now, tell me what I want to know."

Sam leaned in front of Benin while his son tried to disappear behind him. "Fine. Okay, just put the gun away. I'll tell you. Look, let the boy go, and I'll tell you whatever you want."

The general cocked the gun. "My patience is waning."

"All right, she told me everything. I admit it, but I'm the only one she's told."

"And why should I believe you?"

"'Cause it's true. Look, let the boy go. I'm just as good of a bargaining chip as he is. Better even."

"How can that be true? You admitted yourself you've been absent from her life. Why would she care about what happens to you?"

"I don't know, but she does."

The lean man shook his head. "She'll do more for the boy than she will for you, and now that I know she's told you, she's sealed your fate as well." The gun swung toward him.

"Wait! I'm worth more to you alive than dead."

The general's blue eyes narrowed, but his finger quit inching toward the trigger. "Explain yourself."

"I can give you names and locations of three men willing to pay big money for the chance to kill me."

The derringer lowered a fraction. "Why would they do that?"

"Vengeance. I was the one who put their family members behind bars or, in some cases, six feet under."

"So I was right. You are a lawman."

"Yes." For a little bit longer at least. Sam had never taken any oaths like his father, and the line between right and wrong had blurred more times than he cared to admit, but he'd brought many a man to justice over the past five years.

One man dropped his cards and stood. "Hey, I ain't hangin' for shootin' no lawman."

"My man has a point. All right." The gun disappeared. "I'll have those names."

"Not until you let the boy go."

The general studied him for a few heartbeats. "Fine. Ham, untie the lad."

As soon as the boy's hands were freed, Benin threw his arms around Sam's neck. "I don't wanna leave you, Pa."

"I know, but you have to, son." Sam turned his attention to the man standing over them. "Give me a minute to tell my boy how to get home?"

"Why? It's not like he has much chance surviving in those hills alone anyway."

"Please. Just five minutes."

"Two. Mark my words, if either of you tell anyone what you've seen today, I will kill you and every last person in your family, law or no. And you"—the general pointed at Sam—"if you're lying to me, your family's demise is the last thing you will ever see."

"I understand."

"Good." The general motioned to the other men with his head and led them a few steps away. Sam watched them form a huddle, then turned his attention to the clinging child in his lap. "Benin, look at me, son... Come on. There's something important I have to tell you. Good. That's my boy. Now listen closely, okay? Your mama taught you how to ride, right?"

"Yessir."

"Okay. I'm going to tell you how to get to my horse, and then I'll tell you how to get home."

"I don't wanna leave you, Pa."

"I know, but you have to, partner. I've got to have someone to help look after Ma and Gramps for me."

Benin straightened and smeared the tears from his pink cheeks. "Okay."

"Good. Now, do you know your right from your left?"

"No, sir."

"Do you know your letters?"

"Most of 'em."

"All right. Do you know what the letter L looks like?"

"Uh-huh. It looks like this."

Sam smiled when the lad drew the capital letter in the air. "Good. Now hold your hands up with all your fingers straight and your thumbs sticking out. That's it. Which pointer finger and thumb make an L?"

"This one."

"Good. That's your left hand, okay? Can you remember that?"

Benin's dark head bobbed.

"All right. Now, you're going to walk to the end of this gorge. When you can't see the sentries anymore, you climb out and go to your right. Do you know which way that is?"

"The hand that doesn't make the *L*."

"Good. You've got it. So climb to the top of the gorge. Go to your right. You'll walk past a big cactus patch and then see a bunch of trees. My horse is waiting in those trees."

"Sandy?"

"You remember her name?"

Benin nodded. "She's a buckskin. I like buckskins."

Sam grinned as his heart squeezed. "Me too. Now here's how you're going to get home. You hop on Sandy and ride away from the sun. When you come to a fence, put the sun on your left. Do you know what that means?"

"The sun should be on…" Benin held up his hands, then dropped his right one. "This side."

"Good boy. You put the sun on your left side and follow that fence until you get to the opening of our ranch, okay? You think you can do that for me?"

"Yessir, but, Pa, what about you?"

"You don't worry about me. I'll find a way out. I've been in tighter spots than this before. Now you've got to hurry. There's not a whole lot of daylight left. If it gets dark before you can get home, you climb off Sandy and jerk down on her reins twice, real hard. She'll lay down. You stay next to her, and she'll help keep you warm through the night. I've got a bedroll tied behind my saddle too, okay?"

"Okay. I love you, Pa."

Sam swallowed past the lump in his throat. "I love you too, partner. When you see your ma, tell her I love her too."

"Yessir."

"Now you go on. Time's a-wasting."

"Yessir." Benin squeezed him one last time, then scurried off his lap and took off at a run toward the opening of the gorge.

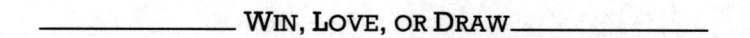

"God, please watch over my boy."

13

Catherine jerked at the sudden movement, then peered back over the edge. Was that Benin running? Abandoning her search for an easier descent, she rushed on quiet feet toward the oak that touched the rim. She peered through the leaves.

That *was* Benin.

Her heart soared but caught when the sentries rose from their stations.

A shout.

The general waved the boy through.

What on earth was happening?

Sam remained tied up, leaning against the log. Had he somehow arranged this?

Benin shot past the sentries and disappeared. Where did he go? Was he running blind, or did he know how to get home? Catherine scrambled away from the edge and gained her feet. Keeping her eye on the direction Benin had vanished, she hastened toward her horse.

A head popped up.

She ground to a stop.

Benin scrambled to his feet, held up his hands, and…headed toward her?

Catherine glanced back at the ravine. Had Sam known she was here? No, wait, his horse. He must've told Ben where to find the horse. Catherine lifted her skirts and ran, climbing over boulders, dashing around cacti.

She skidded to a halt at the tree line and looked out. "Oh, God, please let me find him."

Seconds later, Benin appeared on the other side of the cactus patch.

"Thank You, God." Catherine started to break from the trees but felt a check in her spirit. Maybe running toward a frightened five-year-old wasn't the best idea. She didn't want to scare him more, nor did she want him to shout her name and give away her presence to anyone who might be listening. Perhaps it'd be best to let him find her.

Keeping her son in view, she veered toward the horses, stopping a little bit out of the way behind a larger oak. Benin's eyes widened when he reached the mounts.

"Hi, Sandy. Rusty, is that you?" He stopped patting the horses and turned. "Mama? Mo? Curly? Is somebody there?"

"Benin."

The little boy startled, then turned. "Mama?"

She stepped out from her hiding spot.

He charged toward her, nearly knocking her over in his enthusiasm.

"Oh, honey, I'm so glad to see you." She squeezed him tight, then cupped his face in her hands. "Let me look at you. Are you all right? Do you know why they let you go?"

"Pa talked 'em into it. Is Gramps okay?"

Catherine brushed Benin's hair back from his face and kissed his cheek, her heart overflowing with gratitude toward her husband. "He'll be fine, honey. He was more worried about you. Are you sure you're all right? Nothing hurts?"

"I'm okay, Mama. Pa said to tell ya he loves you."

Her heart skittered. "He did?"

"He also said I had to hurry home 'fore it got all dark."

"I—"

"He told me how. I put the sun behind me 'til I get to the fence, 'n' then put the sun on my left, 'n' follow the fence home."

"That's very smart, but..." Catherine pressed her lips together. How did she get her boy home and help Sam too? She couldn't leave him there to die because of her, no matter what he'd done to her.

"Mama, ya want I should go get help? Oh, no, I can't."

"What? Why not?"

Tears filled his dark eyes. "They said they'd kill you if I told. Papa too."

Catherine well recognized his fear. She'd never wanted this for her son. Tears pricked her own eyes, even as determination to see this end filled her spirit. "It's okay, baby. Mama's not going to let that happen."

"What're you gonna do?"

"We're going to go get help and make sure all these bad men go to jail."

"But what about Papa? He's still tied up, and they'll hurt 'im if we tell. I don't want 'im to get hurted."

She needed a solution that would put Benin at ease, and clearly that included getting Sam out of danger. Her former plan to sneak in during the night came to mind, but what would she do with Ben in the meantime? Keep him with her? Send him home? She'd feel much better if he was safely at home and out of the range of gunfire, but what if he got lost? What if he'd inherited her horrible sense of direction?

Rusty snorted and drew her attention. She'd made it here with God's help. Surely He could see Benin safely home, right? Hadn't she told Roscoe to trust God to bring them all safely back? Who was she to do any less?

"Benin, you think you can do what your Pa said and make it home before dark while I stay here and get him out?"

"You're gonna stay 'n' help Pa?"

"Only if you think you can follow his directions home. I'll get him out of trouble so they can't hurt him when you tell everyone else what's going on. I'll need you to tell Mo to bring help so the bad guys won't get away. You think you can do that?"

Benin nodded.

"All right." After a parting hug and kiss, she set him in Sam's saddle. "You be real careful."

"Yes'm." Benin turned the horse like he'd been riding all his life, which he almost had.

Maybe she should go with him to the fence. Then again, she still hadn't found the perfect spot to descend into the ravine unnoticed, and the sun had already disappeared behind the trees. *Oh, God, I can't believe I'm letting him do this. Please go with him. Keep him safe.*

"Hang on a second."

Benin tugged on the reins. Sandy immediately responded, even with her son's slight weight. Catherine had definitely picked the right horse of the two.

"I can do it, Mama. I know I can."

"I'm sure you can, baby. I just need a couple things to help Pa with before you go." Catherine untied the rope from Sam's saddle and withdrew his rifle. Better to be prepared, and she might need the rope to get in and out of the ravine.

She patted her boy's leg. "All right. You stay with Ida when the men come out to help."

"Yes'm." Benin kicked the horse, and Sandy started walking.

"I love you, Benin."

"I love you too, Mama."

Catherine smiled and swallowed back the tears. "All right. You be your father's son and find your way home."

Benin tossed her a smile and disappeared into the trees.

⁂

Sam's gaze stayed glued to the place where Benin had disappeared from view. Facing down danger himself was one thing. Sending his boy out into it was another. *God, please keep him safe.*

A boot connected with his foot. All five men not on guard duty surrounded him.

"I would suggest you focus on telling us those three names and locations now, because if you even think of escaping, Arizona here has orders to track down the boy and bring him back. I'm sure you wouldn't want that."

Sam shook his head, willing his son to go faster.

"The names."

Ham perched on a log and pulled out a scrap of paper before grabbing up a cooled piece of charcoal.

"Angus McGovern, San Augustine."

Ham scribbled and nodded for him to continue.

"Dakota James, Crystal Falls."

The lies, gunfights, and bleeding bodies traipsed across Sam's mind. He'd narrowly escaped retribution before. Now he was inviting it to his doorstep. What he sowed, he was about to reap.

"And…"

Sam cleared his throat. "And Emilio Ramirez, Laredo."

"Did you get them all?" The general looked to Ham, who nodded. "Good. Grab a horse and get to town. I want those telegraphs sent immediately. Tell them to bring $100 if they want their chance to put a bullet in Sam McGarrett."

"What about the woman, General?" Arizona asked.

Their leader lifted his attention to the fading heavens before offering Sam a sickening grin. "Don't worry. She's known me for a while and knows what I'm capable of. She'll come."

Sam had known her for a while too, and that's exactly what he feared.

14

Catherine waited until light faded from the western sky and lengthened the shadows in the makeshift canyon before tossing the end of the rope down the rocky wall. She knelt a good hundred yards from the outlaws, but she refused to take any chances they might see or hear her descent. Regardless, the horse and rifles waited in the nearby woods. No need to put them in close reach so someone could use them against her.

She tugged on the knot securing her to the man-sized boulder. That ought to do it. Catherine inched to the edge and inspected the fifty-foot plunge. Her stomach took a dip at the sight. Swallowing against the sensation, she dared another peek. Dark water trickled by on the far edge of the collapsed ravine. Licking her lips, she dropped to her knees. *Lord, please let that knot hold.* Her skirt caught when she scooted onto her stomach. That wouldn't do. Standing, she rejoiced she wore jeans under her skirts when riding. She shed the layers of skirt material, immediately missing their added warmth, but she'd rather risk the cold than her neck.

"Sam, you'd better appreciate this." Catherine double-checked the knife tied to her belt, crawled to the edge, gripped the rope, rolled onto her stomach, and backed herself into thin air. Blood pounding in her ears, she planted her boots on the rocky wall of the ravine and scooted lower.

Inadvertently, she peered over her shoulder. "Oh, dear Lord, have mercy."

It was official. She was either insane or insanely in love with her husband. No other woman she knew would dare attempt this. Okay, maybe Sarah Matthews, but Cat couldn't imagine her sister doing something this crazy. Her father had always said she was made of sterner stuff. She had no idea she'd prove him correct in such a way.

Catherine forced her fingers on her right hand to loosen a fraction and slid them to the rope below her left. Her boot skidded on the rock face as she inched it lower to a small ledge. Her heart left residence in her chest to pound in her throat. She could do this. *Just don't look down.*

Hand over hand, inch by inch, she descended the gorge's wall, barely daring to breathe until her feet touched level ground. When they did, she gripped her shaky knees and stared up at the distance she'd covered. Straightening, she grinned. It was oddly liberating facing a fear and overcoming it. Maybe she might yet face the fears she had about Sam and come out the victor.

Shoving the thought aside for later perusal, Catherine kept to the ravine wall and started toward the outlaw camp. First she had to get her husband out alive, then she'd figure out how to live with him.

―――※―――

The general and his men stoked the fire and bedded down for the night. Sam's shoulders ached from the strain of having his hands tied behind him for so long, but the pain wouldn't last. If these no-accounts didn't kill him soon, the ones they'd telegraphed would. He'd finally come home to be the husband he needed to be, to be the father he didn't know he was, and now he wouldn't even have the chance to try.

At least Benin had gotten away, and they hadn't captured or killed Cat. If his death spared them, then it was worth every second of pain. Surely Benin was home now. Safe. He hoped Cat wouldn't try anything stupid and would stay home as well. Hopefully, between her and his father, they would help Benin grow into a better man than him, and they'd remind his son how much he loved him. Even if only for a short time.

The faint call of a whip-poor-will drew Sam from his thoughts. Wasn't it a little late for a whip-poor-will to sing?

A shadow moved to his left. Someone was here.

Sam glanced at the sleeping outlaws. *Father, please don't let them wake up.* They'd go after Benin if they thought he was trying to escape. Sam peered into the night. Whoever lingered in the shadows moved closer. When he saw the person wasn't wearing a skirt, he breathed a little easier. At least it wasn't Cat. Maybe she'd sent one of the hands. He wagged his head, hoping the man would take the hint and stop. His hopes weren't realized.

The shadow scurried closer, and as the firelight reached him, Sam's heart plummeted to his stomach.

Cat hurriedly ducked behind him, a knife in her hand.

He kept his focus trained on the outlaws and lowered his voice, praying the crackling fire would be loud enough to cover his hushed words. "What do you think you're doing? You've got to get out of here."

"Not without you."

"Yes, woman, without me. If they find you here, they'll kill you." The ropes binding him wiggled on his wrist. "Don't cut me loose. Just go."

"I told Benin I'd help you."

"You saw Benin? He's okay?"

"Yes, he's on your horse and hopefully safely back at the ranch by now. He wouldn't leave for help until I told him I'd get you out."

A loud snort rent the air.

Sam's attention flicked to the outlaws, and the ropes ceased their wiggling behind him.

One of the men snorted again, then rolled away from them onto his side. A couple heartbeats later, his raucous snores filled the night.

Air seeped from Sam's lungs, and warm pressure touched his back, most likely Cat's forehead.

The jiggling of the ropes resumed.

"Cat, you've got to go. Now. If I even try to escape—"

The binds slackened and slid from his wrists.

He caught her arm when she moved toward his ankles.

"Let go. We don't have much time."

Sam tugged her closer, grabbed her other arm, and spoke directly into her face. "You have to tie my hands back together."

"What? Why?"

"If they even think I've tried to escape, they'll go back after Benin, after you. I didn't sign my death warrant just to have my family killed."

Her brows pulled together. "Death warrant? What are you talking about?"

"Other men want me dead, men whose families I put in jail. Some I even put six feet under. They'll pay to see me dead. I had to tell the general their names so he'd let Benin go. He's already got someone sending wires to them. You have to get out of here."

"But...we need you."

His heart warmed in his chest even as it broke for what he'd be leaving behind...unwillingly this time.

Catherine shook her head. "No. No. I refuse to let you die like this. I did not get you back just to lose you again. Benin is safe on the ranch. Help will come. We just have to get out of here." She pulled from his grasp and started on the ropes at his ankles.

That was his Wild Cat. Never say die.

Sam reached forward and took the knife. She glared at him until he snapped through the bindings with a single swipe. Then she smiled.

He did the same. "Let's go."

They hurried to their feet and rushed for the shadows hand in hand.

"Wait. My guns."

"Forget them."

He'd been wanting to of late, but they might need them to get out of this alive.

"Look, you can always get them later. I've rifles up top if you really need to shoot something."

"All right."

Ignoring the stinging needles of the blood reentering his feet and hands, Sam let her lead him along. The fact she willingly touched him didn't go unnoticed either.

His wife was willing to fight. For him. He smiled.

His shin banged into a rock, and he grunted.

"Sorry. You okay?"

"Good. Fine. Keep going." Sam dragged his attention off his wife and onto their surroundings, striving to see into the silvery darkness of a night illuminated by a nearly full moon. The walls looked almost sheer in this part of the gorge. "Where'd you come down?"

"I climbed down with your rope. We should be almost there." Her hand slid along the wall while they hurried along.

"Thank you."

"For what?"

"Coming after me. I was ready to give up, 'til you showed."

"Can we continue this discussion later? I don't want to miss the rope." She gasped.

"What is it? What's wrong?"

Cat stopped. "I cut my hand."

"How bad is it?"

"I don't know. I think it's bleeding."

Sam reached into his pocket and unearthed his handkerchief. "Here, let me tie this around it. That should help until we can get a closer look." He worked quickly. "Better? You want me to take the lead?"

"No, that helps. I know where we're going. I think we're almost there."

"You know where we're going? That's a switch." He chuckled.

An elbow connected with his gut.

"Hey, that was a little uncalled for, don't you think?"

A pause.

"No."

Sam grinned into the darkness. Even yards from half a dozen outlaws and stuck in a dark ravine, he wouldn't want to be anywhere else. He'd always loved bantering with his wife. He collided with Cat's back but caught her around the waist before she tumbled to the ground.

"Are you trying to get back at me?"

Sam put his other arm around her and set his face beside hers. "Sorry. My mind was wandering."

"Yes, well, rein it in, will you?" The smile in her voice belied the stern words.

"Yes, ma'am."

"Samuel."

"Hmm?"

"I can't climb the rope with you hanging on me."

"Oh, you found the rope?"

She giggled.

Surely heaven's bells sounded so sweet. Regrettably, he released her.

Cat grabbed the rope and pulled. With a gasp, she dropped it like a hot poker.

"What? Oh, your hand. Is it that bad? Can you climb?"

She held the appendage against her waist. "I think so. Just give me a second."

"Here."

"What?"

"Put your arms around my neck and hop on."

Cat glanced upward. "You can't climb that whole way with me on your back."

"Thanks for the vote of confidence. I'm not going to let you hurt your hand more. I'm getting older, but I'm not that old. Now climb on."

"Are you sure?"

"Cat, we can stand here and argue this all night 'til those no-accounts wake up, or you can climb on."

"Fine. Squat."

He did so. She wrapped her slender arms around his neck, and her legs hugged his waist.

Sam grabbed the rope.

Cat slid off his back. "I don't think I can do this."

"*You* can't do this? All you've got to do is hold on."

"But what if we fall? What if the rope breaks? What if the knot doesn't hold?"

"Hey, you climbed down it, didn't you? This is the same thing, only in reverse."

"No, it's not the same thing. I weigh less than you. We go up at the same time, and that's just doubling the weight. The rope might not be able to take it."

"Cat, you said you used my rope, right?"

"Yes."

"That's a good rope. We'll be fine."

"But what about my knot?"

"How'd you tie it?"

"I did two half hitches."

"Well, that's not going anywhere."

"What about the—"

"Cat, you wouldn't still be afraid of heights, would you?"

"It's different when I have something to hold on to."

They had to get out of this slice in the ground, and her fears were eating up their precious time. Sam cupped her face in both hands. "Then hold on to me."

He felt her swallow, then nod. "That's my girl."

They repeated their movements from moments ago. Sam reached for the rope, then paused. "Darlin', I've got to be able to breathe if I'm going to climb."

Her arms slackened a fraction, and precious air seeped into his lungs.

"Ready?"

She nodded, her face next to his.

"When we get to the top, you climb over me and onto the ledge, okay?"

Another nod.

"All right. Here we go." Sam tightened his hold on the rope and started walking up the wall. Cat buried her face in his back and remained motionless. Hand over hand, step after step, he listened for a threat below and tried to pick the best placement for his feet going up. His muscles protested her added weight as they neared the top. Doing his best to ignore them, he pressed onward.

"Cat?"

She didn't move.

His arms began to shake. "Cat, we're at the top. Climb up."

Cat finally lifted her head, then clambered up his shoulders and onto the ledge. She surprised him by turning and gripping his forearm. When he finally sat on level ground, she sank onto her heels.

The moon pressed back more of the shadows from their new height and made her blond locks shine like an angel. Sam reached over and touched her cheek, wishing he had the time and permission to pull her close and kiss her. Any other night this would've been a perfect time for romancing his wife, but anytime now those bandits would find him gone and go after Benin.

They needed a plan before that happened.

Sam let his hand fall to her shoulder, gave a small squeeze, and pushed to his feet.

15

Catherine closed her eyes, opened them, but Sam kept coiling the rope. What happened? Had she imagined his intention to kiss her? Surely not. She'd been kissed by him enough in the past that she wouldn't read him that wrong. Why hadn't he?

Of course. Her stipulations.

Catherine dropped her gaze, then went to the boulder and untied her knot. She was surprised by how much she'd wanted Sam's kiss, by how much she'd wanted to kiss him, despite all he'd admitted to earlier that day. Truly, it made sense though. They'd survived a harrowing ordeal. She was grateful. Grateful for the way he wouldn't let her use her injured hand. The way he calmed her fears. Carried her. Held her.

"You okay? You've gone awful quiet on me."

Catherine turned her head, surprised to find he held her now like he had at the bottom of the rope, arms around her from behind. His masculine, musky scent invaded her senses. Her lips pressed together. What would it hurt to kiss him, to be kissed by him? He'd nearly died today because of her, and the trouble wasn't over. There were still outlaws below that would put a bullet through them both without a second thought if given only half a chance. If she didn't kiss him now, would she regret it?

She turned in his arms. Studied the heightened angles of his face in the moonlight.

"Ca—"

Her fingers touched his lips, then slid along the stubble of his jaw until they buried themselves in his thick, dark hair. Sweet memories swarmed her and warmed her insides. Was it better to remember the good that they'd shared or the wrong that he'd done? It was up to her. He stood here, willing to risk his life for her and their son. Those weren't actions of a man wanting to throw everything away. Those were actions of love, caring.

She played with his locks where they curled on his neck while she toyed with the idea of forgiving him. This might be her only chance. The outlaws might find them and kill them. Did she really want to traipse into a gunfight while walking in rebellion to God's command to forgive? Jesus clearly taught in the Sermon on the Mount that if she wanted to be forgiven, she had to forgive. If she chose not to forgive Sam now and died of lead poisoning, she was dooming herself to an eternity in hell. But if she chose to forgive, heaven and her Savior awaited. God had forgiven her of so much; who was she to do any less?

Catherine gently tugged Sam closer.

He obliged. His breath mingled with hers, and desire radiated from him, yet he didn't kiss her. He did wet his lips though.

Her other hand found its way up his chest. "I forgive you."

His breath caught, and his arms tightened around her. Tilting his forehead against hers, he questioned, "Did I hear you right?"

Catherine touched his cheek and saw the moisture glint in his eyes. "How much longer are you going to stand there until you kiss me?"

Sam sucked in a sharp breath. "Give me permission."

"I thought I just di—"

His lips pressed against hers, first gently, then gradually with the fervor she remembered. Or at least she'd thought she'd remembered. This was oh so much sweeter, so much better than a thousand memories combined. How could she have forgotten?

Catherine yielded to the yearning to pull him closer. When Sam deepened the kiss, tears seeped out of the corners of her eyes. How she'd missed him, this nearness, this completeness. His thumbs moved from her cheeks, and he began to kiss the tears away one by one. Her heart too full, she buried her face in his chest. His steady arms tightened around her while she clung to his sturdy frame.

After a long moment, after his heartbeat slowed to a steady rhythm and his snug hold relaxed, she tilted her chin and met his gaze.

His soft smile warmed her. "I don't know how I forgot what that was like."

"Me either."

Sam tucked a flyaway behind her ear. "You're beautiful, you know that? And I don't just mean on the outside."

She smiled, and another tear squeezed out. "Now what?"

Brushing away the wetness, Sam drew a shuddering breath. "Now I have to force myself to stop thinking of that kiss so I can figure out a plan to keep that gang from escaping before help arrives."

"Right." Catherine took a small step back and immediately missed his warmth. "Shall we, uh, go get the rifles?"

"Did you leave them with the horse?"

She nodded.

"A stroll might help." He stooped and retrieved the coiled rope. "What's this?" When he stood, a dark drape of cloth dangled from his long fingers.

"Oh."

"Oh?" Sam glanced her over. "Your skirt?"

Catherine licked her lips. "I had to take it off so I could climb down. Hand it here so I can put it back on."

"Do I gotta?"

She gave him a playful smack on the arm. "Yes, you've gotta."

When she reached for it, he held the material behind his back and tugged her close with his other hand. "On one condition."

"What's that?"

"That you wear those"—he nodded toward her jeans—"for me another time when I can actually see them."

Catherine sobered. "You really believe we can survive this?"

"Hey, what happened to the gal who refused to let me stay in that ravine?"

She shrugged.

Sliding his finger under her chin, he lifted it. "We're going to get through this, darlin'. Just you wait and see." Sam kissed the tip of her nose. "Come on. Let's go get those rifles before the guards rotate and figure out I'm gone."

A shout carried from below.

"I think they figured it out."

"I think you're right." Sam shoved the skirt into her hands. "Get my rifle. Meet me at the opening of the gorge."

"Right." Catherine draped the material over her shoulder. "Wait. What are you going to do?"

"I'll figure that out when I get there. Now get the guns. But be quiet about it."

She nodded and dashed toward the trees.

Sam hurried along the ravine's edge, all the while trying to invent a way to keep the band of outlaws from escaping. He only had a rope and a knife on hand. That wouldn't do him much good against seven men with one or two guns apiece. Make that six men—one hadn't returned from sending the telegrams yet. In other words, there was a man who could come up behind them and shoot them in the back. Wonderful.

Maybe he shouldn't try to trap the men inside the makeshift canyon. Even shoving rocks to try to close the opening would only be giving away his position, and if he didn't get it closed in time, then he'd just invited them to come find him. Besides, he had Cat's safety to consider, and these men wouldn't spare her because she was a woman. Men who would even threaten to shoot a woman were of the lowest sort and the most unpredictable.

But what about Benin? If those bandits got out, they'd head straight for his son. That settled it. These men weren't getting out of that hole unless they were hog-tied and draped over a saddle. Now to figure out how to make that happen.

Sam tossed a look into the ravine to try to see what the gang was up to. The light of a meager fire glowed against the group while they scampered here and there like ants, saddling horses and grabbing gear. Two mounts raced back toward the opening. Probably the two sentries.

His window of opportunity was shrinking fast. Maybe if he

distracted them, that would buy him more time. That boulder ought to do the trick. Sam skidded to a halt at the next waist-high rock and put his shoulder into it. The boulder budged a fraction.

"Come on." He couldn't let them go after Benin.

Sam shoved again. The rock tottered. He stepped back and kicked it. The boulder tumbled over the edge, bouncing and cracking and sounding almost like a stampede of cattle as it crashed its way to the bottom.

Crouching, he peeked over the edge. The sentries shouted and pulled up, then hurried toward the small rockslide. Thankfully, their horses wouldn't be able to climb up the rocky incline toward him. The angle was still too steep here.

He scooted back and hurried ahead. Pausing, he scooped up a handful of rocks the size of his fist and hurled them toward the other side. They pinged and bounced down the opposite side, causing the guards to swivel in their saddles. The pounding of galloping hooves strengthened.

Sam slung the other rocks and sprinted as fast as he dared in the silvered darkness. Shouts and unintelligible voices carried to him when the thundering of hooves lessened. That distraction wouldn't last long. Where was Cat?

Splitting his attention between the path ahead, the men below, and the trees on his right, Sam hurried around the curve where the ravine thinned and then opened and widened to a lesser incline. Stopping, he scanned the area and searched for a way to trap the outlaws who'd come his way any moment.

Crunch.

Sam whirled toward the trees, his hand going for the knife in his boot.

"It's me."

He heaved a sigh and waved Cat closer. "How good is that horse at pulling?"

"Rusty? He's strong. Why? You got a plan?"

"Maybe." Sam swung into the saddle, tied a quick lariat, and nudged the horse closer to the edge of the narrow curve of the canyon.

Directly across from them sat a large boulder. Standing in the stirrups, he circled the lasso above his head, then let it fly.

The rope slapped the giant rock and fell downward into the ravine. With a growl, he yanked the rope, pulling it toward him.

"Sam, they're coming. Hurry."

"What do you think I'm doing?" He put the lasso back into a spin and, with a prayer, released it.

Air whooshed into his lungs when the circle found purchase. He cinched the rope tight and wrapped it around the pommel in the same motion.

"Come on, Rusty. Give it all you got." Sam tugged on the reins twice. The gelding stepped backward. "That's it. Come on."

The horse strained and pulled, leaning back on his hind legs. Rocks skidded and crunched while his hooves moved farther from the edge. Sam's focus stayed fixed on the boulder opposite them.

A mounted rider neared.

"Come on. Fall, you stupid rock!"

The boulder tipped. Rusty countered backward, taking up the slack.

Men shouted below and reined up when the rock careened downward, carrying multiple stones of various sizes with it.

Sam hurriedly brought the rope back, then patted Rusty on his sweaty neck. "Attaboy." He swung down and stopped beside Cat where she watched the gang below, who stared at the rockslide blocking their exit.

"Now what?"

Sam placed a hand on her waist. "Now we wait. And deter anyone who even thinks of climbing out." He reached for the rifle in her hands.

"Get your own gun."

Sam chuckled under his breath and gave her a small swat on the backside when he moved toward the horse. He grabbed the Sharps from the scabbard on the saddle.

"Honey?"

He hurried back to her side. "What's wrong?"

"You missed one."

"What?" Sam peered in the direction Cat pointed. Sure enough, a mounted rider picked his way up the incline, angling toward the north. Sam wanted to slam his fist into something. "Can you keep these men here? Will you be okay by yourself?"

"Take the horse. Go. Don't let them get Benin."

"I love you." Sam pecked her on the lips, then vaulted into the saddle.

16

Catherine watched Sam and Rusty disappear into the darkness, until voices raised in frustration carried to her from below. *God, please don't let them get to Benin. Protect my boy. Protect Sam.*

Two outlaws strayed toward the rocks. *Help me too.* Catherine licked her lips and chambered a round. What would she do if they tried to escape? Could she really shoot a man? Even ones who'd threatened to shoot her and her family? If she didn't, they'd have no qualms coming after her or her men. They'd proven that true already.

The bandits started to climb.

There was no denying it. They had to be stopped.

Catherine licked her lips and leveled her sights on a rock a good three feet above them. The rifle's loud retort rang in her ears. The men glanced up and reached for their guns while they ducked behind their horses or any available boulder.

Dirt and rocks kicked up from the edge and splattered her face as a gunshot echoed from below. Catherine shrank back and searched for a better perch. Two waist-high boulders leaning against one another looked promising. She ducked behind them and propped her rifle barrel in the *V* of the rocks. Another bullet pinged off the boulder on her left. Catherine dropped, her heart pounding in her chest.

After a moment, she peeked through the *V*. The men remained hidden, or at least she didn't see their dark forms contrasted against the pale rocks anymore. She was scared spitless, but at least they weren't climbing. Or were they? She couldn't see the rock wall on her side anymore from this position. Maybe it'd be best if she moved back to where she'd been, but that meant a higher risk of getting hit should they return fire again.

Catherine swallowed the lump threatening her wind supply, grabbed her rifle, and crawled around the rocks. Lying on her belly, she peeked over the edge.

Chilly wind whistled around Sam while he chased a moving shadow through the silver-lighted trees. He praised God the moon glowed bright enough to see by, but which way was the man headed? Cater Springs? Lampasas? Or The Bar M and Benin? Sam wasn't quite sure yet. Maybe the outlaw wasn't sure himself.

The shadow darted to the right into an opening and jumped a wooden fence.

The Bar M.

Sam's heart lodged in his throat as Rusty jumped the fence with ease. The tired horse seemed to sense their location, and somehow his speed increased. Sam debated shooting his rifle and ending this before it got started, but he'd never shot a man in the back, and he wasn't about to start now. He wasn't above deterring the bandit though.

Sam retrieved the rifle and steadied it as much as possible. Taking aim, he hesitated before squeezing the trigger. How familiar was Rusty to gunfire? Would the horse spook with the shot and throw him? Was the warning worth the risk? Sam pursed his lips and brought the gun down. If he got thrown and injured, he wouldn't be of much use to his son.

Sam blinked when he realized Rusty gained on the other horse. The moonlight illumined scattered buildings in the distance. Sam rotated the gun until the cool barrel rested in his grip. *God, please keep this horse's feet from stumbling, and give him wings.*

"Come on, boy." Sam leaned over Rusty's neck.

Inch by inch, foot by foot, they narrowed the gap. Sam's heart pounded in tandem with the galloping hooves. When Rusty's nose reached the other horse's flank, Sam swung the rifle, slamming the butt into the outlaw and knocking him from the saddle as they charged into the barnyard.

Sam slowed the panting horse and swirled the rifle in his hands. He rode back toward the outlaw, who laid gripping his head with both hands and groaning.

"On your feet."

The large man's hand inched toward the guns on his waist.

Sam cocked the rifle. "Give me a reason."

The outlaw froze.

"On your feet. Hands in the air." Sam glanced about while the man slowly followed instructions. A door slammed behind him and to the right. "Mo, that you?"

"Mista' Sam?"

"Yeah. Get a rope and lend me a hand."

"Yessuh." Footsteps hurried away, then a door creaked.

Seconds later boot steps hastened toward him. A ring of yellow light fell on the ground beside Rusty and moved to the outlaw's back. Dishwater-blond hair glowed in the lamplight. Larry. He should've known.

Mo deposited the lantern, moved forward, and bound the no-account. "Sho' is good to see ya, Boss."

"Benin make it home?"

"Benin, suh?" Mo's eyes widened in his dark face.

Sam's heart stilled. "He's here, isn't he?"

"No, suh. You means he escaped them there outlaws?"

Sam forced himself to breathe. He licked his lips. "Take this man and tie him to a porch post. Then I need you to get Curly and go round up as much help as possible. Tell everyone to meet up here."

Sam walked Rusty toward the other horse and grabbed the free reins while Mo grabbed the outlaw's collar and shoved him toward the house.

"How's the sheriff?"

"Shut your mouth, Larry, or I won't be responsible for what happens to you." Sam urged his horse up beside Mo as they strode toward the house. "Where is he?"

"My Ida's keepin' watch ov'r 'im in yo' house there."

So Pa was still alive. Air flooded Sam's lungs. At least something had gone right tonight.

A door slammed.

"Here comes Curly." Mo shoved Larry onto a porch step and tied his hands to the nearest timber.

Sam moved around to the hitching post, swung down, and tossed the reins around the post. "Make sure you get all his weapons. We don't need him getting away and causing us more trouble. Have Curly put these two in the corral and saddle us up some fresh mounts. I'll be right back to fill y'all in on what's going on."

"Right, Boss."

Sam strode into the house and got a face full of warmth. A small fire glowed in the fireplace on the far wall, and a soft light sifted into the living area from the bedroom on his right. He moved that direction but stopped in the doorway.

Pa, looking pale and old, lay cocooned in quilts on the bed. A large white bandage swallowed his right shoulder. Red, blue, and black colored the skin around his left eye. When Sam stepped toward the end of the bed, Ida stirred in her rocking chair by the bedside.

"How is he?"

She blinked her dark eyes, then glanced at the older man before standing and motioning Sam from the room.

He touched his father's blanket-covered foot and followed her out.

"He'll be fine." Ida crossed her arms as if she was cold. "Miz Cathy got you out?"

"Yeah, but the trouble's not over. Will you be all right holding down the fort while I take the men to finish this? We've got Larry tied to the porch post."

Her brows rose. "Shore. I'll keep my skillet handy. Have Ben 'n' Roscoe come stay in here with me."

The grin that tugged at Sam's lips wilted. "Mo said Benin wasn't here."

"Didn't y'all bring him back with ya?"

"No, ma'am, I convinced them to let him go and told him how to get home, but he hasn't made it here yet. We'll make sure he does. I'll have Mo bring your boy over." Sam moved toward the door.

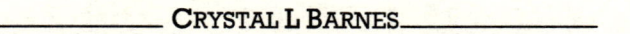

"Where's Miz Cathy?"

"She's fine. She's keeping the other outlaws pinned for me 'til I get back." Or at least he hoped she was.

17

Catherine sent another warning shot toward the shadow that moved along the farthest wall.

Another barrage showered her way.

She ducked and reloaded her rifle. How many bullets did those lowlifes have? Only a dozen bullets remained in her formerly bulging pockets. Why hadn't she allowed Sam to retrieve his pistols? "Sam, you'd better hurry up."

If he didn't get here soon, she would have to stop warning these idiots and start winging them, or she'd be a sitting duck when she ran out of ammunition. Catherine shook her head. What a horrible comparison. Was she going daffy? No, she just really didn't relish being stuck here by herself any longer.

Catherine scooted to a new spot a little ways down and peeked into the gorge. Nobody climbed the wall on the far side…or this side…or the pile of rocks trapping them in. She peered toward the curve where they'd tried to sneak around before.

There went another one.

Gritting her teeth, she re-aimed her rifle. Clearly, the galoots didn't think she meant business. Would they quit testing her patience if she hit an arm? No, they'd probably shoot at her with the other hand and run. If she got a leg, they at least wouldn't be running.

Catherine tilted her rifle lower. *Oh, God, please don't let me kill anyone on accident. I just can't let them get away and come after us.* Emptying her lungs, she slowly squeezed the trigger. The gun butt shoved her shoulder, her ears rang, and the shadow dropped. Her breath caught. Gunfire sprayed her direction. She rolled away from the edge, but not before she saw the shadow move.

"Oh, thank You, God." She hugged the rifle to her chest, the smell of gunpowder tickling her nose. "Please let this be over soon. I don't think I can take much more of this."

How much longer would it be before the sun rose? She looked toward the east—or at least she hoped it was the east—and tried to see through the trees. Would daylight bring relief? The Lord's mercies were renewed every morning. Surely that would help. "Lord, I could use whatever mercies You've got left for the day right about now."

Catherine drew a steadying breath and rolled back to her lookout.

Rocks crunched in the distance to her right.

Her heart skipped, then charged away without her. She considered calling out, but then again, it might be Sam or it might not. The rifle made its way to her shoulder.

The crunching grew louder.

Sweat broke out on her forehead. Blood pounded in her ears.

"Cat."

Never had a nickname sounded so sweet. Air flooded her lungs and made her lightheaded as tears touched the corners of her eyes. "Over here."

Muffled voices carried to her, and the crunching stopped.

Hallelujah, he'd brought help! Catherine rested her head on her forearm and wanted to weep. *Thank You, Father.*

"Cat?"

"Here. I'm here near the two leaning boulders." She tossed a glance into the ravine before pushing onto her knees. A large, lanky shadow strode her direction.

Sam knelt beside her and gathered her into his arms. "Are you okay?"

She nodded against him and tried to stop the shaking that overcame her. The trouble wasn't over. She couldn't fall apart yet. Catherine drew a steadying breath and straightened. "I think they're all still down there. I just got one of them in the leg. They weren't taking my warnings seriously anymore."

He rubbed her upper arm, a grin in his voice. "They don't know you too well, do they?"

"Sam?" A man's voice called from the trees.

"We're over here."

"Who'd you bring with you? That sounded like Joe Matthews."

"That's because it is me." Joe knelt with his hand on the nearest boulder. "Sounds like y'all are having too much fun tonight."

"Trust me. I'm ready for the party to end."

"That's what we're here for." The cowboy chambered a round. "Sam, we got this. Y'all go help find the boy."

"The boy? Benin? Didn't he make it home?"

Sam's hold tightened. "Not while I was there."

Her heart dropped. "This is all my fault. I knew I shouldn't have let him go off alone. We've got to go find him. He could be hurt. He—"

"Now, don't panic. We're going to find him, darlin'."

"Where's me a horse?"

"I'm just as anxious as you are to find him, honey, but first tell Joe where the men are hiding below."

Catherine forced down the panic that threatened to consume her and tried to focus. She peered over the edge and pointed out the locations to the best of her knowledge.

Sam clamped Joe on the shoulder. "If we find our son before y'all get in, I'll come back and help."

"Don't worry about us. Get."

"Thanks, Joe. I owe you one."

"What are friends for? I'll be praying. Give Benin a hug for me when you find him."

"Will do." Grabbing her hand, Sam rushed toward the trees.

Catherine clambered atop the first horse she came to. "Which way do we head?"

"Toward the fence line. Maybe he got tired and stopped along the way like I told him to."

Hope rose in her chest. "All right. Which way is that?"

"Thataway." He turned his horse. "Follow me."

Catherine didn't need to be told twice. Her horse's nose nearly touched the flank of Sam's palomino as they wound their way through rocks and trees. A thought struck after they'd ridden a short distance. "Sam, didn't you follow the fence line earlier? Wouldn't you have seen him?"

"No, we hopped the fence and charged cross-country across our land."

"Oh."

"Don't worry. We'll find Benin. We're nearly to the fence line now."

That was good news. Maybe her son could hear her now. She started calling Benin's name, Sam echoing her while he lit two lanterns and handed her one.

No response.

They traveled a bit farther. More shouts joined theirs.

"Who else is out here?"

"Your nephew Amos. Mo and Roscoe are out here too."

"What about Curly?"

"He's helping Joe and two others at the ravine."

Catherine had nearly forgotten about the outlaws. She craned her neck and scanned the area. "Benin!"

No answer.

"Sam, he's got to be out here somewhere. What if he's hurt and he can't answer us?"

Sam moved to her side and caught her hand. "He's going to be all right, darlin'. Just keep praying. We'll find him."

She nodded, but her prayers didn't seem to have enough faith to boost them above the treetops. "What if he got home after you left?"

"Ida's there. Everyone knows to set off three shots to let us know when he's been found."

Catherine licked her lips and nodded. "Benin! Where are you?" She yanked back on the reins. "Did you hear that?"

"What?"

"I heard a horse snort, and it wasn't ours. You think it could've been Sandy?"

Sam draped his reins around the pommel and cupped his hands to his mouth. The mournful call of the dove whistled from his fingers.

Shuffling came from their right.

Catherine's heart leapt into her throat, then sprinted away. "Do it again."

Sam obliged.

A soft whinny.

"That's got to be them." Catherine moved her horse toward the right. "Benin! It's Mama, baby. Where are you?"

They moved further into the oaks and mesquites, shouting, but still no response came.

"Sam, do it again."

The dove call filled the air.

A frustrated whinny answered.

"Thataway." Sam pointed to the left and moved ahead of her. "Benin!"

"Pa?"

"Oh, thank God. Benin, where are you?"

"Mama?"

"Yeah, honey, it's us. Just keep talking so we can find you."

"I'm scared, Mama."

"It's going to be okay, honey. We're coming."

"Are you hurt, son?"

"I'm sorry, Pa." Tears filled the lad's voice.

They ducked under a low-hanging branch.

"It's okay, Ben. Everything's going to be all right."

"Sam. There." Catherine pointed toward a dark shadow in the hollow of a wash.

"I see him. Watch your step."

Their horses picked their way down, slipping occasionally on the smooth stones, their hooves sucking in the mud when not. Finally, their lantern light fell on the boy where he stood in front of the buckskin kneeling on the ground. Mud streaked his face and covered his hair and clothes. She'd never seen a more beautiful sight.

"Mama!" Benin scrambled over the rocks toward them.

Catherine leapt from the saddle and scooped him up. "Oh, baby, I'm so glad you're all right."

Sam placed a hand on her back and ruffled the five-year-old's mud-caked hair. "Me too."

"I'm sorry, Pa."

"What for?"

Benin pointed at Sandy, who on second glance stood in mud up to her withers in the creek bottom. "It's my fault Sandy's stuck. I couldn't see, 'n' she got in the mud 'n' couldn't get out."

Sam patted their son on the back. "It's not your fault, partner. It's dark out here. Are you hurt?"

When the boy wagged his head, dirt flew in all directions. "Mama, does this mean I gotta wash 'fore I get supper?"

Catherine laughed and squeezed him. "I think we can make an exception this time."

"Is Sandy gonna be okay, Pa?"

"I'm sure she'll be fine. Let me let everyone know you're okay, and we'll work on getting her out, all right?" Sam moved to his mount and withdrew his rifle.

Putting Benin down, Catherine knelt in front of him. "Cover your ears, baby."

When they'd both done so, Sam fired three consecutive shots into the air. He put away the gun and then walked toward Sandy, talking to her in a soothing tone. Catherine and Benin followed and watched at a distance while Sam joined the horse in the mud. The buckskin nickered a greeting.

Catherine kept a hand on Benin's chest. "You think we can get her out?"

"I reckon so. There's a solid-enough bottom. Get me my rope, will you?"

"Sure. Stay here, Benin. Mama'll be right back." She placed one of the lanterns on a high rock and scuttled over to their mounts.

Sam flung mud from his fingers. "I thought my pa said it hadn't rained in days?"

"It hasn't. I guess things haven't dried up all too much from the other times it's stormed." She grabbed the rope and started back.

"Bring the other horses too if you can get them closer without getting them stuck."

"You couldn't have said that sooner." Catherine retreated, grabbed the reins, led the horses up the embankment and around opposite Sam. She walked them down next to Benin, slipping on occasion. How on earth were these horses going to be any help in this boggy condition? "Here's the rope."

"Can you lasso her from there?"

"Can I—" She frowned, readjusted her grip, and set the lariat into a spin above her head. With a flick of her wrist, the loop glided through the air and settled around Sandy's neck.

Sam turned and cocked a grin at her. "Maybe I should've let you rope that boulder earlier."

Her insides warmed as she returned his smile. Most men despised her skills, but Sam never had. He'd encouraged them. At least that much of him hadn't changed.

Another rope glided over Sandy's neck.

Catherine startled and turned. "Amos? Where'd you come from?"

Her nephew smiled and wrapped the end of his rope around his pommel. "I wasn't too far away when I heard the shots. Figured I'd see if y'all needed any help."

"Amos!" Benin scrambled closer.

"Hey, kiddo." The twenty-one-year-old pulled his cousin up onto his lap, mud and all. "What're you doing getting lost at this time of night?"

"I weren't lost."

"You weren't?"

"No, my ride got stuck."

Amos chuckled. "Well, how about we help get her unstuck?"

Benin nodded.

"Cat, why don't you take Ben over there away from the horses while we give this a go?"

She rotated to face Sam, who squished his way out of the mud. "You don't want me to help?"

"I'd rather you take the boy where neither of y'all will get hurt if something breaks. I'll let you know if I need you closer." He winked at her and slid the rope from her hands.

Heat crept up her neck and into her cheeks. "All right."

Biting her lip, she fetched Benin from Amos's lap and carried him to a safe distance. Oh, she would have her hands full with that husband of hers when they got home. She could see it now. There would be no safe distance from him anymore. Her heartbeat accelerated in her chest, and it wasn't just from the scene unfolding before her as the men backed up their horses and tightened the ropes. Was she ready for Sam to move closer? She'd told him as much through that kiss earlier, that tantalizing, heart-throbbing, set-your-knees-to-wobbling...

Catherine drew a deep breath and yanked her mind to the present. Oh boy, did she have it bad, but the passion they'd shared had always overridden her good sense. What if that was happening again?

Benin cheered in her arms and urged to be put down.

Catherine gave herself a mental shake and followed the boy toward the men and the mud-dripping horse. "That was quick."

"Yeah, it was easier than I expected." Sam swung from Pecos's back and picked his way over to Sandy.

"You and me both." Amos started coiling his rope once Sam cleared it from the horse's neck.

"Now what?" Catherine asked.

Sam handed Sandy's reins to her. "Now you two head home and clean up."

"Aren't you coming too?"

"Not yet. I promised Joe I'd come back and help round up that gang."

Her heart skidded. He planned to go back? They might shoot him. Catherine glanced at their son, who watched them intently, then took Sam's hand and drew him a short distance away. "Do you have to go?"

A smile played on her husband's lips. His fingers slid from her grip and settled on her waist. "What do you suggest? I told them I would."

"But Joe said you didn't have to worry about it."

"I *will* worry about it 'til I know both of y'all are safe." His fingers massaged her back, doing funny things to her insides.

"Aren't we safer with you here?"

"It's all right. Amos will see y'all home. I'll meet y'all back at the house later."

"What about the man that went to send the telegrams? Did y'all stop him?"

Sam's gray eyes widened. He released her and slapped a hand against his thigh. "I can't believe I forgot all about him." He let out a huff and jogged toward his mount.

"Where are you going?"

"I've got to go help Joe and the others. They think the only ones worth watching are in that ravine."

"You mean…"

"Yeah." He swung onto the palomino and shoved his dark hat firmer onto his head. "Amos, see them home safely."

"Sure, Uncle Sam."

"Cat…"

She returned his gaze, the lantern light allowing her to read what he didn't say as his focus shifted to their son. Her hand settled on Benin's shoulder. "We'll be okay. You be careful."

Sam nodded and heeled his mount, disappearing into the darkness.

18

Sam strained to see into the darkness, wishing he could relight the lantern but knowing he'd be touting his location if he did. He stopped in a clearing and looked toward the stars, trying to regain his bearings. Was it him, or was the sky beginning to brighten in the east? Maybe this wretched night was nearing an end.

Pow!

Sam jerked to attention and scanned the trees before him. That could either be a shot to stop the outlaws or Ham catching someone by surprise. Sam prayed it was the former. Tightening his grip on the rifle, he urged his horse forward.

A return volley echoed up ahead. Sam stopped Pecos and slid from the palomino's back, with only a slight creak of leather. He dropped the reins to the ground and slunk forward, praying he wouldn't find his friend bleeding.

A large shadow contrasted against a pale boulder. Was it Joe or Ham? Considering the broadness resided more around the middle than the shoulders, his guess leaned toward Ham. Then where was Joe?

Sam shouldered the rifle. "Lower the gun nice and easy."

The shadow swiveled and fired.

Sam ducked behind the nearest tree. Yep, definitely the outlaw. "Ham, you might as well give it up unless you want to die by lead poisoning like your friends."

Bark splintered above his head in response.

"Don't say I didn't warn you." Sam shouldered the Sharps and sighted down the barrel.

The shadow shifted above the boulder.

Catching his breath, Sam squeezed the trigger.

Ham flew back.

Sam chambered another round and moved from behind the tree. "Joe?"

"Here." The deep voice came from Sam's left and was layered with pain.

A wave of relief washed over Sam as he skirted around the boulder. Ham gripped his shoulder, writhing and cursing.

Sam kicked the gun away from the outlaw's hand. "Your ma ought to wash your mouth out with soap. You're lucky I didn't kill you."

"You shot me."

"Yeah, now shut your trap before I do it again." Sam tugged the bandana from his neck and knelt, keeping his gun well out of reach from the lowlife. He cinched Ham's hands behind him with the scrap of material, turning the man's moans to a hiss of pain. "Now sit still, and don't make me regret not putting that bullet a little more to the left."

Ham glared at him.

Sam ignored him, grabbed the guns, and moved toward Joe. "How bad is it?"

"I'm lucky he's a bad shot."

"Where'd he get ya?"

"On my side. I think he might've cracked a rib, but I can breathe okay." Joe grunted and moved his hand from under his right arm, then after a grimace, returned it. "I thought you said they were all down below?"

"I forgot about the one who went to send the telegrams. Sorry."

"Telegrams?"

"More trouble."

"You just can't come home quietly, can you?"

Sam shrugged and peered into the ravine. "Weren't for lack of trying. The others all still down there?"

"Yeah. I think Schreiner might've clipped one of them. Not very many are wasting bullets returning fire anymore."

"Sunrise is coming soon. You okay to stay and finish this, or do we need to get you patched up?"

"I can make it."

Sam studied his friend a moment and could almost hear Aunt Isabel's fussing. If he didn't send Joe back, he was liable to get an earful when they got home. "I don't like having that lowlife lingering here. You reckon you're up to taking his sorry hide to the jailhouse? Maybe you could stop by and get the one tied to my porch post too."

"And maybe have Ida patch me up while I'm there?"

Sam grinned. "Too obvious?"

"Just a bit." Joe grunted while he moved to a crouch. "I'll see you back in town."

"Joe."

"Yeah?"

"Make sure Cat and Benin are at the house before you leave there."

"The boy okay?"

"Hungry and a bit on the muddy side, but other than that he's fine."

"Good."

Sam caught Joe's hand in a firm grip. "Thank you."

Joe nodded. "See you in town. Try not to get shot. Gals might like scars, but it's not much fun getting them."

"I'll remember that."

Joe clamped him on the shoulder, then snatched up Ham by the collar and strode for the trees. Sam returned his focus to the ravine. All seemed quiet. He peered at the sky. The black had receded to gray.

Another hour or two and this would all be over.

That was until the next batch of men seeking to put a bullet in his hide came to town.

Sam sighed and shifted his attention to the pile of boulders blocking the outlaws' escape. He was about as trapped as the five bandits below. Why did trouble have to dog him? It seemed the harder he tried to leave it behind, the more it nipped at his heels. *God, I sure would love to see this come to an end without more bloodshed. If You could see Your way to doing that, I'd be mighty grateful.*

All things are possible to him that believeth.

Lord, like that man who brought You his son in the Bible, I say, "I believe. Help Thou mine unbelief."

Sam nudged his hat up a fraction and checked his rifle. This night, this trouble had to end soon so he could get back to Cat and finish what they'd started. *Father, that's another thing I could sure use Your help with.*

His mind drifted to their kiss earlier. No, his memory hadn't done her justice at all. Did she realize the effect she had on him? She made his senses spin and the whole world fade from existence. When she rested in his arms, nothing else mattered. Not outlaws, not sore muscles, not empty stomachs. She touched a part of him he'd never let anyone else see, and to be forgiven...sweeter still. He might not understand her whole motivation for doing so, but he'd also been taught not to check a horse's teeth when someone gifted one to you. Sam would strive to make Cat not regret letting him back in her life. He'd work alongside her, show her how much he loved—

A shot ricocheted below.

Sam yanked his mind back in focus. While berating himself for woolgathering, he studied his surroundings. Pink painted the sky and enhanced the shadows and rocks below.

The outlaws were making a move.

He put the rifle butt to his shoulder and stared down the barrel, aiming at the man hiding between his horse and a boulder while they moved toward the heart of the canyon. Stilling his breathing, he squeezed the cool, metal trigger.

The shot rang in his ears and connected with the outlaw's foot. The horse reared on his hind legs and bolted, leaving his owner bouncing and clutching his boot with both hands.

Sam chambered another round and shouted into the ravine, "Surrender now if y'all want to walk out of that hole alive."

The wounded man glanced up, then hopped behind the boulder.

Dirt kicked up into his face as gunfire exploded below.

"Why those dirty, rotten—" Sam clamped his lips shut and shoved his hat down lower. Apparently, these idiots were dumber than he thought. What did they want to do, keep this standoff going for days?

They'd starve before he let them escape to hurt his family again.

Sam studied the rocks and trees across from him, searching for the others keeping watch. A snatch of blue caught his eye between two leaning boulders. A lone boot peeked out behind a downed tree. Schreiner and Henderson were still with him, but he'd feel better if they moved and reassured him they weren't bleeding out behind their hidey-holes.

Crunch.

Sam rolled, aiming his rifle at the nearby trees.

"It's jus' me, Mista Sam." Mo moved from the shadows.

Sam's shoulders relaxed, and his finger slid from the trigger. "You alone?"

"Yessuh, I sent Roscoe back with Miz Cathy. I thoughts you might need an exter hand."

Sam nodded and motioned the black man closer. "You seem to be pretty good at moving undetected. You reckon you can check on the others guarding across the way and let me know how they stand on ammunition and such? Looks like we might be here a spell longer. I might have to send you back to town to get me some more bullets."

"Sho' thang, Boss. Where they be?"

Sam pointed to their locations and directed Mo on the path to take across the ravine so he wouldn't get shot by mistake.

"I'lls be back in two shakes."

"Thanks, Mo."

White teeth gleamed against dark skin before Mo hurried to the trees and snuck away on silent feet. After a moment, his lean shadow skittered down the slope with the agility of a mountain goat and clambered up the opposite side. Sam's brows rose. For a man with a touch of white in his coal-black hair, he sure could move. Cat had done well picking Mo for a foreman.

Splitting his attention between Mo and the outlaws, Sam waited to see how the others fared. Mo disappeared for a few heartbeats, then reappeared at the next man. In no time at all, he scrambled across the collapsed ravine and back to Sam's side.

"So?"

"Schreiner be the one behind them boulders, 'n' Henderson be keepin' watch behind the tree."

"Either of them shot?"

"No, suh, they's all be in one piece. Curly's farther up, 'n' he be good too."

Sam had forgotten about Curly. The man knew how to blend with the landscape. He hadn't detected him at all. "How are they doing on bullets?"

"They's still got a bit. They's wantin' to know if'n you've come up with a plan."

"I don't want to kill anyone if I don't have to. Tell them I'd rather we wait them out. Then do me a favor, and go find me some more bullets, just in case."

"Sho' thang, Boss. I'll tells ya how's yo' family be doin' when I get back too."

Sam shared a smile with the insightful man. "My wife did good hiring you."

Mo nodded his appreciation before he disappeared into the trees.

Sam returned his attention to the ravine. *God, let this end soon.*

19

Catherine paced from the snapping logs in the fireplace to the front window, where daylight streamed in. Mo had left hours ago with the extra bullets for Sam's rifle. Surely this would end soon.

"We gonna have to replace that board if'n you keep traipsin' 'cross it."

Catherine spared Ida a glance where she knitted in the rocker by the fire. "How can you be so calm? They should be home by now."

"'N' you should be sleepin' like yer boy 'n' the sheriff."

"I'm too wound up to sleep. What if something's gone wrong? What if that's why they're not back yet? What if Sam's been—" Her throat closed around the word, squeezing it to death. Catherine pushed away the image that carted across her brain and fetched her rifle. "I'm going back there. I'll go crazy staying here."

"Miz Cathy."

Catherine shoved her hat on her head. "What?"

"Grab the men some grub 'fore ya head out."

Catherine tossed her cook a smile. "Tell Benin I'll be back after a while"—she opened the door—"with his pa."

She closed the latch and hurried through the sunshine to the corral. Buster cantered over to her. "You raring to go again, big guy?"

Catherine opened the gate, closed it behind the horse, and scurried into the barn. Buster followed her like an overgrown puppy, and she soon had him saddled and headed out the door. After grabbing some cold ham, cheese, and biscuits, she heeled the horse and galloped off toward Gable's Gorge, hoping the multitude of tracks would lead her the right way.

Boulders and oaks, mesquites and prickly pear slowed her progress at times, but soon the beginning of the rift in the ground came into view. Breathing a sigh of relief, she pressed forward until she spotted Pecos, who nickered a greeting.

"Show yourself."

"It's me, Sam."

Dirt scratched. "Cat, what in the world are you doing here?"

She hopped down, grabbed his rations from the saddlebag, and dashed toward him, staying low. "I thought you might be hungry."

Placing the towel-wrapped food beside her, she laid in the dirt next to him, ignoring his frown.

"You shouldn't be here. Who's watching Benin?"

"Ida. Besides, he's asleep."

"You should be too."

"Tried. Couldn't." Catherine untied the towel and shoved a chunk of ham under his nose. "Eat. I'll watch for a bit."

"You need to go home." He tore off a bite of meat.

"Later." She focused on the fissure below her, welcoming Sam's presence beside her and the knowledge he was still in one piece. "How much longer are you going to keep this up? What are you waiting for?"

"Their surrender." Sam plucked a chunk of cheese from the open cloth and shoved it inside a biscuit. "You bring something to drink?"

She smiled and handed him the canteen lying on her opposite side. "Glad I came?"

"Perhaps."

Catherine bumped her shoulder into his. "Admit it."

He grinned and pressed a kiss to her cheek. "All right. I admit it. My belly button was playing patty-cake with my backbone. You bring anything for the other men?"

"Yep, there in my saddlebags. I had to see you first."

"Oh yeah?"

Heat crept into her cheeks. Had she really admitted that? She focused on rubbing a dirt streak from her rifle barrel. "Of course. I knew you'd want to know how Benin was doing."

"Mmhmm." He tore off another bite, the smirk still on his mouth while he chewed.

"I'd rather you were there to see for yourself. Why must you wait for them to surrender?"

His gaze finally swung to the gorge, and a full breath entered her lungs.

"It's the only way I can figure to prevent more bloodshed. I doubt these men are prepared to meet their Maker yet."

It was her turn to stare. She hadn't given those men's eternity a second, or even a first, thought. "You really are a good man."

Sam's haunting gray eyes met hers. "No. Just forgiven."

Catherine looked away, fully chastised over her lack of compassion, and flicked a pebble over the edge.

"You do still forgive me, don't you?" Sam brushed a strand off her cheek.

She nodded even as her stomach tumbled into knots at the warmth of his touch.

His finger crooked under her chin and turned her face to his. "I still want us to have a talk when this is all over."

She pressed her lips together. Part of her wanted that. Another part feared whatever he had to say. She'd already endured so much. What if she couldn't handle more of the truth? Maybe it was better not knowing.

Sam's thumb brushed across her mouth, drawing her attention back to him. An unmistakable yearning resided in his eyes, both thrilling and terrifying her at the same time. Letting him close meant he could hurt her again, but having him close was a soothing balm to her lonely heart.

"I should take the other men their food."

"In a minute." Sam slid the gun from her hand, leaned forward, and claimed her lips with his own.

He tasted of sweet, honey-wheat biscuits and bittersweet memories, a thousand dreams fulfilled in a single moment. His strong arm snaked around her, drawing her against his warmth while he plied her with his tantalizing kisses. Her reticence began to wane. The guard around her heart slipped. She pulled away a fraction, but he stayed with her as if he could sense her wavering and how close she was to completely losing herself to him again.

The kiss deepened.

The world faded away.

All she knew was her husband and the love, passion, and pleasure that radiated from him straight to her heart. Her fingers gripped his collar, holding him to her. She never wanted to lose this again. She never wanted to lose him. Why did he have to do this to her? Why did he have to make her love him? Make her never want to let go?

Sam finally drew back, his labored breathing mingling with her own. His fingers kneaded her back, making her even dizzier. His Adam's apple bobbed while his darkened blue-gray eyes searched every inch of her face. "I, um..."

Words seemed to have abandoned him like they had her, but then again, sometimes words got in the way. Her finger settled on his mouth.

He kissed it, then tilted his forehead against hers. "What am I going to do with you?"

Catherine stiffened. Do with her? What kind of question was that? He was the one who'd started all this. Why did he have to make it sound like her fault? Like she'd messed up his plans?

Sam jiggled her. "Quit it."

"Quit what?"

"Assuming I meant something bad by that."

Catherine leaned back, her brows pulling together. "Didn't you?"

His hand brushed her cheek. "Not in the least."

"But—"

He silenced her with a peck on the lips. "I meant that I love you, and I don't know how I'm going to let you go long enough to be of use to anyone. You scramble my brains, woman."

"You? Brains?"

His chuckle rumbled through her, tugging a smile to her lips. "Yeah, they're in there somewhere, contrary to what some may think."

Catherine leaned into him. "I really should go give the others some food."

Sam's sigh fanned across her cheek. "I know."

"Are you going to let me go?"

"Do I have to?"

She smiled and pecked him on the mouth. "Yes."

"All right, if you insist."

His arms slid from around her as another idea took root in her mind.

"Would you rather stretch your legs and take the food to the others? You know where they are better than I do."

"That's not a bad idea. You sure you don't mind?"

Catherine wagged her head.

"You're a treasure." Sam moved to a crouch and pressed a kiss to her cheek.

His hat flew from his head as a gunshot echoed below.

Sam dropped to his stomach beside her, his arm pressing her into the dirt. "Why, those dirty, rotten—"

Return fire boomed from three other locations around the rim.

Reaching back, Sam snatched his black hat. A stream of light shone through a bullet hole in the brim. "This is my favorite hat."

"Your favorite hat? Is that all you have to say? They almost killed you."

He wiggled a finger in the dark fabric. "Can this be fixed?"

Catherine shoved his shoulder. "They almost killed you."

Sam's gaze returned to hers. "Almost only counts in horseshoes."

"What? How can you be so nonchalant?"

"Ain't the first time I've been shot at. Probably won't be the last." He shoved the hat on his head. "We're going to have to be more careful now that the sun's up. You go grab that food and take it to the men, then high-tail it back to the house."

"No, you need—"

"I *need* to know you're safe." Sam looked to the rocks below. "Whistle at me when you get done with the food to let me know when you're leaving."

"Yes, master." Catherine tightened her grip on the rifle and scooted away.

Sam caught her hand. "Hey. I'm only trying to take care of you. One of us has to live through this so our son isn't orphaned."

"Don't you think it'd be better if both of us lived through it?"

"Of course."

"Then let me stay an—"

"I'm not arguing with you on this one, Cat. Get back to the house where it's safe." Determination glinted in his stormy blue eyes.

This wasn't a battle she would win. Surprisingly, respect rose in her at his stubborn stance. "I love you."

His eyes softened. "I love you too." He nodded toward the trees with a slanted grin. "Now, get."

Catherine returned his smile before she darted for the nearest oak.

Sam watched his wife disappear, then shook his head. Of all the times for her to admit she still loved him, he hadn't expected it right after telling her no. That woman was something else. What, he still wasn't sure. He grinned and turned his gaze to the gorge. Hopefully, he'd live to enjoy solving that mystery for many years to come.

Sam scanned the boulders and horses below. Which one of those idiots tried to shoot him? Was there any way to end this quicker? He had to figure out a way to force their surrender with something besides hunger. After all, who knew what rations they had stashed in their saddlebags?

Waving grasses in the ravine's bend caught his eye. He scratched his chin, a plan forming.

A whistle called from over his shoulder.

"Cat, wait."

She emerged at the tree line. "What is it?"

"I need you to do me a favor."

An eager grin played along his wife's lips. "Yeah?"

He bit back a smile. She was as bad as a kid. "You got any rags or bottles in your saddlebags?"

Cat peered over her shoulder, then back at him. "The only rags I had were the towels that the food was in, but the others still have those.

Why?"

Sam scooted from the edge and hurried to her side. "I've got a plan. I need you to go back to the house. Get some rags, and some kerosene, and at least half a dozen jugs or bottles."

"What for?"

"We're going to smoke them out."

Her brows rose. "What if the fire gets away from you?"

"They're in a ravine surrounded by rocks. I think we'll be okay."

Her mouth pressed into a line.

"Unless you have any better ideas?"

"What happened to waiting them out?"

"That could take days, days I'd rather spend with you and our son. Besides, I still have to figure out what do when those other men get to town."

"Other men? What other men?"

Sam yanked off his hat and smacked it against his leg. Why did he have to go and remind her about that? He hated the worry that puckered her brow.

"Sam? What men?"

"The ones coming here to kill me."

Cat frowned before her eyebrows shot to her hat brim. "The telegrams."

"Right."

"I'd forgotten all about those."

"I'm sorry I reminded you."

"I'm not. We've got to tell the others and come up with a plan."

Sam couldn't help but smile at his Wild Cat. They'd have won the war a lot quicker with her fighting.

"All right, Mrs. Never-Say-Die. You work on that, but first, get me those supplies."

"What? Oh. Right." In five steps, she reached her horse and swung into the saddle. "I'll be back in a jiffy."

Sam chuckled. "Cat."

She swung the horse around to face him. "Huh?"

"Home's thataway."

Pink climbed into her cheeks. "Right. That way. I knew that." Cat turned Buster and moved off at a trot.

"Don't get lost."

"Yeah, yeah." She waved off his comment, but he still sent up a prayer that she'd find home safely and easily.

Propping his rifle on his shoulder, Sam strode toward Mo's lookout.

It was time to inform the men.

The waiting game would soon be over.

20

Catherine tore another dishrag in half and added it to the pile. Hopefully, Sam's plan would work, and this would be over soon. She longed for some normalcy. Did she even know what that was anymore? She'd never known what having a husband *and* a son at home was like. A sigh seeped from her, and she rubbed at the headache forming between her eyes. Would life ever feel normal again?

"Here're the bottles, Mama."

"Thanks, baby. Is Roscoe watering Buster for me?"

"Yes'm."

"Catherine," GW called from the bedroom.

She shoved the half-torn rag into her son's hand. "Here, finish tearing this for me, Benin, while I see what Gramps needs."

"Sure, Mama."

Catherine strode to the bedroom door and peeked inside. "What are you doing?"

"What does it look like I'm doin'? I'm puttin' on a shirt. Help me with these dumb buttons so I can go with you."

"You're not coming with me. You're staying right here in that bed. Do I need to go get Ida?"

GW peeked her direction but kept on with his button-fiddling. "I ain't sittin' around like an ole man when my family needs my help."

"You *are* an old man, and I want to see you get a lot older. Now stop this foolishness and get back in that bed."

"Nothin' doin'. Have Roscoe saddle up Pecos for me."

"He can't. Sam has your horse, which is all the more reason for you to stay here."

GW pulled up a suspender onto one shoulder and stepped closer. "Save your mollycoddlin' for Benin. I don't need it. I'll take any horse you wanna put me on."

"I don't want to put you on any of them. I want you to listen to me and get back in that bed before you faint and I have to figure out a way to get you back there myself."

"I ain't gonna faint."

"Tell that to your white face."

He gripped her arm and moved her out of his way. "I'm goin'. I'll take your horse, and you can stay here with your son."

"You most certainly will not."

GW brushed past her to the small table in what used to be the kitchen. "Ben, can you and Roscoe put those things in your ma's saddlebags?"

Benin looked to her.

"That's fine, honey. You can use that basket there to carry it all out."

The bottles clanked into the basket next to the cloths and kerosene.

"Wrap those rags around the bottles, son, before you put them in the saddlebags, okay?"

"Yes, Gramps."

Catherine opened the door for her boy, then shut it behind him. Folding her arms, she faced her father-in-law.

GW stepped forward and placed his hand on her forearm. "Tell me Sam didn't want you safely at home, and I'll let you go."

"He asked me to bring him that stuff."

"He never mentioned wantin' you to stay home where it's safe?"

Catherine pressed her lips together and studied the floor.

"That's what I thought." He unhooked his gun belt from the peg beside the door. "Stay here, and let the men handle it this time."

"But you're hurt." Catherine gestured to the sling on his right arm.

"Don't worry. I've had scrapes worse than this. Besides, I shoot better with my left hand anyway."

She handed him the other end of the gun belt when it slipped from his grasp. "You know I don't like this."

"I know. Don't worry. I didn't get this old by acting the fool." GW pressed a kiss to her forehead. "Take care of my huntin' partner for me. Tell him we'll still try to bag that turkey for the holidays."

Blinking away the tears that threatened, she moved from his path. "You better not go and get yourself shot."

"Yes, ma'am." GW stepped onto the porch but turned back to face her when she followed. "That boy needs you right now a whole lot more'n me. He's been through a lot in the past twenty-four hours. Give him a bit of normalcy. Let him know it's all gonna be okay."

Normalcy. Hadn't she just been longing for that herself? Catherine nodded and gave him a quick hug. "Be careful."

"Always, darlin'." GW pecked her on the cheek, then met the boys in the yard. After ruffling their heads and speaking to them a moment, he swung up in the saddle. He gave her a salute, then rode out of the yard.

God, keep them safe. I don't want to lose any more family.

Sam shifted at the crunch and clomp of an approaching horse. Catherine hadn't gotten lost. He smiled and scurried for the tree line. And stopped short. "Pa? What are you doing here?"

"Is that any way to greet your ole man?"

"I...I apologize. I was expecting Cat. Is she behind you?"

"Nope. You're stuck with me."

"You convinced her to stay?"

"Let me tell you, it weren't easy." Pa swung down from the saddle, the silver star on his jacket glinting in the sunlight. "The things y'all asked for are in the saddlebags. You wanna tell me what you have in mind for all this stuff?"

"You look a mite peaked."

"I'm fine. Tell me the plan."

Sam wanted to argue. His father looked ready to keel over at any moment, but surely at his age he knew what he could handle. Cat had let Pa come too. Praying he wasn't making a mistake, Sam lifted the leather flap on the saddlebags and fished out the rag-wrapped bottles.

"I'm thinking to give those men an incentive to surrender." He withdrew the kerosene, lined the bottles up, and started pouring a small measure into each one.

"You're plannin' on smokin' them out."

It was a statement, not a question, but Sam nodded anyway. "Why don't you go take a peek at what we got while I finish getting these ready?"

Pa nodded and slunk to the edge, keeping the boulders between him and the drop-off.

Sam stuffed a rag in each bottle and watched the yellowish liquid wick up the cloth. Now all they needed were matches. He strode back to the horse and unearthed a set, which he stuffed in his shirt pocket.

With three bottles in each hand, he moved from the trees. "Pa."

The silver-haired man stole back his way. "Where're the others?"

"Mo's further up the rim on this side. Henderson, Curly, and Schreiner are across the way. I figure you can take these three to Mo, and I'll take the others around to Curly. I'll grab Schreiner and Henderson, and we'll plant ourselves at the top of the rocks barricading the gang in. When we're in position, Mo and Curly can light the cloths and chuck them into the grasses at the bend. That'll force the outlaws to us. You three on the rim can keep guard in case something goes awry."

"Sounds like a plan." Pa took three of the bottles and half the matches in his left hand. "Let's get this over with."

Sam nodded, and they split up. Sam tried to keep the glass from clinking while he scraped his way down the rocky incline and up the next. He waved at Schreiner and Henderson but didn't stop until he reached Curly. The younger man lay in the dirt, his tan shirt and pants blending well with the surroundings.

"Curly, it's Sam. Hold your fire."

The wrangler peered over his shoulder. "What's happening?"

Sam crouched and crept forward. "I need you to take these bottles. We're going to smoke these men out and bring this to an end. You can see the rocks blocking their escape from here, right?"

"Sure."

"I'm going to take Schreiner and Henderson, and we'll station ourselves there. The sheriff and Mo are on the opposite side. At my signal, you and Mo will light those rags and chuck the bottles into those grasses down there. Got it?"

The mop of light-brown curls bobbed.

Sam handed Curly the matches and grabbed his rifle. "Remember, wait for my signal."

Another nod.

"When we've got them all secured, mount up, and you can help us escort them back to the jail."

"Sure."

"Thanks."

Curly nodded, then focused on the canyon. Sam hurried to the trees and over to Henderson's location. He signaled the cowhand to join him and led the way to where the blacksmith hid behind the leaning rocks. Once he had the two together, he explained the plan.

"Do one of y'all have a rope?"

"Yep, on my saddle there."

"Bring it."

Sam waited long enough for Henderson to retrieve the rope, then guided them onto the landslide of boulders.

"Ready?"

The men checked their guns and nodded.

Sam waved the barrel of his rifle in the air. Seconds later, shattering glass ripped the silence. Scraping issued from the far side of the rocks as smoke spiraled into the sky.

Sam planted his feet, his aim steady at the top of the blockade. A shot boomed from his left. Who had Mo shot at, or was it Pa? Sam resisted the urge to climb the rocks and find out. One shot might simply be a warning.

Coughing joined the crackle of fire. Rocks slid and clattered. Sam glanced at the others and widened his stance.

A riderless horse topped the boulders and charged toward them. White shone around his eyes as he galloped past. Two more chestnuts soon followed his harried path.

"This is the sheriff. Throw down your weapons, and come out with your hands up."

More coughing.

Sam had all he could do to stay where he was and not make himself a target at the top of the boulders. Surely the outlaws would start climbing the rocks soon. A couple were injured. Maybe that's what took them so long.

His shoulders tightened when the sounds of scraping and shifting rocks carried to him again. A flat-brim hat and then a scarred face appeared.

"That's it." Sam motioned the gang's leader forward with the tip of his rifle. "Come on over nice and easy with your hands where I can see them."

The general's darkened gaze speared Sam, but after the outlaw glanced over his shoulder, he scaled the rocks. Another crawled over, a bandana around his calf. The other man who'd played sentry appeared with a hole in his boot—Arizona helped him slide down the boulder opposite Schreiner and limp to a seat at the bottom of the landslide. One more dusty, soot-smeared outlaw brought up the rear.

With the five grouped together, Sam stepped closer, Henderson alongside. "Henderson, you got that rope handy?"

"Yep."

"Put it to some good use, will you?"

The older man handed his rifle to Schreiner and strode forward.

With the gang bound, Sam worked his way to the top of the boulders and motioned to the others. Curly and Pa met them at the opening of the gorge with their horses, plus the empty mounts of the captured men.

"Missin' somethin', son?" Sam's gun belt, minus the extra bullets normally in the slots, dangled from Pa's hand. The bone-handled six-shooters were probably empty too, but at least the Peacemakers had found their way home.

Sam took the end of the leather belt and strapped them on. "Where's Mo?"

"He's gonna keep an eye on the fire. Make sure it don't get outta hand." Pa handed Buster's reins to Sam.

"Hey, I was riding Pecos."

"Not any more you ain't." Pa grinned, then prodded the nearest outlaw. "Get to steppin', boys. You got a long walk back to town."

"Walk? But you got our horses right there."

"Your point being? I like this arrangement better. Besides, this oughta give y'all plenty of time to consider the error of your ways. I'd suggest y'all make peace with your Maker too 'cause I doubt any judge will take too kindly to men who threaten women and children."

Sam shoved his feet into Buster's stirrups. "Don't forget the man they murdered."

"That what started all this?"

Sam nodded and moved his horse alongside the five. Schreiner took the opposite side while Pa, Curly, and Henderson followed behind.

It was getting on toward sunset when their troop sauntered into town. Residents stepped from their homes and businesses to watch their progress to the jailhouse.

Joe met their group on the threshold. "About time y'all showed up. Managed to bring them all in alive, huh?"

"Not too bad for a day's work." Sam swung from the saddle and thanked Schreiner as he passed by on his way to the livery.

"In you go, boys. There's two cells in there with y'all's names on it." Pa motioned the men inside with his rifle barrel.

"We'll meet you back at the ranch, Curly. Thanks for the help."

"Not a problem, Boss." The wrangler turned and headed south.

With the gang locked away, Sam turned to thank Joe and Henderson, when the door swung inward.

Amos stopped. "Oh, y'all are back."

Joe motioned the younger man inside. "I thought I sent you back to the ranch. What are you doing in town? Is something wrong?"

"Nothing's wrong, sir. Your wife was getting anxious, so I told her I'd come check on things."

"Well, we're done now. Me and Henderson'll ride back with you to the ranch."

"Don't y'all need someone to watch the prisoners?"

Pa stepped forward. "You volunteering, Amos?"

"Sure...I mean, if that's all right with you, Sheriff."

Pa looked to Sam and Joe for their consent, then turned back to Amos. "You know how to use that Peacemaker?"

"Yes, sir."

"All right. Don't open the jail door for any reason. I don't care if one of them is choking."

"Yes, sir."

Joe settled a hand on Amos's shoulder. "I'll stop by your ma's on the way home and let her know where you are."

"Hope you don't mind, but I already took the liberty, sir."

"That's fine. Henderson..." Joe and Henderson bid their good-byes and exited.

Pa shoved on his Stetson and faced Amos. "I'll have Mrs. Ritter bring over some meals from the boarding house."

"Thank you, sir." Amos hung his hat by the door and moved toward the desk.

Sam tossed him the jail cell keys. "There's a pack of cards in the desk there if you get bored, unless Pa moved them."

"No, they're still there." Pa grinned. "I can flick nearly a full deck into my hat without a miss."

Amos slid out the drawer, dropped the keys inside, and withdrew the deck. "Y'all have a good night."

After expressing his thanks, Sam followed his father from the office. They made their promised stop at the boarding house before they headed for the ranch.

"You gonna be able to make it there without fallin' asleep in the saddle?"

Sam blinked and covered a yawn. "If I can't, just grab the reins and lead me home."

Pa chuckled. "You know I used to have to take you for a ride to get you to take a nap when you were younger."

Sam tried to conjure a smile, but the last two days—make that the last month—were quickly catching up with him. Surely Cat wouldn't still relegate him to the barn after all he'd been through for her today.

He studied his pa, who remained a bit too pale except for the bright shiner coloring his left eye. "Why are you coming home with me instead of finding your own bed?"

"I figured Catherine and Ben would need to see for themselves that I was okay. I can head for home after supper."

"Mmmhmm. You just wanted a supper invite."

"In case you don't realize, it's Friday. I have a standing invitation, remember?"

"Oh." Sam frowned. "Is it already Friday? Where did Thursday go?"

"I don't know. I'm still tryin' to find it myself."

"Do you believe I only rode into town three days ago? I don't think I've ever packed so much in a couple of days in my entire life."

"I've been there. Have ya gotten any sleep since you got back?"

"Only a few hours in the barn and then a few in Anderson's old cabin." Sam scratched his chin. He really needed a shave, but that'd have to wait until morning after he got some shut-eye. He'd be liable to slit his own throat if he dared the feat tonight.

The sway and creak of the saddle lulled him to a state of semiconsciousness. By the time they reached the Bar M, he only yearned for a place to lay his head. Lacking the energy to argue with Cat for a spot in his home, Sam simply rode into the barn. He took the reins of his pa's horse and nodded Pa toward the house. Once the saddles were put away and the horses in the corral, Sam looked for the freshest stack of hay and collapsed.

<hr>

Catherine hurried across the yard toward GW. "Where's Sam?"

"Puttin' away the horses."

Relief sloshed through her as Benin charged past. "Careful. Gramps's shoulder is hurt."

Benin slowed a fraction but still threw his arms around his grandfather's legs. "Mama was worried, but I knew you'd come back."

GW crouched to the boy's level with a muffled groan. "Oh yeah?"

"Mmhmm. You're the bestest lawman ever."

"I don't know. You're pa did mighty good out there."

"Really?"

GW tousled Benin's dark hair and stood. "How 'bout I tell y'all all about it over some grub?"

"Miss Ida fixed up chili with crackers."

"No cornbread?"

"Mama had cornbread."

"Oh, I see, and you had crackers."

"Me and Roscoe."

"Uh-huh. Catherine, did Mo make it back okay?"

She dragged her gaze from the barn where Sam hadn't emerged yet. "Y-yeah. He made it back just fine. The fire's all out." She looked back to the whitewashed building. "How long does it take to put away two horses?"

"Why don't you go check on him? Benin can show me where the chili is, can't you, son?"

"Yessir."

"I think I'll do that." Catherine strode to the barn. The door creaked under her hand. "Sam?"

No answer.

She lit the lantern on the hook by the door.

No horses waited to be unsaddled.

She peeked back at GW, whom Benin towed toward the kitchen. Stepping inside, she shut the door against the cool wind. "Sam? Are you in here?"

A muffled snort carried from an empty stall near the back. Frowning, she headed that way. She paused in the opening. Sam lay sprawled across a mound of hay, sound asleep.

"Sam." Catherine hung the lantern nearby and knelt beside him. He never moved. Considering the way he'd awoken at a mere word in the cabin the yesterday morning, he had to be exhausted.

The barn door swished open, carrying in a draft of cold air and a merry whistle.

"Mo?"

"Miz Cathy?" Footfalls padded her way, then Mo's dark face peered back at her. "What you be doin' in here? Is that Mista' Sam?"

She nodded. "I think he's tired."

"I don't falls 'sleep like that 'less I'm beat, ma'am."

"Yes." Catherine peered at her husband and made a quick decision. "Mo, would you do me a favor?"

"O' course."

"Would you ask GW if he'd mind staying in the house with Benin tonight?"

Mo glanced between her and the sleeping Sam and smiled. "Sho', Miz Cathy. There be extra blankets on that shelf there."

"Thanks, Mo."

"G'night, Miz Cathy."

"Good night, Mo. Oh, Mo?"

"Yes'm?"

"Would you ask Ida to make biscuits and sausage gravy for breakfast? They're…they're Sam's favorite."

"I reckon he's done earned 'em. I'll milk Bessie right quick 'n' let Ida know."

Catherine smiled her thanks and listened to Mo's whistle and the cat's pleading yowls while she grabbed two woolen blankets off the shelf and returned to the stall. She spread one on the straw beside Sam, knelt on it, and then spread the other across them both. Shortly thereafter, the whistling stopped, Mo bid her good-night, and silence filled the barn.

Catherine climbed to her feet long enough to extinguish the lantern before she slid farther down onto the blanket beside Sam. His body heat radiated through her skirts, and a muffled snore carried from his lips, but he couldn't be all that comfortable with hay poking him in the face. Catherine removed her shawl and tucked it under his cheek.

Sam snorted and rolled toward her, his arm settling across her waist.

She smiled and studied his profile in the meager light from the setting sun peeking through the cracks in the boards behind them. How she'd missed this. *God, thank You for bringing him home safe and sound.* Catherine brushed a dark lock off his forehead.

Sam shifted. "Cat?"

"Shh, just go back to sleep. I'm here."

His arm tightened around her, and he nuzzled his face in her hair. "I'm glad."

Seconds later, a soft snore brushed her neck.

Catherine smiled and rubbed his arm. "Me too."

Leaning her head against his, she savored the moment. More people were headed their way bent on killing her man. She could only pray they wouldn't succeed.

21

Sam brushed at whatever tickled his nose and shifted to get more comfortable, but when his arm wouldn't move, he pried his eyes open. He found Cat's head pillowed on his right bicep, her soft curves spooned against him absorbing his heat. Sam rubbed the fist of his left hand against his eye, yet she remained.

What a way to wake up.

He cupped the smaller fist resting on his chest and cuddled her close, breathing in the sweet lemony scent of her golden hair mingled with the rich aroma of fresh hay. Not questioning Cat last night had clearly been the right choice, but when had she joined him in the barn? The last thing he remembered was putting up the saddles in the tack room and collapsing in the first empty stall.

Debating on whether to wake her, Sam tucked a wayward strand behind her ear. Mornings with Cat had always been his favorite. Her kisses were sweeter, her affections unclouded. She'd awaken with a sleepy smile and snuggle close. Nothing could be better. A rested Cat was a happy Cat, and she'd often made leaving her side such a dreaded chore. Maybe that's why he'd loved having her tag along to check the horses and handle the milk cow each morning, even if it meant a later breakfast.

His mind drifted to those mornings in the weeks before he'd left. She'd rarely woken in one of those good moods. Looking back, Sam realized she'd been in the family way at the time and probably hadn't felt rested in the least. Mares were temperamental when in that condition. Why hadn't he made that connection? Why had he immediately assumed her bad humor had something to do with him?

Sam snorted. Probably because she'd taken every chance to point out what he'd done wrong or how her way was always better. He'd never measured up.

Sam studied her sleep-flushed cheeks and the way her pale lashes curled against them. Did he have such pleasant things to look forward to every time their family increased? He rubbed a hand across his face. What was he getting himself into?

"Mama, you in here?"

Sam stiffened at Benin's voice, but Cat didn't move. He quickly eased his arm from under her head, tucked the blankets back around her, and moved to intercept the boy.

Benin shuffled through the center of the barn, a blue blanket trailing behind him.

"Hey, kiddo, Mama's still asleep. Will I do?"

"Pa, you came back."

"Well, sure." Sam lifted the lad into his arms, smiling when his son's small arms wrapped around his neck. If more little people like Benin were the result of Cat's temporary bad moods, he'd endure them every time. "Did you sleep okay, partner?"

"I guess so."

Sam carried his son toward the milk pail hanging near the front door. "You guess so?"

"Yeah, Gramps snores. Loud."

Sam chuckled. "I forgot. Louder than a hound dog with his tail caught in a door, isn't it?"

Benin giggled. "Uh-huh. Real loud. Where we goin'?"

"I figure since I'm up and I'm in here, I might as well milk Bessie. It's a little early yet, but I don't think the other men will mind. After that I plan to check on Mama's new horse."

"The sick one?"

"That's the one." Sam grabbed the bucket and strode toward the farthest stall.

"Mama says I ain't s'posed to go near 'im."

"Well, then how about you sit over there on one of those barrels so neither of us gets in trouble?"

"Would he like a sugar cube? I know where Miss Ida keeps 'em."

"I don't know…"

"Please? Mama lets me give 'em to Buster, 'n' he likes 'em a whole lot."

"All right then, but just one. If you see Mo, tell him I'm handling the milking." Sam set Benin down and grabbed the milking stool. The boy thundered down the aisle and banged out the barn door. Sam winced and prayed the loud noise didn't wake Cat or upset Thunder. Why hadn't his wife taught their son not to make such sudden sounds and movements around the horses? He was old enough to learn how skittish horses were at times.

Sam glanced down the aisle at the long faces that'd moved to their stall entrances to stare at him. "Sorry, fellas. I'll warn him next time."

"Warn who?" Cat pushed to a sitting position on her blanket, one hand rubbing her eye.

"Your son. Sorry he woke you."

She waved a hand and staggered to her feet. "It's all right. If he's up, I need to be up."

"Why? I'm here."

Cat paused, her hand on the stall wall. "For now."

After all they'd been through in the past forty-eight hours, she had to throw that in his face again? Sam folded his arms. Surely his actions should've earned him some of her respect. If she still felt so caustically toward him, then why had she climbed in the hay with him? What happened to her *I forgive you* and passionate kisses from yesterday? "Care to explain that remark?"

She swiped the hair from her face. "What's to explain? More men are coming here to kill you. Maybe I'll be able to accept that you're here to stay when I don't have to worry about you being shot every waking moment."

Oh, so that was it. "You're just borrowing trouble." Sam strode to the milk cow's stall, grabbed the three-legged stool, and sat in position.

"Trouble seems to have a way of finding us, if you haven't noticed."

Unfortunately, he had. Trouble ought to be his middle name, they were so intertwined. Why had he thought he could escape it now?

Cat paused outside the stall, stifled a yawn, and shifted the folded blankets in her arms. "I'm going to put these away and go help Ida. The men should be in here soon to start moving the horses from their stalls. I hope you have a plan to share with us during breakfast, because I stayed awake half the night and came up empty."

Right. A plan. Sleep so clouded his mind yesterday evening he hadn't given those telegrams another thought.

The barn door banged open. "Here's the sugar cube, Pa."

Cat pivoted. "Benin. What did I tell you about barging into the barn? What if a horse got spooked by your shouting and hurt someone?"

"Sorry, Mama. I forgot. I'll 'member next time."

"See that you do. I'd hate for your next reminder to have to come from a talk behind the woodshed."

Benin's eyes widened. "I promise. I won't forget."

The desire to contradict Cat and soothe Benin's angst gripped Sam as milk pinged into the pail, but Cat was right. The cow might've stepped on him if she wasn't half-asleep. The boy needed to remember how to act in the barn so he didn't endanger himself or others with his actions.

Sam leaned his forehead against the cow's warm side. What of his actions? Had he been self-centered by coming back when he had? Should he have done more to settle things with those who had aught against him before he'd returned home?

"Good. Now, come give me a hug so I can go help Mrs. Ida." Cat squatted to Benin's level and squeezed him once he'd run into her arms. "You be a good boy and stay away from Thunder."

"Yes'm."

Meow.

The pinging of milk stopped. A chill raced down Sam's spine as he looked about for the source of that horrific sound. Menacing green eyes in a dark furry face glared at him from atop the stall divider. All at once, Sam was four years old. Two felines with flaming, intertwined tails raced toward him, claws gleaming, fangs bared. Yowls of torment pierced his ears.

"C-c-c-c-cat."

"Yes?" Hay shifted. "What's the matter, Sam?"

"No, c-cat." He pointed at the gray beast that looked ready to add to the faded scars on his neck at any moment.

"Oh, hi, Soot." His wife stepped toward the maniacal monster.

"Don't!"

The feline dropped to the hay. Peeked at him from under the cow. Sam toppled off the stool and scrambled backward with a shout. Bessie bellowed and stomped on the bucket. The gray menace yowled and streaked from the stall as milk swirled into the air. Sam snatched up his son, grabbed his wife's arm, and dragged them in the opposite direction.

"Sam! Sam, what is the matter with you?" Cat yanked her arm away and swiped a stream of cream from her face. A dark line of moisture streaked down her purple apron. Milk dripped from the hem, making a splattered pattern in the dirt.

"I...you...the cat." He set down Benin and gestured in the direction the fiend had disappeared. "When did you get a cat? I told you, no cats."

"We had mice. What's the matter with cats?"

"What's the matter with—" He bit off the rest of the question and turned to his son. "Benin, why don't you go outside and give that sugar cube to Buster?"

"Are you scart of cats, Pa?"

"I, uh...let's just say your ma is the only Cat I've ever wanted."

"I like Soot. He's nice."

"Benin, the sugar..."

"You're not gonna get rid of Soot, are you, Pa?"

Cat put her hands on Benin's shoulders and rotated him toward the door. "No, he's not going to get rid of Soot. Now scoot. Go play, or better yet, go see if Mrs. Ida needs more wood in her kitchen."

"Okay. Can I still give Buster the sugar cube?"

"Yes, that's fine. Just stay outside the fence."

"Yes'm."

Sam's gaze darted to every corner of the barn, searching for the four-legged monstrosity his wife lovingly dubbed Soot, while his son ambled out the door. He was almost positive he'd told his wife he would never own one of those feral fur balls.

A giggle turned his head.

Cat's fingers hovered over her lips, but they didn't hide the smile that peeked out. "I can't believe it. You're scared of cats."

Sam frowned. "No, I'm just...cautious."

"Cautious. Of course. I've seen plenty of men fall off milking stools because they're *cautious* around cats." Cat stifled a laugh, removed her apron, and wiped a wet strand from her forehead. "Are you okay? You didn't hit your head or anything, did you?"

"I'm glad to see you're so concerned." Sam stalked away and snatched the dented milking bucket from the ground, his eyes ever watchful for the sneaky Soot. First the woman came at him with a pitchfork, then turned a gang of outlaws his way. Now she had a cat. What would she throw at him next? A stick of dynamite?

"Come on, honey. You have to admit it's a little funny. Besides, if anyone should get upset, it should be me. I'm the one who got a milk bath, after all."

"I'm sorry." He strode toward the door. "Excuse me while I rinse this out."

She caught his arm and pulled him to a stop. "I'm sorry I laughed. Really, are you okay?"

"I'm fine." Except for his wounded pride.

"Why don't you like cats?"

"Forget about it. It's not worth mentioning."

"Sam. Please?" Her coffee-colored eyes held his, pleading with him, until his shoulders sagged.

He switched the bucket to his left hand and used his right to sweep the hair away from his neck a few inches from his ear.

Cat rose on tiptoe. After a moment, her fingers traced the three parallel scars that remained after twenty-five years. "A cat did this to you?"

Sam recovered the scars. "Two. Tied together."

She cringed. "I'm so sorry I laughed. I had no idea. Why didn't you ever tell me?"

"You think I wanted the woman I married to know I'm scared of something the size of my boot?"

Her thumb caressed the scars beneath his hair, her ministrations slowly worming past his wounded pride to warm his heart. "I would've understood. Do you want me to get rid of Soot?"

He settled his arms around her. "Do we really have a mouse problem?"

"Before Soot we did."

"I guess he can stay then."

"I'm sorry I didn't warn you. Mo and Curly usually feed him when they're milking Bessie."

"It's all right. You didn't know."

"Would a kiss make it better?"

Sam felt a smile coming on. "It might."

He leaned closer. A breath before his lips touched hers, she darted sideways and pecked him on the neck.

"Hey!"

Cat laughed, ducked under his arm, and darted for the door. Sam raced after her and caught her around the middle before she could escape. The squeal that elicited from his wife wriggled a chuckle from his chest. With a playful growl, he tickled her sides until she squirmed.

The clang of the triangle broke through their laughter.

"Sam, breakfast." Cat gasped.

"Not until I get my morning kiss."

"I gave you one."

"Oh, you did?" He wiggled his fingers against her ribs again.

"Okay, okay."

Sam moved his hands to her waist with a triumphant grin.

Cat's smile softened. She tugged him nearer and brushed a sweet, soft kiss against his lips. "Better?"

"Much." He intertwined their fingers together, lifted her hand, and kissed the back of it before leading her to the kitchen.

Sam hesitated in crossing the threshold when he opened the door.

"What's that smell?"

Cat tugged him inside. "A special surprise I arranged last night."

"Smells like sausage gravy and biscuits."

"That's 'cause it is." Ida set a pot of coffee on the table. "You two don't hurry up, they gonna start without you."

Sam squeezed his wife's hand. "Have I told you lately how much I love you?"

Cat's smile reached from ear to ear and never left her face.

That was until Pa pushed his plate away and brought up yesterday's troubles. "All right, Sam, that's your third helpin'. The kiddos are outside. Now tell me 'bout these men that were sent wires, before I have to go relieve Amos at the jail." Pa shoved his coffee cup away. "How long will it take for them to get here?"

Sam peeked at his wife, who still had a piece of straw sticking from her bun, and shoveled the last bite of soppy biscuit in his mouth. He chewed while considering the option that had played through his mind before Soot made his appearance. His wife and son needed his protection, but his presence only put them in greater danger.

"If they left right away, they'll probably be here the middle of this coming week." His heart breaking, Sam folded his napkin, wiped his mouth, and forced out the words that left a bitter twang on his tongue. "But I won't be here."

Cat stiffened. "You won't? What are you talking about?"

He wished he could put the smile back on her face, but there wasn't any other way. "Cat, I'm not bringing trouble to your doorstep. Y'all've already been through enough. I should've taken care of these things before putting y'all in danger."

"You're leaving?"

A thick silence settled on the room, so heavy the crackle of the fire in the kitchen stove could be heard.

"I'm sorry. I wish there was another way."

"Do you?" Cat pushed her chair back and rose to her feet. "If you run away this time, Sam McGarrett, don't be surprised if I'm not here when you come back." She slammed her chair in and banged out the door.

Run away? Sam blinked at the door, too shocked by her response to be angered by it.

"She's right, ya know." Pa folded his arms. "This isn't a battle you run from. There's no shame in acceptin' help, son."

"What if she gets hurt in the process? Or Benin?" He shook his head. "I'd never forgive myself. At least with me taking the battle elsewhere, they'll be safe."

"You don't know that."

"What?"

"Have you forgotten what we've gone through the past day and half? Catherine found that trouble all on her own, and if it wasn't for you, she'd still be stuck in it. There's nothin' sayin' she won't fall into trouble again with or without you here. Your presence or the lack thereof won't change that." Pa selected a toothpick from his shirt pocket and shook it at him. "You're the one person she'll really open up to. That ain't somethin' you throw away, son. You might not want to admit it, but you need her as much as she needs you." He rose. "Think on it. I've gotta go relieve Amos."

Sam nodded and stared after his pa and the hands as they filed outside. Were they right? Was he running away like a coward? He'd stood down multiple outlaws, collected multiple bounties. That meant he wasn't a coward, right? Then why did their words make him feel like a dog with his tail tucked between his legs and scurrying for the trees? He felt worse now than after that humiliating scene with the cat in the barn.

He jabbed his hands into his hair. What if things went south? What if Cat got hurt, or worse? A fist squeezed his heart. No easy answer existed for this one. If he stayed, he endangered his family, but if he left, they might be in more danger, and he'd not be there to help. Did it take more courage to stay or to go? What was the answer? *God, I don't know what to do.*

Trust me.

But I don't see a solution that will keep everyone safe this time.

His pa's words about Cat getting into trouble with or without him replayed in his mind.

So is it better that I stay?

For this cause a man shall leave his father and mother and cleave to wife.

"All right, God, but You've got to keep us. You got us out of the mess the other night. Get us safely out of this too."

"Now you talkin' like you got some sense." Ida swiped a towel across a dish.

"Sorry. I thought I was alone."

"Ya never are. Now go tell Miz Cathy 'bout yo' decision before she gets too worked up to listen to ya."

22

Catherine stalked into the barn and barely caught herself before slamming the door behind her. Maybe the barn wasn't the best place to work off her frustration. Normally the scent of hay, horses, and grain soothed her, but right now they only conjured memories of the fun she and Sam had shared that morning, the way he'd looked last night, all vulnerable and exhausted on her account. She was such an idiot.

"Oh, that man! He makes me so mad I could—*ugh*!" She yanked up the handles of the wheelbarrow and shoved it into the middle aisle. She snatched a shovel from a corner and marched to the first empty stall with soiled straw. There was no want for chores on a horse ranch, and for once, she was glad of it.

With a thrust and toss, she dumped the first shovelful in the wheelbarrow. "Why does he have to do this every time? Why do I let him do it? Why—"

"Cat?"

She gripped the handle of the shovel tighter and pushed away the unction to turn around and swing the thing at Sam's head. Barely. "If you've come to say good-bye, I don't want to hear it."

The harsh scrape of metal against dirt echoed in the barn, then dirty straw plopped into the wheelbarrow.

"Cat, can we talk a minute?"

She had nothing worth saying to him, the selfish, unthinking, no-good, dirty rotten skunk. If he thought for one minute he could sweet-talk himself out of this one, he was greatly mistaken.

Plop.

Footsteps approached. "Please."

He could pretty-please until he was blue in the face. She wasn't wasting another moment on his sorry carcass. She was through. Done. Finished. "I don't need to hear your lies or explanations, Mr. McGarrett. If you want to leave, there's the door. Don't let it hit you on the way out."

Plop.

He'd shoved her love and care back in her face for the last time.

"Cat, I'm not leaving."

"Why not? That's what you do whenever things get rough, right? Why wouldn't you do it now?"

Plop.

"'Cause you need me."

Cat stopped her shovel and swiveled to face him. "Need you? Need *you*? The only one I need is God. He got me through the last five years without you. He can help me through the next fifty. I'll make it with or without you, Samuel McGarrett, so don't deceive yourself in thinking I need you. If you want to go, there's the road. Don't stay on my account."

"Then who's account am I staying for?"

Plop.

"Don't you want me to stay?"

"I don't care what you do anymore, Sam. I. Just. Don't. Care." Catherine threw down the shovel and stalked from the barn. When she crossed the threshold of the cabin and shut the door, she let the tears flow unchecked. She leaned against the wood and sank to the floor.

Why had she ever trusted the man? Why had she opened her heart?

Galloping hooves pounded outside and faded in the direction of town.

Curling into a ball, Catherine sobbed.

"Sam? What on earth? What're you doin' here?"

"I'm staying here tonight." Sam chucked his saddlebags into the corner of his father's living room and strode toward the back door of the small cabin. "And before you start in on me too, know I've about had my fill of talking for the day."

Sam stomped outside and snatched the axe from the chopping block. After setting a chunk of wood in its place, he divided it with one fell swoop.

"Don't stay on my account."

Swoop.

"Why should I care?"

Swoop.

"Who needs you?"

Swoop.

Glass shattered.

"Hey!" Pa's face appeared in the broken window. "If I want more wood, I'll come fetch it myself."

"Sorry. I'll replace it."

"You bet your sweet Sunday you will. Get in here and clean up this mess."

"I'll be right there, Pa." Sam sank the edge of the blade into the stump, tossed the other half of the splintered log onto the pile, and stalked into the house. He grabbed the broom from the kitchen and set about cleaning up the broken plate glass, grumbling the whole way.

Pa strode into the living room carrying his cup of coffee. "If you want me to respond, you better speak louder'n that."

"I don't want to talk about it."

"You ain't quit talkin' since you showed up, so clearly, you do. Now spit it out. What's got your nose outta whack?"

Sam dumped the shards into a pail. "She threw me out, that's what."

"Catherine? I know she was upset, but she'd never—"

"Well, she did. Flat out told me she didn't need me, didn't care what I did, and there's the door." Sam stood and carried the bucket and broom back to the kitchen. "After all I've done for her, this is how she repays me? It'd serve her right if I did get on my horse and keep riding."

"You already said you were at breakfast."

"But I went to the barn after you left and told her I wasn't."

Pa took a sip of coffee. "And?"

"She didn't believe me."

Pa strode back to the kitchen. "Why should she?"

"Why should she? I've not once lied to that woman."

"Then what're you doin' here, standing in my house?"

"I—"

Pa set his cup on the table. "The only way you're gonna prove to that woman you're here to stay is to do just that. Stay."

"I already told you I was."

"You can't expect to erase five years in five days, son."

"What are you getting at?"

"It's gonna take time. She's gone five years without a word from you, and you expect her to treat you like that never happened."

"No, I don't."

"You could've fooled me."

Sam gripped the back of a kitchen chair. "All right, so maybe I have expected her to treat me with some respect, but surely all I've done in helping her with that gang has meant something."

"Not if you up and leave again."

"I told you I wasn't leaving. Doesn't anybody around here believe me anymore?"

"Then you better finish coolin' off and get your tail back home." Pa set his mug in the sink and strode toward the front door. "Don't forget to board up that window before you go."

"You still coming out later to help with a plan for those other men heading my way?"

Pa donned his gray Stetson. "Don't worry. I'll drop by around suppertime and make sure she ain't killed ya."

"Ha-ha." With a shove to the chair, Sam turned and headed for the shed out back. Maybe after pounding nails into some boards to cover the broken window, he'd be able to talk to his wife with a civil tongue, or maybe he'd just teach her a lesson and wouldn't go home tonight. Maybe then she'd think twice about telling him to hit the road.

Catherine swiped the evidence of tears from her cheeks at the footfalls outside the door. She couldn't hide inside all day. No matter how much she wanted too.

"Miz Cathy, you al'right?"

"I'll be fine, Ida." Someday.

A dark, round face peeked inside the door. Ida's brow rose. "Them red-rimmed eyes tell another tale."

"Really. I'll be just fine." Catherine stuffed the hankie in her apron pocket.

"You wanna tell ole Ida why Mista Sam took off outta here like a scalded gander?"

Tears pressed in behind her eyes. "That was him then?"

"What happened, honey?"

"Oh, Ida, I think I messed up everything." Catherine retrieved the handkerchief. "I wouldn't listen, and I said some horrible things. I didn't want him to go. Well, maybe I did at the time, but I was mad, upset. I didn't really mean it." Catherine squeezed the bridge of her nose, but the tears still flowed. "I'm a horrible wife."

Ida's warm arms engulfed Catherine, bathing her in comfort and the smell of cinnamon. "Suga', it can't be as bad as all o' that."

"Oh, but it is. I don't think Sam will ever talk to me again." Catherine jerked back. "And he might be killed by one of those men. Oh, what have I done?" She buried her face in Ida's shoulder and bawled.

"Mercy, chil', it's gonna be al'right. If you've done somethin' wrong, you can still make it right. He ain't dead yet."

"But you said so yourself—he left."

"Well, he ain't been gone that long, 'n' I know you can ride like the wind."

"You mean go after him?"

"'N' why not?"

"Women don't chase men."

"Women maybe. Wives, on the other hand…"

Catherine shared the cook's smile and brushed at the last of her tears. "Ida, have Mo saddle Buster for me?"

The older woman chucked her under the chin. "Thatta girl."

Catherine galloped into town and plowed to a halt outside the sheriff's office. Kicking her feet from the stirrups, she vaulted from the saddle. She hoped against hope that Sam had mentioned to his father where he'd be headed.

"I'll be right back, Buster. Stay put." Catherine banged inside.

A cell full of outlaws glared back at her.

"GW?"

"What's up, Aunt Cathy?" Amos set down the coffee pot on the potbellied stove in the corner.

"Well, look who finally came to pay us a visit." Larry draped his arms through the bars. "You have a pang of remorse?"

"Yes, but not over you." She turned back to her nephew. "Where's the sheriff?"

"He's not here yet."

"Have you seen Sam?"

"No, ma'am. Is something wrong?"

"Nothing I can't handle. If you see GW before I do, tell him I've got a question for him."

"Sure."

Catherine dashed out the door and sprinted down the alley between the jail and the livery. GW's house sat only a hundred yards or so from the back of the jailhouse. Hammering broke the silence of the midmorning. Good, he was home.

Grabbing the doorknob, she pushed inside.

And ground to a standstill.

"Sam?"

Her husband glanced through the broken window as the hammer swung toward the board. His eyes widened in shock, and a shout of pain burst from his lips. "Gracious, woman, who taught you how to enter a house?" He shook his hand, then shoved his thumb in his mouth.

"I...I'm sorry...I was in a hurry."

"No fooling." Sam leaned through the broken window and retrieved his hammer from the floor.

"I was..." She drew a deep breath and plunged forward. "Actually hurrying to find you."

Sam propped the hammer on the windowsill. "What for? I told you I wasn't leaving."

"You weren't? Then what are you doing here? No. Wait. I didn't come here to argue. I...I wanted to apologize."

"You? Apologize?"

Catherine folded her arms. "Well, are you going to let me or not?"

"Go ahead. No one's stopping you." Sam lifted the hammer and drove in another nail.

"Aren't you going to stop long enough to talk to me?"

"Why? You could muck stalls and talk to me."

"Why I—"

"Ain't much fun when the shoe's on the other foot, is it?" He gave her a humorless smile before the gap in the window closed with another board.

"Samuel Houston McGarrett, quit acting like a child. Get in here so I can apologize."

Something clattered to the ground, followed by determined footsteps across the back porch. Finally. Maybe they could actually have an adult conversation now.

Sam marched through the door. It banged shut behind him as he continued to stride toward her, an unwavering glint in his stormy eyes. She backed up a step, but he kept on coming. Maybe she should've apologized through the window. Clearly, his humor hadn't improved during his ride to town.

"Now, Sam..." Catherine continued to counter his approach until her back met a wall.

Sam towered over her, his steel gaze trapping her as much as his large frame. "Look here, woman. I've had it about up to here with your bossiness and know-it-all attitude. I am not Benin, and I am not one of your ranch hands. You'd better get that through your thick skull real quick like, and another thing...I am coming back to *my* ranch tonight, and I'm sleeping in *my* bed, and if you don't like it, *you* can sleep in the barn. I have given and given until I'm blue in the face, and do I get an ounce of respect from you for all I've done? Not a lick!"

"That's not true."

"Oh, it isn't? Then who was that blond-haired woman who told me to hit the road just a while ago? She looked an awful lot like you."

"I was angry and upset. You told me you were leaving after you'd already said you wouldn't."

"If you'll recall, I also told you I changed my mind and wasn't leaving after all."

"And how many more times am I going to have to worry that you're going to change your mind?"

"I told you I'm not leaving."

"Are you sure? Because I've heard that before. What if your pa needs help? What if more outlaws come to gun you down? Will you stay even then, or will you pick up and pack up regardless of who or what you're leaving behind? Tell me so I can be sure, because I still have no clue why you even left in the first place!"

"That's not true. The day after I got back I—"

"Yes, it is true. You only said you had something to take care of and you couldn't take any more of our..." Catherine gulped, her gaze falling on their touching boot tips. "Fighting."

Silence reigned for several heartbeats, except for their heavy breathing.

Sam stepped back a fraction and stuffed his hands in his pockets. "I never have told you the whole story, have I?"

"No, you haven't." Catherine swiped the wayward strands from her face and hugged herself, feeling exposed and raw. She hadn't intended to admit so much. Why did he always have that effect on her?

"I guess now's as good a time as any. Have a seat. I'll tell you whatever you want to know."

23

Sam added a couple logs to the fireplace to help ward off the chill from the boarded window and resisted the urge to pace. They'd planned to have this conversation before, so why did he feel so unprepared? Maybe because he had no clue how Cat would react. He sank into a chair. She deserved the truth, but would she look at him the same once she knew? Would she want anything to do with him? He'd said he wasn't leaving, but what if she couldn't stand the sight of him afterward?

Swiping a hand through his hair, Sam forced himself not to pull the strands from their roots. He popped from the chair and strode the short distance to the mantel. Head bent, he gripped the wood. No. No more running. Not from her or any of his problems.

"Sam?" Cat stood from her seat on the couch, her arms wrapped around her middle.

"You cold?"

"Not really." She rested her hands on the back of the chair he'd vacated. "Am I going to regret this?"

"I told you I'd answer your questions. If you're not ready to hear this, we can have this talk later."

"How many people did you kill?"

Sam rubbed his chin and moved to the couch. They were really doing this. "Five, but they were all in self-defense. Three were kin to the men who were sent telegrams."

Cat stepped from behind the chair and filled his empty place by the fire, her back to him. He wished she'd turn around so he could read her face.

"Why?"

"Lots of reasons." He sighed and rested his elbows on his knees, his mind going back six years. "For months before I left, Pa got multiple reports of a group of cowboys who'd hired on to take herds of cattle from several ranchers and drive them to market. Most of them were small outfits. The agreement was for the drovers to keep a portion of the profits for their troubles and send the rest back to the ranchers. Only their money never showed up. These men were stealing the ranchers' livelihood, and they were demanding Pa do something about it. He was going to investigate himself, but I volunteered."

Sam chanced a peek in Cat's direction. She'd turned and watched him steadily. More questions didn't come, so he continued.

"I figured too many people knew Pa was a lawman. He needed someone who could slink into the gang undetected and catch them red handed. I figured that was me. You didn't seem to need me or care what I did except to argue with me—"

"That's n—" She pressed her lips together. "I'm sorry. Please go on."

A wry grin tugged at the corners of his mouth. Some things never changed. "I thought maybe if I succeeded in finding those drovers and brought them to justice, it would impress you enough to make you see me as capable, to maybe earn your respect again. Although I'm still not sure how I lost it. But that was the only reason I could come up with for why we argued so much, why you constantly disregarded my opinion." Sam breathed a sigh, his focus on his locked fingers. "Anyway, I told Pa I'd hire on as a horse wrangler with an outfit, and work to find the group stealing from these ranchers, and bring them to justice."

Cat moved to the empty seat beside him. "That took five years?"

"No, that took about two, but when other towns heard how I'd helped, they sought me out. It was nice to be needed, and I…I didn't have the courage to face you after all I'd done, so I went wherever they asked me to." Sam raked a hand through his hair. "I'm sorry, Cat. If I'm honest, I wasn't just running from you and our troubles. I was runnin' from God. I was sick of all the demands, the *do this, don't do that.* I could never measure up, and after I killed someone, I didn't figure He would ever forgive me anyway, even if it was in self-defense. The guilt was eating me alive. I remember actually praying someone would kill me."

Sam stood and moved to the mantel. He stared into the flickering flames, seeing the eternity he would've had if God hadn't spared him. "I got shot earlier this year."

Cat's soft gasp interrupted, but he pressed on.

"Nearly died. A family by the name of Stone took me in, nurtured me back to health. Stuck there in that bed day after day, I had plenty of time to think, and for the first time, I couldn't run from my thoughts." A dry grin pulled at his mouth. "Couldn't run from Stone's preaching either."

Sam faced his wife, relieved to see the openness emanating from her instead of the condemnation he'd feared. "For the first time I understood God wasn't there waiting for me to mess up. He was there loving me, waiting for me to understand that not only did He want to be my Savior and Lord, He longed to be my Friend."

A tear slid down Cat's cheek.

He knelt before her and wiped it away. "It was God's love and forgiveness that gave me the courage to finally face you. You have no idea how much I prayed and prayed on my way back to Cater Springs. Then when I saw you, every word I'd practiced flew out of my head. You were so beautiful and angry, standing there beside that wagon. I was so afraid you wouldn't give me the time of day, let alone forgive me…" Sam stood and paced back to the mantel. "And then there was Benin. I couldn't believe what I'd done. And when you said you'd forgiven me, I couldn't believe my ears."

"Well, to be fair, I hadn't forgiven you as much as I thought I had."

His stomach dropped. Here it came, the rejection he'd expected.

Cat picked at a fingernail. "Roxie's letter had kind of planted some doubt I hadn't realized was there, and then when you admitted to kissing someone else…"

He moved back to her side and gathered her hands in his. "Cat, I promise you nothing happened. I admit I used any means necessary to infiltrate gangs and bring troublemakers to justice. Sometimes that included sweet-talking their sisters or cousins or friends. I figured the end justified the means. But I knew it was wrong, and it curdled my stomach."

"They really meant nothing to you? You never..."

"No. I swear to you I never betrayed you like that. Darlin', you're the only one who's ever meant anything to me, the only woman I've ever given myself to." He squeezed her hands, begging her to forgive him, to believe him. "That's part of the reason I had to come back. I knew my heart would never be whole again until you were back in my arms."

Cat gulped and swiped at more tears. "Why do you have to be such a sweet talker?"

Sam dared to inch closer. "Does that mean you forgive me?"

She nodded, and his heart soared.

"How did I ever get blessed with such a wonderful woman?"

Cat leaned into his hug. "I'm not so wonderful. I wanted to wring your neck a short while ago."

"I kind of gathered that, and just for the tally books, I would've deserved it if you had."

"No, I shouldn't get upset so easily." She picked at a button on his chambray shirt. "So now what do we do?"

"I'm not sure." He chuckled. "I never really thought I'd make it this far."

"I've dreamt of the day you'd finally come home."

"I bet it wasn't at all like what happened."

Her quiet laugh warmed him. "Not quite." She lifted her face to his. "Promise me two things?"

"Hmm?"

"You won't leave again?"

"Done."

"And that when these men come gunning for you, you won't get killed?"

"I'll do my best." He bent closer but hesitated. She might not be ready to accept his kisses again. He gave her the angled grin that'd always made her smile in the past. "I rather like the idea of staying and being your husband again."

A lovely pink stained her cheeks. "I've kind of missed being your wife."

His heartbeat moved from a walk to a canter. "Yeah?"

"I had to…to make myself forget just to survive."

"Oh, darlin'…"

"Then when you kiss me, I can't help but remember what it was like between us, and I…" Her gaze settled on his mouth. "I miss you even more."

"I miss you too." Sam dared respond to the yearning in her eyes. His lips grazed hers, and unlike the day before, it took only a little coaxing for her to kiss him back. Cat's arms slipped around his neck, reminding him of the unity they'd once shared. Breathing in her scent, he deepened the kiss and brought her closer.

"Glad to see y'all've made up."

Sam jerked away, his senses swirling and his blood pounding in his ears. "Pa, what are you doing here?"

"It's my house, remember?"

"Oh. Right." Sam forced himself to distance himself from his wife and swiped a hand through his hair, pretending nonchalance. "Was there something you needed me for?"

"No, Amos said Catherine had a question for me."

Cat stood and rotated away from him, giving Sam a lovely view of her golden hair. The wavy masses had pulled free from their confining bun sometime during that kiss and reached nearly to her knees. It'd grown longer in his absence. His fingers reached out of their own accord to feel the silky softness.

"It was nothing, GW. I was just looking for Sam."

"I see you found him."

"Uh, yes."

"You two headed home now?"

"I, um, think that's a good idea. Yes." She scratched her neck, then drew her hair together at the nape, dislodging his fingers. "GW, would you mind bringing my horse around from in front of your office?"

"Sure." Pa donned his hat with a wide grin and touched the brim before stepping back outside as quietly as he'd come.

Cat started twisting up her hair.

"I wish you wouldn't do that."

"Sam, I can't go through town with my hair down." She plucked a pin off the floor and shoved it in her hair. "I definitely can't ride with it loose like this either. It'd be a rat's nest by the time I got home."

"I wouldn't mind helping brush it out. You used to love it when I did that."

"Well, I'd love it right now if you'd help me find the rest of my pins before your father walks through that door again." She anchored more hair in place with another pin. "I can't believe he walked in when... Oh, what must he think?"

"That we're married?" Sam offered Cat the other pins with another smile.

"Don't you look at me like that. I have never been so embarrassed."

Sam settled his arms around her while she shoved in the last hairpin. "Cat, we're married. Pa knows what it's like. I might not remember my ma, but I'm sure he does."

"If that's meant to make me feel better, it's not helping."

Sam chuckled. "How about this?" He brushed another kiss across her sweet mouth.

She spoke against his lips. "Honey, I...think we have more...to discuss before you...move back into the house."

"I'll sleep on the same side as before." He grinned and stole another kiss.

"Sam—"

A knock rattled the door.

Sam slid his hands to Cat's waist and squeezed. "We'll finish this *discussion* later." With a wink, he moved to answer the door.

24

Catherine wiped her sweaty palms on her dress and locked her knees to keep from collapsing onto the couch. Her pulse raced, and she had no doubt the grin on GW's face said he knew what they'd been up to in his absence. She resisted the urge to fan her face with her apron and moved outside into the cool November air. Could this day get any more trying?

Catherine approached her horse as father and son said their good-byes on the porch. "Buster, ole boy, you better be thinking straight enough for the both of us to find our way home, because I'm not sure I am."

"You say something, Cat?"

"Not to you."

The men chuckled.

Ignoring them, Catherine gathered the reins, then a fistful of skirts.

"Hang on a second, and I'll help you."

Liking the idea of his hands on her again more than a little too much, she hurried into the saddle. She needed to put some space between them or she'd be saying yes to any notion that entered her husband's head, and she knew exactly what he was thinking. Her mind had strayed there too.

"I guess she's in a hurry to get home."

Heat crept into Catherine's cheeks at GW's remark, and she didn't dare look at Sam.

"It would seem so. Don't worry about coming out tonight. We'll just plan on you joining us for dinner tomorrow after church."

"Sounds like a plan."

"I'll go fetch Sandy from the corral so we can get a move on."

"Don't forget your saddlebags. Never mind. I'll get them."

"Thanks, Pa."

The men disappeared in different directions, and Catherine's lungs filled with relief at the momentary interlude. If her morning was any hint, this would be one very long day. She'd meant what she'd said about there being things they still needed to discuss. Their actions wouldn't just affect them. They'd affect their son too. How would Benin react to having Sam in the house, staying in her room even? Would he be uncomfortable or happy? Considering the boy's reaction to everything "Sam" so far, probably the latter.

Then there was her. Was she ready for that kind of intimacy with Sam again? The part of her that made her cheeks flush at the mere idea shouted yes.

"Snap out of it, Catherine. The man just threatened to leave a few hours ago." She propped her chin on her fist and stared at Buster's red coat. "But he did promise to stay too. Oh, who am I kidding? I've gone completely batty. Letting him kiss me and hold m—"

"You talking to me?"

Catherine started. Sam had rounded the house and was nearly upon her.

"No, just talking to myself." Yet more proof that she was crazier than a loon.

Sam grinned knowingly, and a horde of butterflies took flight in her stomach.

Oh, God, what am I going to do? Hadn't her time carrying Benin taught her anything? Did she want to end up pregnant and alone again? After all, Sam had done it before. That was the trouble with him; he made her completely forget herself and her surroundings. She couldn't—no, wouldn't—repeat the mistakes of her past, but how did she accomplish that when she couldn't keep from arguing with the man like before? Was history repeating itself again? How did she break the cycle?

Catherine's gaze lifted heavenward, and the church steeple caught her eye in the distance. Like a moth to a flame, she felt drawn to visit the building. She needed answers, and God always had them. Laying her reins to the right, Catherine turned Buster toward the church.

"Cat, home's thataway." Sam pointed in the opposite direction.

"I'm fully aware of that. I have some place I need to visit first."

"Visit? Oh great. Here we go again." Sam rode up alongside her, draping his saddlebags into place. "Tell me something. Why can't you be satisfied to leave what happens between us *between us*?"

"What?"

"Don't act like you don't know what I'm talking about. Every time we've fought, you've always felt the need to blab our problems to somebody. Why can't we handle things without you bringing someone else into the mix?"

"I don't blab. I seek advice." With a sigh, she pulled her horse to a stop in the grassy area behind the mercantile. Sam did the same. "I've never been married before. I know I don't have all the answers. What's so wrong with asking for help?"

"'Cause you always make me out to be the bad guy, and then no one looks at me the same, and don't tell me your sister has a better marriage than we do. Her husband hides in a whiskey bottle half the time and in the saloon the other half."

"Melvin wasn't always that way. He changed after the war. Besides, I wasn't going to talk to my sister. I was headed to the church house."

"The church? Why? We'll be there tomorrow."

Catherine nudged her horse and angled past the last building in town. "We need God's help, Sam. I can't go on repeating the same mistakes. You're welcome to come along or go home without me, but I have to stop there."

"What do you mean by 'the same mistakes'?"

"The fighting. We still fight like cats and dogs, and you said that's part of what drove you away before. I don't want to do that again."

"Well, I don't call you Cat for nothing."

"I'm serious."

The horses' hooves clippity-clopped on the bridge that crossed over Cater Spring.

Sam bumped his hat higher on his forehead. "I know. I just don't see how we can fix it. That seems to be the only way we really communicate."

"Don't you think there's something inherently wrong with that?"

"Sure, but what's that got to do with coming here? There's nobody around anyway."

Catherine halted by a live oak and drew her leg over the saddle horn until she faced her husband. "All my life God has been the answer to every problem. He has a way to help us with this."

Sam followed her in dismounting. "And you think we'll find that solution here today?"

"It's worth a try, don't you think?"

"All right. Lead the way. Maybe we can find a solution for this week while we're at it."

Catherine ground-hitched her horse and strolled toward the church steps.

Muffled voices carried from within when they neared.

"Sounds like someone's here after all. I didn't see any horses. Must be the preacher." Sam opened the door and moved to the side.

Catherine stepped over the threshold, and the voices stopped when her heels clicked on the wood floor. A white-blond head popped up from the first pew while Reverend Becker waved from his spot at the front.

"Mrs. Cathy!" Asta, the Beckers' four-year-old daughter, scampered from her seat and scurried down the aisle, her twin braids flapping behind her.

Catherine welcomed the smiling pixy into her arms and lifted her onto her hip. "Hi, sweetie. What are you doing in here?"

"I'm helping *Vati* ready for tomorrow."

"You are? Well, that's mighty nice of you." Catherine grinned at the reverend, who set down his notes and sauntered toward them.

"Who's he?" Asta pointed at Sam.

"Asta, don't be rude. If Frau McGarrett vants you to know who he is, she vill introduce you." The short German man extended his hand toward Sam. "Guten Tag."

"Morning."

"It's all right, Reverend. Asta, this is my husband, Mr. McGarrett. Sam, this is the Beckers' oldest daughter, Asta."

"Howdy, little lady. It's a pleasure to meet you."

"I'm pleased to meet you too, Mr. McGrett."

Catherine chuckled. "That's why she calls me Mrs. Cathy. There's something about that *a* that she can't quite seem to squeeze it in there."

Sam grinned and tugged one of the child's braids. "Well then, how about you calling me Mr. Sam? If that's all right with your pa, that is."

Asta looked to her father, who nodded his consent. "Okay. Howdy, Mr. Sam."

The adults laughed.

"She becomes more Texan every day." The brown-haired man reached for his daughter, planted a kiss on her cheek, and set her on the ground. "Go tell *Mutti* I have company, and play vith your sisters, ja?"

"Yes, Vati. Bye, Mrs. Cathy. Bye, Mr. Sam." The four-year-old waved and disappeared out the door. A short time later her blue gingham dress blurred past the window on the way to the parsonage.

Sam folded his arms. "She's quite the charmer."

"I am glad you think so and vere not offended."

"Oh, no, not at all. It's good to see you again under better circumstances. I appreciate your help rounding up men to search for Benin the other night."

"It vas my pleasure." Reverend Becker motioned them toward a pew. "Now vhat brings you here today? Is there something I can help vith again?"

"Well..." Catherine settled in the pew beside her husband while the preacher sat in the seat in front of them and hooked his meaty arm over the back. She'd had no idea her talks with others had bothered Sam so much. Maybe she should tell Reverend Becker they wanted to pray. Better yet, maybe it'd be better if they just left. She didn't want to upset Sam again, and if keeping her mouth shut this time would keep him happy, she'd manage somehow. "I'm sorry, Reverend. We shouldn't have interrupted. We—"

Sam settled a staying hand on her thigh. "We actually came hoping for some advice."

Catherine's eyes widened as she searched his face. What happened to not wanting to air their problems?

"You know I vill do vhat I can do help."

"I'm sure we can trust you to keep what's said here to yourself?"

"Ja, of course."

Sam's hand slid around hers. "We argue. A lot."

Catherine squeezed his fingers in a silent *thank you*. "And we don't want things to continue that way."

"All married couples argue at times."

"Is that the only way your wife will tell you what's going on in her head?"

Catherine frowned. He could've found a better way to put that.

"Vell, no. Normally, ve only fight vhen she vants to do something a different vay than I vould, but most times I give in because she is right—her vay is better." The reverend chuckled. "But don't tell her I said so."

Catherine leaned forward. A man who'd admit his wife was right would surely set her husband straight. "How do you keep from fighting over other things?"

"Ve learned to dance."

"Pardon?"

"I know not everyone condones dancing, especially not the valtz, but I have found it can teach a husband and vife much about marriage. Come, come. I vill show you, ja?" Reverend Becker shooed them from their seats to stand in the aisle.

Catherine stood next to Sam and crossed her arms. She did not dance. Not that she was against it. No, she'd just never learned. Blame it on her father dying when she was young, blame it on marrying young, blame it on whatever one might, but she did *not* dance. She admired those who reeled around at barn raisings—even wished at times she could join in—but she'd never, *never* dared step out on that dance floor to make a fool of herself. She wasn't about to start.

Sam extended his hand toward her with a meager bow and a slight smirk. Why was he looking at her like that?

"You know how to valtz, Bruder McGarrett?"

"I've made use of it a time or two. Saved a town once from a money-hungry fella who loved to throw elaborate shindigs. I had to dance or stick out like a coyote in a hen house."

"Oh, I see. Frau McGarrett?"

"I've never heard of the waltz. Is it like the dances they do at barn raises and such?"

"Not quite. There are no trading partners."

Okay, if that was true, then she could see why the reverend had compared it to marriage, but she still wasn't going to do this and make a complete ninny of herself.

"To start, you place your right hand in his left."

"Isn't there some way you could show us instead?"

Sam cocked an eyebrow. "Why? You chicken?"

Yes, but she wasn't about to let him know that. She'd never hear the end of it.

"Fine." Catherine placed her hand in his.

Sam immediately tugged her to within a foot of his chest and placed his right arm around her back.

"Sam!"

Reverend Becker waved off her objections. "No, no, this is right."

"People don't dance like this. Why, it's…it's…"

"Romantic?" Sam offered with a roguish grin.

"Frau McGarrett, I do not teach this to unmarried couples, but trust me, you vill learn from this."

Catherine urged her galloping heart to slow to a walk. If this would help her marriage and help keep Sam home, then she'd learn. She could do this. She'd scaled into a ravine, hadn't she? It couldn't be any harder than that, right? "All right. What next?"

"In the valtz, it is the man who leads. If two try to lead, it no vork. Just like in marriage."

Sam's heated remark about her bossiness echoed in her mind and drew her gaze upward. Was she trying to do more than she should and sabotaging things? But how did she trust a man to lead who'd left and remained absent for years? What if she trusted him to lead and he left with her heart again?

"You must follow your partner's leading and trust him to steer you away from any obstacles or people in your vay. The leader must communicate clearly as to vhich vay he is going or his partner vill not understand and get stepped on."

Sam's brows bunched.

Well, at least they were both learning something here.

"Marriage is about clear communication. Make sure your spouse understands vhat you are saying. Do not assume." Reverend Becker chuckled. "Except on one thing. I tell my vife, if I say something and it has two meanings, and one meaning hurts her feelings and the second does not, assume I mean the second."

Sam grinned. "I know exactly what you mean."

In other words, she was supposed to believe the best, not the worst. One of the middle verses from 1 Corinthians 13 blazed across her memory. Love *beareth all things*, believeth *all things, hopeth all things, endureth all things.*

What faulty assumptions had she made of late?

The preacher, with Sam's help, went on to show her the basic one-two-three step pattern. Half the time Catherine found herself moving backward and the other half moving forward.

"Like the valtz, marriage involves giving and taking. It is not one sided. Both must give so that both can take. Marriage is no place for selfishness. You must put your spouse first."

Catherine swallowed hard as Sam continued to waltz her around the front of the church. She kept a sharp eye on the toes of her boots to minimize the torture to Sam's feet and her own.

Sam leaned in when he stepped forward, forcing her to counter back. "Relax. Enjoy yourself."

She peered up and immediately stomped on his toe. "How am I supposed to relax? I don't want to hurt you."

A lazy grin spread across Sam's face. "I'm tougher than I look. Now come on. Relax. Nuh-uh-uh, look at me. Not your feet."

Catherine forced her gaze to remain on her husband and soon began to sense the pressure in his grip vary when he moved to change directions.

She smiled. "I'm getting it."

"That you are, darlin'. Want to try a turn?"

"I...I don't know."

"Trust me. It's easy. Just follow my lead."

Catherine gave a hesitant nod. A few steps later, Sam's grip on her hand shifted to her fingers, and his right hand pushed her back, turning her to the right under his left arm. With the turn complete, he settled her again in his arms, albeit a bit closer than before.

A smile spread across his lips. "See, I knew you could do it."

"Looks like you two have found your rhythm. I am confident you can find it in your marriage now, ja?"

Sam drew them to a halt and released her as they stopped in front of the preacher. Catherine twined her fingers together, not sure what to do with them now that she wasn't holding on to her husband. That had gone much better than she'd hoped. Actually, she was sad it'd ended. She could've danced all night.

"You've given us plenty to think on, Reverend. Thank you." Sam shook Reverend Becker's hand.

"You are velcome. I vill see you tomorrow, ja?"

"We'll be here."

"*Sehr gut.*"

"That means great," Catherine translated when Sam looked at her quizzically. "Thank you again, Reverend Becker. I hope we haven't taken too much of your time."

"I am alvays here to help. Safe travels home."

Sam placed his hand on her back, and as in the dance, Catherine instinctively moved with him toward the door. Maybe she was learning after all.

Perhaps there was hope for her marriage yet.

25

"He sure gave us a lot to think on, didn't he?"

"Yeah." Sam hooked his knee around the pommel of his saddle as they headed out of town toward home. He hadn't expected things at the church to go so well. He *surely* hadn't expected to find himself waltzing with his wife. Who would've imagined such a scenario? The preacher made some good points. Maybe he should've talked to one in the past instead of volunteering to help his pa and leaving. If he'd done that, he wouldn't have to work so hard to regain Cat's trust.

"Do you have something you want to discuss?"

"About what he said?"

Cat nodded.

"Not yet. I'm still chewing on it. Can we talk after a while?"

"Sure."

The familiar rhythm of creaking leather and plodding hooves kept them company as they moseyed up the next hill.

Cat thumbed her hat back. "Have you figured out a plan for this coming week? Do you know how we're going to handle the vengeance seekers?"

"Vengeance seekers? Is that what you're calling them?" Sam shrugged. "I guess it fits. They all want me dead."

"Do you have to put it so bluntly?"

"It's the truth." He straightened in the saddle. "Hey, you helped out at Gable's Gorge. You reckon you could help again?"

Cat's brows rose. "Me? I thought you didn't want my help."

"Since I'm staying, I figured I'd take you up on your offer."

"What would you want me to do?"

"I know you're good with that rifle. If I put you in a high post in town, out of harm's way, you reckon you could help keep me from getting killed?"

"It sounds like you've already got a plan."

"I'm working on it. It'd help if I knew how many men we're going to be up against, but we have no way of knowing when these men will get here and whether or not they'll be bringing anyone with them. If we're lucky, all three men will come in on the Tuesday stage."

"How do you figure that? Wouldn't it be *better* to split them up? You know, divide and conquer?"

"Not the way I figure it."

"How's that?"

Leather creaked as Sam returned his foot to the stirrup. "If we can have them together, we can finish this all at once."

"Okay, I can understand that, but how do you plan on doing it?"

"The way I see it, we'll have at least three, maybe even six or more, with loaded weapons coming in on that stage. I'll meet the stage and tell them we don't allow guns in our town."

"But that's not true."

"It will be for that day."

"What makes you think they won't shoot you the second they lay eyes on you?"

"I'll just have to take that risk." Sam glanced over at his wife. "And that's where you and the others come in."

"Others?"

"I figure to ask the blacksmith and a few others to have their rifles ready. When they resist surrendering their guns or try to kill me, Pa and the others can move in and arrest them."

"So what do I do?"

"You reckon the stage office man would let you use his upstairs as a perch?"

"Mr. Palmer? Probably, but, Sam, wouldn't it be better to take the fight out of town? Have them send the men to you?"

"Where would you suggest?"

"I don't know. Our ranch?"

"I don't want Benin anywhere near this if I can help it."

"No, I don't either." Cat settled her hands on the pommel as they ascended the next hill. "What about Gable's Gorge? That place worked for our last shootout."

"How're you going to lure that many men past all those rocks?"

"Good point."

"Wherever we do this, we have to have extra guns ready at a moment's notice. The best I can tell, that means the town or the ranch. I know no one would say anything about me defending my property, but that still leaves Benin and Roscoe."

"We could send the kids to my sister's."

"Didn't you say she's pregnant?"

"Yeah...and they don't have much as it is." She scratched the back of her neck. "Sam, what if they don't come in all at once? What if they don't even use the stage?"

"Then we'll have to get Pa to send someone to warn us when anyone asking for me arrives."

"You do realize they could ask for directions in the next town over and never step foot in Cater Springs. Many people know how to get to the Bar M. I've sold horses to lots of people."

"I know that's a possibility. I don't like this any more than you do."

Cat heaved a sigh. "I guess that means we'll keep our guns handy in the meantime and plan to meet the stage on Tuesday."

"And go to church tomorrow so I'm prepared to meet my Maker should something go awry."

She slapped at his arm. "Don't say that."

"You'd rather I not be ready?"

"That's not what I meant, and you know it."

Sam reined his horse closer and caught her hand. "It's going to be okay, darlin'. I've gotten out of bigger scraps than this before."

"Truly?"

"Yeah. In fact, there was this one time—"

"No. Don't. I don't think I can take hearing much more today. Just remember you promised me you wouldn't get killed."

"I told you I'd do my best not to, and I will. You've nothing to worry about."

The furrows on Catherine's brow touted that he hadn't convinced her, and honestly, he hadn't entirely convinced himself. He could name more than a dozen things that could go wrong.

※

"There's nothing to worry about, big fella. I don't mean you any harm. We're just going to get you a bit of exercise so I can clean out your stall. That's it." Sam finally hooked a lead on Thunder's halter. The black stallion reared, but Sam held on.

"Whoa, whoa, easy now. I'm not going to hurt you none. That's it. Easy does it." Sam backed from the stall. "Glad to see you're coming to life on us. Do you act this way for Mo and Curly?"

"No, he don't let us get that close. He nearly bit me. Twice." Curly hooked his thumbs in his pockets. "How'd you get him to let you do that?"

Thunder shook his head and strained against the lead rope.

"Easy, boy. Curly's not going to hurt you none. He's just going to help open the barn door and the gate to the side corral."

"I am? Oh, right, I am." Footsteps receded, and then the creak of metal and wood announced the hand's exit.

Thunder's eyes widened, and he tried to rear again.

"Easy, big guy. That's nothing to get bent out of shape over. Just a little squeaky wood. You've heard that plenty of times. Come on. Let's go find you some sunshine, huh?" Sam crept backward, keeping his tone light and soft as he led the beautiful black from the barn. A few more steps and he released Thunder into the corral.

Curly hastened to close the gate. Once it latched, the young man leaned on the top railing and watched the stallion investigate the water trough. "I still can't believe it. How did you do that? Mrs. Cathy's the only one Thunder lets get anywhere near him. I figured that was just because she's a woman."

"Probably is."

"How come you can get close to him then?"

"It's a gift, I reckon. I've always been able to understand horses better than people."

"Yeah, especially women."

Sam shifted to face the curly-haired wrangler. "I thought I was the only one with woman trouble."

"They're a plague to us all."

Sam chuckled and withdrew a sugar cube from his pocket. "You catch more flies with honey than vinegar."

"Who wants to catch them? I'm trying to get them to leave me be. They think just because I'm male and breathing I want to be hitched. Although, all the free food ain't too shabby."

"I used to have the same problem." Sam draped his hand over the fence and noted from the corner of his eye Thunder's head came up.

"Really? How'd you fix it?"

"I got married."

"No, thank you."

"It's not so bad."

"So you say, but I ain't deaf, Boss. I've heard you and the missus lock horns on more than one occasion, and you ain't been back a week."

"You make that sound like a bad thing, but that's part of the fun." Sam grinned, considering how their fight had ended earlier. He looked forward to revisiting that *discussion*.

"Okay, now you're just stringing me along."

"All right, well, not all the time. There are times when her snipping gets on my nerves, but really, consider how boring life would be if she always gave in right away. Naw, having a woman who speaks her mind makes life more interesting."

"Maybe, but there ain't any of those around here."

"I doubt you been looking either."

"Not exactly." Curly's eyes widened. "Boss, Thunder's coming closer."

"I know. I've been watching him. Just keep talking normal. Ignore him like you were doing."

"Uh, okay...um, I heard you and the missus arguing earlier. Was that because you're leaving?"

"I changed my plans. I'm staying."

"She's upset you're staying?"

"No, the leaving idea was what got her all hot under the collar." Warm air blew onto Sam's fist. "I thought I could better protect her by leaving, but the more I think about it, the more I realize staying is the better option. It's like with this horse here. If I'm not around, how can I help him?"

Sam inched open his hand without looking directly at the stallion. The black backed up a step, then clomped closer and stole the treat from Sam's palm. Sam turned when Thunder cantered away.

"Well, I'll be... You and Mrs. Cathy definitely are a pair."

"She's done well with him. Looks like he's been through a lot, by the number of scars I see healing."

"That she has. Thunder's finally starting to get some shine back to his coat. It was mighty dull when she brought him to the Bar M." Curly leaned his back against the gate and propped his elbows on the rung behind him. "You know, Mrs. Cathy has more patience and heart than anyone I ever met. I reckon that's why she's so good with the horses. They seem to sense it somehow. Thunder ain't the first one she saved. I've watched her restore more than one horse back to fine form. She'll spend endless hours working with them, and she doesn't even seem to get tired doing it."

The word *restore* snagged Sam's attention as Curly prattled on about two other horses Cat had rescued. Sam's gaze gravitated to the house. Had his wife been practicing with horses in hopes of doing the same restorative work on their marriage? Bringing something, anything, from near dead back to perfect health truly did take hours and hours of work plus loads and loads of patience. Was he being patient and understanding enough with Cat? Was Pa right? Was he expecting her to forget the past five years in less than five days?

Those heated moments before his father barged in strolled across Sam's mind along with every other kiss and advance he'd made toward his wife since coming home. Perhaps he was being too pushy, and that's why she balked. Or fought him. Sam folded his arms on the fence railing and studied the black as he greeted the geldings in the adjoining corral. The stallion acted skittish with people because of how he'd been treated in the past. He didn't want to be hurt again, and who could blame him, with the number of scars lining his hide?

Sam peered over his shoulder at the house. Had he taught Cat to be defensive with him? Was she afraid of him? She'd admitted as much the first day he'd come home, but when she'd shared about the general, he'd reckoned that was the source of it all.

His heart squeezed. Her fear was the last thing he wanted. Gracious, he treated his horse, Sandy, better than he treated Cat. He took Sandy everywhere with him, protected her, made sure she was fed, brushed, and cared for, and his mare trusted him completely. Cat deserved better treatment than his horse, and clearly he hadn't been doing such a good job at that.

He never wanted to pressure her into anything, but it seemed Pa was right. That's exactly what he'd been doing of late, ever since she'd kissed him on the canyon rim. The preacher was right too. Maybe Sam had been taking when he ought to be giving. Well, from here on out, Cat would lead where their intimacy was concerned. She would get all the time she needed to trust him, and hopefully, by the time he finished convincing her he was trustworthy, she'd be the one coming to him.

A chiming rang from behind them.

"Sounds like grub's on the table. I'll muck out that stall real quick while you've got Thunder out here, and meet you inside."

"Save it till after we eat."

"Thanks, Boss, but I better not if I'm going to get cleaned up for church tomorrow before I hit the sack tonight. Tell Mrs. Cathy I'll hurry." Curly jogged into the barn.

Cleaned up, huh? That's right. It was Saturday. Sam caught a glimpse of Cat as she disappeared inside the kitchen, Benin on her heels. He scratched his chin, an idea forming in his mind.

26

Catherine picked at her food, her mind replaying her morning with Sam yet again, the review culminating to the time spent dancing in his arms. She'd learned so much today her brain couldn't take it all in, and what she'd learned about herself had her stomach so twisted in knots it'd take a month of Sundays to straighten them out.

She chewed slowly, wishing not for the first time that her mother still lived and could offer another perspective. Catherine didn't remember much about her mom, but she'd always had the knack for making anything wrong better. Catherine sank against the back of her chair. She could do with some better right about now. She was so tired she didn't have the emotional energy to handle thinking for herself.

"Miz Cathy, you feelin' al'right? You look a bit peaked."

"Huh? Oh, I'm fine, Ida. Just have a lot on my mind." Catherine tried not to look at Sam as she made that last comment, but failed. His wink added another kink to the already twisted mess of her insides.

If he would just quit smiling at her, maybe she could think straight. He hadn't stopped since they'd gotten home. Not only that, but he'd gone out of his way to be nice to her, taken over her chores, pulled out her chair, filled her plate. She didn't know how to handle it anymore. Was he acting that way because he wanted to or because he wanted something? His reminder that they'd revisit their *discussion* hadn't gone forgotten. How could it with that twinkle in his eye?

What would their evening together hold? Would he understand if she admitted to him how she really felt? Would he even give her the chance to speak, or would he demand his way like he had earlier today? She hadn't seen him that upset in ages. If ever. Catherine pushed a chunk of stewed squash around on her plate, then forced herself to eat it. If she said the wrong thing, would she be driving Sam away again?

His kisses and that dance said she'd done the exact opposite, but why did she and Sam clash so? Was there something wrong with her? Was she too bossy, like he'd implied? The Bible taught that a wife should submit to her husband. Reverend Becker had emphasized that point, even added they needed to communicate clearly, but how did that work when every time she opened her mouth she seemed to mess something up?

Sam caught Cat's hand when she moved to follow the others out the door. "Mrs. Ida, me and Cat will do the dishes this evening."

"We will?"

Sam winked at Ida and slanted his eyes at his wife.

The cook's dour expression evaporated. "That's mighty thoughtful of ya, Mista Sam. Thank ya, sir. I'll handle your boy's Saturday night scrubbin' over at my cabin for ya, Miz Cathy."

"I, um, okay. Thank you, Ida."

Sam captured Cat's other hand once they were alone. He rubbed his thumb along the inside of her wrist and felt her heightened pulse. She was a bundle of nerves that evening. No doubt because of him. "Cat, I need to tell you something, and I hope you'll understand."

A muscle in her throat bobbed. "I'll do my best."

He drew a deep breath and repeated the words he'd rehearsed during supper. "See, here's how it is. I realized today I haven't been very fair to you. I've been trying to force things to happen, to force you to accept me and trust me, instead of giving you the time to come to those conclusions yourself. For that, darlin', I am well and truly sorry. You deserve all the time you need, and from here on out, I'm going to do my best to see that you get it."

"Thank you." The pulse under his thumb slowed, and Cat wet her lips. "Sam, I..."

"Yes?"

She pulled her hands away and picked at a fingernail.

"Cat, whatever you have to say, just tell me."

"Promise you won't get upset?"

He nodded.

She squared her shoulders and drew in a deep breath. "I'm not sure I'm ready for us to share a bed again." The words came out in a rush and were coated with desperation.

Sam reclaimed her hand. Her pulse was racing. He'd have to tread lightly here. Her actions earlier had told him the exact opposite. Maybe she truly didn't know what she wanted, but like when working with a frightened horse, he wasn't going to make any big moves and frighten her more. "Can you tell me why?"

Cat rose and started stacking plates. Wondering if she was gathering her thoughts or simply trying to avoid answering, he joined her in carrying the dishes to the dry sink. Silence settled over the kitchen except for the clank of dishes. Cat shaved soap into the washbasin and filled it with hot water from the stove's reservoir.

With a nearby towel, Sam started drying the clean plates she handed him. "Cat, you don't have to tell me if you don't want to, but I really would like to know what you're thinking."

Pressing her lips together, Cat plunged her dishrag into the water and started scrubbing. And scrubbing. If she kept at it, she'd scrub the design right off the plate. Maybe he should've shared his other idea first, but he'd wanted to give her a chance to speak her mind. Clear communication, that's what the pastor had recommended. They worked through half a dozen more dishes before her movements slowed and a sigh seeped out of her.

"I'm conflicted, Sam. Part of me is afraid history will repeat itself. Then again, part of me doesn't want to be filled with regrets, if—heaven forbid—something goes wrong next week."

"What do you mean 'history will repeat itself'?"

"That...I'll be stuck pregnant and alone again."

Sam caught her hand before she reached for another cup and turned her to him. "I know I've already said this, and I know you might not believe me, but I'm not going anywhere."

"You say that now, but what if you do or you're...shot?"

"I don't want to spend my life on *what ifs*. No one knows what a day will bring. Only God."

She nodded, her gaze hovering somewhere around the buttons on his shirt.

Sam held her loosely and waited for her to look up. "Darlin', nothing has to happen right now. I meant it when I said I'm not going to pressure you. I'll even sleep in the barn if that's what you want."

"With the cat?"

He gulped. That feral fur ball had completely slipped his mind, but his wife needed to understand the lengths to which he'd go for her. "Yes, even with that feline."

"Truly? You'd do that for me?"

Sam cupped her cheek. "I just faced down a gang of outlaws for you, darlin'. A flea-infested menace can't be much worse."

A corner of her mouth curled upward. "You're not mad that I need more time?"

"Nope. Not in the least."

Cat fiddled with his collar. "Sam?"

"Hmm?"

"Could you abide by simply holding me for now if we shared a bed, or would that be too hard for you?"

"It would be a privilege. I'm fine with whatever you're ready to give. In fact..." He untied her apron strings and lifted the cloth over her head. "I have something to give you this evening."

Her brows rose in question.

"You, my dear wife, get to clean up for tomorrow while I finish the dishes."

"You? Finish the dishes?"

"I'll even claim Benin and knock on the door before I come in, so you can have a good soak."

Cat gaped at him.

"Where do y'all keep the tub, by the way? I'm assuming Ida doesn't have the only one around here."

She pointed at a curtained-off section in the back corner of the kitchen. "Y-you mean it?"

"Why're you still standing here? Shouldn't you be getting your things?"

"I... Thank you." She bounced up on tiptoe and pecked him on the cheek, then scurried outside.

Sam chuckled, his heart lighter. Cat's smile was worth every ounce of sacrifice.

Catherine yanked the curtain closed around the steaming tub. "Aren't you about through with those dishes?"

"Only a few left. I promise I won't peek."

"Quit smiling."

Sam chuckled. "Who said I was smiling?"

"I know you, Sam McGarrett."

"Oh, enjoy your bath, woman. I'll be out of here in a few minutes."

Catherine toyed with the belt on her dress and decided to take him at his word. Seconds later, she sank into the lemon-scented water with a sigh. The soft clank of dishes and Sam's humming carried to her while the heat soothed her tired muscles. She loved Benin to death, but oh, she could sure get used to this. She couldn't remember the last time she hadn't needed to jump in and out of the tub in the same breath, and normally the water remained lukewarm at best after Benin's scrubbing. Hot water and near silence was like heaven on earth. Even Sam's presence on the other side of the curtain couldn't spoil the moment. If he was trying to worm his way into her good graces, well...it was working.

"I'm headed to check on Benin. You going to leave me any hot water?"

"Doubt it."

Sam chortled. Footsteps grew fainter, and then the door creaked open and closed.

Alone at last.

Catherine leaned her head back against the smooth edge of the copper rim and closed her eyes. She'd worry about scrubbing and climbing from the tub in a little bit. For the time being, she'd enjoy herself. Who knew when she'd get to do this again?

<hr />

"Cat, darlin', you okay?"

Catherine yanked upright with a splash. Sam's shadow loomed on the other side of the curtain. The water was tepid. Had she fallen asleep?

"Catherine, you better answer me, or I'm coming around that curtain."

"I...I'm fine. What time is it?"

"Well past dark. I've already put Benin to bed and had my own bath in the creek."

Yes, she'd definitely fallen asleep. "Creek? Wasn't that cold?"

"Very. You coming out soon?"

"I, uh, need a bit longer." She hunted frantically for the soap. "Oh, where is it?"

"Where is what?"

She sloshed around in the tub, feeling the bottom. Nothing. The floor got her perusal next. "I was sure I had it with me."

"Sure you had what? Cat, what's going on? Do I need to come back there?"

"No! Don't you dare come around that curtain." She stared at the wall, trying to imagine the last place she'd seen the soap. What had she done with it? She'd grabbed her soap with her robe and gown. It must be with one of those. Catherine looked to the stool where she normally set her things. Where were they?

"Samuel Houston McGarrett, you better give me back my clothes."

"Your clothes? What are you talking about, woman? I haven't touched your clothes."

"Then why aren't they on the stool I always put them on?"

"I don't know. What'd you do with them?" Sam's shadow pivoted, then faded away.

"Where are you going?"

"You're not by any chance looking for a pale-pink robe, a

matching gown, and..." Something clattered to the floor. "A bar of soap? You fell asleep back there, didn't you?"

"So what if I did? Give me my things."

"But you told me I couldn't come back there."

"Just put them on the floor and slide them under the curtain."

"Oh, I couldn't do that. They might get wet."

"Samuel McGarrett!"

"Oh, I love it when she says my name."

"This is not funny."

"Then why am I laughing?"

Abrupt tears clogged her throat. "You said you wouldn't pressure me."

The chortles died a sudden death. "I'm not, darlin'. Really. Here."

Her clothes appeared under the curtain a fraction off the floor. She took them and set them on the nearby stool.

"You want some more hot water?"

"It doesn't matter." Catherine plucked up the bar of soap and started scrubbing.

Clanking metal and sloshing water resounded from opposite the curtain. Footsteps neared, then a filled pot slid her direction.

"I'm sorry I teased you."

"Forget it."

"Aww, now don't be like that, darlin'."

Catherine swiped at the stupid tears and finished scrubbing her hair, then used the fresh water to rinse it. His teasing shouldn't have bothered her, but it did. Maybe the stresses from the past few days where finally catching up with her, maybe she was being overly sensitive, but all she wanted to do was bury her head in her pillow and sob.

"Cat?"

"I'm busy."

Quiet reigned in the room except for the occasional splash of water. Catherine finished her bath and dressed in record time. She gathered her discarded clothes, moved the curtain, and headed for the door.

Sam blew out the lantern and hurried to her side. "I didn't mean to make you cry, darlin'. Really, I'm sorry."

"Forget it." She strode inside their cabin, not even waiting for Sam to open the door for her. The tight rein on her emotions was slipping. She yearned to be alone, but Sam followed her straight to the sanctuary of her room.

Catherine started to demand he leave, until she made the mistake of meeting his stormy gray eyes. Distress and worry had settled in the lines of his face, and making him feel bad only made her feel worse.

"I'm sorry. I don't mean to be so touchy. I just…" She dropped her things in a chair and sank onto the side of the bed.

"Wasn't in the mood to be picked on?"

She shook her head.

Sam perched on the mattress beside her. Longing to be held and let someone else be strong for once, she leaned into him.

He obliged, his warm arms encircling her. "I am sorry."

"I know." A tear slid from her eye and dripped off her nose. "There's just been so much happening so fast. This is the first time I've really stopped."

"I know." He rubbed her back, then reached over and tugged the covers. "Come on. Get some sleep. Things'll look better in the morning."

Catherine laid her head on the pillow, and Sam slid the blanket up to her chin.

"I haven't been tucked in in years."

He kissed her brow and brushed the damp tendrils from her forehead. "You deserve to be taken care of for a change."

More tears flowed.

Sam brushed them away before he stepped toward the door.

Her heart snagged. "You're not leaving, are you?"

"I'm just going to check the fire. I'll be right back."

She hadn't even considered the fire in the fireplace. Come to think of it, the bathwater still filled the tub. She'd never acted so lazy. What must he think of her? Catherine reached for her robe, slipping it on as she left the room.

Sam pulled the grate in front of the fireplace and stood. "Where are you going?"

"I forgot to take care of the tub. I didn't even check the fire in the kitchen stove. I'll be right back."

Sam caught her by the shoulders and swiveled her toward the bedroom. "I checked the fire while you dressed. The water can wait till morning." He slid the robe from her shoulders. "There's nothing else that needs doing tonight."

"Are you sure?"

"I'm sure." He held back the covers and waited until she climbed in before re-tucking them around her. "Now get some sleep so I can too."

"Are you positive?"

"Absolutely. Sweet dreams, darlin'."

Catherine closed her eyes, making the last few tears seep out. Within moments, sleep claimed her.

Sam settled in beside his wife and waited for sleep to come, but it evaded him. Not very often did Cat let herself be taken care of. He'd caught her off guard tonight, and in doing so she'd done the same thing to him. He'd seen the chink in her armor, and it'd only served to remind him of how much he loved her.

The firelight from the living room gave off enough light he could make out her lovely profile in the darkness. How much had his Cat had to handle on her own through the years? When was the last time someone had seen to *her* needs? *God, why could I never see how much she needed me?* The pastor was right. Marriage required both giving and taking.

Sam smoothed Cat's damp hair from her face and let his fingers linger against her warm cheek. The sweet, tangy scent of lemons filled his nostrils. He'd always been partial to lemon drops, and somehow he'd found a woman who smelled sweeter than his favorite candy.

Father, help me do right by her this time. Help me survive the coming storm so I can be the husband I'm meant to be, the husband she needs me to be. I know this mess is mostly of my own making, but if You could see Your way to help us get out of this alive, I'd be mighty grateful. I want to be around to be a pa and a husband, but without Your help, I don't see that happening.

27

Catherine smoothed a pleat on her burgundy dress for the fifth time as she watched Sam scan every face that walked through the church house door. "Stop it. You're making me nervous."

He patted her hand. "Sorry."

"I heard some of the other ladies talking. Do you realize Thanksgiving Day is this Thursday?"

"I'll be plenty thankful if I'm still alive by then."

She frowned. "Don't you realize how many people will be coming into town to visit family? The streets will be filled with strangers."

"What do you reckon our chances are those gunmen will wait 'til after the holidays?"

"Sam, we've got to come up with another plan. There'll be too many people in town that day who might get hurt. They'll be meeting family, buying last-minute items for their turkey dinners. We can't let a showdown happen in the middle of that."

Sam rubbed his thigh. "You might be right."

"I know I am."

"I'll try to come up with something else."

"So will I."

He smiled and squeezed her hand. "I'm glad you're on my side."

Catherine opened her mouth to respond the same moment Reverend Becker's German-accented voice brought the service to order.

After the opening prayer, Sam leaned close to her ear.

When he didn't say anything, she looked up. "Yes?"

He cleared his throat and glanced away, but not before she saw the undeniable interest in his gaze. "With Pa's help, we'll try to settle on a different plan at dinner."

Catherine nodded, her gaze glued to the front of the church. She chose to ignore Sam's continued perusal of her, just like she had most of the morning. Part of her was flattered by his attention and longed for it. The other part was filled with fear and refused to let her enjoy it.

She lifted her voice in harmony with the others until his unnerving study got the best of her. "Can you see the words okay?"

"Oh. Yeah, here let me hold that for you." His fingers brushed hers, sending a streak of fire up her arm.

Shaking away the sensation, she focused on the singing, determined not to let his presence make her miss a moment of the service. Her heart cried for a word from God, something to stem the fear that ate at her. She'd thought the fearfulness would end once the general sat in jail, but it hadn't. The fear had simply spilled into other areas, tainting everything. It was getting on her nerves.

When the singing finished, Catherine took the hymnal, put it away, and sat. Benin left his seat beside Roscoe and climbed onto Sam's lap. He hitched the boy higher on his leg and reached for her hand. To all those around her, they seemed like a normal, healthy family, but they still had a ways to go to get there.

"'There is no fear in love.'"

Catherine stiffened at the preacher's words.

"'But perfect love casteth out fear: because fear hath torment.'"

She knew torment. She'd spent the last three years under the fear and torment of those bandits Sam had in jail, not to mention the torment of not knowing when, or if, her husband would return home.

"'He that feareth is not made perfect in love.'" The preacher moved away from the podium and stared out at the congregation. "Friends, those verses from I John 4 I have read many times, but God showed me something new about them this veek. That is vhy I am sharing them vith you instead of thoughts on thankfulness, as you vould expect at this time of year."

Catherine got the odd feeling this message was for her.

"Ve all know from II Timothy that 'God hath not given us the spirit of fear; but of power, and of love, and of a sound mind,' but look vith me in Matthew 18 at the parable Jesus told of a king who demanded payment of a debt from a servant who owed him a vast sum of money. The servant pleads for mercy, and the good king pardons his debt. However, the servant vas later found demanding a smaller debt from another and showing no mercy to his fellow vorker. Vhen the king heard of the servant's actions, read vith me vhat he did in verses 34 and 35..."

Reverend Becker returned to the podium. "'And his lord vas wroth, and delivered him to the tormentors, till he should pay all that vas due unto him. So likevise shall my heavenly Father do also unto you, if ye from your hearts forgive not every one his brother their trespasses.'"

Unexplainable tears pricked Catherine's eyes.

Reverend Becker shut the Bible. "Friends, have you opened yourself to being tormented by holding unforgiveness in your heart against your fellow man? Remember, I John says fear hath torment, but perfect love drives out fear. Love and mercy are the answer. Ask God to give you that spirit of love that can rid your heart of the spirit of fear."

A tear dripped onto the pages of her Bible. *God, I thought I'd forgiven Sam completely, but the fear in my heart testifies against me. I don't want to be tormented anymore. Help me to love him like You do and forgive him completely from my heart.* She tugged the handkerchief from her sleeve and dried her face. *God, I choose to forgive him. I want Your mercy. Help me to show him the same mercy I want from You.*

Sam settled his arm around her shoulders and dipped his head. "You okay?"

She mopped her face some more. "I'm sorry."

"You've got nothin' to be sorry for."

"Yes, yes I do. I've been holding your past against you, not forgiving you completely like I should have." She sniffled. "Please forgive me."

He pressed a kiss to her forehead. "Forgiven and forgotten."

Catherine turned into him and cried silent tears while the service continued around them. When the others stood to sing the closing hymn, she struggled to compose herself. Her nose and eyes had to be red and puffy. She'd cried more in the past two days than she had in the last two years, but the peace that settled on her soul was worth every ounce of salty water.

"Better?"

Catherine nodded.

Sam stood, shifting the dozing Benin into his arms, and offered her his hand up. She clung to it as they made their way from the small clapboard building.

He paused outside the church. "I'll get the wagon ready. Pa, you still joining us for dinner?"

That was right. They still had to come up with a new plan of offense.

GW closed their small circle. "You sure y'all got enough?"

"Always enough for you." Sam hitched Benin higher in his arms. "Besides, we've got some more things to discuss."

"I'll be there like stink on a fly."

Catherine groaned. "Please don't teach that one to my son."

GW grinned. "Too late."

"Wonderful."

Sam chuckled. "Come on. Let's get home. We've got a busy week ahead of us."

―――――

Catherine blinked at her husband, who sat at the head of the table full of adults. "Are you daft? Not do anything? What happened to the busy week you said we'd have? I thought that meant you had a plan."

"The plan is to leave it in God's hands."

"That doesn't mean we can't be prepared."

"I'm not saying that we shouldn't have our rifles ready and be prepared for the worst." Sam took hold of her forearms where they rested on the table, and his steady gaze insisted she listen carefully. "I want many years to come with my family. God knows that's my desire. I'm trusting Him to see that it happens."

His words warmed her heart and terrified her at the same time. Not plan? Surely there had to be some way to make these no-accounts not shoot her husband. "So the plan for meeting the stage Tuesday is out?"

"Hey, why don't we stop the stage before it gets to town?"

GW leaned back in his chair. "Curly, we *do* want people to visit our town again."

"It was just a thought." The wrangler sank further into his chair, then suddenly straightened. "What if someone goes and keeps watch at the last stage stop before Cater Springs?"

"It's not a bad idea, but I'm the only one who has any idea what these men look like." Sam flicked at a breadcrumb on the table in front of him. "Who knows whether they'll actually be taking the stage anyway?"

Catherine rubbed her forehead. She'd wanted a husband who would lean on God and put Him first, but she'd had no idea how hard it would be to trust his judgment when put to the test. Mercy, forgiveness, trust. Enjoy the moments God gave them together and not worry about the rest. She took a deep breath and interlaced her fingers. "All right."

All eyes swung to her.

Sam's large hand settled on top of her folded ones. "You're with me on this?"

"I'm trusting you. Don't make me regret it."

"You're trusting God."

Catherine nodded. Indeed she was.

"All right, everyone. You heard the little woman. Keep your rifles clean and loaded—"

"And nearby."

"And nearby." Sam smiled at her. "Pa, if anyone comes into town asking about me, we need to get me a warning before they're sent my way."

"It'd be best if I could just bring them out myself."

Sam scratched his chin much the way GW often did. "That would be best, but we'd have to get people to notify you somehow. Let's see—who would people ask first?"

"How about Schreiner?" Catherine offered.

"Probably Palmer at the stage office too. Actually, he might already have an inkling of what's goin' on since he's the telegraph operator." GW stopped stirring his coffee. "Did you check to see if the telegrams actually got sent?"

Catherine straightened. There was a chance there might not be anyone coming after all?

Sam nodded. "They were sent. Joe wrung the information out of Ham, then verified it with Palmer."

Catherine wilted in her chair and shared a concerned glance with Ida. Would that this trouble were already over. Waiting was nigh unto torture. Then again, normally that was only true when she got impatient. Like now. A sigh seeped from her. *God, get me through this.*

"Did I tell you that we also got the general fella to admit his real name?"

Catherine's gaze swung to her father-in-law. "Really? What is it?"

GW chuckled. "Nimrod Nelson."

Sam's shoulders bounced with silent laughter. "No wonder he preferred to go by the title general. I don't care if it is in the Bible. I'd've found me a different name too."

"Me too." Curly hid a smile behind his hand.

All seriousness, Mo folded his arms on the table. "Did he e'er go fightin' in the war at all, Sheriff?"

"If he did, he weren't no general. Nobody would've forgotten that name." GW sobered. "But that is a true Confederate general's hat he wears. Makes me wonder how he came by it."

Smiles melted off of faces as everyone contemplated the sheriff's words. With as much evil as Catherine had seen Nimrod Nelson do, she hated to wonder at the fate of the man who'd previously owned the hat.

Curly propped his chin on his fist. "Don't most go to the mercantile for information?"

Catherine straightened and stared at the wrangler as he swung them back to the previous topic. "That's right, Sam. They do. Brother and Sister Koch should be warned too."

She could just imagine that old couple facing armed gunmen. Someone would have to wipe them up off the floor.

"Why don't we call a whole town meeting while we're at it?" Sam threw up his hands.

GW tapped his spoon on the rim of his cup. "Ya know, that ain't such a bad idea."

Catherine knew that glint. They'd be having a town meeting before the day was out.

28

Sam paced at the front of the church while people filed in. He stopped in front of his pa. "I can't believe I let you talk me into this. What if someone tries to play the hero and gets hurt because of this? It'll all be on my head."

"Settle down and quit your pacin'. Knowledge is power."

"That's exactly my point. Some of these people probably don't even like me."

"Give them a chance. The more who know, the better prepared we'll be. Now sit down."

Sam plopped onto the front pew beside his wife. "I hope I don't live to regret this."

"I hope you do."

He met her worried gaze. "That's not what I meant. I don't plan on dying."

She patted his arm. "I know. Remember, you're the one who said we're trusting God in this."

With a sigh, Sam raked his hands through his hair. "You're right. Trust." He twined his fingers with hers. "Keep reminding me of that."

Cat smiled and squeezed his hand. The peace that radiated from her was nearly palpable.

"You're different this afternoon."

"God can do that in a person." She tugged him closer and whispered in his ear. "I'm sure you'll see the difference later tonight too."

Her beguiling grin struck a spark in him. "Oh?"

"Did I mention that Benin is staying with Roscoe tonight?"

"All night?"

"Mmmhmm."

The spark ignited to a flame. How on earth was he supposed to concentrate on anything but her now? "You, Mrs. McGarrett, are a cruel woman. You just had to tell me this now?"

Cat giggled. *Giggled.* "Worried about the emergency meeting anymore?"

"Forget the meeting. Can we sneak out the back?"

She laughed, clamping her hand over her mouth to cover the outburst.

Pa stepped to the podium. "Friends, friends, I know you're wonderin' why I called this emergency meetin'. Most of you have heard about the trouble at Gable's Gorge the past few days and about the men now sittin' in our jail." Pa set down the gavel and stepped into the aisle between the pews. "My son, Sam, helped bring that to an end, but not before they stirred up a hornet's nest of trouble for him."

A murmur wove through the crowd.

"Hold it down. Let me finish."

The murmuring waned.

"During my son's absence, he brought many outlaws to justice. Many of whom have a vendetta against him. This gang got a hold of some of these names and sent off wires to three men, who will most likely be coming to our town armed and ready to kill anyone who gets in their way."

Questions on top of questions rang out from the townspeople until their voices formed a quiet roar. The burn of many glares seared the back of Sam's head. He'd known this was a bad idea. Why hadn't they listened to him? Pa went to the podium and banged the gavel for order, but the shouts continued.

Cat sobered, then without warning moved from her seat into the middle aisle. She crossed her arms and waited until one by one the people sank into their pews. "GW, do you mind?"

"Go ahead, sweetheart."

Cat stared down the crowd. "I'm ashamed of you folks. My family has never asked anything of you before. Not when my sister and I were orphaned. Not when our home was taken from us and we had to move in with our aunt. Not when she was taken by the influenza. Not ever. You've offered your hand in friendship and stood beside me through hard times."

Cat spared Sam a glance. "That's all I'm asking of you now. Men are coming, determined to tear apart my family now that it's finally whole again. We're not asking you to take up arms against anyone. We're not asking you to fight our battle for us. All we're asking is that you warn us should someone start asking for our whereabouts."

"You have our help and our guns."

Sam turned at Joe Matthews's voice.

One by one other townspeople stood and added their support.

Sam looked in shock at Cat, who blinked back tears. He felt like doing the same. These people weren't doing this for him. They were doing it for his wife. She'd earned their respect all on her own. And if possible, she'd earned more of his.

"Thank you." Cat nodded to the crowd, then moved to her seat beside him.

He wrapped his arm around her and felt her shaking under his touch. "You're amazing, you know that?"

She offered him a weak smile and leaned her head against his shoulder for a second.

"Sheriff, tell us more about these men who're coming."

"Son?"

Sam gave Cat a squeeze and moved to the spot she'd vacated. "I'd like to add my thanks for your help. Like my wife said, all we're asking for is a warning. We know it's the holidays and you have your own families to see to."

He took a steadying breath and hooked his thumbs in his pockets. "There were three men that were sent wires late Thursday evening: Angus McGovern, Dakota James, and Emilio Ramirez. They all had a son, brother, or cousin that I wasn't able to bring in alive. I wish I could tell you that I had." Sam had all he could do to continue to look the townsfolk in the eye.

"Ve understand, Bruder McGarrett. Tell us vat they look like so ve can help."

Sam blinked at the preacher and cleared his throat. "Right. Well, you won't be able to miss McGovern. He's Irish and has the bright-red hair and brogue to go along with it. Emilio Ramirez is from Laredo. Spanish accent and skin tone to match. Dakota James won't be one to stand out in a crowd. He has dark hair, dark eyes, and no particular accent. The only thing that sets him apart is a scar on his neck, which he mostly keeps covered with a high collar." Sam rocked back on his heels. "Any more questions?"

A hand went up in the back from an elderly woman he didn't recognize.

"Yes?"

"How do we get a warning to you?"

"Tell the sheriff. Also, he's willing to hire on a few deputies for the next week or so until this is over, so if you're interested, see him when the meeting's over."

Nods met his response.

"Any more?"

Silence reigned.

"Well, if that's all, I want to again express our thanks for your help. May God richly bless you." Sam dipped his head, then stepped toward Cat.

"Vait." The preacher's voice brought everyone to a standstill. "Ve must pray for this family before ve dismiss."

Sam reached for his wife. She rose and joined him in the aisle while the townsfolk swarmed them. A tear slipped down her cheek when the others began to pray. He tugged her closer before joining in. This wasn't nearly the reaction he'd expected from these people. He didn't deserve this, but then nothing he could do would earn him the grace and compassion God chose to shower on him in spite of his many mistakes. All he could do was be grateful and live a life reflecting that gratitude.

Everyone echoed the preacher's amen and began to disperse. Some took the time to shake his and Cat's hands. A few stopped his pa to talk. Sam needed to know who the other deputies would be, and the sooner he got things taken care of here, the sooner he could get on with the rest of his evening.

Sam leaned near Cat's ear. "Let me speak with Pa for a minute, then we can go, all right?"

Once she nodded, he strode toward his father.

Pa clapped him on the shoulder when he neared. "Sam. Good. I was hoping you'd find your way over here. These three men have volunteered to be deputies for the time being."

Sam started to scan the group but paused on the first. His wife's nephew. "Amos? I thought you were one of Matthews's hands?"

"I checked with him. He's fine with it. Uncle Hap and I are going to trade off so nothing's left undone. Before you say anything more, I'm well over my majority. I don't need anyone else's permission. She's my family. I'm going to help see she's kept safe."

Sam's respect for the young man rose a notch. He extended his hand. "Welcome aboard."

He turned to the next man. Broad in build, brown wavy hair, and a brownish-red handlebar mustache.

"Sam, meet Hap Martin. Amos's uncle." Pa gripped Mr. Martin's shoulder, a broad grin on his face. "He just got into town the other day, but I've known him for years. If he smells like cattle, don't hold it against him."

The brawny cowboy chuckled.

"Pleasured, Mr. Martin."

"We're practically family. Call me Hap."

Sam nodded and accepted the firm handshake. The man wasn't at all like Cat's brother-in-law, except for maybe the shade of his hair.

"And this is Logan Ritter."

"That the same Ritters that own the boarding house?"

"My sister."

Sam nodded and shook the shorter man's hand, surprised at the strong grip from such an older fellow. "Thanks for the help."

"Mrs. McGarrett's been good to us. Just returning the favor."

Sam dipped his head in acknowledgement.

Pa folded his arms. "I've talked with the men, and they each have a horse and a gun available to them. You'll see at least one of us each day this week. We'll keep you informed of anything that's happening and bring you any supplies you may need. I reckon keepin' y'all home as much as possible will be best. Thataway no one can catch you unawares on the road or in town."

"Fair enough. Well, fellas, if you'll excuse me, I'd better be getting the missus home. I'll be seeing you." Sam shook their hands in parting, then hurried his wife toward the wagon, which sat parked beside a pair of large live oaks. When she gripped his hand to board, he dragged her around the trees instead.

"Sam!"

He silenced her with the kiss he'd been aching to give her for the past hour. When he finally came up for air, she'd melded to him like sap on a tree.

"Mmm. What was that for?"

"That was to tide me over till we get home."

The promise in her smile made him want to race the horses, but somehow he kept them to a reasonable pace. When he pulled to a stop outside the house, dusk coated the yard in grays. Sam disembarked. Cat moved to follow, and he swung her into his arms. Her squeal turned into laughter as he toted her into their home.

"Sam, the horses."

"What about them?"

"You can't leave them hitched all night."

"Who says?"

"Come on…"

"Fine." He deposited her in their bedroom doorway and pressed a kiss to her sweet lips. "Don't you go anywhere. I'll be right back."

"I'll be waiting."

29

Catherine lit a candle and slipped into a frilly nightgown while she waited on Sam to come from the barn. Fear tried to remind her of the risks she was taking, but she shoved it aside, determined to not hold Sam's past against him anymore and to enjoy every moment she was blessed with as his wife.

Seconds trickled by. Darkness deepened outside her window. Why hadn't Sam returned yet? It didn't take that long to put away a wagon. Had he changed his mind about coming back inside? She pulled aside the bedroom curtain and peered toward the barn. The door stood wide open, but no lantern burned inside.

Something wasn't right.

Her stomach twisted into a knot. Catherine snatched up her robe and threw it on while she strode to the living room. After removing the rifle from above the doorframe, she checked the load and hurried outside.

Scuffling and grunts met her ears. A horse whinnied.

She pointed the barrel into the air and squeezed the trigger, then leveled the weapon on the shadows within the barn. "That's enough."

The scuffling stopped.

A sickening thud echoed.

"Sam?"

"I'm all right."

Air inundated her lungs.

Seconds later, a scratch birthed a flickering light. Sam touched the match to a lantern and gripped his knees.

"Honey, what happened?" Catherine hurried forward, keeping the gun aimed at the unconscious redhead on the ground. "When you didn't come back, I got worried."

"McGovern. He got the drop on me. I'm glad you showed up when you did."

"Miz Cathy, what's goin' on? Who's shootin'?"

"I did, Mo. One of those men showed up early."

"Y'all al'right?"

"We're fine." Sam grabbed a rope and tied McGovern's wrists together. "Fetch Curly."

"Sho' thang, Boss." Mo disappeared from the barn entrance.

Sam stood and moved toward her. "You can lower the gun now, Cat."

"Looks like you're going to have quite the shiner." Catherine peeled his shirt collar back a fraction. Angry red marks marred his tanned skin. "Oh, honey."

"I'll be all right." He covered her hand with his own. "Here, let me take the rifle. Tie your robe before the men get back."

Her eyes widened at the thin fabric peeking out. She jerked the wrap closed as hurried footsteps neared the doorway.

Sam stepped between her and the door.

"What's going on? I heard the shot. I was halfway across the yard when Mo told me to go back and get my boots."

Catherine cinched the belt tight and touched Sam's elbow.

He peeked at her, then drew her against his side. "McGovern showed up quicker than any of us expected."

"Is he dead?"

"No. I need you and Mo to load him up and take him into town. Have the sheriff or whoever's on guard duty put him under lock and key."

"Sho' thang, Boss. Let's git some fresh hosses, Curly."

Mo and Curly strode past the wagon in the middle of the barn and out the back door toward the corral.

"Let's go check on Benin and let Ida know what's going on."

Catherine fell into step beside Sam. "Are you planning on going with them to town?"

"No, I think I'll let them handle this one. I might have to help load him up though. McGovern isn't no small sack of taters."

"No, he's not. Are you sure you're okay? You're shaking."

"I'll be fine. Nothing a little time won't heal."

"Maybe you should let me look at that eye. It's already swelling. Is your lip bleeding?"

Sam lifted a hand to his mouth. "Maybe a little. You can play doctor all you want once we're through checking on Ben."

He knocked on the door of the small cabin. It snapped open.

Ida took one look at Sam, stepped outside, and shut the door. "Boy, you look like you been run through the wringer."

"I feel like it. Are the boys awake?"

"Yessuh, but I told 'em the shot was probably just someone huntin'. What be goin' on out here?"

"McGovern surprised Sam in the barn and tried to kill him. I distracted him long enough with a shot to give Sam the upper hand."

"I've got Mo and Curly taking him into town. Will y'all be okay 'til they get back?"

"Y'all's only a shout away. We be fine. Lookin' like you could use some doctorin' though. Miz Cathy, the tincture of arnica is settin' in the medicine basket on the back shelf in the pantry."

"Thanks, Ida. We'll see you in the morning." Catherine grabbed Sam's hand and started towing him toward the kitchen before the cook closed the door.

"Hold it. I need to go see if they need help loading McGovern."

"Well, I'm not letting you out of my sight. We'll get the medicine, then I'll walk with you to the barn."

"Barn first. Doctoring second."

She heaved a sigh. "Fine."

In no time at all they had the dazed and semiconscious McGovern in the back of the wagon, the medicine in hand, and were sitting under the lamplight on their living room rug. Catherine dabbed at the bruises darkening on Sam's face while he held a cold rag to his split lip.

He pulled the rag away a fraction. "I'm sorry McGovern ruined our evening."

"Don't fret about it. I'm just glad you're all right."

"Maybe God's trying to tell us something."

Catherine's hand stilled. "What do you mean?"

Sam removed the rag and draped his arm on his bent knee. "Maybe it's best if we do wait until all this settles down. I wouldn't want to leave you pregnant and alone again."

She resumed her doctoring. "You're not going to die."

"We don't know that. Tonight just proved how unpredictable life can be. We didn't expect to see anyone until later this week."

"Take your shirt off so I can see what other damage has been done."

"You're not listening to me."

"Yes, I am. You didn't think we'd be seeing anyone until the stage arrived. Now let me get at those bruises on your neck."

"That's not what I said," Sam argued but did as instructed.

"That was the jest of it." As she dabbed at the finger-sized marks surrounding his throat, her doctoring slowed. "He nearly killed you, didn't he?"

Sam's jaw twitched, and he broke eye contact. "I'd nearly blacked out when that shot went off." He faced her. "You saved my life."

With a gentle hand, Catherine cupped his cheek. "I'm glad God sent me out there when He did." She dropped her fingers to her lap and set the rag aside. "Come on. Let's get you to bed. You need your rest."

"Wait." He caught her hand and cradled it between his own. "You deserve so much better than me, Cat. If...if something does happen, I want you to—"

"Stop. I won't listen to that kind of talk." She cupped his face. "We're going to get through this. Both of us."

"You don't—"

Catherine set her thumb over his lips. "We're *going* to get through this."

The corner of his mouth lifted a smidgen. "How did I ever make it this far without you?"

"I don't know, but if you ever try to lone-wolf it again, you'll be picking buckshot from your backside."

Sam chuckled, then grimaced and gripped his left side. "Oh, don't make me laugh."

"Did he break a rib?"

"No, I can breathe okay. I think it's just bruised a bit."

She stood. "Come on. To bed with you. You've had enough excitement for one day."

Sam grunted as he gained his feet. "Let's pray tomorrow isn't this exciting."

The kitchen door banged open.

Curly gripped the doorframe. "Miss Cathy, you might want to get out here. We tried to talk him out of it, but he just won't listen."

"What? Who won't listen?" Catherine wiped her hands on a dishrag even as she strode toward Curly.

"Mr. Sam."

"Dear Lord, have mercy on me. What now?" Tossing the rag aside, she ran out the door behind the curly-haired wrangler.

Curly angled toward the barn. Angry snorts and deep voices filled the air. Sam had nearly gotten killed last night. What on earth was he doing?

Catherine rounded the corner of the whitewashed building and ground to a halt. Her heart leapt to her throat and her mouth went dry at the sight of Sam trying to keep his seat on the black stallion she'd rescued. She bit her lip to keep from shouting at Sam and frightening Thunder more. The horse side-hopped, bucked, and twisted, the whites of his eyes clearly visible. If Sam lived through this, she was going to kill him.

"I tried to talk 'im out o' it, Miz Cathy, but he wouldn't listen."

Afraid to open her mouth for what might come out, Catherine acknowledged Mo's words with a nod and approached the corral fence. Maybe her presence would help calm the stallion.

Thunder reared, nearly falling over backward and finally succeeded in ridding himself of the parasite on his back. Sam hit the dirt with a sickening thud, but Thunder wasn't through. He turned, stomping up dust with his heavy hooves as he tried to trample Sam into the dirt.

Catherine's heart lurched. Snatching a rope from a nearby post, she hopped the fence. Sam scrambled backward while she formed a quick lariat and laid the rope around Thunder's neck. A second rope sailed from opposite her to do the same, pulling the stallion back as Sam bailed over the fence.

Dark hands settled on the rope in front of hers. "I got it, Miz Cathy. Go make sure he's al'right."

She was going to do a lot more than that. Catherine relinquished her hold to Mo, crawled through the fence, and marched toward Sam, who stood outside the corral beating pale dirt from his clothes with his black Stetson. Her eyes scanned the length of him. He seemed no worse for wear, except for the black eye from last night.

"Are you okay?"

"I'm fine. Just got the wind knocked out of me, is all."

"Good." Her pulse slowed a fraction. "Because there's something I want to ask you."

Sam straightened. "What's that?"

"Have you lost your ever-loving mind? What do you think you were doing in there? That man nearly killed you last night, and now you're trying to get killed by a horse today. Do you have a death wish or something?"

"I'm fine. Don't overreact."

"A horse trying to trample you is not fine. Who said you could get on Thunder anyway? How dare you endanger him like that without my permission?"

"Endanger him? What about me? That beast just tried to kill me."

"It would've served you right too. You had no right getting on Thunder without discussing it with me first. I bought him. He's mine. I've put months of effort into bringing him back to health, and you probably just injured him with your thoughtless actions."

Sam stepped closer, towering over her. She planted her fists on her hips, refusing to back down.

He spoke over her head. "Y'all can let him go now, fellas."

The others dispersed. They probably didn't want to witness a murder.

Without warning, Sam grabbed her hand and swung her into a waltz.

"This is no time for dancing." Catherine only moved to keep from being stepped on.

"No, I think you need the reminder." Sam one-two-three-ed her a few more steps until she was moving backward again.

Of course he wanted to remind her he was the boss, but that was *her* horse. Sam couldn't be the boss in this. She was the one who'd put all the time and effort to get Thunder this far. Sam was ruining everything, and she was supposed to sit back and be okay with it? Catherine wanted to growl and cry all at the same time.

"Let's get one thing straight. My actions were not thoughtless, and the last I checked, there was no yours and mine. There was only ours. I don't need *your permission* to work with *our* horse." Sam drew them to a stop. "But you're right. I should have talked to you first."

"Thank you."

Sam broke contact and angled toward the fence.

Catherine caught his arm. "What do you think you're doing? You're not getting back on that horse?"

"What if I am? Are you going to stop me?"

The helplessness squeezed at her throat, but she couldn't stop the words from coming out. "Did you not hear what I said? You can't rush the restorative process, and your actions probably set me back a whole month, maybe a whole year."

"I'm not rushing anything, Cat. He's ready."

"No, he's not. Besides, if anybody's going to ride him, it should be me."

"No." Sam's unyielding tone nailed her boots to the ground. "I won't have you getting hurt. That's part of the reason why I did this."

Part of the reason? What did—oh, so that was his trouble. Catherine laid her hand on his arm. "Sam, I've done this before."

"Not with a stallion, you haven't. Curly told me the other two you rescued were geldings."

"So?"

"So. You and I both know stallions can be temperamental, unpredictable."

Catherine folded her arms with a smirk. "Don't I know it. What has gotten into you today?"

Sam donned his hat. "Nothing."

"That's not true. You've been a bear all morning. Now what is it?"

Sam peered about. Thunder had settled down, and drank water from a trough on the opposite side of the corral.

"Cat, I've done a lot of thinking, and I think you, Ida, and the boys ought to go to your sister's or into town to stay with Pa."

"What?"

"And I want you to stay away from the barn and not go anywhere by yourself."

"The barn? Is this about last night?"

"Cat, if anyone's going to get hurt, I'd rather it be me, not you."

"Have you forgotten that if it wasn't for me, McGovern might've killed you last night?"

"No, I haven't forgotten, but that's exactly why you need to go. It's not safe for you here."

"It's not safe for you either, but you're staying. I'm not going anywhere, Sam McGarrett, so you can wipe that silly notion right out of your head."

"Ugh, it's my job to protect you, woman. Why won't you let me?" Sam's shoulders drooped.

Catherine settled her hands on his broad chest. She fiddled with his collar, her eyes falling on the angry bruises on his neck. "I understand last night rattled you, honey, but think about it from my perspective. If there was the possibility you were only going to get a few days with me or even a few hours, would you let me push you away? Wouldn't you want to spend every waking moment together?"

Sam sighed and settled his hands on her waist. His forehead touched hers. "What am I going to do with you?"

She smiled and tipped her face up to his. "Kiss me."

He happily obliged. "You know this isn't going to keep me off that horse."

"Sam…"

"He's ready, Cat. He let me put that saddle on him no problem."

"Well, he didn't let you ride him no problem."

Sam scratched his jaw. "No, he didn't, did he?"

"If anyone should ride him, it should be me. I think he's had his fill of men for a time."

"He's got to learn we're not all bad."

"No, you're not all bad. Some of you are even quite nice."

"Well, thank you."

"But that doesn't mean I'm letting you back on him right now."

"Cat—"

"Thunder's been around me more. If you think he's ready to be ridden, then let me do it. Trust me. Please."

"You're going to do it no matter what I say, aren't you?"

"You're a quick learner."

"And you've got more guts than good sense."

"I could say the same about you."

Sam chuckled. "You know, Curly's right."

"About what?"

"We are a pair. A pair of what, I'm not sure yet." Sam squeezed her waist. "All right, you can take a turn, but promise you'll be careful and you'll bail if he starts getting too wound up."

"You mean so I don't land in the dirt like you did?"

"Ha-ha, very funny. Seriously, Cat, I don't want to see you get hurt."

"I know, and I love you for it." Catherine went on tiptoe and pecked him on the lips. "Have that rope ready in case I need it."

"Yes, ma'am."

30

Sam gripped the lariat so tight his knuckles hurt. That horse had done his best to kill him, and here he stood letting his wife go alone into the corral with the maniac. Maybe those punches last night had knocked loose what good sense he had left. He shot a prayer heavenward for Cat's safety and perched on the top rail, ready to spring into action at a moment's notice.

Thunder skirted the fence away from Sam, his eyes darting to the woman standing in the middle of the corral. Cat stood silently, waiting, her quiet manner gradually calming them all. Sam rested his hands on his knees when the horse neared of his own accord. After a time of inspection, Thunder snuffled her hair.

Cat's smile lit up her whole face. With slow movements, she pivoted on her heel and rubbed the stallion's nose while she retrieved the reins that hung limp by his neck. "How you doing, big boy? You miss me?"

Thunder's snort blew free strands of her blonde hair across her face.

"Sam says you're ready to be ridden." Her hands stroked the horse's neck until she stood beside the stirrup.

Sam wasn't sure she could get her boot that high. The stallion had to stand at least sixteen hands. Her head barely reached his withers.

"I know you didn't much like him riding you, but you think you could give me a chance?"

The black bobbed his head, and Sam gripped the fence beneath him to keep from falling off. He'd yet to see Cat work with the horse. Maybe he'd been wrong. He hated to admit it, but maybe the horse did like her better than him.

Cat somehow managed to lift her boot to the stirrup, and a peek of denim brought a smirk to his lips. When had she snuck into those breeches? Well, she had awakened and dressed before him this morning. He'd have to remind her to let him see those denims again without the swarm of skirts hiding her long legs.

With a bounce, Cat popped up and swung her right leg over the saddle. Thunder never moved. Then again, the beast hadn't when he'd done the same. It wasn't until he'd nudged the stallion into action that the horse reacted. Sam held his breath as she bent her knees and settled her weight on the leather.

Thunder looked back at Cat. Was he going to bite her? No, he faced forward again when she rubbed his neck. Air seeped from Sam's lungs with a quiet swoosh.

"That's a good boy. Seems like Sam was right." Cat smiled, but her focus remained on the horse. "We've walked around this corral before. What's say we do it again today, but with me up here, huh? Sound like a plan?"

Cat clicked her tongue, and the black stepped forward.

Sam slouched, his chin falling toward his chest. *Well, I'll be...*

Why hadn't she told him she'd trained him with clicking? It made sense though, with all the scars on the stallion's flanks. She didn't want the animal to associate her with its former owner. Sam shook his head. And what had he done? Nudged him along those scars. Was he that out of practice, or was this just another example of Cat's amazing abilities? The old sensation of his insufficiencies swamped him. Did Cat need him at all?

The night when he'd tucked her in traipsed across his memory. She'd needed him then...

Cat clicked her tongue, and the black moved into a trot as they passed by him.

...but she surely didn't need him now.

Sam gave himself a mental shake. He might go to meet his Maker any day now. He should be glad Cat could do without him. She'd been doing without him the past five years. Why shouldn't she be able to handle a stallion without his help? He should be happy.

But he wasn't.

Sam's shoulders slumped, and with a sigh, he threw his leg over the fence.

A door slammed across the yard.

Thunder whinnied and reared. Cat gripped the reins in one hand and the saddle horn with the other, managing to keep her seat. She tried to calm him as before, but Thunder wasn't having any of it. He kicked up his heels, trying to catch the sun with his belly.

Sam watched in horror as Cat tumbled over the horse's ears and into the dirt.

"Cat!" He bolted from his perch, and with hardly a thought, his hand set the lariat to spinning in the air.

Thunder's hoof landed near her shoulder in his next frightened bound.

Oh, God, no!

"Cat, move."

She stayed still as death.

Sam threw the rope. The horse bobbed and weaved, dodging the lariat, but at least he veered away from Cat. Sam scooped up his wife and charged toward the fence. Thundering hooves neared from behind. Scaling the fence one handed, Sam vaulted to safety. His feet and knees stung with the impact as he hit the packed dirt with his wife in his arms.

Thunder whinnied and galloped the perimeter of the corral.

Sam peered at his wife to find her blinking up at him. *Oh, thank God.* He sank to the ground before his knees could finish buckling with relief, and wrapped his arms around her.

With a groan, she reached for her head. "What happened?"

"You got thrown. I knew I shouldn't have let you on that horse."

"No, what startled him? We were doing so good." She brushed the flyaway strands from her face but continued to lean into him, not that he planned on releasing her anytime soon.

"That'd be my fault, Miz Cathy."

"Roscoe?"

Sam peered up to see everybody on the ranch gathered around them. Benin's bottom lip was caught between his teeth, and he looked scared to death. Sam knew the feeling.

"I'm so sorry, ma'am. The wind stole the barn door from me, 'n' it slammed 'fore I could catch it."

"Well, that explains it." Cat shifted to sit up more.

Sam hurried to help when she grimaced.

"Mama, 're you all right?"

"Sure, baby. I just took a tumble. That's all. Nothing to worry about. It's not the first time. Probably won't be the last." Cat lowered her voice. "Sam, let me up."

"Are you sure?"

She cocked an eyebrow, so he moved to help her stand, his hands never releasing her.

"I really am sorry, Miz Cathy."

"I know, Roscoe. It was an accident. I'm fine. No harm. No foul. Y'all go on and go play quietly near the house while we put Thunder up, okay?"

Roscoe looked to his pa, who nodded. Sam expected them to scamper off immediately, but the lads came close and hugged Cat first.

Sam observed the barn doors as the boys wandered off. "First thing next week I'm going to look into making those doors slide instead of swinging open."

Cat paused in dusting her skirts. "I'd never considered that. You think we could?"

"I'm going to figure out some way to keep this from happening again. That should've never happened. Cat, why don't you go with the boys and take it easy? We'll handle putting Thunder away."

"No, if anything, I need to do this." Cat approached the fence he'd bailed over a short while ago.

Sam stayed on her heels. "Why? So you can get hurt again?"

"No, because he threw me. No horse is going to get the best of me. Not now. Not ever." She looked him up and down. "If anything, we should both be doing this."

The slight shake in her hand when she reached for the top rail said she wasn't *suggesting* he go with her back into that corral. No, she *wanted* him there. She just refused to let anyone see how shaken she was.

A faint smile tugged at his lips. He laid his hand atop hers and squeezed. "You're right. We'll do this together. Mo, Curly, y'all have those ropes ready, just in case. Mrs. Ida, will you open the back door to the barn on your way to the kitchen and make sure the other door is still shut?"

"Surely. Y'all be careful now, ya hear?"

"Yes, ma'am, we will. Curly, is Thunder's stall ready?"

"Sure is."

"All right." Sam gazed at Cat, who had a smear of dirt across her cheek. "You ready?"

Drawing a deep breath, she nodded. "Stay behind me, and let him come to us."

"I was fixing to say the same thing."

"Well, I said it first. Besides, I'm a woman. He likes me better."

"I like you better too."

A smile graced her lips, calming Sam considerably. She was going to be all right.

He leaned near her ear and whispered, "I won't let him hurt you."

Cat rotated her hand and squeezed his, then climbed the fence. Sam followed and stayed a step behind her until they stopped in the middle of the corral. When the big black slowly approached after a short time of perusal, Mo nodded at him, lariat ready.

Cat touched his arm. "Sam, I'm going to ride him into the barn."

"N—"

"He needs to know I'm still the boss."

Why did she have to make such good sense? "All right. I'll keep hold of his bridle."

"Thanks, honey."

When the black neared, Sam did as he'd said and waited for Cat to mount. They must've worn the fight out of Thunder—that, or he knew where they were taking him, because the stallion offered no trouble as they escorted him to his stall.

When the massive horse was safely put away, Curly collapsed against a barn support beam. "Boy, am I glad that's over. You two sure do know how to make life interesting."

"We sure do." Sam draped his arm around Cat's shoulders. "Y'all mind finishing things up in here while we go wash down the bucket of dust we swallowed in all that hullabaloo?"

"Don't mind at all, do we, Mo?"

"Not a lick. Y'all go on 'n' take it easy. Dinner oughta be ready here right quick like."

"Thanks, fellas."

Once they'd cleared the barn, Cat leaned her head against him.

He squeezed her shoulder. "You all right?"

"Fine, just a touch of a headache. How about you?"

"I'll be all right."

"Admit it. You ache from hitting that ground as much as I do."

"Maybe a bit." Sam grinned and angled them toward the water bucket sitting outside the kitchen door. He offered her the ladle first. When she'd finished, he slaked his thirst. He dropped the ladle back in the bucket. "I guess I'll head into town once lunch's over."

"What? Why?"

"I need to find out what's going on."

Cat shook her finger at his nose. "No, you don't. You said last night on the way home that GW told you to stay put."

"He also said he'd send someone out. We haven't seen hide nor hair of anybody."

"Pa, somebody's comin'."

Cat smirked in triumph.

With a frown, Sam started for the hitching post.

"And I thought I was the impatient one."

"I heard that."

Cat's footsteps followed at a slower pace. "Benin, head inside until we see who it is."

"Aw, Mama."

"Benin." Sam tossed the warning over his shoulder.

"Yessir." The door swung shut behind the five-year-old.

"I don't think I recognize that man, do you?"

Sam lifted a hand to his brow. A second later, his grip slid from the butt of his bone-handled six-shooter. "That's one of Pa's new deputies. Hap, I think he said."

"Hap Martin? Connie's brother-in-law?"

"Yes. You've met him, haven't you?"

"A time or two. I didn't know he was back in town. Normally he's only here during spring roundup."

"Is he Melvin's younger brother?"

"Yes."

They waited side by side until Hap dismounted with a creak of leather.

Sam stepped forward and shook the cowboy's hand. "Hap. How goes it in town?"

The mustached man extended a folded slip of paper. "This came in for one of our prisoners. Thought you'd want to see it."

Cat edged closer. "What is it?"

"A telegram." Sam shifted it toward her. "Ramirez is dead."

A rush of relief washed over him, but guilt at rejoicing over another's death followed close behind.

Hap thumbed his brown hat back. "Two down. One to go."

With a nod, Sam returned the paper. "Thanks for letting us know. Anything else?"

"Not yet. I'll be getting back unless y'all need help with anything."

Sam's hand settled on the small of Cat's back. "We're fine."

"Fine, but impatient," Cat interjected.

He frowned at her.

She ignored him. "Would you like some dinner or coffee before you go, Mr. Martin?"

"It's Hap, ma'am, and no thanks, but I appreciate the offer. I've got guard duty tonight and a bowl of Mrs. Ritter's chicken and dumplings headin' my way." Hap put his boot in the stirrup and mounted in one easy motion. "Nice to see you again, Mrs. McGarrett. Sam."

Cat lifted a hand in farewell before they watched the chestnut kick up dirt on its way up the hill.

Benin charged from the house. "Who was it? A bad guy?"

Cat ruffled his hair. "No, one of Gramps's deputies. He was bringing your pa a message. You can go back to helping in the barn. Better yet, why don't you go see if Mrs. Ida needs more wood in her kitchen? Maybe she'll let you peek in the pots before the noon meal."

"Oh boy!" Benin raced for the building set away from the house.

"Does food always distract him?" Sam leaned against the porch post and watched him go.

"Only if I'm lucky." She folded her arms. "Will it work on you?"

"I'm not hungry." An angled smile pulled at his lips as he pushed away from the post. "But I do know something that will distract me."

"Now, Samuel…"

"What? You said you wanted to distract me." He reached for her waist. She dodged, but he caught her apron string and reeled her in.

Cat rested her hands against his chest after he'd stolen his kiss. "How're the ribs?"

"Not too bad."

"And the eye?"

"I won't be giving in to many vain thoughts, if that's what you're wondering."

She giggled and toyed with his collar. "And your neck?"

"Sore, but I'll live. Is there a reason behind all these questions?"

"Just seeing how you're doing, is all."

"You sure you're not thinking about later?"

A lovely blush stained her cheeks. "Why would you think that?"

"'Cause I am." His lips touched hers. "You know there's only tonight before the stage comes in."

"Then perhaps we should finish this conversation later. That is, if you feel up to it?"

"Oh, I feel fine." Sam took a moment to convince her of such until the dinner bell rang. He drew back with a sigh. "Have you noticed my distractions keep getting interrupted with more distractions?"

"Well, hopefully, I'll be your only distraction tonight."

"Amen to that."

31

"Mama?"

Sam jerked away from his wife's distracting kisses. Benin stood in their bedroom doorway, holding his blue blanket by the corner.

Cat touched her mouth and rolled over. "What is it, baby? Why aren't you in bed?"

"I had a bad dream. Can I sleep with you?"

Sam flopped back against his pillow, his forearm across his forehead. Cat's brows dipped, but he didn't care. So much for her being his only distraction that evening.

"Why don't you tell us about it, and then maybe you can go back to sleep?"

Benin scrambled onto the foot of the bed and crawled in between them. Sam swallowed a sigh and scooted over.

"What was the dream about, honey?"

"I dreamed 'bout those bad men. They got outta jail 'n' hurt Gramps again."

Sam moved his arm from his head and for the first time saw the tears glistening in his son's dark eyes. "Hey, partner, it's okay. Nobody's going to let those bad men out of jail."

"So they can't come here 'n' hurt you too like they did in my dream?" A tear tracked down Benin's cheek.

Cat brushed his hair back. "No, baby."

"I like havin' a pa. I don't want you to die."

Sam sat up and lifted Benin into his lap. "I like having a son too, kiddo. Don't worry. Everything's going to be all right."

"Promise?"

Sam shared a look with his wife. They both knew the uncertainty of tomorrow. Clearly, Benin had picked up on that too. A child his age shouldn't be worried about the people around him dying, especially not his pa. "God will take care of us, Benin. No matter what happens, we can be sure of that."

"Does that mean He won't let you die?"

"You sure don't ask easy questions." Sam draped his arms around his son and shifted him in his lap. *God, what do I say?*

As Sam considered his response, an assurance washed over him. If he died, he'd be in heaven with Jesus. If he lived, he'd be with his family. Either way he'd win. Either way God was still in control. For some reason, the future didn't look so uncertain anymore.

"Benin, there will come a day for all of us to die. Me included. I don't know when that will be, but I do know that when it happens, God has promised to take me to be with Him in heaven because I've believed on Jesus and asked him to forgive me of my sins."

"I done that too."

"Good. That means one day we'll be together in heaven."

"Mama too?"

Cat smiled and patted his knee. "Mama too."

"Okay."

"You think you can sleep now, partner?"

"Do I have to go back to my room?"

The sad touch to Cat's lips said she'd reached the same answer as him.

"You can stay this once."

"Thanks, Papa." Benin pressed a kiss to his cheek and crawled under the covers.

Cat touched Sam's arm while he tried to get comfortable in a bed built for two that held three people. He lifted his head to see her over Benin's dark top.

She mouthed, "I'm sorry."

Sam blew her a kiss, then reached over and extinguished the light. After five minutes of his son's squirming, he had no doubt he was in for one very long night.

Catherine blinked against the glaring sun streaming through her bedroom window and moved Benin's foot out of her face. That boy put a worm to shame. She slid out of bed and grabbed her robe, her gaze going to the other side of the bed. Where was Sam?

She tied the housecoat and tiptoed to the living room. It lay empty. Had he already gone outside? His hat and coat still hung by the door, but he might've dared the outdoors without them. Yesterday had been on the mild side. Sam wouldn't go out without his guns though. They'd been a permanent fixture since his encounter with McGovern.

Catherine traipsed back to the bedroom. The gun belt lay on top of the chest of drawers where Sam had put the guns last night. Where was he? Her heartbeat picked up the pace. Had something happened in the middle of the night, and she not hear it?

"Sam?" She turned back to the living room.

A grunt, then a gravelly "what?" answered from behind her.

"Where are you?"

"I'm on the floor."

"The floor?" Catherine hurried around the bed. Indeed he was. "What are you doing down there?"

Sam rolled over on the makeshift pallet he'd made of the rag rug and extra blanket. "After about the fiftieth time of that boy kneeing me in the ribs, I decided he could have my share of the bed."

"Why didn't you take his?"

Sam frowned and sat up. "If I'd've been thinking clear enough, I would've." He scrubbed his hands across his face and yawned. "I hope Ida makes an extra pot of coffee this morning. I've a feeling I'm going to need it. How come you look so rested? Didn't that boy's squirming bother you?"

"I guess as a mother you learn to take it in stride. Most of the time, I make him go back to his own bed."

"Well, tonight he will." Sam stifled another yawn and pushed to his feet. "I guess since I'm up, I might as well make myself useful and milk the cow."

"The stage comes in around noon." Catherine reached and touched his arm. "What do you plan on doing?"

"I was thinking I might do some target practice."

"Can I do it too, Pa?"

"I thought you were asleep."

"Please, Pa."

Catherine frowned at Sam.

He put his mouth beside her ear. "Just let me teach him how to use it properly so he won't hurt himself."

She folded her arms.

"It could save his life, Cat. Besides, I told him I would someday, and who knows what will happen this afternoon. I might not get another chance."

Her hand slipped from the crook of her arm, and she finally nodded. "Fine, but you're doing it with me there."

"I'm good with that."

"Mama nodded. Does that mean we get to, Pa?"

"Sure, Benin, but only if you eat all your breakfast."

"Oh boy."

"No bouncing."

"Sorry, Mama. I forgot." Benin slid off the bed. "I'm gonna go tell Roscoe."

The back door banged shut seconds later.

"You do realize you'll be teaching both of them now?"

"I kind of gathered that." Sam's warm arms slid around her. "Thank you."

"Just don't make me regret it."

"Speaking of regrets, there's one thing that boy's going to have to learn right quick like."

Catherine frowned. Benin was a good boy. "What?"

A roguish grin touched Sam's lips as he leaned closer. "He's going to have to learn to knock when our door is closed."

"The door wasn't closed."

"It will be next time."

A certain giddiness washed over her. It was so good to have her husband back.

"Come on. Let's get this day over with." He pressed a kiss to her forehead and swatted her on the backside. "Get dressed."

"Oh, you." Catherine threw him a frown that quickly transformed into a smile. She selected a brown calico with yellow flowers and draped it on the footboard.

"Put on the jeans first."

"The what?"

Sam stepped away from the now closed bedroom door. "The jeans. You know, the ones you wear under your skirt when you go riding. I haven't gotten to see them in good lighting yet."

"We're not going riding today."

"Who says?"

Catherine rolled her eyes and grabbed the denims from a shelf in the armoire. "Fine. Get dressed."

"I want to see."

"I know." Putting her back to him, she opened the robe and donned the jeans and a fresh camisole. When she hung up the robe and reached for the dress, she felt his hands on her waist.

"Thank you."

"You got your wish."

"Mmhmm." Sam trailed kisses along her shoulder, sending a delicious shiver down her spine.

"Do I get to finish getting dressed now?"

"I shut the door."

"I know, but there's a little boy who hasn't learned your new rule yet."

His sigh tickled the hair on her neck. "It's different with children around."

She turned and rested her hands on the front of his gray shirt. "We'll figure it out."

"Does that mean we can finish this later?"

Fear stemmed the excitement that rushed through her. "Ask me that after the stage has come and gone."

His fingers massaged her back. "It's going to be okay, darlin'. You remember what we told Benin last night."

"I know." But this morning it didn't make her feel any better.

"Don't borrow trouble. We don't know what'll happen today or if someone will even show."

"I know."

"You know I'll do my best to see that I'm here for you and Ben."

"I know."

Sam pecked her on the lips. "You sure do know a lot. Do you know how much I love you?"

Catherine clung to him. "Please don't die today."

Sam gave her a lingering kiss full of promise, but she still noticed what he didn't say. There was no guarantee how this day would turn out. She could only pray to God that it would turn out for good.

~~~

"Y'all picked a good spot, boys. Hand me those nails and that hammer, and we'll get started."

Catherine stood opposite the dead oak and watched Sam hammer three nails in partway.

"Pa, what you doin' that for?"

Her question exactly.

"I'll show you." Sam rejoined them and drew one bone-handled six-shooter from his holster. He leveled the barrel at the tree, cocked the hammer, and let off three rounds. White smoke sifted through the air and tarnished the breeze with the bitter taste of gunpowder.

Her ears still slightly ringing, she followed the trio to the tree. Each nail sat countersunk into the chipping bark.

"Whoa." Roscoe felt at the holes.

"How'd you do that?"

"Lots of practice, Ben." The corner of Sam's mouth turned up when he walked past her. "Careful, you're liable to catch flies like that."

Catherine clamped her lips shut. "I never knew you were that good with a gun."

"I had to be. Boys, why don't you set up those wood chunks on that log over there, and then I'll let y'all try."

Catherine caught his hand while they walked a short distance away. "Thank you."

"For what?"

"For suggesting we do this. Knowing you're that good somehow puts my mind at ease."

"Good. I'm not partial to the worry in your eyes." Sam pressed a kiss to her temple. "I'll do my best to walk away from this trouble."

"You better."

He squeezed her hand, then released it as the boys clambered toward them.

"Me first."

"No, me."

"No, your ma's going first."

"What? I'm only here to watch."

"It won't hurt you none." Sam opened the chamber, showed the boys how to load the bullets, and set the pistol in her hand.

"It's heavier than I remember."

"Weighs about five pounds. Feel free to use both hands."

Catherine gripped the handle and eased back the hammer until it clicked twice. Releasing a deep breath, she squeezed the trigger. The barrel kicked upward, and the bullet zinged toward the middle target. Nothing fell.

"That's okay, Mama. Try again."

"Site it along the barrel. Just like with your rifle."

Catherine lifted the Peacemaker a fraction higher, aimed, and squeezed off another shot. The chunk of wood spiraled off the log.

Sam's smile warmed her when she handed back the gun. "I knew you had it in you."

Benin jumped up and down. "My turn. My turn."

Sam squatted behind his son and set the Colt in the five-year-old's hands, with his larger one safely wrapped around both of Ben's. He pointed the tip of the gun toward the dirt.

"Remember, a gun isn't a toy. You always treat it like it's loaded. That means you never point it at something you don't aim to shoot at."

The boys nodded, entranced. Sam continued to instruct the lads, then allowed each to fire off a few rounds. He never moved an inch from their sides, and the two lapped up his attention.

God, Benin really needs his pa. Don't let this be the only memory he has of him. Please give us favor today.

~~~

Sam stuffed the rag and oil back in its pouch and pieced his Colt Peacemakers back together, mindful of the young boys who watched his every move. He'd never forget the gift of spending time with his family today. He prayed his son wouldn't either if this afternoon didn't go as well as he hoped.

After cleaning his hands, Sam slipped the timepiece from his pocket. The stage was scheduled to have come in more than an hour ago. If anyone planned on coming, he'd see them soon. He loaded the bone-handled revolvers, leaving the hammer of each resting on an empty chamber. The cool, familiar swish of metal against leather filled the room as he slid the guns into their holsters. Maybe after today he could set these aside and never wear them again.

"I ain't seen nobody tie 'em to their leg before. Why ya do that, Mr. Sam?"

"Makes it easier to get the gun out faster if the holster doesn't move." Sam poked his arms into his vest. His jacket would just get in the way. "Remember, you two play inside."

"Sure, Papa."

The rattle of a wagon sounded outside.

"Stay here."

The boys bobbed their heads in acknowledgment, so Sam exited the house, his stomach a hard knot. A buckboard approached, carrying what looked like his pa and...a woman? Sam moved to the edge of the porch and waved Cat over when she popped her head out of the barn.

She hastened across the yard. "What is your father doing, bringing a woman out here?"

"How should I know? I'm as baffled as you are."

"You don't think she's come to shoot you, do you?"

"I wouldn't think so, but I'm not ruling anything out just yet. Why don't you go inside with the boys?"

"No, I'm staying with you."

"Cat..."

"I'm staying, Samuel, until I know who she is."

He released a sigh and shook his head but still settled his fingers on Cat's waist.

The wagon neared, and Pa waved a greeting.

Sam returned the gesture, then settled his free hand on the butt of his gun. "Can you make out what she's carrying?"

"I'm not sure, but if I didn't know any better, I'd say it was a baby."

"A baby?" He squinted and put a hand to his brow. "Now I'm even more confused. Does she look like one of your friends from town?"

"No. I've never seen anyone with a colorful skirt like that."

Sam scratched his chin. There was something oddly familiar about the young woman, but he couldn't place her. Maybe it was the skirt. The Mexican women down near Laredo wore tons of bright colors. Maybe that was it. Maybe he'd met her in Laredo. Laredo... Did Ramirez have a sister?

"Afternoon." Pa slowed the wagon and set the brake. He then helped the scant of a girl, who looked to be maybe nineteen, from her perch on the wagon seat. "This young lady came in on the stage and asked for directions to your place. Said she had a message for you. I took the liberty of escortin' her out."

"How do you do? I'm Catherine McGarrett, and this is my husband, Sam McGarrett."

"I know who he is."

"You do?" Sam cocked his head and studied the dark eyes and brown skin. "You kin to Emilio Ramirez?"

"*Sí*, why do you act like we have not met? You only seduced me and killed *mi hermano*. I come here to make you help with him."

Her heavily accented words were clear enough, but she wasn't making any sense. "Him who?"

"*Su hijo.*"

"My *what*?"

"His *what*?" Pa stared at the woman, then at Sam. "Somebody better start explainin'."

32

Catherine unfolded her arms. "Start explaining what? What does *hijo* mean?"

"Look, ma'am. I admit I killed Eduardo Ramirez 'cause he took a potshot at me, but I didn't do nothing to Emilio, and if you think I'm going to be cornered into caring for some kid I've never met by some woman I can't hardly remember, you're plumb loco."

The teenager started spouting off a steady stream of Spanish and gestured at the sleeping child in her arms.

Catherine peeked past the striped blanket at the roughly seven-month-old baby. Was this girl claiming the child belonged to Sam? Catherine's heart lodged in her throat. Surely not. That wasn't possible...was it?

"Enough!"

Everyone snapped their mouths shut and stared at Catherine.

"Look, I don't know Spanish like these men do. What is going on? What is your name?"

"Lola Ramirez."

"Why are you here?"

"*Señor* McGarrett killed my brother, and now he must help take care of his baby."

"This is your nephew? Your brother's child?"

"No, it is his." Miss Ramirez nodded at Sam.

Catherine's knees threatened to collapse. She gripped the hitching rail and forced herself to remain upright.

"That is a bold-faced lie." Sam turned to Catherine. "Don't believe a word she says. I don't know what she's up to, but she's lying. I am not that child's father."

Catherine swallowed. Hard. Whom did she believe?

Love beareth all things, believeth all things…

She licked her lips and peered between the two. Lola Ramirez, a woman she'd never met, who claimed to be kin to a desperado Sam admittedly shot. Then there was Sam, a man she'd known and loved and chosen to forgive, to not hold his past against him. Was this a test to see if she'd abide by her choices?

"Cat?" Sincerity and palpable fear radiated from his blue-gray gaze.

Catherine touched Sam's arm and moved between him and the newest onslaught on their marriage. "Look, Miss Ramirez, or whatever your name is, I don't know what you're up to, but you'd better tell us the truth."

Sam's sigh tickled her neck. His hand settled on her shoulder. Catherine straightened. This was as it should be—Sam and her against the world. She peeked at her husband, who stared at her with a light sheen in his eyes.

GW folded his stocky arms. "Besmirchin' a man's good name ain't no small matter, young lady. Why don't you start this story from the beginnin'? What're you doin' here?"

"I will talk when mi hijo is out of the cold."

"Fine. We'll talk in the kitchen." Catherine hooked her arm through Sam's and strode toward the dwelling. The sooner they got the girl to admit the truth, the sooner they could unscramble this mess. She paused on the threshold as a thought took hold. "GW, why don't you take our guest inside, and have Ida fix us some coffee? Sam and I will be in shortly."

"Sure." The sheriff looked at her askance, then faced the stranger. "This way, ma'am."

When the door shut behind them, Sam's brows bunched. "What is it? What's wrong?"

"You've really never met that woman?"

"I promise you, Cat, I don't know her from Adam. I met a lot of people in Laredo, but I can't recall her face."

Catherine lowered her voice. "Do you think it's possible then that she's supposed to be a distraction?"

"What do you mean?"

She surveyed their property, looking for anything suspicious. "The telegram from yesterday—do you think it could have been a lie? That maybe Emilio Ramirez is alive and using this woman as a distraction while he waits for the perfect opportunity to shoot you?"

Sam's eyes widened before he scanned the area as well. "That's something I could definitely see a Ramirez doing."

"Then we'll keep our eyes and ears open and see if we can't figure out what they're up to." Catherine moved forward and reached for the door latch.

"Wait." Sam's hand landed on her arm. His Adam's apple bobbed. "Thank you."

She touched his cheek. "I love you, Sam. The past is behind us. I'm determined to leave it there. No more secrets between us. No lies."

With a turn of his head, he kissed her palm before taking her fingers within his own. "We move forward together." He reached for the door. "You go on inside. I'm going to go warn Mo and Curly so they'll be on the lookout. Are they still working with the geldings?"

"Should be."

"Okay, I'll go tell them and be right in. Try to hold off the questioning until I get back. I want to hear what that woman has to say."

"I'll do my best. Be careful." Catherine watched Sam hurry around the barn, and then she stepped inside. GW sat across from Miss Ramirez at the table. The babe, now awake, sat with a heel of bread in his tiny hands. He had the same dark hair and eyes as his mother and could almost pass as Benin's brother. Had she been wrong? Catherine gulped. Love believed all things. Sam wouldn't lie to her. He said the child wasn't his, so the child wasn't his. She drew a deep breath.

God, please don't let me be wrong.

"Where's Sam?" GW stirred cream into his mug.

Catherine accepted the empty cup Ida handed her and poured

herself some water. She was wound up enough as it was without complicating the matter further with coffee. "He had to see to something real quick. He'll be right back. Would you like a snack to go with your coffee, Miss Ramirez? Ida baked some fresh gingersnaps this morning."

The young woman bobbed her head. "Sí, gracias."

Catherine took that as a yes and fetched a handful from the cookie jar on the worktable, where Ida covered another steaming loaf of bread.

"What's going on, Miz Cathy? Who's she?"

Catherine matched Ida's hushed tone while she arranged the cookies on a plate. "That's what we're trying to figure out. She claims to be kin to that man we got the telegram about yesterday."

Ida's dark brows rose. "The dead one?"

"That's the one. She claims the babe is Sam's too."

"Land sakes! Do you believe her?"

"I think she's up to no good. There's something about her that just doesn't ring true."

The kitchen door swung open.

Catherine pivoted, plate in hand. "Hi, Sam. Would you like some cookies with your coffee? I was just getting some for Miss Ramirez."

"Sounds good." Sam hung his hat on the peg by the door and joined her at the cookie jar. Ida moved back to the stove.

He lowered his voice. "Has she said anything yet?"

"Not yet. I distracted her with cookies." Catherine lifted the plate.

Sam plucked a gingersnap off it. "Let's see what we can find out."

Once they were both seated on the bench across from the stranger, GW folded his hands on the table. "All right, Miss Ramirez. You're inside where it's warm. Are you ready to answer our questions now?"

The young woman selected a cookie from the plate but otherwise remained stoic, if not a bit pale.

Sam leaned forward. "Ma'am, I have never met you. How did you learn about me, and what's this about me killing Emilio? I did no such thing."

"Sí, you did. He caught pneumonia trying to find you."

"He should've left well enough alone. His brother asked to be shot. He was running with the wrong crowd."

"That is not true. You kill them both. Now I have no one."

"So that's it. You're looking for charity."

Catherine squeezed Sam's hand under the table. There was no sense in making the woman defensive.

He looked her way and bent close. "What?"

"You catch more flies with honey than vinegar, dear."

Ida set a glass on the table. "Here's your milk, ma'am. Ya want I should add another settin' to the table for suppa', Mista Sam?"

Sam lifted his brows in question at Catherine. She nodded.

"Sure, Ida, then Pa can take her back to the boarding house."

"I have no *dinero* for lodging. I used the last of mi hermano's money to come here."

The theory of Miss Ramirez seeking charity raised another notch on Catherine's scales. That was, if Ramirez was even her name. Was money how Emilio had convinced her to lie?

"That sounds like a personal problem."

"Sam." Catherine frowned. They didn't need this woman in town spreading her lies. Besides, if she left, they couldn't ask more questions. "She can stay here."

Sam crossed his arms. "Fine, but she's not staying in my house."

Where should they put her then? The barn? "Ida, would it be all right if Roscoe stayed with Benin for the night and Miss Ramirez sleeps in his room?"

"Sho', Miz Cathy. I don't think Mo'll mind."

"GW, will you be staying for supper too?"

"No, I think I better scoot on back to town if y'all have got things under control here."

"I'll walk you out, Pa. There's something I wanted to ask you while you're here." Sam nodded at Cat and followed his father out the door.

Catherine studied the woman across from her. The babe had crumbs scattered all over the tabletop, but Miss Ramirez kept her half-eaten cookie far from his reach.

"Miss Ramirez, now that the men are gone, you want to tell me what's *really* going on?"

"I have told you. Your señor must pay for what he's done."

"For what *you say* he's done, but I'm finding it hard to believe you're telling me the truth."

"Why would I lie about a thing such as this?" The dark-haired woman started to rise. The color drained from her face quicker than sand through a sieve, and she dropped back into her chair, a hand to her head.

Catherine rushed around the table and caught the woman before she toppled to the floor. "Miss Ramirez, are you all right? Ida, get her a damp cloth."

Catherine pulled the babe from Miss Ramirez's lap and set him on her hip as Ida rounded the table with the requested rag.

"*Perdóname.* I think I need rest, *señora.* Our travel was long."

"Ida, would you mind showing Miss Ramirez to her room? I'll keep an eye on the bread for you."

"Sho', Miz Cathy. I'll grab up a few things for Roscoe to take to Ben's room while I'm at it. You want me to take the babe?"

Catherine peeked at the infant tugging her apron. "I guess I can watch him for a while."

"Gracias, señora." Miss Ramirez rose with Ida's help and shuffled out the door.

Baby Ramirez touched a drool-covered finger to Catherine's ear.

She captured his hand. "Little man, I wish you could talk, because something's definitely not right here."

Sam grabbed his father's arm and tugged him farther away from the kitchen door when it opened. A pale Miss Ramirez and a worried Ida stepped off the porch and veered toward the foreman's house on the opposite side. What was going on?

"That woman sure is full of surprises," Pa noted. "Ain't accustomed to lyin' either."

"You caught that too, did ya? Cat thinks she might be helping with one more surprise."

"Besides saying you're the father of her baby?"

"That's a lie, Pa. Don't you dare believe her." Sam ambled toward the wagon, knowing Pa would fall into step beside him. "Look, Cat had an idea, and I think she's right."

"I'm listenin'."

"She believes that woman might be part of a setup. Cat thinks the telegram yesterday was all a hoax so that when Miss Ramirez showed up, she'd distract us from what's really happening."

"What do you think is really happening?"

Sam lowered his voice. "We think Ramirez is still alive and waiting for the right moment to shoot me."

Pa stopped at the corner of the house. "Is Emilio Ramirez the kind of man to do something like that?"

"I don't like to speak ill of people, but that whole family is a bunch of sidewinders."

Pa rubbed his whiskers. "Y'all might be onto somethin'. I'll get some men together and start scoutin' around. If Ramirez is hidin' in the area, we'll find him."

33

After a supper void of Miss Ramirez's company, Catherine put Benin and Roscoe to bed and took her post at her bedroom window. The boys' soft snores floated from the loft as shadows played across the yard, creating an unease that settled into her bones. Sam, Mo, and Curly were stationed in different places around the property, rifles ready. Catherine's rifle leaned next to the windowsill, but she wished Sam had taken his post with her. If she wasn't going to sleep, she'd at least like someone to talk to as she whiled away the hours.

Leaning against the chair's back, Catherine brought her knees up to her chest and tried to see into the shadows, but all she could see was Sam's face next to the Ramirez baby's. So they both had dark hair...so what? Miss Ramirez had dark locks too. Most Mexicans did, in fact. The babe had the same brown coloring of the Mexican people too. Catherine propped her chin on her knees. What was the truth? She reached for the Bible beside her bed and set it in her lap. Only God had the answers. Only He could see past deceptions to the heart of any matter.

"God, I need answers. Please guide me to the truth. Don't let me be deceived. I know I don't want what Miss Ramirez said to be true. I want to believe Sam's telling me the truth, but how can I be sure?" Searching for peace, Catherine relit the lamp and leafed through the pages of her Bible until she found the Psalms. She read psalm after psalm until she stumbled upon the last verses of Psalm 27: "I had fainted, unless I had believed to see the goodness of the Lord in the land of the living. Wait on the Lord: be of good courage, and he shall strengthen thine heart: wait, I say, on the Lord."

What did she believe? Did she believe she'd see God's goodness in her life? For some reason, that's what this seemed to boil down to. Not what Sam had or hadn't done. Not what Miss Ramirez had or hadn't done. But what Catherine herself believed God would do. Would she still cling to His promises? Still trust in His loving care…regardless of the truth? Would she still believe God had good in store for her?

Catherine rubbed her thumb against the thin pages, ruffling them. "Let God be true and all men liars."

The Apostle Paul's declaration fell from her lips, and as the conviction settled in her soul, so did a newfound peace. God would see her through.

"Cat, what are you doing? I said no lights."

Catherine jolted, and the Bible skittered from her lap. "Sam, what on earth… You scared the living daylights out of me." She retrieved the Book. "I thought you were keeping watch outside."

"I was until I saw the light on in here. I thought something was wrong." He stalked over and blew out the lamp. The warm glow from the fireplace in the living room edged back the full darkness. "Why aren't you asleep? I told you that you didn't have to keep watch."

"I couldn't sleep, so I figured an extra set of eyes wouldn't hurt."

Sam leaned his rifle next to hers and settled his hands on her shoulders, his thumbs kneading at the tension there. "Would it help if I kept watch from here?"

Her eyelids fell shut. "Hmm, maybe, especially if you keep doing that."

His fingers worked their magic on her bunched muscles as they trailed from her shoulders to her back to her neck. Catherine leaned into his touch while the frustrations of the day melted away under his ministrations. A girl could get used to this kind of treatment.

Sam's lips caressed the tender skin of her neck, sending a delicious shiver down her spine. One by one the pins slid from her hair until it tumbled into her lap. More tension eased from her temples. She should've done that hours ago.

He brushed tendrils behind her ear. "You think you can go to bed now?"

Capturing his hand, she twined her fingers with his. "Only if you join me."

His smile warmed her through and through as he pulled her from the chair and into his arms. "I was kind of hoping you'd say that."

―――

"Miz Cathy!"

Sam bolted upright at Ida's shout and scrambled from the bed, Cat doing the same. He hadn't intended to fall asleep, but after the bliss of being with his wife, he hadn't wanted to leave. What had happened? Why were they calling Cat and not him? He threw on his discarded clothes, then bounced into his boots as he peeked out the window. With the amount of alarm in the cook's voice, he expected to see a fire blazing against the predawn sky, but he only spotted Ida with a flailing bundle in her arms as she rushed across the yard.

"She's got the baby."

"What? Why?" Cat yanked her dress over her head and tied her sash behind her.

Sam dashed for the back door, with Cat on his heels. Howling cries pierced his ears when he threw open the panel. "Ida, what's wrong?"

"It's Miz Ramirez, sir. She be coughin' up blood. I's got Mo rousin' Curly to fetch the doc, but the babe, he be hungry, and his ma—"

Cat stepped forward. "Give me the boy. I'll see to him. You see to Miss Ramirez."

"Oh, thank ya, ma'am."

She took the screaming infant, and Ida hastened back to her house beyond the kitchen.

Sam shut out the cold air and turned to his wife. "What can I do?"

While she yanked her shawl from its peg by the door, Cat jostled the baby, bringing momentary silence to the cries. "Bring some fresh milk to the kitchen."

"Sure." Sam saw the two safely to the kitchen and jogged for the barn. He soon plopped onto the milking stool amid galloping hooves outside. As his hands did the mindless work, his mind replayed the past few minutes. His rhythm slowed. "Coughing up blood?"

He glanced in the direction of the foreman's cabin. That kind of symptom only meant one thing—consumption.

That woman had brought sickness to his house.

Bessie stomped a hoof near his foot.

"Sorry, girl, no sense in taking my frustrations out on you."

Meow.

Sam's gaze darted to the corner of the stall. "I don't have time for you, cat." He squirted milk in the feline's direction. Soot caught it in his mouth and licked his lips.

"That's all you're getting. Now get lost." Sam kicked hay at the greedy menace, hurriedly finished filling the bucket, and made a hasty exit toward the kitchen. The baby had taken up howling again, his cries carrying through the thick walls. Stepping inside, Sam looked for the source of the painful wails. His wife stood at the stove, stirring a pot, with the complaining infant on her hip.

"Here's the milk."

"Strain it and bring me some."

Sam did as told and brought her the pitcher. "Aren't you going to make him stop crying?"

Cat frowned. "What do you think I'm working on? If you're so bothered, why don't you do something about it?"

He studied the screaming child. Praying he wouldn't break something, he took the babe from her arms.

The cries magically stopped.

Cat raised a brow in his direction.

Sam shrugged. He'd never done this before. He'd never even held any of his wife's nieces or nephews until they were well over a year old. "What's his name?"

She moved the pot off the stove and spooned some oatmeal into a bowl. "I never asked."

The howling resumed. Sam tried the jiggling Cat had done before, but to no avail. She doctored the hot cereal with sugar and molasses and stirred it while blowing against the steam.

"He's old enough to eat that?"

"Benin did when he was his age."

"Benin was this small?"

A smile touched her lips as she reached for the child. "Once upon a time."

Cat sat at the table and placed the baby in her lap. The little one gobbled up the food as quick as she placed it in his mouth, screaming when she didn't move fast enough.

"He sure is a hungry thing." Sam gripped the back of a nearby chair and welcomed the glimpse of the past he'd missed. For an instant, he wished the child was theirs and he'd get to see this touching scene every morning. "I'm sorry, Cat."

Her chocolate eyes met his, a question there.

"I should've been here for you."

"You're here now." She shoved another spoonful into the baby's mouth.

He sank into the chair and squeezed his knees. "Can I give it a try?"

"You want to feed him?"

"Don't act so surprised." Sam smiled and took the spoon from her slackened grip. More of the oatmeal ended up on the child's chin than in between his lips, so Sam tried again.

"I didn't mean that like it sounded. I just...I thought you needed to go help keep watch."

"I probably should." Sam successfully aimed another bite into the bird mouth. "Here, I'll let you take back over." He stood and dropped a kiss on her upturned face. "Yell if you need me."

"I will. Sam?"

He paused on his way to the door.

"Please be careful."

"Yes, ma'am."

Catherine stared at the door Sam disappeared through. Baby Ramirez fussed for another bite. She shoveled in another spoonful, a smile slipping out. The boy really was a cute little fellow. "I don't know about you, young man, but I have some questions for your mama. It's about time we got to the bottom of this, don't you think?"

She wiped the excess from his mouth after he finished the last bite. She then rewrapped the blanket around the infant, slipped on her shawl, and headed over to Ida's small cabin. After two knocks, the door swung open.

"How is she?"

Ida stepped back and let her in. "She's mighty tuckered, ma'am. Keep havin' them coughin' spells. I was just gettin' her some more water."

"I'll follow you back." Catherine waited for Ida to finish filling the glass, then trailed her to the curtained-off room that normally belonged to Roscoe.

The thin girl lay propped with pillows against the headboard, her dark hair fanned across her pale gown. She'd aged overnight, looking closer to her thirties or forties than nearly twenty. "Mi hijo..."

Catherine drew back the blanket, and the little one wiggled and reached for his mama, a smile wreathing his round face.

"You feed him?"

Catherine nodded and set the child on the foot of the bed, for the first time wondering if Miss Ramirez was well enough for all the questions she wanted to place to the woman.

"*Lo siento.*"

"Pardon?"

Miss Ramirez coughed into a hankie and straightened. "I am sorry."

Catherine waited, not sure what exactly the woman apologized for. Lying about Sam? Bringing sickness to her house? Or not showing up sooner?

"I should not have come." Another cough. "A doctor said in Laredo I have no much time. He help me enough for travel, but mi hijo—" Miss Ramirez covered her mouth and broke into another fit. When it passed, she wheezed and collapsed back against the pillows.

Ida handed over the water glass.

"Miss Ramirez, you don't have to explain now."

The young mother shook her head and took a few sips. "I must. I come for mi hijo... My son, he has no one besides me. I receive the message...about your man. I remember his kindness to my village."

"I thought you said he killed your brothers."

"Only Emilio was my brother-in-law, my sister's husband. He die while searching for your Señor McGarrett, but he was *un perro*. He deserve to die, just like his brother."

"Ramirez really is dead?"

"Sí, and my name is not Ramirez. It is Reyes. I sorry I lie to you, but I know not what to do. Your husband, he help free our town from their cruelty." Mrs. Reyes sipped more water and nodded toward her son, who played with the covers. "I come with hope he might help again."

"I don't understand. Didn't you say you had a sister?"

"She is *muerta*, dead."

"Is S—Mr. McGarrett really his father?" Catherine couldn't help holding her breath.

"No, my husband was shot by Emilio's brother. I have no one."

Catherine wilted even as her faith in Sam surged. She wanted to be angry at Mrs. Reyes for her lies and the turmoil she'd caused, but Catherine understood what it meant to be left alone, to have no hope in sight, to be at a loss as to where to turn and what to do next. However, she'd never been as alone as this woman. Even when her parents had died, she'd still had her sister. When Sam had left and she'd discovered she carried Benin, she'd still had help from her sister and Isabel Hatch. Catherine had been more blessed than she'd realized.

This woman had no support, and she lay dying. How could she fault her for fighting for her son? Hadn't Catherine done the same for Benin by ending the turmoil with the general?

Catherine's heart turned over. "What do you want us to do?"

Tears tracked down Mrs. Reyes's face. "Mi hijo, he needs a good man to look up to."

"You want us to help find a family for your son?"

Mrs. Reyes shook her head adamantly and broke into another coughing fit. Catherine instinctively covered her mouth at the bone-rattling coughs. Mrs. Reyes gasped and hacked more. Blood stained her pale lips and seeped between her fingers. The baby started to cry and crawl toward his mother. Catherine lifted him into her arms and backed away.

Ida refilled the water glass and handed over a fresh handkerchief. "Maybe y'all oughta finish this later."

Pushing away the cup, Mrs. Reyes wagged her head. "Please, Señora McGarrett...you...keep mi hijo."

"Me?"

"Señor McGarrett es...good man...will be good father."

"I...I don—"

A knock interrupted.

Ida hurried to the door. The town's new doctor entered the house, accompanied by every man on the property. Except Sam. Who was keeping watch? Wait. They didn't need to keep watch for Ramirez anymore. Somebody needed to inform the sheriff.

"Señora, please." Desperation settled in the lines of Mrs. Reyes's face.

"I...I'll consider it."

A hand touched Catherine's arm.

"Miz Cathy, the doc, he be wantin' you to take the babe elsewhere. Do you want I should take him and go feed the menfolk?"

"N-no, Ida." Catherine gave herself a mental shake and finally looked at the cook. "I'll take care of things this time. You stay with Mrs. Reyes."

Catherine greeted Dr. Pritchett in passing and herded the others from the small dwelling, anxious to get the children away from the sickness. She whipped up more oatmeal, her eyes ever watchful on the kitchen door. Where was Sam? Surely he was hungry. Catherine hurriedly filled a final bowl and added molasses and sugar, the way her husband liked it. She had to let him know about Ramirez and tell him why their visitor had really come.

34

"McGarrett, get your rotten carcass out here."

Sam jolted at the familiar voice and dashed to the barn door.

Dakota James stood on the front porch of the cabin, his dark duster tucked back and his hand hovering over a shiny six-shooter.

Sam's stomach dropped to his toes. Where were Cat and Benin? If Dakota barged into the house to get to him, they might get hurt instead. Sam checked the load on each gun, glad he'd grabbed his gun belt before returning to the barn to keep watch. Why hadn't someone escorted Uriah James's brother out like they'd planned?

The doc.

Anyone watching and listening in town could've easily found out where Curly and the doctor were headed and followed them. Troublesome woman. If it hadn't been for Miss Ramirez, this wouldn't be happening right now.

"I know you're here. Now come out and face me." Dakota slammed his boot into the front door.

Something shattered.

Sam bolted outside, searching for Cat. "I'm over here, Dakota."

The big man pivoted.

Sam spotted his wife outside the kitchen, a broken mess at her feet. *God, please don't let Dakota see her.* Sam stepped farther from the barn and waved Cat off behind his back.

"Well, if it isn't Sam Houston McGarrett." Dakota moseyed from the porch. "You look pretty good for a dead man."

"You've shot me once, Dakota. I learned my lesson. You can turn around and go home. No one has to die today."

"I told you I'd kill you for what you did to my brother." Dakota's hand hovered over his gun. "I'm known as a man of my word."

"You know your brother made his choice. He could've come in peacefully."

"Liar. You never gave him a chance. I'm a better man than you though, so I'll give you what you never gave him. Draw."

"Dakota, we don't have to do this."

"You can either defend yourself or die where you stand. Your choice."

"Have it your way." Sam sighed and eased his hand closer to his gun. *God, please help me. I don't want to kill anyone anymore.*

"No!" Cat dashed in between them. "Sam, you can't do this."

"What is this?" Dakota bellowed. "Woman, get out of the way."

Sam tried to push her from the line of fire. "Cat, get back inside."

"No, I can't let you do this. I love you. You can't die. We need you."

Sam risked taking his eyes off Dakota to look at his wife. Love and desperation radiated from her sweet face. A smile tugged at his lips, and he brushed a hand across her cheek. "I love you too. Now get back inside where it's safe."

"Woman, my patience is growing thin. Matter of fact, Sam here killed my brother. Maybe I should make him watch someone he loves die first."

Cat gasped and whirled around.

Sam jerked her behind him. "This is between you and me, Dakota. Leave her out of this."

The gunman cocked his head to the side. "I'm a fair man. I'll give her five seconds to get to safety. One."

"Cat, run!"

She squeezed his arm.

"Two."

"Now."

Pounding footsteps retreated behind him.

"Three."

Sam's fingers twitched beside his gun.

"Four." Dakota smirked. "That's too bad. I'd so hoped to get to five."

The rising sun heated Sam's back as much as the no-account's words boiled his anger. "Let's finish this, Dakota. Go for your gun."

Dakota's dark eyes narrowed a fraction, and his long fingers flexed beside his Peacemaker.

Sam sucked in a deep breath, refusing to draw first. If he had to shoot again, it would only be in self-defense. No matter how much he wanted to put a bullet in the blackguard.

The man's hand gripped the handle.

Sam drew and fired.

Catherine jerked at the double report of gunshots. Her heart slammed against her rib cage. *God, please...* She peeked around the edge of the house.

Both men lay in the dirt.

"Oh, God, no." She left the safety of the back porch and raced to Sam's side. Blood seeped from a wound in his leg. Why were his eyes closed? Had Dakota James managed two shots? Had Sam not fought back at all? If so, where was the other bullet hole?

"Don't you die on me, Sam McGarrett, or I'll never forgive you." Catherine ripped off the edge of her petticoat and worked it around the wound on his thigh.

Sam groaned and reached for his leg. "Dakota?"

She peered over her shoulder. "He's not moving. Lie still."

A door slammed, then rushing feet approached. "Miz Cathy? Boss?"

"Go get the doctor, Mo."

Air hissed through Sam's teeth. "Mercy, woman, can you tie that any tighter?"

"I told you not to get shot."

"No, you didn't." He grunted. "You said not to die."

"Same difference."

"I beg to differ." Sam pushed up on one elbow as a door slammed again.

Mo and Dr. Pritchett jogged toward them.

Catherine tied another knot in the bandage.

"Miz Cathy, look out!"

A sharp click brought Catherine's head around. The shaky barrel of Dakota's gun leveled her direction. Sam jerked her toward him.

A deafening shot rang over her head.

Silence followed.

She brought her face up from Sam's chest and searched for the smoking gun in his hand, but both of Sam's arms lay around her.

His gray eyes roamed her face. "Are you okay?"

She nodded. Mo and the doctor stared toward the kitchen. Curly stood a couple yards from the door, a rifle in his hands. A glance over her shoulder revealed a prostrate Dakota James.

"Is he dead?" Curly's question spurred the doctor and Mo toward the gunman.

Sam pushed to a sitting position when they passed but kept a steady hold on her waist. "I should've killed him the first time. I'd hoped injuring his gun arm would be enough to deter him. I'm so sorry, Cat."

She patted his arm. "Never be sorry for being merciful."

Dr. Pritchett knelt beside the dark-clad man sprawled in the dirt. After a few moments of inspection, he rose and nodded in Curly's direction.

The younger man gave an answering nod and disappeared back inside the kitchen.

"Remind me later to thank him." Sam retrieved his gun from the dirt and shoved it into his holster.

"Me too." Catherine tucked a stray strand behind her ear and inched over when Dr. Pritchett approached.

The gray-haired man knelt next to Sam, grabbed his right arm, and motioned for Mo to grab the other. "Come on. Let's get you inside, and we'll see what we can do about that leg of yours. Lead the way, Mrs. McGarrett."

Catherine hurried ahead of them and opened the door to her house.

She stripped their bed of the twisted quilt and threw a few extra towels on the bottom half of the mattress.

Sam gritted his teeth when they lowered him onto the bed.

"I'm going to need some hot water, Mrs. McGarrett."

"Mo, would you?"

"Sho', Miz Cathy." Mo disappeared from the bedroom in two strides.

"What else, Doctor?"

Dr. Pritchett unearthed a pair of scissors from his bag and split Sam's pants leg open. "More light."

Catherine yanked open the curtains, then hurried to the living room to retrieve the other oil lamps. She lit two and dispersed them about the bedroom.

The doctor tugged a stool closer and perched next to the bed. "You know, son, after the war I'd hoped I was through treating bullet wounds."

"And I'd hoped I was through getting them." Sam clenched his jaw while the doctor probed the wound. Beads of sweat broke out on Sam's forehead, but he didn't yell out.

"You're lucky. Looks like that bullet went clean through. Missed the artery too. Yes, sir, mighty lucky. You want something for the pain before I start stitching you up?"

Sam shook his head. "Just do what needs doing."

The doctor's gray brows rose. "All right, sonny. Whatever you say."

Catherine twisted her fingers in knots. "Anything else you need, Doctor?"

"Just that water." Dr. Pritchett leaned back a fraction and wiped his hands on a towel.

She hastened to the door and peeked out.

Mo approached the porch with a steaming kettle.

"Oh, good, you're back. He needs the water." Catherine led the way back to the bedroom and moved the pitcher from the basin, setting it closer to Dr. Pritchett. Mo poured some of the water inside the ceramic bowl and deposited the kettle on the floor.

The foreman touched her arm. "Miz Cathy, I knows you'd rather be here, but I'm a-thinkin' Curly might 'preciate your help, ma'am, tendin' to those three boys."

"Three boys? Oh, I forgot all about the baby." Catherine bit her lip and looked between Sam and the door. "Mo, would you please help him just this once? Tell Benin I'll come get him when he can come see his pa."

"I—"

"Please, Mo. I'll come help as soon as the doc finishes with Sam and he's settled."

Mo sighed and patted her hand. "Sho', Miz Cathy. I'll get Ida if'n they get too much for us."

"Thank you so much."

Sam grunted, drawing Catherine's attention to the bed. Dr. Pritchett had cleaned away a good portion of the blood and was suturing the seeping hole in Sam's leg.

She moved closer. "What can I do?"

"Have you got more towels?"

Catherine fetched more from the chest of drawers and handed them over.

The doctor wiped his fingers and continued to work. "You know, Mrs. McGarrett, y'all sure do know how to make a day interesting. First, a woman with consumption. Now a bullet wound." He shook his head. "It's a crying shame, that gal dying so young."

"Is she really that bad, Dr. Pritchett?"

"Sad to say, but she doesn't have much longer for this world." He snipped the thread and set aside the needle. "Mr. McGarrett, we're going to need to roll you onto your side, so I can get to that exit wound. You think you can manage that?"

In answer, Sam gripped the far side of the bed frame and hoisted himself onto his side. His face paled to match the sheets.

Catherine dabbed the sweat from his brow. "Are you sure you don't want something for the pain, honey?"

Sam gave a subtle shake of his head. His teeth remained clamped shut.

"Do you want me to check the babe, Mrs. McGarrett, before I leave here today?"

"He hasn't coughed any, if that's what you mean."

The doctor nodded and tied off another stitch. "Has Mrs. Reyes said what's to be done with the child when she passes?"

Sam's eyes angled toward hers. "Reyes?"

"Well…" This wasn't the way she'd wanted to broach the sensitive subject with Sam, especially considering she hadn't made up her mind how to answer Mrs. Reyes herself.

Dr. Pritchett glanced up from his needle. "Did she mention the father of the babe?"

"He's dead."

Sam opened his mouth but grimaced as the doctor started another stitch.

"That's a shame. Does she have other family?"

"They're dead too."

"So he'll be an orphan. Tsk, tsk. That is a shame." The doctor snipped the thread. "I reckon that'll do it. Son, you stay put in that bed. I don't need you putting weight on it and busting up my handiwork. You'll need to keep that wound clean, too, so infection won't set in."

"I'll see he obeys your instructions, Dr. Pritchett. I can't tell you how grateful I am that you were here today."

"Yes, I can imagine." The doctor washed his hands in the last of the fresh water.

"Yeah, thanks, Doc." Sam had as much color as an apparition.

"Well, I'll get this bandaged up and get on out of here…unless you two are expecting more trouble today?"

"Oh, heaven forbid. I think we've had enough excitement in the past week to last a lifetime."

"Yes, y'all have kept the town hopping." Dr. Pritchett secured the bandage. "How does that feel, Mr. McGarrett? Too tight?"

"Fine."

"You certain you don't want something for the pain?"

"I've had my fill of laudanum this year. I'll pass."

"Well, if you're sure." The doctor put away the last of his supplies and looked to Catherine. "If he needs a little something to take the edge off the pain, brew some willow bark tea. I should have some extra here in my bag…"

"Don't worry, Dr. Pritchett. We have some. Sam, will you be all right for a second while I walk the doctor out?"

"I can walk myself out. Oh, and don't worry about the payment. I'll send you my bill. Might put the payment toward one of them fine horses out there."

Catherine returned the doctor's easy grin, thanked him, and shut the front door behind him. She tiptoed back to the bedroom, where Sam lay against the pillows, his eyes shut. The grimace on his face said he was anything but near to sleeping.

"Are you okay? Can I get you anything?"

"A new leg?"

She gave a halfhearted smile. All this trouble and pain was because of her. If she'd never seen the general kill that man, he never would've sent those telegrams and Sam wouldn't have been shot.

"Hey, don't look so sad. I'll live."

"I know." Catherine put her hand to her mouth and fought back the tears.

"Cat, what is it? I mean it. I really will be okay."

She nodded, and a tear slid down her cheek. She brushed it away. "I'll go get Benin so he'll know you're all right."

"Wait. Come here." Sam grimaced when he shifted on the mattress.

Catherine swiped at another wet escapee. "No, really, I'm fine."

"Cat." He beckoned her closer.

She inched toward the bedside. He caught her hand and pulled her to sit beside him.

His steel-blue eyes held hers. "I'm okay."

"I thought you were dead."

"I'm not."

"I thought I'd lost you again."

"I'm right here."

"I don't want to lose you."

Sam tugged her down into a hug. "I'm not going anywhere, darlin'."

The safety and assurance of his arms were her undoing. The sobs and fears she'd held in seeped into his shirt. "Please don't ever do that again."

"I don't plan to." He rubbed her back. "I plan to leave that life behind and grow old here with you and our children and grandchildren, raising horses 'til we're too old and feeble to lift a curry brush."

She leaned away and wiped her cheek. "I'd like that."

Sam caught a wayward tear and brushed it aside. "We good now?"

Catherine nodded with a smile. "I should go get Benin. He's probably anxious to see you."

Sam glanced about. "Perhaps it'd be best if you helped me clean up a bit first. I don't reckon seeing all this blood will be much of a balm."

Catherine took in the soiled towels, the stained water in the basin, and Sam's ripped pants leg. "I think you're right."

"Miracles never cease."

"Oh, you..." Catherine rose and started tidying the room. It took some doing, but she finally rid Sam of his bloody clothes and helped him into his nightshirt. She stuffed a clean pillow under his heel to help keep his thigh from resting on the mattress. By the time they were finished, any color that had returned to Sam's cheeks was long gone, and sweat streamed down his temples.

"We'll keep Benin's visit short so you can get some rest. Do you want me to bring you something to eat or drink? You never did have breakfast."

"I don't think I could eat right now, but I'll take a glass of water."

"Sure. Rest now. I'll be back with Ben in just a bit."

Sam grunted his acknowledgment and closed his eyes. Catherine stepped from the room. Wails carried from the kitchen as she crossed the yard.

"God, I'm not sure I'm strong enough to handle a squalling infant today." Taking a steadying breath, she pushed open the door separating her from the brunt of the noise.

Curly's eyes widened before he sagged with relief. "Oh, Mrs. Cathy, thank God you're here. How do you make him stop? Mo just left with the doc and the wagon to take that other fella in to the undertakers. I was fixing to send Roscoe to go get his mama. Would you please?" The wrangler extended the infant toward her like he held a rabid dog instead of a small child.

Baby Reyes wailed, his face red and his arms flailing.

She cuddled him close and patted his backside. Her hand came away damp. "No wonder you're so unhappy. Benin, will you get me one of Mrs. Ida's dishtowels from the stack there?"

Benin scampered to the worktable and back to her. "Is Papa okay? Mr. Mo said he got hurted."

"Papa's going to be just fine, thanks to Mr. Curly here and the doc. He did get hurt, but with a little time, he'll be right as rain. Let me finish here with the baby, and I'll take you to see him, okay?" Catherine laid the infant on the table. "Can you pour Papa a glass of water that we can take to him? Roscoe, can you help him get the cup from the hutch?"

Roscoe rose from his chair. "Can I come too?"

"Sure, but we'll have to keep it short. Mr. Sam is very tired."

"I'll help too." Curly scurried away to join the boys.

"Chicken." The man could stare down a hardened gunman, but a squalling child sent him running. Catherine shook her head and made quick work of the wet mess. The infant's cries lessened to whimpers while he rubbed his fists against his eyes.

"Somebody's tired." Catherine grabbed the baby blanket off the back of a nearby chair and bundled the wee one in its softness. "I've really got to learn your name, little man."

Scooping up Baby Reyes, Catherine waited for her three helpers. They returned with two brimming glasses and a pitcher.

"I take it you're visiting too, Curly?"

"If you don't think he'll mind, ma'am."

"I don't think he'll mind at all. I believe he wanted to thank you himself as well."

Curly studied his boots. "Nothing to thank me for, ma'am."

Catherine touched his arm. "I beg to differ. You did a good thing today, Curly, and I'm mighty appreciative."

"Yes, ma'am." Curly peeked past the blanket in her arms. "How'd you do that?"

She let him change the subject. Baby Reyes, clearly worn out from all his screaming, lay sound asleep. "I guess he's a ladies' man. You forget"—she nodded toward Benin with a smile—"I've done this before."

"Please don't ever do that to me again, ma'am."

"You don't like babies, Curly?"

"Not screaming ones."

Catherine chuckled. "I'll try to remember that. Come on. Someone open the door for me. Remember, we're keeping this short. Mr. Sam needs his rest."

A chorus of "yes, ma'am" met her ears, but not another word was spoken while they crossed the yard and entered the house.

Benin reached the bedroom first. He halted in the doorway. "Mama, he's dead."

35

Sam pushed back the pain-numbing sleep and opened his eyes. Tears streamed down his son's face. "I'm not dead, partner. Just tuckered out."

The boy visibly relaxed but stayed by his mother's side.

"Is that water for me?"

Benin nodded.

Cat stepped farther into the room, a bundle in her arms, and nudged Benin toward him. "Go ahead and give it to him, baby. It's all right."

"I brought you some too." Roscoe stood in the doorway, his brows bunched together.

"Me too."

Sam raised his gaze to the curly-haired man behind the dark-skinned boy. "Thank you." Sam hoped Curly understood he was thanking him for far more than the water.

The wrangler nodded and set his pitcher on the chest of drawers.

Sam did his best to sit up without grimacing. "I didn't realize I was getting a whole audience. Forgive me if I don't get up."

"Are you hurt bad, Papa?"

Sam took the cup from Benin and gulped half the contents. "I've been hurt worse, son. It's just my leg, but I won't be able to ride Sandy for a while. You reckon you could take care of her for me 'til I can?"

Benin stood straighter. "Yessir, I can take care of Sandy. I'll make sure she's fed 'n' watered 'n' brushed."

"She'll need some exercise too."

"You mean I get to ride 'er?"

"I wouldn't trust just anybody with her."

Benin finally smiled. "I won't let you down, Pa."

Sam ruffled his hair. "That's my boy."

"Can I help too, Mr. Sam?"

"I'm expecting it, Roscoe. I'm short one wrangler, and with me laid up, it'll be harder on Curly and your pa."

"I can muck the stalls 'n' brush the horses."

"You hear that, Curly? Not every man will offer to muck stalls."

Roscoe stretched to his full height.

Curly set his hand on the lad's shoulder. "Don't let this boy fool ya. He can ride like the best of them too."

Roscoe smiled up at the wrangler. "You think so?"

Cat ruffled his head. "I know so. Now leave your water on the stand there, and go get busy. Mr. Sam needs his rest, and we all have work to do."

"What are you gonna do, Mama?"

"I've got to figure out what's for dinner and supper since Mrs. Ida is busy with Mrs. Reyes."

Roscoe's eyes widened. "You know how to cook?"

"I fixed your breakfast, didn't I?"

"Anybody can fix oatmeal, Miz Cathy."

"Oh, posh." Cat nudged Roscoe toward the door. "Off with you. Go tell your ma I've got the noon meal handled. Curly, bring me Benin's cradle from the barn please. Put it in a warm spot in the kitchen. Sam, do you want me to wake you for lunch?"

"Just bring me some whenever you get through eating."

"I can bring you something before I call the others to the table?"

"Whatever you want to do." Sam pressed his palms against the mattress and scooted lower on the bed, trying to get more comfortable. It didn't work. Sleep seemed to be the only thing capable of easing the throbbing pain in his leg, but he could handle the pain better than the grogginess of laudanum.

A door shut.

Cat stood in the doorway, watching him. "Do you want me to make you some willow bark tea?"

"Not right now. I'll let you know if I can't take it."

She shifted her hold on the baby. "All right, I'll check on you in a little while. Get some rest."

Sam closed his eyes and listened to her traipse through the house and ease the back door shut. He told himself to go back to sleep, but the throbbing in his leg and the replaying of the showdown in his mind made that impossible. He'd done his best not to kill again, and it'd nearly cost him Cat's life. Although he was pretty certain Dakota had been aiming more at him than at her.

Now Curly had to deal with shooting a man too. That wasn't a situation he wanted anyone to face. He'd seen the haunted look in the young man's eyes. Sam could only pray Curly could make peace with it. Finding that peace had taken many a mile and many a year for Sam. Not to mention many a sermon from Elijah Stone. Sam would do his best to help Curly like Stone had him, but ultimately it was between him and God.

Sam rubbed his leg as the throbbing increased. He'd hoped to never endure this kind of pain again. "God, help me not be a grouchy patient for Cat. I know I didn't make things easy on Stone the last time I was laid up. Get me out of this bed quickly, and please help Curly."

―――

"Samuel Houston McGarrett, you get your tail right back in that bed. You heard Dr. Pritchett."

"Yes, he said not to put any weight on it and bust the stitches."

Catherine hurried to take the shirt from Sam's hand. "He also said to stay put. I could wring Curly's neck for bringing you that crutch."

"It wasn't Curly. It was Pa, and before you go wringing anybody a new one, you listen to me." Sam shook his finger under her nose. "I have missed five Thanksgivings—*five*—with my family. I'm not going to miss a sixth."

Catherine let the shirt slip through her fingers when Sam yanked it again. "Why didn't you tell me that's why you were being so stubborn?"

Sam sank onto the edge of the bed, a light sheen of perspiration covering his forehead and upper lip. "I didn't think you'd understand."

"Not understand? I was the one you missed those Thanksgivings with." She moved to his side. "But, honey, I don't want you to overdo it. You're already white as a sheet from getting your clothes."

"I'll come back to bed soon as supper's over. I promise."

Catherine sighed, knowing she wouldn't win this fight and recognizing that as much as Sam wanted to sit at the table, she wanted him there too. In their whole married life, they'd only shared one Thanksgiving together, and she'd dreamt of the day when they'd have the holidays to spend together again. They were some of the loneliest times of the year without him.

"You've gone quiet on me. Does that mean I win this battle or that you're coming up with another strategy?"

Catherine finished tugging the nightshirt from his arms "You win, but back to bed with you as soon as dinner's over."

Sam grinned and slid on a white button-up shirt. "I don't get dessert?"

"All right, fine, after dessert. Can you wear those breeches with that bandage on your leg?"

"Ida might swoon if I left the room without them, don't you think?"

"Oh, don't be fresh. I was just wondering if I needed to let out the seam real quick. Couldn't you have gotten shot somewhere besides your thigh?"

Sam paused in slipping on the jeans and angled his head in her direction. "Where would you have preferred?"

"Oh, you know what I mean. That's just a troublesome spot to work with."

"I think I noticed."

Catherine sighed. "I'm sorry. I'm being insensitive. Do you need some help?"

"I wish I was in better shape to accept that offer."

"What? Oh." Heat crawled up Catherine's neck and spilled into her cheeks. His roguish grin reminded her of the other night and threatened to turn her to mush. "Yes, well…"

Sam caught her fingers. "You know you're a much prettier nurse than the one I had last time I got shot. I reckon I'll like having you to dote on me."

"What makes you think I'll be doting on you?"

"You're here now, aren't you?" He kissed her hand. "Besides, I remember another time when I was sick and stuck in bed. You were quite doting."

"Before you gave me your cold."

"My pa always taught me to share." Sam winked and pushed to his feet before gingerly working the pants over the bandage. "Speaking of pas, how did you know the father of that baby was dead?"

Catherine retreated a few paces and picked at a fingernail. "Mrs. Reyes told me."

"I thought her name was Ramirez. When did that change?"

"Yesterday morning. I was headed to talk to you when... Well, you know."

"So what else did she tell you?"

"She told me Ramirez was her brother-in-law. He really is dead, Sam. No one else is coming to shoot you."

He paused, his shoulders lifting like a weight had been taken from them. "Well, that's good to hear. Why didn't you tell me last night?"

"You were already asleep once I got the baby down for the night. I hated to wake you."

"Does Pa know?"

"Yes." She moved closer when he tottered. "You're starting to look a little pale again. Why don't you sit down? I'll go get Mo and Curly to come help you over to the kitchen."

Sam sank onto the edge of the bed with his leg outstretched. "Just give me a minute. I think I can make it."

"Sam, please, don't fight me on this one."

He sighed. "Fine. Go get the men."

She pecked him on the cheek. "Thank you."

"Hey, if I'm going to give in without a fuss, you can do better than that."

Catherine grinned and gave him a lingering kiss on the mouth.

"Better?"

"For now." Sam winked. "We can practice more later."

"You're incorrigible, you know that?"

"And yet you still married me." His roguish smile grew. "Go on and get the men. I'll be a good boy and sit here until they show up."

She poked him on the shoulder. "I'll hold you to that."

Sam poked his fork into the juicy chicken and wrenched off a drumstick for his wife to pass to their son.

"Pa, ain't we s'posed to eat turkey on Thanksgivin'?"

"Normally, son, but sometimes things don't go like you planned."

"Like you gettin' hurt?"

"Exactly." Sam passed the other drumstick for Roscoe.

"I'm surprised my sister let you come to the table." Constance Martin heaped a pile of mashed potatoes onto her middle daughter's plate and then her own before she handed the bowl to her oldest daughter, who did the same with the younger girl next to her.

"I'm surprised we all managed to fit at the two tables myself." Sam perused the spread before them. "I hope we have enough food."

"I's always make enough, Mista Sam. Y'all eat up now." Ida set another golden bird next to the one he'd nearly stripped bare.

Danny, the youngest Martin boy, grinned and shoveled in a bite of carrots. "You ain't gotta tell me twice."

"You don't have to," Constance corrected.

"I don't haveta what?"

"You do not have to be told twice."

"But ya ain't told me the first time, Ma."

Laughter floated around the table while Amos ruffled his brother's hair and explained his misunderstanding. The lad's mouth formed a silent *O* before he offered a sheepish grin and tucked back into his plate.

"So…" Pa passed a bowl of corn on the cob to Hap. "Who wants to share what they're thankful for first?"

"I do."

"All right, Benin. We'll start with you."

"I'm thankful Pa's home 'n' that Mama smiles more with 'im here."

Sam studied Cat, who offered Benin one of those smiles. Her hair gleamed golden in the lamplight. She looked like an angel. Was Benin right? Did she smile more with him here?

"I's thankful I work with the best hosses around 'n' fer the best people around." Mo's words brought Sam's focus back to the table. Curly seconded Mo's declaration.

Pa cleared his throat and set down his fork. "I'm mighty thankful to have my son back home and that God saw fit to spare us all through our troubles of late."

"Here, here." Multiple people chimed their agreement.

As the voices of gratitude carried around the room, Sam turned his mind to coming up with his own response. A lot had happened in the past year. He'd been shot twice, yet survived both times. He'd found his way back to God and found the courage to face his mistakes. Cat had welcomed him home, introduced him to a son he hadn't known he'd had. She'd forgiven him.

Sam's gaze gravitated to the honey-haired woman by his elbow. She'd forgiven him. Multiple times. She no longer held his past against him when she had every right to. He wouldn't be sitting at this table if it weren't for her forgiving heart.

"Sam?"

He focused on Cat's coffee-colored eyes. "You need something?"

Humor crinkled the lines near their corners. "It's your turn."

"Oh." Sam straightened in his seat, and without another thought, knew exactly what he wanted to say. He removed the fork from Cat's hand and surrounded her fingers with his own. Her eyes widened before she offered him one of those priceless smiles.

"For starters, I'm thankful for Curly's help yesterday. I might not be here without him. Second, I'm thankful for my wife, who's also responsible for my presence here today, but most of all I'm thankful for love and forgiveness. Freely received." He squeezed her hand. "And freely given." Sam leaned close and pecked his wife on the cheek, then whispered in her ear, "I love you."

Cat's eyes gleamed as her smile softened. "I love you too." After giving his hand a squeeze, she shifted the baby in her lap and scanned the room. "I'm also thankful to Curly…and I'm thankful that my family is whole again and that God answers prayers, even the ones you begin to wonder will ever be answered. I'm thankful for hope and love. Forgiveness. Freedom. Life… I could go on all night with how much God has blessed me. Suffice it to say, I'm thankful for you all."

Others concurred and lighthearted conversation rang louder with the passing of bowls and dishes as people asked for seconds. Curly stood and slipped outside, unnoticed by most but not by Sam. He shot up another prayer for the man to find the peace God had provided him. Ida stepped out for a moment to check on Mrs. Reyes, but despite the few hiccups, all in all the evening ended up being everything Sam had longed for through the years.

Ida brushed into the kitchen with a swirl of wind. "Land sakes, it's gettin' mighty cold out there."

Roscoe paused his eating. "Did Mrs. Reyes like whatcha brought her, Mama?"

"Yeah, but I ain't sho' how much she gonna be eatin' of it. That poor thang. I never see'd a sadder sight."

"Speakin' of Mrs. Reyes, she ever say anything about him?" Pa pointed the end of his fork at the infant in Cat's lap.

Sam pronged another bite. "I don't know. I'm still waiting to hear if he's got a name."

"I had Ida ask earlier this morning." Catherine gave the baby another bite of roll. "His name is Antonio."

"But Mama calls 'im Tony. He's gonna be my new baby brother."

"He's what?" Sam stopped midchew. The shocked expression on Cat's face said a lot, but not enough. "Where did he get that idea?"

"Mrs. Reyes asked Mama to keep 'im the same mornin' you got hurted."

"Oh she did, did she? When were you going to tell me about that one, dear?"

"Perhaps it's best if we discuss this later." Cat cast a knowing look

Benin's direction.

"But I heard 'er say that, didn't I, Mama?"

Cat passed a basket of rolls to Ida. "Yes, Ben, you heard right, but I never gave Mrs. Reyes an answer. I couldn't make a decision like that without talking to your papa first."

Sam sank back a fraction.

"Are we gonna keep 'im, Papa?"

"He's not a pet, Benin. Besides, like your mama said, that's a decision best made together. Now finish your chicken."

The clink of utensils slowly resumed, and gazes drifted back to plates. Why did that Reyes woman always have to ruin everything? She had quite the nerve to ask such a thing after trying to blackmail them into the same only days ago. Why would she ask them anyway? She hardly knew them, and why would Cat even consider it? Why would she think *he* would consider it? Surely the child had some distant relative he could stay with.

Pa cleared his throat and pushed away his plate with a groan of satisfaction. "I'd like to tack on how grateful I am for such a fine meal. Ladies, you've outdone yourselves, as always."

"I cleaned my plate, Mama. Do I get pie now?"

Cat peeked at Sam, then rose from her seat. "Sure, Ben. Anybody else?"

Affirmative responses came from all corners of the room. Sam shoved away his plate, his appetite gone.

Ida helped Cat dish out the slices of gooey pecan pie and warm pumpkin pie. "Mista Sam?"

"No thanks, Ida. I've had enough. If y'all'll excuse me, I think I'm ready to get this leg propped up again."

"You want some help, son?"

"No, I think I can manage." Sam retrieved his crutch from the floor and pushed to his foot. He hobbled to the door and made his way back to bed. If he knew his wife, she'd find him as soon as she was free to do so, and she'd want to finish the conversation that had started at the table. Sam lay down and stared at the wood above his head. He'd better get to thinking, because he had no idea how to answer Cat.

Adopting a child was no small thing.

❦

Catherine paused in the bedroom doorway, not surprised to find Sam awake. It'd taken every bit of her willpower not to hurry after him earlier, but she'd needed time to think. It stood to reason Sam did too. She hoped he wasn't mad at her. "Have I given you enough time to think?"

Sam glanced up from the Bible in his lap. "Everyone gone?"

"Yes. Benin's in bed, and the baby's asleep in the cradle in the living room."

Sam studied her for a few heartbeats. "Why?"

"Mrs. Reyes is dying, Sam. You apparently are the only upstanding person she knows."

"No, why didn't you tell me sooner?"

"When would you have preferred? When Dakota James was ready to shoot you, or when the doctor was stitching you up? It's not like things have been exactly calm around here."

"Fair enough." He shut the Book. "What did you tell her?"

Catherine stepped into the room and leaned against the wall beside the chest of drawers. "At first I was going to tell her no, but she was so adamant, and she has no one... I didn't know what else to say. I told her I'd consider it."

Sam picked at the block quilt a moment, then looked at her. "And you remember what it's like being an orphan."

It was a statement, not a question, but Catherine hugged herself and nodded.

He patted the bed beside him, and when she took a seat there, he enfolded his warm hands around her cold ones. "Is this what you want?"

She hitched a shoulder.

"Okay, another question. Do you think this is what God wants for us?"

Catherine returned Sam's inspection. "Maybe."

"You're unsure?"

"No...yes... Don't you have any input on the matter? I mean, the woman tried to force you into doing this."

"Yeah, that didn't sit well with me, but then I got to praying and reading. You wouldn't believe the verse I stumbled upon."

"What's that?"

Sam opened the Bible to the book of James and pointed to the last verse of chapter one. "'Pure religion and undefiled before God and the Father is this, to visit the fatherless and widows in their affliction, and to keep himself unspotted from the world.'" He sighed. "As much as I'd like to ignore this, it would seem God doesn't want us too."

"There's nothing saying we have to do this, Sam."

"But?"

He read her too well.

"But where would he be if we didn't? Her sister is dead. Her family is dead. The boy's father is dead. You can't help but feel sorry for the child. He didn't choose this. He has no say in the matter. Wouldn't it be better if he had two parents who would raise him in the fear and admonition of the Lord? She chose us, Sam, because of how you helped her in the past. I doubt she even knew you were married. Besides, I honestly think she's still alive because she's waiting to get an answer from us."

"I haven't seen her since that first day. Does she look that bad?"

"She looks like she aged overnight. She's holding on for Tony. I'm sure of it."

"I guess it's up to you then."

"No. This has to be *both* our decisions. I won't be blamed for this later should you not like it."

"How did you make up your mind so easily?"

Catherine rubbed her finger over his knuckles. "I held him. There's something about his sweet smile. He already comes to me quicker than Ida or anybody else. I can't explain it."

Sam smirked. "Believe it or not, when I saw you with him that first time... When was that? Yesterday morning?" He swiped a hand through his hair. "Wow, things sure have been happening quick around here."

"Yes, they have. You were saying?"

"Right, I was saying that when I saw you feeding him, I toyed with the idea of the babe actually being ours, but I honestly never expected a request like this to come our way."

"So we're agreed?"

Sam's brows rose as he drew in a deep breath. "I guess so. Are you sure we're ready for this?"

"Honey, you're never ready for children. Even when they're your own."

"The nerves are normal then?"

Catherine giggled. "Yes."

Sam tugged her closer, and she gladly settled in his arms. Even after all they'd been through, she still found them the most comforting, secure-feeling place ever.

He rested his chin on her hair. "This doesn't mean we're not still going to have more children of our own, does it?"

She tilted her face up to his. "How many do you want?"

"Oh, I'm thinking at least a dozen."

"Only a dozen. Well, I reckon that's a manageable number."

Sam chuckled. "You have a better idea?"

"No, a dozen's fine."

"Good, 'cause as soon as this leg is better, I aim to test that theory."

Catherine smiled and pulled him close for a kiss. "I look forward to it."

EPILOGUE

Christmas Day, 1878

Catherine felt Sam's watchful gaze follow her around the bedroom while she cinched her robe in place. "Are you going to lay there all day?"

"It's a tempting offer." He sat up and grabbed her belt when she moved past the bed toward the armoire. He tugged her closer, and she gave in without a fuss as he drew her onto his lap. She'd longed for moments like these during those years he'd been absent, and she'd never grow tired of them.

Sam nuzzled her neck. "You know I can't take a whiff of lemons without thinking of you?"

Her heart warmed, and she leaned into him. "That's me and witch hazel."

His arms encircled her, and he propped his chin on her shoulder. "Do we have to face the world today?"

"If we don't, it'll just come knocking."

The creak of a board warned them a split second before a timid knock rattled their door.

"See what I mean." She moved to rise, but Sam held her fast.

"Shh, maybe if we ignore them, they'll go away."

Catherine giggled even as another louder knock hit the door.

"Mama, Tony 'n' I are up. Do we get to open presents now?"

Sam tickled her side. "You know you're terrible at being quiet. Sure, Ben, we'll be out there in a minute, and y'all can open your presents. You didn't wake up your brother, did you?"

Silence answered.

"That's what I thought." Sam nudged her from the bed and grabbed his pants. "Come on. If we don't hurry, Tony'll start without us whether we like it or not. You remember last Christmas…"

Catherine laughed and moved toward the door. "Yes, I'll never forget seeing Tony under that tree surrounded by ripped paper—"

"And Benin's not-so-innocent look when he said Tony insisted on opening all his presents first."

"Yes, Benin is quite the instigator. I wonder where he got that from." She threw him a grin before she opened their bedroom door. "Oh no. Tony, wait!"

Catherine hurried forward, laughing as she went. She plucked the almost-two-year-old from under the tree. A small package dangled from his finger.

"She caught you this time, huh, squirt?"

Tony wiggled and reached for Sam. "Papa."

Catherine snagged the present while Sam stole the tyke from her arms. "You're right. This is Papa's present."

"Oh really?"

"Open it, Pa. Open it."

"You want me to go first?"

Benin nodded.

"All right." Sam settled on the small couch with a boy on each side and untied the string holding the green paper closed. He peeled it back and froze like a startled deer.

"What is it, Pa?"

Sam lifted the small white bonnet by the string tie and looked at her.

Catherine smiled, unable to contain her joy.

"Does this mean…"

She nodded.

Sam put Tony on the floor and moved to within inches of her. "You're really…"

"Uh-huh."

"Woo-hoo!" He swooped her in his arms and spun her around.

Benin and Tony jumped around too as Sam touched her feet back to the floor.

"How long have you known? Are you okay?"

"A few months. I feel fine."

"Why didn't you tell me sooner?"

"I wanted it to be a surprise. Are you happy?"

"Thrilled. Boys, guess what?"

The two stopped tumbling around on the floor.

"What?"

"You're going to have another baby brother."

"Or sister," Catherine corrected.

Sam straightened and stared at her. "A girl? With your hair." He grinned.

"And your eyes."

He pecked her on the lips. "She'll be beautiful. Just like her mama." Sam caught her hand and tugged her toward the door. "Come on. Let's go tell the others."

"But, Pa, what 'bout our presents?"

"Oh. Right."

Catherine laughed as Sam towed her back toward the tree. She wasn't sure he realized he still held on to her. If he got this rattled simply by the news she was expecting, she couldn't wait to see how he reacted when she went into labor in six months.

Sam handed each boy a wrapped package before he wrapped her back into his arms and began waltzing her around the room.

Catherine smiled, loving the rhythm they'd found together. Sure, there were times she still wanted to wring his neck. It took work to make a successful marriage, but the more they danced, the easier it got.

Benin shouted when he opened the toy train.

Catherine giggled. "You think he likes it?"

A grin turned up Sam's lips. "I can't wait to see his reaction when we take him out to see his other present."

"You sure it's not too soon to give him his own horse? He's only six."

"Thunder sires good colts. Don't worry. Benin and Storm can

grow up together. It'll be good for them. He won't be riding that horse until he's at least nine anyway."

"I suppose you're right. Are you ready to open your other present?" She'd sewn him a shirt that would match his gray-blue eyes perfectly. She couldn't wait to see it on him.

"No." Sam drew her closer and steered her around Tony when he chased after the ball he'd finally managed to unwrap.

Catherine's brows rose. "Why not?"

"'Cause I don't need any more presents."

"You don't?"

"No, you've given me more than I ever expected."

Yes, a baby was quite a gift. "I didn't do this alone you know. There was you. And God."

"Yes, but none of this would've been possible if you hadn't welcomed me back last year. I don't think I can ever tell you how grateful I am that you didn't toss me out on my ear that first day back in town."

"I thought my heart would stop when I saw you. You looked better than I remembered, and I couldn't decide whether I wanted to wring your neck or kiss you."

"I wasn't sure which one you'd do either, although I feared the former. I'm glad I won your trust though."

"I'm glad too." She smiled up at him. "Have I ever told you how glad I am that you came back home?"

Sam eased them to a stop under the mistletoe. "Every time you kiss me."

Catherine smiled and went up on tiptoe. "Then let me say it again."

A NOTE TO READERS

Dear friends:

I hope you enjoyed *Win, Love, or Draw* and that it ministered to you in some way. I know it touched me. This story comes from a place deep in my heart. For you see, I was once that child who saw her family restored, and like Cat, I am waiting to experience my own miracle. Aren't you glad to know God is in the miracle-working business? Don't limit Him, my friends. What He's done for others, He can do for you.

I'd love to hear how this story has touched your heart or interact with you. Please drop me a line through my website (http://www.crystal-barnes.com) or join me on Facebook (https://www.facebook.com/booksbybarnes) or some other social media. On my website, I also offer a chance to sign up for my newsletter, which I use to keep my readers updated on coming releases, grant sneak peeks, and share other fun stuff.

If you enjoyed *Win, Love, or Draw* enough to leave a review on Goodreads or Amazon, please know how very much I appreciate it. I pray for every reader as I write my stories, not only that you'll enjoy the adventure but that the message will help you in your walk with God.

Happy Trails,
Crystal L Barnes

ABOUT THE AUTHOR

Crystal L Barnes is an award-winning author, who also happens to be a born-n-raised Texan. She is an active member of American Christian Fiction Writers (ACFW), her local ACFW chapter, 19th Century Writers, and her local church. In 2012, she was a semifinalist in the ACFW Genesis contest. She has a degree in Computing Science because she loves putting things into their proper place, and she enjoys writing because she gets to share her love of old-fashioned things and the Lord. Find out more about Crystal at crystal-barnes.com or connect with her on Facebook, Google+, or Pinterest.

Want to stay up to date on the latest happenings? Sign up for Crystal's Newsletter on her website.

COMING SPRING 2016!

Dinah's seeking answers but finds more than she bargains for when she gets caught in a shotgun wedding—with the rifle pointed at her. Will a dream for love shatter forever, or will the pair find a marriage worth lock, stock, and barrel?

LOVE, STOCK, & BARREL

Marriage & Mayhem

Crystal L Barnes

ALSO COMING 2016!

An heiress who's fishing for a husband.
A wrangler who doesn't want to be caught.
Could joining forces solve both their problems?

HOOK, LINE, & SUITOR

Marriage & Mayhem

Crystal L Barnes